CRUSH

A BAYONET SCARS NOVEL

JC EMERY

SERIES & TITLES BY JC EMERY

Men with Badges
Marital Bitch
The Switch

BAYONET SCARS
Ride
Thrash
Rev
Crush
Burn (coming soon)

CRUSH

a Bayonet Scars novel
by
JC Emery
Copyright 2014 by Left Break Press

Cover Design by Brenda Gonet at Gonet Design
http://www.facebook.com/gonetdesign

Timeline created by The Illustrated Author
http://www.theillustratedauthor.net/

Copy Edits performed by Michele Milburn

Dear Reader,

While I know the story of the Forsaken Motorcycle Club as surely as I know the sound of my own voice, it's come to my attention that the overlapping storylines of each book can be confusing. The series is set up so that every book overlaps the one before and the one after in some manner. The fast-moving nature of the series and the first person perspective means that you, as the reader, may have to wait for answers until we get into another character's head. I have carefully mapped the series story arc as well as the individual relationship arcs to best tell the story that's in my heart.

In order to make it easier for you to follow along as we move toward our final conclusion, I have added a timeline as a means of indicating where we are with the series story arc. The timeline does not include the prologue or the epilogue. I hope this helps clear up any confusion that's occurred along the way.

Thanks,
JC

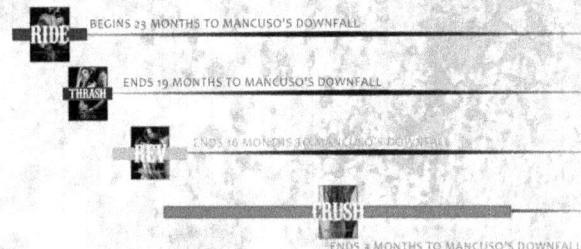

BAYONET SCARS SERIES

TIMELINE

RIDE — BEGINS 23 MONTHS TO MANCUSO'S DOWNFALL

THRASH — ENDS 19 MONTHS TO MANCUSO'S DOWNFALL

REV — ENDS 16 MONTHS TO MANCUSO'S DOWNFALL

CRUSH — ENDS 3 MONTHS TO MANCUSO'S DOWNFALL

JC Emery

Mom,

Thank you.

Always.

PROLOGUE

July

21 months to Mancuso's downfall

Jeremy

I NEVER FEEL more at home than I do right here on Forsaken land. The black vinyl inserts in the high-as-hell chain link fence that surrounds the compound have the word FORSAKEN painted across them in ten-foot high white lettering. Everywhere they can, the club's marked this property. Even if one day Forsaken no longer calls this spot home, their mark will remain. After a small fire that was started, due to no fault of my own, Dad and Jim had to repair and repaint one of the picnic tables. They knew how it started, and instead of laying into me, Dad gave me a knife and told me to mark that table as my own. Beneath the table top, in the fucked up scratch marks of a seven-year-old's handiwork, is JEREMY WAS HERE. I don't get to come by as often as I'd like, but every chance I get, I sit at that table. In a way, it makes me feel closer to my dad. I'd go there now, but there's a crowd around my table watching two of the brothers fight it out.

Nobody's paying attention to me, which is the way I like it. People pay too much attention and they start asking questions. I slip past the crowd and around to the line of Harleys backed up against the fence. There's really no order to the way the brothers park in the lot except that they try to make it as easy as possible to get out in a moment's notice. I don't recognize all the bikes here. Some of them are familiar, like Ryan's bike that he's had custom painted with obsessive detailing that nobody else seems to see but him. Next to Ryan's bike, on the very end, is Duke's. Duke patched in before Dad went to prison, and he's always been good to me. I like the guy and all, but his bike is boring as shit.

I scan the crowd and find the fight is still going on. Taking advantage of the moment, I run my hand along the gas tank of the black Harley. I'd really like to get my hands on Ryan's bike, but he has this thing about people's asses and his dick, so I'll just stay over here with Duke's. Duke won't say it because he's Forsaken and he's not a fucking pussy, but I know he lets me hang around the clubhouse because of my sister, Nic. Even before they hooked up, he let me do shit I know Dad would beat me for. Usually I'll just casually ask him if he's seen Nic anywhere like I'm there for her. I think he caught on that I was full of shit at some point, but as long as I feed him information, he lets me hang out. He even had a Lost Girl show me how to properly feel up a chick once. That was pretty badass.

The seat of Duke's bike is worn. Its cracks show a seat

that has seen a lot of miles with its rider. Dad says when he gets out he's going to hook me up and get me a bike. I can't wait. More than anything, I just want to learn how to ride. I want to earn my cut and sit in Church with these guys. Dudes like me, who don't know shit about books and fucking hate math, only got a few choices in life. But even if I was book smart, I'd still want this. The brotherhood is deeper than family and survives shit most relationships never could. I know my sister loves me, and she does the best she can, but I don't think I'll ever really know my father and feel like I belong somewhere until I'm one of his brothers. I lower myself onto the seat of the bike and lean up against it. I know better, and I don't care. For just a moment, I want to know what this feels like.

There's noise from the crowd. Grady, the club's sergeant at arms, is breaking up the fight. After a few choice words, he zeroes in on Nic. I can't hear what he's saying, but I regret trying to figure it out the moment she eyes me on Duke's bike and gives me that parental chin nod she's been practicing, telling me to get off. I stand from my position on the bike and take a step forward to appease her. Shit. She's not going to let this go later. She never lets anything go.

People are walking away from Diesel and Duke. Both men are heaving in anger just feet away from one another. Everybody seems to be disinterested in what's happening now that Grady's broken up the fun. Everybody but the skinny blonde with a bad attitude who vaguely resembles my sister who's staring at Duke like he's dying or some shit. Crap. I knew Nic had a thing for him, but she's looking at him in a way I've never seen her look at anyone.

Content that her focus is elsewhere, I lower myself back against the bike and indulge in this feeling. Just leaning up against it, I feel powerful. It's not very large, but this close I can see the small Forsaken symbol shining back at me from the top of the gas tank. The Nordic warrior isn't a logo. It's more than that. The warrior is powerful and fierce. He's indestructible, and nobody fucks with him. At least that's how I've always seen him. Placing my hand over the warrior, I let out a heavy sigh. If my dad was here, he'd tell me the warrior's history. He'd make sure I understand what it means to be Forsaken and to be allowed to have this symbol on your bike. It means brotherhood. It means family. It means never having to be alone.

When I lift my head and meet eyes with Duke, I square my shoulders and try my best to not look like a fucking baby. We've always been cool, and I'm just admiring the detail work. He'll understand that.

"Are you on my fucking bike?" he yells. His voice is deep and scratchy and so much fucking scarier than it's ever been before. I keep my jaw set and try to keep my breathing steady as he unhooks his arm from around my sister's waist and walks toward me.

Forsaken doesn't like weakness, they don't like mistakes, and they fucking hate apologies. So I don't apologize, and I don't move. I go for the truth, pat the gas tank, and say, "I like the paint job."

"Off," he says, gesturing for me to get off. "Before I break your fucking kneecaps."

"Chill." I don't finish that comment with what I really want to say, which is a string of nonsensical curses mixed in with some good old-fashioned begging. Because, I remind myself, Duke won't respect begging. As I push off the bike, the chain of my wallet clanks against the perfect black paint job. It startles me, and I move quickly—too quickly—causing a horrible fucking scratch on the gas tank. It all happens so fast, even though he's moving really slowly, but the next thing I know he's shoving me away from the bike and holding my shirt by its collar.

"You scratched," he says, careful to enunciate every syllable, "my bike."

Shit. Shit. Shit.

The time for respect is over, and now I'm well into pansy-ass begging mode.

"Sorry?" I say and hope I don't sound like a total pussy, so I follow it up with a small smirk.

"You're going to pay for this, shithead," Duke says, roughly letting me go. I stumble backward, and when I look up, I find myself guarded by Nic. She's standing in between me and Duke. His chest heaves a little lighter, but he doesn't look at her. He grits out, "Move," as he stares me down.

Gently, she moves toward him and places a hand on his chest as she says softly, "Please. We need to check your head."

He shakes his head like he's trying to fight against, her but he can't. Those two are so fucking stupid for each other it makes me sick. She moves to his side and places her hand on his back. It's a long moment that he stands there glaring at me. He's practically breathing fire, and

5

when I look at my sister, she's not looking any more pleased with me. As fucked as it sounds, I feel like I have Mom and Dad staring me down and about to ground me. Which is weird because although Nic totally goes "mom" on me, it's not like she and Duke are anything official.

He screams, "Fuck!" Then, in the meanest fucking voice I've ever heard, he says, "He's lucky he's your brother, or he'd be in the emergency room right now." His eyes are on me, but the message is meant for Nic. She's the only reason he's not beating the shit out of me. And well, if that's the case, I hope she does something nice for him later, like sucking his dick or letting him fuck her. Because under no circumstances do I ever, and I mean *ever*, want to piss him off that bad again. In one stupid, selfish moment, I lost all those months of trust and respect I'd built up with him. There's no fucking way he's ever going to trust me enough to approach the club about letting me prospect now.

Fuck.

From out of nowhere, Grady walks up and roughly grabs me by the back of my neck. I don't breathe or move. I just stand here and pray he's not as angry as his grip makes him seem.

"I'll babysit while you two talk your shit out," Grady says. The words slide from his tongue in a slither as the hand that's wrapped around the back of my neck constricts, the tips of his fingers coiling around my throat. His dark brown hair is streaked with gray here and there, and he's got lines around the edges of his eyes. Even though I'm sure he's old as hell, his grip is still really fucking strong. Unfortunately, Grady is the least of my problems.

I scratched Duke's bike—his fucking Harley—and with the way he's looking now, I don't know that he and I will ever be cool again. And I need us to be cool. His blue eyes are narrowed and one hundred percent focused on me. It's almost more than I can bear. His shoulders heave dramatically as he struggles to suck in breath after breath. His pink, sun-kissed skin is now red from a lack of oxygen, and his jaw ticks with every sporadic breath he takes.

Standing beside Duke is my sister, Nic. We used to look alike once, but now her small frame and bleached blonde hair make it difficult to tell we're related. Her lips are turned down in disapproval, but her green eyes show her worry. When I was a kid, I used to hate her eyes. I got my dark blue color from my dad and my shape from my mom. Nic has neither. Her eye color and shape were inherited from a man who never bothered to meet her. They're just another fucking reminder of what my dad doesn't acknowledge—that she's not really his kid. Mom was a whore long before the club came along.

Like mother, like daughter, I guess.

The hand at my neck pulls me back from Duke and Nic. I stumble awkwardly, unable to keep my feet from following Grady ask he strides determinedly toward the clubhouse. My back twists with the effort to turn around so I can walk forward instead of being dragged backward, but Grady isn't having any of it.

My steps falter as I make it into the room, trying to avoid looking like a fucking chump as much as I can. We're halfway through the main room of the clubhouse, with Grady dragging me into one piece of furniture after another. My legs smack into wooden tables of all sizes and shapes, and I knock down chairs and am then forced to find a way over them despite the protruding legs that shoot into the air.

Sunlight streams into the room from the high windows that line the edge of the ceiling. They provide just enough natural light for me to avoid getting hit in the nuts by the leg of a haphazardly fallen chair. I'm too young for my junk to get damaged.

The door opens, welcoming the sounds of heavy boots on the concrete below. From the angle at which Grady is pulling me, I see their boots and worn jeans before I see their faces. First Wyatt enters, followed by Diesel. Neither man is smiling. Almost instantly their eyes find me. Diesel bares his teeth in a disturbing smile, but Wyatt's expression remains flat. From the intensity of their gaze, I have no doubt that they're coming for me. I'm smart enough to know how the club deals with crap like this but apparently stupid enough to have— accidentally or not—fucked with one of their bikes.

Grady rounds the corner into the game room at the back of the clubhouse. He cuts the corner close to the wall, but I don't realize how close until it's too late and a sharp pain radiates from the side of my head and my shoulder blade. I grimace in discomfort. My left foot catches on the wall as I'm dragged into the game room. I lose my balance and fall backward onto the hard concrete floor. Grady finally lets go of my neck on my way down but doesn't bother to move back. My head knocks into his knees, but it's my tailbone that throbs. I clamp my eyes shut, trying to block out the world around me. The impact fucking hurt, and it's not really getting any better.

A familiar laugh sounds from a distance. I can't quite

place who it is, and curiosity gets the best of me, so I open my eyes little by little. I'd rather not come face-to-face with any Forsaken. Pushing away the embarrassment at my reaction to the throbbing pain in my tailbone is a challenge. I want these guys to give me a chance to prospect one day, and that won't happen if they think I'm a little bitch. I open my eyes a little more and hope to find that Wyatt and Diesel have something better to do than to fuck with me. I expect to be disappointed and find them feet away, with their arms folded over their chests, staring down at me in disapproval.

Blinking away the spots of light that partially blind my view, I struggle to see what's in front of me clearly. Something is closer than I expect. I can feel its presence crowding my space, but it takes another moment to clearly see what's in my way. Black hair atop pale skin with gray eyes and cracked lips. It's Ryan, and he's less than a foot away.

"Hey, asshole," Ryan says with a large smile on his face. His breath smells like a combination of whiskey and something else I'd rather not try to place. It just fucking stinks. I let a scowl form on my face and bite back the comment that's on the tip of my tongue. I want to tell him to fuck off or to suck my dick. But I don't. I'd rather deal with Grady—who I know to be a fair man—than Ryan, who I have on good authority is a fucking psychopath. Not that I think that's necessarily a bad thing. Actually, I've been doing everything I can in the last year or so to show Ryan that I'm more than a punk kid with a big mouth. He seems to respect a strong personality, so that's what I want to show him. Still, I don't know that right now is the time to try to show him that.

Ryan stares at me with little to no emotion. It's a long, insufferable moment before he raises an eyebrow and his lips spread into an awful smile. But it isn't until he's smiling so wide that he's showing his teeth that I know I am really in for it.

I don't see it coming, but the impact from the palm of his hand slamming into my cheek sends a stinging across my face. I try to block out the moment, but all I can think is that I just got bitch-slapped by Ryan. This is bad—really fucking bad. I try to scramble backward, looking for an out, but the back of my head and the top of my shoulders are stopped by Grady's shins. His wavy hair hangs low, practically touching my forehead. The stench of alcohol and onions wafts over my face. Just once, I'd like for one of these guys to have fucking brushed their teeth before getting in my face. Like Ryan, Grady could really use a goddamn mint. Once again, he grabs ahold of my neck and stands slowly, pulling me up with him and bringing me to my feet.

Aware of how unsteady I am, I keep my back straight and bring my chin up just enough to show the men around me that I can handle the shit they're dishing out. Even if I'm not entirely convinced they aren't going to beat the shit out of me, I don't want my fear to show. Ryan stands just as Grady pulls me backward, deeper into the room. With more distance between us, I'm able to see who else is in here with us. Sure enough, Diesel and Wyatt are standing with their arms crossed over their chests. I don't know either well enough to judge the expressions on their faces. We're in the center of the room right next to the pool table when Grady releases me. I take a deep breath and try to blow it out inconspicuously.

"You fucked up, kid," Wyatt says. I say nothing as he looks me up and down. His left nostril lifts in disgust.

"Butch would be very displeased," Diesel says with the shake of his head. I'm pretty fucking well aware that my dad wouldn't approve of me scratching Duke's bike. It doesn't matter if it was an accident or if I did it on purpose. All that matters is that I fucked with something that belongs to Forsaken. Leaning against Duke's bike was stupid. Right now I can't even remember why I did it. Sometimes it feels like I can't get anything right no matter how hard I try.

"What punishment do you think you should get?" Wyatt asks. Punishment? Fuck if I know. I'd like to say that this intimidation bullshit is enough, but I know better.

"We're going to have fun, kid." Ryan is smiling as the words come out of his mouth. I've never seen him smile this much before. It's starting to freak me the fuck out.

Grady clears his throat, and I turn just slightly to wait for his admonishment but am surprised to find that he's shaking his head. He says, "Down boy," and his eyes slide over to Ryan.

Thanks to my sister and her big-mouth friend Chel, I know all about the trouble between Grady and Ryan. Apparently Ryan's looking to get himself hooked up with some bitch they call Princess who ratted on her pops. If there is one thing I know about Grady, it's that he is one by-the-book motherfucker. There's a way you do things and there's a way you don't do things, and in Grady's world, there's little room open for interpretation of the "code of silence." I wish I was smart enough to find a way to redirect Grady's attention to Ryan and the beef they got going, but I can't think of anything that won't get my ass beat.

"You got any idea how bad you fucked up?" Ryan asks. Judging by the fact that I have four members of Forsaken staring me down like I'm dog shit, I think I have some clue. "Fucking answer me."

I try to respond, but it's more than a little difficult to get my vocal cords to cooperate. All I can think about is my dad and how he'd flip out whenever I fucked up. He would ask me all these questions he never intended for me to answer. It's what you call a rectal question, or whatever you call it. Even when he'd demand an answer, he didn't really want one and never gave me time to give him one. He just likes to yell—something he still does when he manages to stay out of the Hole long enough to get a phone call in, and unfortunately, my sister pretty much always rats me out.

"Yeah, I got it," I mumble after some serious thought on the subject.

"Don't think he gets it," Diesel says. His voice booms in the ever-shrinking room.

"Nah, he don't get it," Wyatt grumbles.

"Give the boy a chance to prove it," Grady says. His attention is still focused on Ryan. I thought these two weren't getting along, but maybe I was wrong. "He's been comin' around for some time now, saying he's man enough to wear the cut."

"He's just a kid," Wyatt says in a huff.

"You were all just kids once." The words come from a

deep voice that's familiar but I don't quite place until I see Chief's long black hair and broad shoulders. He moves into the room, and everybody grows silent. Grady, who is one scary motherfucker, seems to take a step back as he acknowledges Chief's presence. If I didn't already know Chief's longstanding history in the club, I would be well aware of it now. According to my dad, Wyatt is vice president because he wanted the job. Chief could have had it, but it wasn't his end game. Great power, great responsibility and all that shit.

"Fucked up, didn't you?" he asks. His brow and jaw are relaxed. I remain silent, expecting this to be another one of those questions I'm not supposed to answer.

"Answer me," he barks.

"Yes, sir."

"Come on, Chief," Ryan whines. I'm not talking about a manly whine—if there is such a thing—I'm talking about this full-on, high-pitched fucking whine. His brows furrow and he stomps his foot. Diesel snorts, but Wyatt and Grady both look annoyed at his antics. Only Chief doesn't react.

"Fine," he says. A small smirks appears in the corner of his mouth. My attention shifts to Ryan, who is smiling full of teeth that look as though they're growing sharper by the moment. He lunges forward with his right foot but stops suddenly. I make the mistake of jumping back quickly. Like a wild animal, the action spurs him on. Before I know it, he's stepped forward with his left foot. It's happening so fast that I'm not really thinking—just reacting—and I take several steps back.

"Let's play a game—I catch you, you get to suck my

dick," Ryan says as he reaches out to grab ahold of me. Before I know it, I'm running away and he's rushing after me. Chief, Grady, Diesel, and Wyatt move off to the side, watching me about to get the "privilege" of being mouth-raped. It's likely a few minutes, but it feels like hours as we run in circles around the room. I make a pass by Diesel, who is smiling like a madman. I'm so focused on his face that I don't see his foot sticking out in front of me. My palms slam against the concrete only a second before my knees do. I don't have time to focus on the horrific pain traveling up from my knees to my hips, because Ryan hunches over me, wraps one hand around my throat and the other on my hip. I thought he was kidding about making me suck his dick, but now I've got my asshole clenched as tight as I can, fucking terrified that he's more interested in my ass.

Ryan leans in close with his mouth to my ear when he whispers, "Call me Trigger," and he shoves me to the pavement. As he walks away, the sound of his footsteps are drowned out by the echoes of the other men laughing heartily. I give myself a solid minute to regroup before I push up from the concrete. The chuckles subside, and in their place, hushed murmurs fall over the room.

"Hey, Chey," Grady says. "What are you doing here?"

Brushing myself off and straightening my back, I turn toward Grady. Now is *not* the time for Cheyenne Grady to see me. Especially in the clubhouse. Her short, thin legs are covered in worn jeans and she's wearing a pink-and-black flannel button-up on top. She's cute, like really fucking cute. She's the kind of cute that's been giving me blue balls ever since I discovered that shit was good for more than just tugging on the damn things because I was bored. She runs a hand through her dark brown hair and lifts her chin in my direction.

"Tracie and I want to go to the movies," she says.

"And what does that have to do with me?"

"I need my allowance for the week."

"I gave it to you already," Grady says.

"What am I supposed to do, then?" she asks. Her bottom lip pops out, and she blinks up at him with her big green eyes. "I don't have any cash left."

"I don't know. Sneak in or stay home. Either way, it's not really my problem, is it? Told you before—I'm not a fucking bank."

"But, Daddy," she whispers. She bats her eyes at him. She's goddamn dangerous. She bats her eyes like that at me and I'd probably just hand her my fucking wallet. But Grady doesn't react.

"Oh, come on, Grady," Chief says. He smiles down at his goddaughter and waves her over. She moves immediately into his arms. Once there, he wraps one large arm around her and uses the other to dig into his pocket where he pulls out a twenty-dollar bill and goes to hand it to her.

She shakes her head and sighs. "No, Uncle Chief. I can't take the money from you. It's okay. I can stay home." Her voice sounds so small, and she looks so defeated.

I redirect my attention to Grady, who is glaring at Chief. The two men exchange a look, with Chief nodding toward Cheyenne and Grady shaking his head. It goes on until Diesel and Wyatt—who I almost forgot are in the room—are casually urging Grady to give Cheyenne money for the movies. Soon enough, Grady loses his patience and pulls out two twenties. He shoves them at her with narrowed eyes.

"Con artist," Grady gripes. "You two are a couple of fucking con artists."

Cheyenne gives Chief a squeeze before practically skipping toward her dad. She grabs the money and wraps her arms around Grady's midsection. He pats her back reluctantly and then shoos her away.

With Grady's attention diverted, Chief takes the opportunity to shake his head at me as he mouths, "*Grady will kill you.*"

I stare at him in confusion and shrug my shoulders, trying to pull off this whole I-don't-have-a-crush-on-Cheyenne-Grady thing. He doesn't buy it. He just chuckles and smirks, then says, "Pussy."

"Thanks, Daddy," Cheyenne says and rushes out of the room excitedly. Now that she's gone, I'm reminded that I'm still in a good amount of trouble with the guys around me.

CHAPTER 1

November

17 months to Mancuso's downfall

Jeremy

THE SOGGY GRASS squishes beneath my heavy black boots as I stomp my way across the football field. I've been out here standing in the shadows of the bleachers for the last hour, and only now am I able to show myself to Cheyenne and that douche bag she's flirting with.

I have orders. I'm to keep an eye on her but not to interfere unless the situation warrants it. I've always respected Grady as the sergeant at arms, but I'm starting to like the guy on a personal level now. His instructions were clear: watch Cheyenne and make sure there's no inappropriate touching or anybody suspicious in her vicinity. As far as I'm concerned, Clinton Bruce, quarterback for the Wolverines, having his hands on Cheyenne anywhere is inappropriate, and the uptight, pretty-boy asshole is definitely suspicious. Grady would sanction this.

"Hey!" I shout and shove an index finger in Clinton's direction. Clinton. Who the fuck names their kid that, anyway? My mom's one fucked up bitch, and even she had the decency of giving me a legit name. I shake my head. Clinton.

Good old Clint jumps in place as his hands still on Cheyenne's hips. His eyes narrow as he slowly realizes I got a bone to pick with him. He's fucking slow, but Cheyenne isn't. She steps back, swatting Clint's hands away, and shakes her head at me. Her eyes are focused on the black leather that rests on my shoulders.

This is the first time she's seen me in my cut.

"You got a problem?" Clint asks loudly. His gray-and-purple practice uniform is spotted with mud here and there, but he doesn't look like he's been really sacked yet. Maybe I should change that.

"Hands off Miss Priss."

"Miss Priss?" he questions. Yeah, slow.

Cheyenne folds her arms over her chest and gives Clint a quick look that reeks of an apology. She ain't got shit to apologize for, but that she thinks she has to pisses me off even further. She's always trying to fit in with other people. For as long as I can remember, she's gone for the jocks. Occasionally she'll pay attention to a band geek, but not often. She's always stayed away from the loser druggies and anybody who never really fit into a particular crowd—like me.

"My dad and his friends call me that," she says to him barely loud enough for me to hear.

"Is Whelan one of your dad's friends?" Clint asks.

Cheyenne levels him with a frustrated gaze. "You don't see the cut?"

"I mean, yeah," he mutters only half-coherently. Then his voice rises in irritation. "Don't get bitchy with me."

I stride up into his personal space and bump my chest against his gear. "Do we have a problem here?"

I've been working on keeping my expression flat when I need it to be, so I hope I'm able to pull it off. Duke is kind of a hard-ass, but I'm thankful for it. Without having him breathing down my neck every other minute, I wouldn't be wearing this cut. And, God, do I love this cut. I wouldn't exactly give up my dick for it, but I'd consider hacking off a few toes if I had to.

"I don't know, do we?" Clint the Dick says.

"Step off, or all the body armor in the world isn't going to save you." My chest constricts with the desire to hit something. Anything. My skin heats at the thought of making this asshole bleed. My lungs strain for air my body doesn't want to accept. If he pushes me much further, I'm going to snap. It's always been like this, my temper. I get so pissed off over the littlest shit that I have to break something before I feel better. His jaw looks like a decent enough target.

"You got in my face, asshole."

My heart beats frantically in my chest as I tighten my fists at my sides to keep from swinging at him too early. If I get busted for hitting this prick, I want to make sure it's a good shot. But I don't have the chance, because just as the tension in my body gets too much to bear, I hear Cheyenne's voice.

"Jeremy, please stop," she says quietly. "Please." She's pretty much begging at this point. It's like she's been silently asking me to back off, and when it came out loud enough for me to hear, it's nearly a cry.

I open my fists and take in deep breath after deep breath until I can see clearly. He was touching her in a way I don't like—at all—but he wasn't hurting her. Grady didn't task me with this so I could control every little thing she does. I'm not supposed to interfere. I'm only supposed to keep her safe. And she's safe.

I take one step back slowly and then another. When I look to my side, I find that Cheyenne's face is beet red and her green eyes are large. She doesn't look embarrassed. She looks fucking mortified. Shit. That is so not a way to get a girl to suck your dick. I would know because that is one of Duke's most important tips about women—don't upset them, or they won't blow you. They probably won't do any other nice stuff for you either.

I probably should have learned not to piss off women from being raised by my batshit-crazy sister, but I'm what Duke calls a slow learner. He's such a fucking asshole sometimes, but I'd be lying if I said I don't want to make him proud that he vouched for me.

"You wanna tell Daddy's lapdog to get lost now, Chey?" Clint says. My attention snaps to his face so fast that I'm practically dizzy when I catch the smirk forming in the corner of his mouth. "Run along, bitch boy. I'm busy with my girl."

I open my mouth to cuss the guy out, but two things distract me. The first is the football coach trotting over, and the second is the bony elbow digging into my side as Cheyenne passes me and strides up to Clint. For a brief second, I think she's going to wrap her arms around him and tell me to fuck off. But she doesn't.

"You talk big out here on the field, but you damn sure wouldn't be saying that in front of my daddy," she says in the same mocking tone he used a moment prior. "Go ahead and talk shit about Jeremy, but leave his cut out of it."

And I'm in love. This chick is Forsaken through and through, even if she wants to pretend like she's some preppy bitch. She's got the club written all over her, from the way she keeps her chin up to the bite in her tone. I see so much of her father in her right now that it's going to make my shower jerk-off session a little awkward.

"Know what? I'm done with your fucking tantrums, Cheyenne."

"And I'm done with you being such an asshole!" she yells. The calm angry girl from a moment ago has been replaced by a crazy little screamer.

"Oh—oh no—" he says with his mouth turned down in a faux pout. Jesus Christ, she's into some assholes. It's a wonder she never hooked up with me. "Bitch."

I take a deep breath to keep from shoving Cheyenne to the side in an effort to reach this guy and break every bone in his body. On the first deep breath, Cheyenne calls him an asshole. On the second deep breath, she kicks him in the shin. Neither effort has any effect on him. He just looks down at her with a bored expression.

"Bruce, back on the field," the coach shouts from several feet away. He's an older guy in his fifties with gray hair and a pot belly. I should probably know the guy's name since he taught my history class last year, but I don't. I failed that fucking class.

"We're not done here, Coach," I shout without taking my eyes off Clint. I know I'm on the verge of getting expelled, but I don't really give a shit. Holly, Grady's girlfriend, is trying to keep me in school for as long as she can. But word on the street is she's got a temper on her, too. I don't think she'd be too mad at me if she found out I got expelled because this little pussy thinks he can run his mouth whenever he wants.

"Son, what is that you're wearing?" the coach asks. Grady gave me the rundown—no wearing the cut during school hours or on school property. But it's after school, and Coach Whoeverthefuck can suck my right ball. Of course he would want to know what I'm wearing. Some pigs think this cut is a gang symbol. They have no idea.

"Jeremy," Cheyenne says. Her voice is much stronger now. She seems frustrated and a little guilty all at the same time. "Let's just go."

I nod my head to keep from saying or doing anything that's going to cause a scene. We turn away and walk side by side toward the parking lot. Diesel is bound to be waiting for her there, like he does every day. I don't know the lowdown on everything that went down, but someone showed up on campus and scared the crap out of her, so Grady asked me to make sure she's safe during school hours. Maybe I'll earn some bonus points by keeping an eye on her after school.

"Enjoy my leftovers, bitch," Clint shouts. Both Cheyenne and I turn around and glare at Clint as he turns and heads back toward the field where the coach has already returned.

"Do me a favor," Cheyenne says as she places a hand on my back. I look down at her to find her lips have formed into a devious smile. A glint of vengeance shines in her eyes. It's hot. Like, really fucking hot.

"Anything," I say like the pussy-whipped asshole I am.

Her smile gets impossibly wider. "Make him suffer."

I'm unable to hold back the laugh as I give her a wink and take off in a sprint. He doesn't see me coming as I throw myself onto his back and shove his face in the mud. My left hand pinches at the back of his neck with all my strength. My knee digs viciously into the small of his back. I've seen men tortured and abused for far less—and for far less important people than Cheyenne. This bitch is lucky he's getting off with a warning.

"I know where your dad works, and I know where you live. I know your sister and how good her pussy tastes," I hiss into his ear as he struggles to breathe through the mud he's inhaling. "I could have your mother, but that bitch is fucking nasty. Just remember this—I represent Forsaken. *Cheyenne* is Forsaken. You don't want on Daddy's bad side, and you sure don't want to piss off any of us. As far as you're concerned, she doesn't exist. And if I hear any different, I'll make sure her father knows every bit of this conversation."

I shove his face farther into the mud, dig my knee harder into his back, and then stand. My boot slams into his side before I walk off. Every bit of what I told him is the truth, with the exception of the part about his sister. I'm not picky, but she's as fucking gross as her mother is. No way I'd stick my dick in that.

Cheyenne is waiting for me at the edge of the field. When I reach her, she says nothing and just turns to walk toward the parking lot once more. We make it to the concrete before she speaks.

"You're kind of dirty," she says with a wrinkle of her nose.

"Word around the clubhouse is they call you Miss Priss because you're kind of a pain in the ass," I retort.

"I'm so not." She doesn't even sound like she believes her own lies. "But can I ask you something?"

"Depends."

"Who is that guy who showed up at school?"

"What guy?" I know damn well who she's talking about, but I don't know what I'm supposed to say. It's club business, which means it's none of hers.

"I'm not an idiot. That creepy guy shows up at school, and now I have an escort everywhere I go? So who is he?"

"Your escort? It's Diesel," I say with a nod of my head across the lot to the motherfucker with the buzz cut who's resting on his bike.

She shakes her head. "Nice try. I have questions, and I know you have answers."

There's absolutely nothing I can tell her that won't cost me my top rocker. So I swipe some mud from the knee of my jeans and wipe it across her cheek.

She swats my hand away with a surprised laugh and steps back with a screech. "Ew, gross!"

"You're so fucking high maintenance," I say, keeping my tone sounding bored. Just as she looks offended, I swipe another dollop of mud from my jeans and go straight for her nose, but she swipes it off my finger and takes a step closer to me.

In a quiet voice, she says, "Are you trying to distract me?"

I clear my throat. "No, I'm trying to get you dirty, baby."

Shit. I sound like a moron.

A thick cold goo clogs up my ear, and it's only then that I feel her removing her finger and realize she's shoved the mud in my ear. My fucking ear. I narrow my eyes at her as she steps back, waves her finger to direct me to stay put, and grins wildly.

"You're in for it," I say as I take off after her. She screams and takes off running through the parked cars. I could outrun her, but I want to let her think she has a chance.

"D, help! D! Help!" she screams. I look up to find her hiding behind Diesel, who is in the corner of the lot, perched on his bike. His helmet rests on his handlebars, and his tanned muscles are exposed by the black wife-beater he wears under his cut.

"Back off, prospect. The lady wants to be left alone," Diesel says through a smile. He stands from the bike and ushers her over to him where he tosses an arm around her shoulders and then walks her to her car. It takes me a moment to realize that I'm standing in the middle of the parking lot, smiling like an idiot. Alone.

Cheyenne climbs into her Bug that's parked in the center of the lot. Once she's securely inside, Diesel makes his way back to his bike. I parked the bike Grady gave me just a few feet from his, so I follow his path.

"Grady is going to chop your dick off and eat it for breakfast," Diesel says. He's way too smiley right now. It's creeping me out.

"Probably." We grab our helmets and climb on our bikes. Before I start my engine, I say, "But it'll be worth it."

CHAPTER 2

November

17 months to Mancuso's downfall

Jeremy

DIESEL STARTS UP his bike and takes off after Cheyenne, who's turning out of the lot. I follow suit and spend the short ride home thinking about ways to get her to talk to me again. She's cute to look at but better to actually talk to. Maybe I need to beat up more football players. Or I could tease her some more. Maybe I could just talk to her, but that might be too weird.

When I pull up to the house and walk in, I'm met with my sister, Nic, and her old man, Duke. They're hogging up the couch as per usual. He's wearing a pair of old jeans and nothing else, and she's in one of his shirts and I hope something else. Their legs are entwined, and one of his arms is stretched over her shoulders, tucking her into his side. His other arm is stretched out with his hand palming her stomach. Her small frame is dwarfed by his large one in all areas except for her growing belly.

Despite the constant half nudity in the house, he's good for us. He's going to be good for my niece or nephew, too. I just like having a guy around here. For one, we out-vote Nic on almost everything, and for two, I've finally learned how to ride. It's the only thing I ever wanted to do—ride a Harley just like my dad and his brothers. But none of that means he can't be a serious fucking prick to live with. In *my* house. He's like a bossy squatter that can rip my dick off if he so chooses.

Duke had offered to teach me a few years back, but Jim put the gavel down on that. Nic didn't even know I was showing up at the clubhouse as often as I could get away with. If one of the guys had taught me to ride, she would have had a fucking fit, and if there's anything my sister is a pro at, it's throwing a fit.

"You're all muddy," Nic says with a raised eyebrow. She points her index finger in my direction as if to tell me to stay in the hardwood entry.

Duke lifts his chin in greeting. He catches sight of the mud on my jeans and the bottom of my cut. I just shrug my shoulders and shake my head. I'm not about to shoot the shit about Cheyenne to these two assholes. The second I tell Nic I got my eye on a girl, and not just my dick interested in her, she won't fucking let it go. Ever. Nic's like that—she nags endlessly—and somehow I just know if I refuse to give her what she wants, she's going to pester the fuck out of Duke until he makes me. So yeah, I ain't saying shit about the mud or the girl, and I hope that Diesel doesn't find the little scene he witnessed earlier newsworthy.

"Yeah." I leave it at that.

"Hey, since you're up, grab me some food. Eileen called me in since Mindy didn't show, so I have to get to the shop soon," she says.

"Fuck no. Do I look like your bitch?"

The words fly out of my mouth before I can think about what I'm saying. When it was just me and Nic, we had an understanding. She kept food in the house, and I kept out of her way. She stepped on my toes, and I'd step on hers. It was just sibling shit mostly, but sometimes it got pretty fucking heated. She may be a foot shorter than me, but when she's pissed, she fucking loses it. She would get to bitching about the dumbest shit. It bugged the crap out of me, but she never stayed mad long. It worked for us. But now that Duke's here, everything is different. I can't say a single fucking thing that he doesn't approve of without getting my ass reamed for it. I raise an eyebrow at her. She and I get into a fight where she makes me yell at her, and I get hit for it.

We have good times. It's not all hitting and fighting, and Duke always takes time later to explain his bullshit reasons for doing what he does. He's taking this whole daddy-practice thing too far, but it's not like I can say that to him. I don't want to go back to having to call him "sir" every time I see him.

"If you're not going to show your sister some respect, at least show that cut some respect and get the fucking mud off it," Duke says as he untangles himself from my sister.

It's not the response I was expecting. Instead of questioning him like I'm prone to do, I just nod my head and back into the kitchen. Duke stands from the couch and follows behind me.

I've never cleaned my cut before, so I don't really know what I'm doing. I eye the dish soap before deciding to just use water. I don't know why he's bitching about my leather. I mean, Dad always says that a man's cut tells his story. He never cleaned his cut, really. Maybe once or twice—for a wedding or a funeral—but other than that, he let it get dirty and gross. He said he earned the dirt and the wearing of the leather on behalf of his patch. It's a source of pride. But if Duke wants my cut clean, I guess I'll clean it.

He strides in the room a minute later with his boots on. He's pulling on a dark blue V-neck as he shakes his head at me. I turn the water on and reach for the nearest dish towel, but he points to the kitchen table. Instead of cleaning off the mud, I head where he's pointing and sit down. He plops down across from me and rests his elbows on the table.

His voice is low as he says, "Got a job for you."

"A job?" Not that I'm not grateful he's not threatening to kick my ass for smarting off to my sister or anything, but he's acting weird as all hell right now.

"I need you to facilitate a meeting between Princess and Junior."

Shit. Alex gave me a brief rundown on the shit she caused during one of her visits to the house. She's cute but not my type—not my type being the kind of pussy that comes with a hundred and eighty pounds of asshole attached at her side. I asked her what was with all the drama about her and Trigger hooking up. It was a short and weird conversation. I mean, what the fuck do you say when someone tells you they accidentally ratted their dad out, now their cousin wants to kill them, and they inadvertently started a war between Forsaken and the Italian mafia? I mean, fuck. Nic is clumsy, and she tends to break shit, but she's never destroyed an informal, decades-old peace treaty between two outlaw entities. That kind of power is both terrifying and impressive— and I want none of it. So facilitating anything for Alex is above my pay grade, I've decided.

"Why is something this important being passed down to me?"

"Princess requested it. Trigger won't even hear of letting her near him, and if I set the meeting up and he finds out, he'll ride my ass like I'm a Lost Girl."

"And what the fuck do you think he's going to do to me!" I mean, goddamn it. Even Duke doesn't want to piss Trigger off about this shit, so why the fuck does he think it's a good idea to send me in?

"As far as Trigger knows, you don't know shit. You're just doing a favor for Ruby's kid, so it's like doing a favor for the Pres."

"You think he's going to let me slide on that excuse?"

"Probably not," Duke says.

"He's going to fuck me up," I whine. I'm not proud of whining, but facing off against Trigger when it comes to Princess—or Cub or whatever the fuck I'm supposed to call her—is a goddamn death wish.

"So don't get caught," Nic says, startling me. She's leaning against the doorjamb. Her arms are folded over her chest, pulling up her shirt and—thankfully—revealing a small pair of cotton shorts. Decency—I guess she has some of it. "Look, Jer, this is important to Alex. She asked me to talk to Duke."

And suddenly it all makes sense. My sister is the mastermind behind this little plan. If it was Duke's idea, he'd just do it himself and fuck Trigger if he didn't like it. But this is Nic being Nic and trying to protect the people she loves—and she loves Alex like the sister she never had. Apparently she loves Duke enough to spare him Trigger's wrath. I'm her fucking brother, and she can't spare me? If I sent Christmas cards, my bitch sister would be off my list.

Duke silently watches Nic push off the doorjamb and shuffle over to the fridge. I watch his eyes travel from hers down to her protruding stomach and then slide down her legs to her bare feet. Duke looks at Nic in a way I've never seen a man look at a woman before. I mean, people say they're in love all the time. They say they care about people, but then shit happens. They leave, or they get sent away. But none of them ever look at the person they say they love the way Duke looks at Nic. It's like he's making sure she's okay and she's got all her limbs.

Duke told me the last time we were changing the oil in her car that he needs help painting the spare bedroom for the baby. He doesn't need help, and I called him on that, but then he told me that being a man means being involved. It means sometimes doing lame shit like painting a room and putting together baby furniture, and that as the kid's uncle, I have a responsibility to make sure he or she is taken care of. It kind of freaked me out—made the whole baby thing that much more real.

Everything is changing, and I don't know how to deal with half of it. Like now, being told to set up a meet between Alex and her brother. It's heavy shit that I worry I'm going to seriously fuck up.

"Neither of you want to take the heat," I mumble.

"No," Nic says. She opens the fridge and pulls out the peanut butter and jelly, then sets them on the counter and turns back toward me. She turns her attention to Duke and nods her head. "Tell him, baby."

"What you're about to hear stays between us, got it?" he says, and I nod my head. I know better than to run my mouth—usually—about shit a member tells me. It's been months, and I haven't told anyone about the bitch Ian had me get rid of. I can keep my mouth shut when it matters.

"We put it to a vote—moving Junior to a more permanent location—and Trigger lost his shit. As far as the club's concerned, whether or not Princess and Junior see each other again is up to her old man. She's not voted in and likely won't be unless she can win Grady over, so it's not a club problem. But it becomes a club problem if a member interferes with another member's personal life. We can't have tension among the brothers."

"Yeah, that policy is bullshit. You all are always up each other's asses. This is going to cost me my patch."

"Not if you didn't know you weren't supposed to do it," Duke says.

Bullshit. These assholes talk about their policies and codes, and they never fucking follow them. It's just a convenient excuse to avoid getting their hands dirty.

Nic sighs loudly from her spot and taps her foot on the

floor. She opens her mouth but waits a moment before speaking.

"The club can't handle any more stress, Jer. We lost Chief, and with this Italian in town, everybody is on edge. The guys are all on security detail every single day, and Ian is still looking for Darren's parents. Duke isn't going to be able to focus and keep us safe if he's distracted with thinking that Ryan is going to go off on him at any moment." Nic puts a hand on her stomach, and it's fucking unfair because she knows using my niece or nephew against me works every time. The way I see it, motherhood doesn't really run in her genes, and I don't want to do anything to make being a mom more difficult on her. Growing up without a mom sucks, and I don't want that for my niece or nephew.

"Fine. Fucking fine," I say. Pushing back from the table, I glare at Duke whose expression is as flat as it has been for the last several minutes. He doesn't like to talk about all the shit that's fucked in our world right now, and I don't blame him, but hell. Why couldn't either of them tell Alex that she's just going to have to deal with Trigger over this shit? Pussies, the both of them.

"By the way," I say, "Miss Priss was asking about the Italian."

"Don't tell her shit," Duke says. "Club business."

"I know that. Just letting you know. She was pushy."

Nic's back is to me as she works at making her sandwich. She turns around mid-bite and says, "Tell her it's being taken care of and she doesn't have anything to worry about."

"Club business, Nic," Duke says with a harsh tone. "He doesn't have to tell her a fucking thing."

"Yeah, because that line has worked so well for you boys in the past," she mumbles and takes another bite of her sandwich. She has a point. The guys are all about living by the code, but the second their old lady denies them some pussy, they become a bunch of chatty bitches. Doesn't matter, though. Duke gave me my orders.

"Speaking of club business," I say a little quieter and lean in, "Ian still doesn't have a lead on where Darren's parents went?"

"Nothing," he says and eyes Nic, who isn't even trying to pretend she's not paying attention. "It's like they've fucking disappeared off the face of the earth." I do the same, and while she doesn't appear terribly concerned, that doesn't mean shit. She's fucking tough as nails. She got that from our dad.

A chirping noise sounds from across the table. Turning my head back to Duke, I see him pull his cell out of his jeans pocket and read the screen. A few seconds later and he's staring at me with narrowed eyes. "Safe house—now."

"Wait. I'm supposed to set up this meeting *now*?" I ask. The safe house is where we're keeping Michael for the time being. I'm not supposed to know that, or where it is, but the brothers aren't so great at keeping their mouths shut outside of Church. The more I walk around with a confused look on my face, the more they think I'm either too distracted or too stupid to be listening in. Assholes.

Duke hops to his feet, strides over to Nic, and kisses

her cheek. "Don't wait up, babe. Shit's going down. Tell Eileen to run her own goddamn shop." Then he turns to me and jerks his chin at the front door. Understanding the order, I make my way outside.

Once he's shut the door behind him, he turns to me with a serious expression. "We're about to do some shit. Mancuso's guys showed up at the safe house, so it's probably going to get ugly. Grady's called the full table, but Mancuso's guy wants Jim alone."

I nod my head like I know what the hell he's talking about before I realize that bullshitting could be dangerous. So instead of doing what I normally do and acting like I get it, I just ask him. "What does the full table mean?"

"It means that Jim needs everybody to the safe house fully armed, so let's go."

"We should probably leave the bikes at the clubhouse, then. Take one of the vans or the SUV."

Duke slaps my face lightly and forces a tight smile to his face. "Good. You do pay attention. I need you fully armed."

"I got my piece," I say and reach behind my back, lightly patting the holster that the gun Trigger gave me rests in.

"No, I mean serious fire power, not that piece of shit." He just shakes his head and starts walking to his bike but stops when my cell starts ringing.

Quickly, I yank it out of my pocket and check the caller ID. It reads PRES. My thumb slides over the answer button on the screen, and I bring the phone to my ear.

"Prospect," I say. It's stupid, but Trigger gave me the order to answer my phone that way, and I'm not inclined to piss him off any more than I already do.

"We got trouble. Need you to check on Sweets and Bean," Jim says solemnly on the other end of the line. "They're MIA."

"Apartment, coffee shop, and high school. Anywhere else?"

"Not unless you get a lead. See what you find out and then call Knuck."

"Yes, sir. I'm on it." The line goes dead, and before I shove the phone back in my pocket, I check the time. It's well after four, so I doubt Holly will still be at work. Walking up to Duke, I lower my voice so that I'm not broadcasting club business to my nosy fucking neighbors.

"Change of plans. Pres says Sweets and Bean are MIA."

"Fuck," he shouts. Angry veins pop out of the sides of his neck as he stomps his heavy boot into the ground in a move that tells me he and Ryan have known one another far too long. "What the fuck is wrong with this fucking club that we can't keep track of a few goddamn women in a town this fucking small!"

I stay silent for a moment before I realize he's still grunting and screeching so loud that our neighbors are starting to take notice. It might be a bad idea, but I lean in and whisper-shout, "Dude. I get it, but we have an audience."

"Fuck you," he yells. His narrowed eyes travel from

my face to the grass. He takes a few deep breaths, still obviously seething, and stomps off to his bike.

I don't wait for my orders and head for my bike as well. He takes off toward the club house, and I head the opposite direction toward the girls' apartment. The coffee shop is closer, but the way Knuck feels about Holly, she takes priority. My hands shake the closer I get to the apartment, and my palms make my grip on my handlebars almost too slick to ride without eating dirt. But I can't slow down. Knuck needs Holly, and I need my patch—and if I fuck this up, ain't nobody getting what they need.

CHAPTER 3

November

17 months to Mancuso's downfall

Jeremy

STANDING IN THE middle of Holly and Mindy's living room with pieces of splintered wood around me, I'm suddenly nervous that Grady's order to "stay put" didn't mean busting into the place. When I called him a few minutes ago to give him the bad news that I can't find the girls anywhere, he hung up before I could clarify what his order meant. So really this is his fault.

I step over the shards of what used to be part of the front door and its frame and head into the small kitchen. Everything looks normal in here, and until I broke in, the place was secure. So, at the very least, there wasn't anything violent going on here from what I can tell.

Leaving the kitchen and heading down the hallway, I first check out Holly's room. Her bed is messy, and clothes are piled in the corners, but it's not too bad. A beige bra sits on the edge of her bed, distracting me. It's nothing really sexy, but I've been thinking about motorboating her tits for a while now.

Before I find something else to check out, I dart out of the room and into the bathroom, then Mindy's room. Nothing appears out of place until I notice the tipped-over nail polish bottle on her nightstand. The bright pink polish is half-dried on the wooden surface and has dripped down the side, creating a colorful blob on the carpet.

Shit.

I have no fucking clue what I'm doing anymore. I pull out my phone and try to dial Grady again, but he doesn't answer. Calling Jim turns out to be useless, and so does calling Duke. Finally I decide to check the shop once more and hope to find Mindy there and totally clueless as to why I'm freaking out.

My boots scrape at the concrete curb as I rush across the street and up onto the sidewalk at the corner of Main and Laurel on my way to Universal Grounds for the second time this afternoon. The first time I was here, Nic's bitch boss was at the counter. With Bean nowhere in sight, I hopped back on my bike and rushed to the high school. On my way, I found Sweets's and Bean's cars in the drug store parking lot just a few blocks from their apartment. The doors were all unlocked, and there was nothing in Mindy's trunk or the back of Holly's Jeep. Not a single sign of struggle and, thankfully, no fucking blood. The spilled nail polish in the apartment tells me the cars were dumped there. I sent Duke a quick text about the cars and then was back on my way to the high school. I didn't find shit there.

Only Margot was in the office, and she went off, bitching at me about missing classes and this apparent problem people have with my attitude, which is total bullshit. I'm a fucking peach to be around. But whatever. After she shut the fuck up, I got it out of her that Holly got a call and then ran out to take her lunch and hadn't returned since. She was supposed to be off half an hour ago. The fucking busybody wanted to know if she was in trouble—or causing trouble—and if I saw her first that I could let her know she's on thin ice at work. I can't be concerned with whether or not Sweets has a job after today. It's not like the club is going to let her get fired. But so what if she does? Grady can keep her comfortable. But again, none of this shit matters if I don't fucking find her. *Fuck. Fuck. Fuck.*

In a matter of seconds, I'm in front of the coffee house. My lungs strain for breath that's not coming as easily as I need it to. Getting that call from Jim has fucked me up big time. Out of all the guys and the prospects, he called *me*. And it's not like he called me for some bullshit errand.

I know a little about what's going on with the club. Enough to know that shit ain't right around town right now, but not enough to feel like I have my footing. Grady and Duke have both given me the rundown about the Italian who showed up at my school and gave Chey and Holly some shit about the club, but I have a funny feeling that I don't have a clue how real shit is about to get. But this? Holly means something to Grady, which means she means something to the club—whether she likes it or not. It's bad news—bad fucking news—for any of our women to be this vulnerable. That's one thing Dad always made sure I understood—we protect our women. Always.

Through the dirty window pane, I can see Nic. Stupid woman directly disobeyed her old man's orders. Fucking A. She's wearing one of her tight strappy tank tops that shows off Duke's good work. She started showing a while ago, and it seems like she's just getting bigger every week. I don't really know how pregnancy works. I mean, I know how it happens. I'm not that stupid. But as for how this shit works while the kid is baking, I'm at a loss. All I know is that she's not fitting into her clothes anymore, but she wears them anyway. Her face is relaxed as she rings up a customer at the register and then gets to work on their coffee. I don't want to fuck up her day, but I don't have any more time to waste.

Just as a customer opens the front door and the overhead bells chimes, I slide in, completely ignoring the customer who is next in line. I lean against the counter, still struggling for air and say, "You seen Sweets or Bean?"

Nic's eyes travel over to mine, and she purses her lips. She narrows her gaze as she works on the drink at hand, and it's only when she's done that she looks my way. Irritation radiates off her as she says, "No. Miss Perky Face never showed up for her shift. I'm fucking tired, and I think I'm going to barf at some point. I wasn't even supposed to be here today."

And just like that, the bitchy sister I don't miss and kind of fear makes her return. I knew the last few months were too good to be true. She was all in love and shit and acting happy. I was almost worried this baby business had resulted in a personality lobotomy. But nope. She-Demon is apparently alive and well.

"Speaking of that—your old man told you to stay home," I say loudly and hope she knows I'm using my Forsaken voice—the one where I talk a little deeper and with more purpose.

"That's not what I heard," she says and shifts her eyes across the counter with a raised brow and a dismissive tone. She knows damn well what he meant, but fucking typical Nic. She don't care.

The customer at the counter clears his throat behind me and grumbles, "Can I get some help, please?"

Nic takes a deep breath and puffs her cheeks out, like a squirrel who's hoarding for winter, and then blows it out. I'm getting antsy with every wasted second. My neck cranes in the customer's direction. He's a middle-aged man with a distended gut and a button-up that doesn't stretch well enough to fit his midsection. He taps his leather wallet on the counter top impatiently like he's the most important fucking person in the room.

He's not.

"Hang on a minute, buddy," Nic snaps at him. Her eyes flit to mine. "And for the record, I can't abandon Eileen, because *somebody* made me leave work so many times I'm on thin ice as it is."

"Don't blame me because you're unprepared for motherhood," I gripe. Her left nostril lifts in irritation. "But seriously, I need to find them. Like now. It's *important.*"

"Come on. I'm running late to a meeting," he says. He pauses before continuing, but he doesn't get the rest of his complaint out.

"Step off," I yell as I close the distance between him and me. I'm not looking for a scene any bigger than we're already making, so I do him a favor and give him a foot of space. "You think you're late now? Keep fucking talking."

He backs up from me, his eyes flicking to my leather vest, and heads for the door. I don't bother discouraging his exit. I've wasted enough goddamn time in here.

"Shit." Nic walks around the counter, gets close, and whispers, "What's wrong?"

"That visitor from New York?" I say in a whisper-shout. "In town. Had some trouble. Jim's got reason to think that's why nobody can find Bean or Sweets."

"Great," she grumbles. Her bitchy mood is slowly sinking into a quiet fear. I'm not a fan of Bitchy Nic, but I'm even less excited to see Sad Nic. "Tell me if you find Minds, 'kay?"

"Sure," I say and head for the door.

"Boy," a voice shouts from behind me. I turn around to find an old dude who's staring at me from a nearby table. He's got a newspaper opened up before him and a mostly empty mug of coffee in his right hand. Giving me a slight nod, he says, "You looking for the Mercer girls?"

"Yeah," I say. This guy is clearly a local with how he's made himself at home in the shop and the way he's addressed me. Tourists are usually pretty easy to spot. "Who are you?"

"He's kidding, right?" he asks. The old man's look transforms into disbelief as he redirects his attention to my sister.

"He's an idiot," she states.

"I own the hardware store your dad used to take you to all the time. Every time you left, my store was a candy bar lighter than when you came in."

"Oh, hey." Now I remember him. Dad was always taking me to get shit for the house. It was either paint or new cabinet door knobs or other shit Mom wanted for her showplace. Dad would get to buying stuff for the house, and I'd get to deciding which candy bar I wanted to shove in my back pocket on the way out. "Huh, thought I didn't get caught."

"Your father's a good man. He always paid for the candy you thought you were stealing."

What a dick. Makes me want to go in there now and lift something and see what the fuck he does about it.

"Listen. I get that you want to walk down memory lane while you still can, but I ain't got time for this shit. You know where Holly and Mindy are or not?"

He narrows his eyes and studies me for a moment before pursing his lips and saying, "About an hour ago I was closing the shop for the night when I saw them getting into a black sedan outside their apartment. Fancy car."

"Goddamn it," I yell and cover my eyes with my hand. Mancuso's guy has them for sure. Given the threat Grady got from the Italian, I got no doubt. "Nic, I need to get you to Jim's."

"I'm in the middle of a shift." Stubborn Nic is making an appearance, which makes me want to toss her ass in a trunk. Darren was surprisingly easy to move, so Nic can't be any harder. "I'm fine here."

"No, you're not protected," I say.

"She's fine, son," the old man says. The more I look at him, the more I remember about him. I dropped a hammer on this dude's toe when I was a kid. Dad calls him Old Man Hill, if I remember right. He nods slowly and pats the front pocket of his khakis. He pulls out a handgun just enough to show me the butt of it and then slides it back in. "I'm old, but I know when something's wrong. I'll keep an eye on your sister until her old man shows up to take her home."

"You even know how to use that thing, Grandpa?"

"Forsaken aren't the only ones who know how to take care of their shit," he says and lifts his chin.

"Need your help, sis," I say and stride up beside her. Leaning down just slightly, I whisper into her ear. "Knuck told me to stay at the apartment."

"Call Duke," she says with a nod of her head. "Grady will be pissed you disobeyed his order for a little while, but the guys might need you at the safe house."

I lean in and place a kiss on her forehead and then dart out the door. Outside on the street, I call Duke.

"Where the fuck are you, boy?"

"Girls are MIA, and Knuck gave me orders to stay put," I say as quickly as I can.

"Fuck that," he says. "Get up here. I know your nosy

ass knows how to get here. Get Nic's car from the house and park far enough away that I can't hear you pull up. I'm about a mile up from the highway. You'll spot Fish by Ruby's Suburban."

I had a feeling he knew I'd figured out where the safe house is. Shit, but now's not the time to think over what that means.

"Yes, sir," I say automatically. Before I think better of it, the words fly out of my mouth. "Nic went in to the shop after all. Claims she didn't hear the order to stay home. Old Man Hill's got a piece, and he's keeping an eye on her."

"Fucking hell. She never fucking listens. Good that she's with him, though," is all Duke says before he hangs up the phone. I guess he knows something about the guy that I don't.

Back inside the shop, I cut off another customer—this one a woman—and level Nic with a glare. "Need your keys."

"Why?"

"Duke's orders," I say. She gives them up easily, but detaches the small ring with her house keys before tossing them my way. On my way out the door I shout, "Stay with Old Man Hill, or it'll be your hide."

CHAPTER 4

November

17 months to Mancuso's downfall

Jeremy

THE DRIVE TO the safe house is no more than fifteen minutes on my bike—not that I've timed it—but it takes over twenty in Nic's car. There aren't many speed traps in town, but once you get to the outskirts, along the highway, the highway patrol sits around with donuts around their dicks just waiting for some asshole to fly by. They can't see my cut from inside the sedan, and getting pulled over would take time I don't have. So I suffer.

Soon enough, the SUVs come into view. They're parked on the side of the narrow highway, seemingly unattended at first sight. I pull off to the side about fifty yards away and kill the engine. On foot, I approach the SUVs with caution, retrieving my gun from the back of my jeans, unlocking the safety, and rounding the back of Ruby's Suburban.

The crunching of a pinecone surprises me, redirecting my attention to the other side of the Suburban. Fish stands just off the side of the road, with an AR-15 in his hands, the business end pointed right between my eyes. It takes him a moment to relax before he lowers the gun and narrows his eyes in frustration. His chest heaves from the shock of being snuck up on. My own gun is still at my side, having not reacted quickly enough to draw it. Fuck. This is the shit that Duke is talking about when he says that I need to pay better attention or I'm going to get my ass killed.

"Scared me, man," he complains.

I shake off the fear of being done-in by friendly fire, and blow out a heavy breath. "You're fucking telling me." Nodding my head to the woods and raising my brows, I say, "Duke wants me with him. Where is he?"

"About two miles in, straight ahead. But you can't go in like that," Fish says.

"Right." Sneaking up on a bunch of guys with military-grade firepower and a life or death situation is a sure way to turn myself a pair of shish keballs. "Better tell him I'm coming."

"That, too, but I need to debrief you first," he says. Resting the large weapon on its strap over his shoulder, Fish casts a suspicious glance down each side of the highway before he rounds the SUV and unlocks the back passenger door. He pulls out another semi with a scope attached and hands it to me. Then he grabs two smart phones and eyes them before deciding they're what he's looking for.

I grab the rifle by the barrel, and my arm sags with its weight. I haven't shot an AR-15 since Dad was around and he used to take me shooting on Jim and Ruby's property for practice. Since then, the only thing I've practiced on are some of Dad's old handguns Nic has hidden around the house. My sister doesn't dislike guns—she just thinks I'm going to blow my foot off because she's convinced I'm nothing more than a stupid fucking kid.

Fish raises an eyebrow. "You got any idea what you're walking into?"

No, not really. I mean, on some level I guess I got an idea. But I ain't ever done this shit before, so how am I supposed to know what I'm walking into? All I know is that they decided to let me start earning my top rocker during a really fucking dangerous time—not that I'm complaining. The pride that comes with the patch is worth the risk.

"Didn't think so." He shakes his head and points me to the tree line. "W formation. Two in front, three in back, a mile up. Duke's front right by himself. Ian took off to find Sweets." As he talks, he turns the phones on and brings up two different apps. Wyatt's voice sounds from one of the phones before Fish turns the volume down. On the other phone, he messes with the screen. Jim's voice booms on the line before he turns that phone down, too.

"She okay?" I ask, still half-focused on the phones as he hands them over. I awkwardly place the strap of the semi over my shoulder and hold the phones, not sure what to do with them.

"For this asshole's sake, she fucking better be," he says. "Knuck will skin him alive. Now listen up. This one is a one-way radio so you can hear Jim and the Italian. This is the most important tool you have right now. Priority is keeping Pops whole, got it?" he says as he points at one of the phones.

I nod my head and focus in on the phones. I don't recognize either app, but they seem awesome as fuck. Who knew Forsaken had such cool toys?

"On the other phone, you can press the button on the screen at any time to talk to the guys. It's like a conference call. We can all communicate as need be. It's not a toy, and this isn't time to shoot the shit, got it?" He pulls out a wireless earbud. "The earbud is synced to Pops, so if you have trouble hearing him over the other phone, just turn its volume down."

"Serious business," I say and pop the earbud into my ear. "Got it."

Just as I'm heading in what I think is the right direction, he pulls a phone out of his pocket and presses the button on the screen. "Baby Boy is heading your way, boys. Try not to shoot him."

"Got it," Duke barks back, his voice echoing in not only the phone in my hand but on Fish's as well. In my ear, I'm hearing bits and pieces of Jim's conversation with this guy. It's mostly filled with huffs and few words, none of which I can understand.

"Bring my bitch forth," Ryan says with a chuckle. The sick fuck. I can actually hear the smile in his voice.

"Gave the kid one of our signatures," Fish says,

referring to the AR-15 that Forsaken's been fond of ever since I can remember. Dad once told me the club's got over a hundred of these babies floating around town in various places.

"Bet ya haven't handled anything that powerful since I let you deep throat my dick, huh?" Ryan says.

I want to just keep my mouth shut and walk toward the woods, but I also want to know how this thing works. So I bring the conference phone to my mouth, press the button, and say, "No, sir, Duke's is bigger."

"Damn straight. Now shut up unless it's business," Duke says. The chatter on the conference stops immediately.

I've made it about a half mile or so before I finally think I see something in the distance, but it turns out to be a wayward branch. It's all trees and a few birds here and there. I can't find anybody. Little River is a tiny as fuck place that has like no population at all. The safe house sits far enough back from the highway—a few miles, I think—that I didn't even know it was here until I took it upon myself to follow Ryan one day when he made it down this way to have a little "talk" with Michael. Nobody told me to follow him, but with how pissed off he was, I didn't think it was a good idea to let them kill Ruby's son. Thankfully I didn't have to do shit because he hopped off his bike before turning off the highway and kicked the shit out of a poor fucking redwood that did nothing but grow in the wrong damn spot. After he calmed his shit about being pissed that I followed him, he wrapped his hand around my shoulder really fucking tight and gave me a nod. It's the closest he'll ever get to saying thank you. As much as he's hating on Michael right now, he doesn't really want to hurt Ruby.

Trying to walk through woods and not make any noise is probably the stupidest fucking goal ever. If it's not a pinecone I'm stepping on, then it's a fallen branch that cracks beneath my boots or a pile of leaves that aren't wet enough to not make crunching sounds. Sure, let's hide in the woods. Because that shit makes sense.

Since I'm just a prospect, they don't tell me shit. But I'm starting to pick up on a few things. The guys who are the best shots are always in the front. That includes Duke, Ryan, and Ian. Ryan tries to take the lead a lot because he's a cocky motherfucker, but it is actually Ian who consistently has the most accuracy.

"I think I'm lost," I say into the conference. I feel like I've been walking forever and can't find anybody. Pretty soon I'm going to panic that I'm going to be found and get a bullet to my skull.

"Pull up your pants, shithead," Wyatt says over the line.

I pause in place and slowly look around but don't see anything. I take another step before pulling my pants up a little and adjusting my belt so they stay up with my hand that's not holding the gun.

"Where are you guys?" I ask. I'm fucking failing at this shit. Bad.

"Another twenty feet forward, Jer. And don't fucking trip on me," Duke says.

Without arguing, I keep moving forward and don't see Duke lying in the grass and leaves until I'm almost tripping over him. Shit. He told me *not* to trip on him.

Fuck this noise. I can't go on these missions—I'm going to get my ass capped.

As I approach Duke, he seems to notice my presence but does not turn around. Instead, he lifts his left arm in the air and raises his closed fist, telling me to stop what I'm doing, and says, "Show yourselves, boys,"

I slowly turn around to find Ryan, Wyatt, and Bear taking a step away from three separate redwoods, each about twenty to thirty feet apart. I walked right between Wyatt and Bear without noticing them. They're all wearing their own clothes and their cuts—no fancy uniforms or camouflage. Just as quickly as they've stepped forward, they've stepped back into the shadows of their trees and have completely disappeared from view again. Shit. How long do these assholes train for this shit? I thought I was joining a club, not signing up for special ops or something.

Turning back to Duke, I move forward, and as quietly as I can, I lie down on the mixture of grass and fallen leaves beside him. I don't get too close, but I don't want to be too far away either. There's a fine line between two men lying next to each other at a professional distance and two men coming close to cuddling. And I ain't fucking cuddling Duke.

He begins to talk as I awkwardly set up my position with the rifle. I try my best to mimic his stance. His AR-15 has a bandana over the top of the scope. He sees me eyeing it and pulls a spare out of his pocket and hands it to me. I fumble with tying the fucking thing on without messing up anything. Just because Dad let me shoot these things when I was a kid doesn't mean I know much about working a scope.

Duke shifts a little. "These two have been fucking gabbing forever now. I really kind of wish that we could just shoot the fucking WOP."

"We find out who he is yet?" I ask.

"Leo Scavo is our best guess. Seems to fit the bill, but aside from that, we ain't got shit on him."

With that, Duke directs his attention back to the magnifying scope on top of his rifle and continues to watch the conversation between Jim and this guy Leo. I adjust the scope on my own rifle so that I can see what's going down a little bit more clearly. Jim scuffles his boots in the dirt and places his hands on his hips. Ever so slyly, he adjusts the phone in his pocket. It almost goes unnoticed, but the sound in my earbud is so much clearer now. I can actually understand the shit they're saying. I've never been good at distance or nothing, but from here it looks like we are probably a half mile or so away. Thanks to the phone, I can hear him like he's a few feet away.

"Why the fuck are we so far away?" I hiss. Sure, I can hear and see everything from here. Fine, whatever. But I'd like to be closer just in case this fucking asshole tries anything on Jim.

Duke turns and glares at me. "The whole idea is to hide. How the fuck we gonna hide if they can see us?"

"Shit. Sorry," I mumble. Fuck him and his attitude. I still want to be closer.

"Now shut the fuck up, and don't shoot unless I tell you or there's a bullet in my skull, okay?"

I keep my mouth shut because I'm not a fucking

pussy, but I'm not cool with the image of my brother taking a bullet. Nic couldn't handle that shit, and neither could I.

"None of this answers my question, Mr. Stone," the Italian says.

"You been bullshitting me so fucking long, I forgot your question," Jim says with a smirk.

"Sampling too much of your own product, then?"

"I'd give you a sample of our product, but we seem to have this issue about you and yours trying to take what belongs to me." Jim's tone is dark, and he's no longer smirking.

"What's yours, Mr. Stone? Alexandra was promised to me. That means she is mine and that she belongs to the Mancuso family."

"So what you're saying is Alexandra was *stolen* from you?"

"You transported her across the country without her father's permission, did you not?"

"Don't know how shit works in New York, but I've been trying to get my old lady to listen to me for years. Ain't fuckin' working. Got any tips?"

"If you're unable to properly lead your woman, there is nothing I can say to guide you," the Italian says. He rolls his shoulders. I can't really see his face, as I mostly have view of his back, which is fine since it's a wider target.

"Like your boss has control of his women?" Jim asks.

"Shit's about to get ugly," Duke says into the

conference. When he lifts his finger off the button, he says only to me, "Ryan has a thing about people talking about his mom."

"Got my target on his skull," Ryan says.

"Stand down, momma's boy," Wyatt says. "Can't shoot the guy unless he moves first."

"Shit," I say. "Good thing Ian's not here." If there's one thing I've learned about Ian it's that as attached as Ryan is to Ruby, Ian is worse. I wouldn't call him a momma's boy, though. I like breathing too much.

"Mr. Mancuso is a traditionalist," the Italian says. "But your sergeant let on that you know more about Mr. Mancuso than you have lead me to believe."

"I know shit about the cocksucker that would surprise you. The stories I could tell you about my old lady and *Mike*. Too bad none of them are happy."

"Curious choice of words you've used, Mr. Stone."

"Which one—*cocksucker* or *Mike*?"

"Nobody refers to Mr. Mancuso by his first name, much less such an informal nickname."

"Well, I am his daughter's stepfather. I don't really think formalities are necessary."

"You see, while you and your sergeant seem quite taken with this twist on reality, the Mancuso family buried Alexandra and Michael's mother some years ago."

"The woman who mothered those kids is not the woman who gave birth to them. The woman who had Princess and Junior *stolen* from her has scars you can't possibly imagine, but I can because she's in *my* bed every fucking night. I wouldn't worry too much about your place on the totem pole, though. Mike kept that shit quiet for years. Unfortunately for him, he fucked over the wrong woman."

"While this little walk down memory lane is intriguing, I do have to be on my way. Now, please answer my question. What will it take for you to safely return Michael and Alexandra to Mr. Mancuso?" The Italian's voice wavers ever so slightly before he rectifies his show of weakness.

"You're not listening," Jim says. His voice turns cool and disinterested. If I didn't know better, I'd think he's bored, but it's exactly the opposite. Ryan is so much like his father. They both grow cold and quiet before they lay waste to anything within reach. Duke tenses beside me, and I do a quick check of my equipment to make sure I'm on my game should I need to pull the trigger. "This isn't about money. It's about righting the wrongs of the past. A man stole a woman's infant children from her, and then he sliced up the face of the only child he let her keep. He forced her sister to raise her stolen babies as her own. You want to know what price I'm willing to accept? Mancuso dead and served up to everyone he's ever hurt. Anything less is an insult."

"Very well," the Italian says. "I will relay your message to Mr. Mancuso. My two men here will follow me out. I have certain contingency plans in place that will ensure my safe exit, so please spare yourself the trouble and don't bother following me."

"I'm on it," Wyatt says through the conference.

"Road's clear," Fish says.

The Italian strides to his black Mercedes and climbs into the driver's seat. From there, he slowly makes a three-point turn and then stops. His men climb onto the closed trunk and sit down, their rifles comfortably propped on their laps as the Mercedes crawls down the dirt drive and toward the highway.

"Fuck," Duke says. "Shit is either about to get bad, or we might have made a breakthrough."

"You mean this *isn't* bad?" I say.

He snorts and smiles in my direction. "You ain't seen nothing yet, Baby Boy."

We stay put for a few minutes before Fish gives us the clear, and then we pack up and head down to the highway. Once we're there, I return the rifle and phones to Fish and climb back into Nic's car. I've started her up and am about to pull away when Duke climbs into the passenger seat and adjusts his dick as he gets comfortable.

"Fucked your sister in this car," he says with a nod. My stomach roils at the thought.

"That's great," I say through gritted teeth. He does this—talks about porking my sister, knowing it irritates the hell out of me—all the fucking time.

"Clubhouse," he says. "Fucked her there, too."

I try to ignore the comment about Nic and drive for the clubhouse. On the way, he manages to tell me he's had Nic in every room of the house and in my bed. Then he says he's joking. Then he says he's not. By the time we pull up to Forsaken Custom Cycle, I'm ready to run us off the road and end my suffering. We're the first guys back, and the lot is empty beyond the clubhouse gates save for a red-and-black Harley that I don't recognize. Sitting on a picnic bench near the front door is a tall dude about Duke's age, with light blond hair that rests on his shoulders. He's wearing a leather cut that looks like it belongs to us, but I ain't got a clue who he is.

"Who's that guy?"

"Guy from Detroit," Duke says. "He's looking to transfer. Think his name is Daniel." There's a few tense moments between us before he speaks again, this time much more agitated.

"I would really like a fucking update on Bean and Sweets," Duke says. His leg bounces nervously.

Just moments after we pull up, Ruby's red Suburban peeks through the opening gates behind us.

"Ian's back," Duke says with a shout and hops out of the car. He slams his door behind him as he jogs for the Suburban that parks a few spaces down. Ian had Ruby's SUV when he and Grady left to work on the clues that Scavo gave about where Holly and Mindy might be. If Ian is back, then I can only hope that means he found the girls.

I cut off the car and step out just as Ian walks around to the passenger side and opens the front passenger door. The first thing I see emerge is a pair of long, jean-clad legs, and then I see it—her pretty blonde hair. Mindy.

"Fuck, Mindy. Are you okay?" I ask as I rush toward her.

Looking up, she blinks, slightly taken aback, but then forces a tired smile to her face. "I'm not sure that's the right word for it, but I'm unharmed," she says with frustration clear in her voice. Can't fucking blame her.

"How's Holly?" My voice is drops a few decibels, and a gnarly squeak appears halfway through the question. I sound like a fucking kid, but I don't care right now. I need an answer. If Holly isn't okay, I fucking give up.

"Again, she's unharmed."

Ian gives Duke and me a flat look and nods his head toward Mindy. "Sweets is going to stay at Grady's house. Mindy will be staying with Duke and Nic."

"Shit, that motherfucker has got it bad," Duke says with a laugh. He shakes his head and doesn't even try to hide the smile on his face. Mindy huffs and looks at the ground beneath her, but I catch the smile on her face as she tips her head down.

"I'm just glad you're both safe. I get to keep my nut sack for one more day."

Taking a deep breath, I turn and walk toward the clubhouse for a moment to think by myself. It's been a mostly shit day, but knowing the girls are safe helps some. Just as I'm entering the clubhouse, the deep, guttural sound of the brothers' Harleys rumble in the distance, growing ever closer, and I know I won't get any time alone. I guess I can deal with today's shit later. Right now I got to put on my prospect face and suck it up.

CHAPTER 5

December

16 months to Mancuso's downfall

Cheyenne

"THERE'S SOMETHING HERE that I'm missing," I mumble under my breath. Christmas is nearing, and I've been working on this for a month now, and this is all I have to show for it—a scattered collection of sticky notes and business cards strewn about the kitchen table. I can't make sense of anything I'm looking at, and yet there has to be something here.

Over the past several weeks, things have been getting crazy around Fort Bragg. First it was the crazy-hot and crazy-scary Italian guy showing up at my school. Then it was Dad trying to put the moves on Holly, my administrative advocate. Then it was Holly liking Dad putting the moves on her—which was totally cool because he's way less of a jerk when he's got someone in his life. He doesn't think I notice stuff like this because he never used to bring women home, but he's way obvious. Plus, Grandma has a big freaking mouth and complains about his "nocturnal habits" often enough that I have learned to stomach the idea that Dad isn't the exception to the Forsaken rule. He likes the company of women. He just doesn't like them to talk.

I can't keep letting myself get sidetracked—which is really easy because research so is not my thing, but hey, somebody has to do it. I sat back and let Dad convince me that everything was okay when the Italian guy approached me at school, and I let him tell me it was okay when suddenly Holly was basically living in our house even though she and Dad couldn't stand hearing the other talk. They so were not dating, but whatever. It wasn't until Dad got into a screaming match with Grandma—which he lost—about Holly and her cousin Mindy being kidnapped by the aforementioned crazy Italian guy that I knew everything was absolutely, most definitely, no way in hell, totally not okay.

So I've been listening in and pretending to be ignorant when my dad and his brothers talk about club business, because if they know I know things are going south in town and with the club, they'll all clam up tighter than the last time they were under DEA surveillance. Every single one of those guys act like I'm a baby and I can't handle them being honest with me. I can, but they won't give me the chance. So I'm going at it alone in my investigation.

I was sidetracked for a few weeks after poor Mindy was raped—not that anybody told me that's exactly what happened, but again, I listen in. Holly was in her own head for a long while after that. I can't even imagine having to watch something like that. For days on end she just kept saying the numbers seven and one. I've asked Dad about it, and then Aunt Ruby, and then anybody who I could grab ahold of, but they just all keep saying that everything is okay, and that is a huge freaking lie.

So fuck them and their patronizing crap.

I have a few business cards from a guy named Larry Jennings, the dad of a local who's in the hospital in a coma. He's been there for several weeks, and the news has all but forgotten about him, but for some reason, his dad's business cards were in with Dad's stuff on Mindy's rape.

I cast a quick look at the clock that hangs just off center above the bay window beside me. Beneath the clock is a string of garland with colorful blinking lights that Holly hung up when Dad wasn't looking one day. He's not a fan of Christmas decorations, but he's putting up with them the best he can to make her happy.

Crap. It's well after four now, and Dad and Holly will be home any minute. I shove the business cards back in the folder and finger through the various documents inside the manila folder for one last look before I sneak this sucker back into the garage where it belongs. Toward the bottom of the stack, a name catches my attention on one of the papers from the hospital. I do a double take. There are so many papers in the folder that I'd taken it for granted that they were all Holly and Mindy's records from the attack, but on the paper in question, it says JENNINGS, DARREN under the patient's name. The paper is crumpled and spotted in dried blood. First his dad's business cards and now Darren's medical records?

What could Mindy's attack possibly have to do with Darren's? They have to be connected—or Dad thinks they are—otherwise they wouldn't be in the folder together. I'd never looked this closely at the paperwork. The last time I snuck the file out of its place in Dad's tool box, I ran into the police report of Holly's statement. I think I cried for about ten minutes before I gave up on looking at the rest and put the folder back. I couldn't tell Grandma why I was crying, so I just ran up to my room and told her that boys are stupid. I think she bought it, because she came up to tell me that any boy who makes me cry isn't worth the time it takes to shed a single tear. I wanted to tell her the truth. I needed to talk to someone about what I read, but she would have snitched on me to my dad.

Why would someone want to hurt Mindy like that?

Why would someone want to hurt *anyone* like that?

Maybe I'm just stupid, but I didn't know that stuff like this could happen in my town. Dad always says the club takes care of their own and the town belongs to the club, so that means that we're safe here and I don't have to worry about anything. But that's a lie, because if someone can hurt Mindy Mercer like that for no reason, then nobody is safe. Not even the daughter of a Forsaken club member.

"Fuck!" Dad shouts, scaring the crap out of me. "I hate that fucking thing. Next time it ho ho ho's at me, I'm shooting it. Don't care how much you like it."

"Don't blame Santa for recognizing a ho when he sees one," Holly says with a giggle.

"You're in for it, woman!" Dad says loudly and with a disgruntled tone.

My eyes widen and my heart skips a beat. His voice is distant and muffled. I scurry to the hallway to find that the front door is shut, and Dad's head bobs on the other side of the glass pane. His keys jingle as he works the lock.

"Do me a favor and just once act like a gentleman!" Holly says, her voice high and full of irritation.

The door creaks open, and the alarm beeps as he grumbles, "You sure didn't want me to act like a gentleman when I bent you over the kitchen table last night."

"Oh, shut up," she says with a laugh. "Be good and I'll let you bend me over our bed tonight."

I back away from the hallway and rush to the breakfast nook and vow to never eat at the table again. My hands reach for the manila envelope, and just as I'm about to grab it and run, I cringe.

"So freaking gross," I whine as I shuffle the papers into the manila folder as best I can and scoop them up from the defiled kitchen table. "No freaking boundaries. I need to move out like right the hell now."

Dad's heavy boots clap against the wooden floor in the hall, growing nearer as I round the living room and run down the side hall to the garage where I slowly turn the knob and slip inside. Across the garage, in a tall red tool chest, is Dad's stash of folders that have information on cases that are of interest to the club. He doesn't keep many paper files, not around the house at least, except when he's in the thick of an investigation. A few years back there was a series of car break-ins around town. Nothing really went missing, and the club didn't care much, but then Aunt Ruby's Suburban got hit, and Uncle Jim got the club involved. Dad said either the club was going to figure it out or Aunt Ruby was going to start shooting people who look suspicious. I don't think they ever did find the people responsible, but while they were looking into it, Dad had about twenty manila folders stashed in various drawers. If there's one thing Dad hates more than teenage boys, it's probably unsolved mysteries.

I shove the folder back in the third drawer down and sneak toward the partially open door. Holly's voice trails from the living room but is soon overshadowed by several deep, masculine voices that are undeniably familiar. Uncle Wyatt's baritone bark demands a beer from Dad, who then redirects, asking Holly to grab beers for the guys. My palms grow slick as my heart rate picks up. Nervously, I eye the old refrigerator in the corner of the garage where Dad keeps his expansive supply of cold beer for when the guys come by.

"Sure thing," Holly says. Her high-heeled boots make pointed little clicking noises that get louder with every step she takes closer to the garage. Once she hits the hallway, her steps falter. "Are we expecting anyone else?"

"Baby Boy should be by any minute," Wyatt says.

Dad makes an unflattering noise. "Babe, keep Chey in her room while the guys are here. Last thing I need is her distracting the kid any more than she already does."

"Fuck if that ain't right," Duke says. "She blows up his phone, and he can't stop fucking smiling. Doesn't hear a word I say either."

A blush covers my face at the thought of Jeremy wanting to hear from me.

Holly gives him a snort and a little laugh. Well, I'm glad she thinks this is funny. If Dad has his way, I'm going to die a freaking virgin. She takes a few more steps and wraps her hand around the door knob. Scrambling backward, I nearly knock into the bike Dad's been building for the past few months and give away my location. I don't want Holly catching me in here. Not that I'm not allowed in the garage, but without an explanation and feeling as guilty as hell like I do, I'd bet they'd have me singing like a canary before Dad got the question out.

"Right, you don't want any… distractions. Sure.

Couldn't possibly have anything to do with you trying to keep her a little girl forever, could it?" she says a little too sweetly.

"Beer. Now," he says. His tone darkens slightly, something he always does in front of the guys. I really hate when he acts like this. It's not happened often, with how Holly's only now slowly leaving her near catatonic state, but the better she gets, the more he starts to act like his old self—and that is most definitely not a compliment.

Turning away from the door and running to the tall red tool chest, I dart behind it, duck down, and hope I'm not visible from the other side of the room. The door swings open, and in trots Holly with frustrated steps that slam against the concrete floor. Her face is red, her chest is rising and falling in quick succession, and she's counting to herself. He pissed her off all right.

As she crosses the garage and swings open the door to the fridge she mutters, "Keep being that bossy, Sterling, and you can suck your own dick tonight."

My throat constricts as my stomach rolls, and I start gagging. Gross.

Holly reaches into the fridge and grabs as many beers as she can safely carry in her arms before trotting out of the garage and letting the door slam shut behind her. I give it a few minutes before heading toward the door and peeking out. Deep voices sound from the living room, a mixture of grunting and barking out what sounds vaguely like disagreement among the brothers. Not that I'm surprised. Those guys can't seem to ever get along.

I creep down the hall and peek around the corner at the sight before me. Dad is perched on the arm of the couch, something Grandma hates. She always says his "big ass" is going to destroy every stick of furniture we have. Anyway, he's sitting there with one hand on his knee and the other holding a beer. His shoulders slump and then shake as his eyes dance with mischief. In the middle of the couch with his hands folded in his lap like the good little boy he certainly is not is Jeremy. His face is a mask of indifference, but his body language tells me he's nervous. Across the room is Uncle Wyatt. The muscles of his broad shoulders constrict and flex as one hand clenches in a fist and the other welcomes it into the palm of his hand. His brown hair sweeps across his shoulders, and his chest heaves. Uncle Wyatt is normally one of the calmest of the brothers, so it must be bad if he's this upset.

A guilty part of me is looking forward to seeing what this little impromptu meeting is about. I might get some information out of this that will prove useful to my investigation.

"It's bullshit," Dad says with a nod, his eyes firmly fixed on Wyatt. "Kids will do that to you—fuck you up."

I bite back the urge to throw something in his direction. He's one to talk. If he thinks having me as a kid is hard, then I should let him know he's no freaking picnic either.

"They're not fucking kids, man. They're goddamn

adults," Wyatt says.

Dad just shakes his head. "Doesn't matter. Your kids are your kids for life. Jim's a fucking hard-ass, sure. But he's a father. He's got two sons at each other's throats over Junior and Princess. Can't be easy, trying to decide whose needs are more important—Ryan wanting to beat the shit out of Junior to protect Princess, or Ian trying to keep Ruby happy. Personally, I'd side with keeping the woman happy, but ya know…"

Wyatt just grumbles something and turns toward the fireplace, where he places his hands on the mantle and lets his head hang low. Duke's voice sounds from around the corner from me where I can't see him. My heart leaps in my chest, and I suppress the feminine squeak that would give away my location if anybody were paying attention to me. Duke must be in the recliner near the fireplace on the other side of the wall I'm hiding behind. I'd peek around to see him if I didn't think I'd be spotted.

"Yesterday I came home to find Trigger fucking terrorizing Junior," Wyatt says almost too quietly for me to hear. "Had to move him to Ian's."

Dad nods. "Good. Trigger isn't stupid enough to fuck around at Ian's house."

"Told Jim. All he had to say was he thought that was a good move," Wyatt says.

"He's slipping," Duke says loud and clear. All eyes swing to where Duke must be. Jeremy's are wide and fearful, while Dad's are solemn. Wyatt's head is turned in Duke's direction, but other than that, he hasn't moved. I don't know the exact details of what happens when a member challenges the presidency, but it's a big freaking deal. It's not just a big deal, but it can completely destroy a man or an entire charter, depending on how it's handled.

"And who's going to tell him that?" Dad asks of Duke with a prodding gaze.

"Fuck you, dude. I ain't telling him shit. Pop's the only father I got. I say we just ride it out and try to reason with Trigger and Sin."

"Sin?" Jeremy asks. He unfolds his hands from his lap as he repositions himself on the couch, much more relaxed. A smile plays at his lips, all signs of tension now gone. Dumbass has been around the club his entire life, and he's never learned Ian's nickname—as stupid as it may be.

"Ian," Duke says. Jeremy's head tips to the side like a confused puppy, and it's so freaking cute I can't help the blush that rises on my cheeks and makes me hot under the collar. Seeing him sitting among my dad and Uncle Wyatt in his prospect cut looking so confused and young and like he's trying so hard to fit in is freaking adorable and sexy in ways I don't know if I can verbalize. Duke was just as cute once, but then he got a little too old for me, and now that he's with Nic, I force myself to quash every thought that he's attractive. Besides, once I nail Jeremy down, Duke's going to be like my brother-in-law—which brings me to another thought. Duke and Nic's baby is going to be like my niece.

Well, first things first. I need to get Jeremy to ask me out, and then I can figure the details out later.

Cheyenne Whelan.

"Stop it," I tell myself quietly. Sometimes I hate myself for being that girl who gets so into a guy that she imagines his last name with her first and strategizes ways to wiggle into his life in a way he'll never want to let her go. But then I look at Jeremy, and a happy sigh escapes me and I forget what I was thinking about.

"How the hell did he get a nickname like that?" Jeremy asks, but Dad shakes his head.

"You have to ask, you don't deserve the answer," Dad says. "And I don't know if you realize this, but prospects aren't supposed to ask questions." His tone is light and he's almost... smiling? But the message is clear—shut the fuck up.

"But Duke told me—" Jeremy starts up, and Wyatt swings around from his position at the mantle, and his bulking frame strides toward Jeremy on the couch. He shuts up immediately—something he should have done before he opened his mouth that one last time. He's cute and got a great smile, and I'll bet a solid heart, but he's got some learning to do if he doesn't want to be Ryan's butt-buddy.

"Shut your fucking mouth, prospect," Wyatt snaps. His deep baritone strikes me in my soul. I've never heard him sound so angry or so serious. His arms shake with fury as he places his hands against the back of the couch on either side of Jeremy's head and closes in until they're nose to nose. Jeremy's perfectly still under Wyatt's thundering voice and intense physical presence. "My patch reads Vice President. I don't give a fuck who tells you what unless their patch reads President. Got that? Don't fucking look at me, don't fucking breathe on me. Do not talk back to me, and don't ever let me catch you forgetting your place."

"Wy," Dad says in warning. I can barely see him beyond Wyatt's bull-like frame, but I catch the telltale clink of his now-empty beer bottle on the end table as he stands from his place on the arm of the couch. He doesn't approach and makes no move to break it up, but he's at the ready if he needs to be. The brothers don't usually stop a patched member from banging up a prospect, but this is Butch's son. Dad won't ever admit it, but I think he likes Jeremy, which bodes well for our future relationship.

Wyatt huffs heavily into Jeremy's face before he pushes back and walks back to his place at the mantle.

It's a long moment before Dad speaks. "First up, we need to find that prick Scavo. Had the balls to approach me on Forsaken land and take my woman. Asshole needs to pay for that shit."

"Agreed, but finding the Italian is kind of hard when our intel guy is tied up babysitting his half-brother and keeping Trigger from fucking killing him, all the while avoiding Princess," Duke says with slight humor in his tone. "This is so fucked up."

"You're think you're having trouble with it? Jim's got

his hands full," Dad says with a nod. "But soap opera shit aside, I want that Italian dead."

"Bad move letting that shit with your woman cloud your judgment. I still think the Italian can be useful," Duke says, his voice rising slightly. "Junior trusts him, and I'm starting to trust Junior. Plus, that prick could have hurt Sweets, but he didn't. It was a fuckin' scare tactic."

"Scared my old lady," Dad says as his voice lowers into a timber.

"Pissed you off—I get that. But he could be of use to us. Junior swears Leo is more interested in finding out the truth than he is in causing real trouble."

"Still want him dead," Dad gripes. He's a hard-ass, sure, but the way he's so protective of Holly makes my stomach do crazy weird butterflies. For a long time I was pretty much convinced that Grandma and I were going to be the only long-term women in his life—and that's just sad.

"Okay, let's say Scavo isn't of use to us—how do we go about that when we don't even know where he is? What about Jennings? Can't find him either," Duke says.

"He's close," Jeremy says quietly. His eyes are fixated on the floor, his brows furrowed, and he seems to be speaking more to himself than the men in the room.

"Heh?" Duke says, his voice showing his confusion. Dad and Wyatt both turn their attention to Jeremy as they wait for him to speak.

"He found the safe house, he knows our routines, and he even found Miss Priss at school. He knows who we are, he knows your kids, and he knows our weaknesses, even if we don't. Scavo went after Holly and Mindy before you two were together, and he went after Cheyenne when he could have gone after getting Alex and Michael back," Jeremy mutters as his attention shifts to Dad.

"He can't get to them. They're protected," Duke says adamantly. I know he's smarter than that—there's always a way if you're determined—but he doesn't want to think about it. Considering that Alex isn't totally safe reminds him that neither is Nic and their baby. He can't handle going down that road, and I get it.

"Cheyenne was protected," Dad says. "And the safe house was invisible for over thirty years, but he fucking found it."

"Baby Boy's right," Wyatt says as he grabs his beer off the mantle and finishes it off. "Scavo is close. We just have to find him." The men around him nod and murmur their agreement as they all seem to stretch their muscles at the same time and stir in place. They don't like to sit still for too long.

CHAPTER 6

December

16 months to Mancuso's downfall

Cheyenne

THE ROOM FALLS silent, except for the faint sound of slurping. Everything else the brothers seem to be able to drink quietly, but not beer. It's like some kind of big event every time one of them brings a beer bottle to their lips.

The alarm sounds at the front door, startling everybody in the room. They each jump to their feet, draw their guns, and train them on the front hall. The telltale click clack of high heels grows near as Aunt Ruby flies around the corner. Her eyes are wide, her face is pale, and her hair is a total disaster, as if she's been pulling at it relentlessly for the past hour. Each of the brothers relax and lower their guns before returning them to the back of their waistbands.

"Sorry, big fucking problem," Aunt Ruby says. I highly doubt that. But this is Aunt Ruby, and she's a major badass, so she gets a certain amount of wiggle room that the rest of us don't.

"Where's Pres?" Jeremy asks, obviously not in the know.

"Transport mission. He's got Trigger with him," Wyatt says. The president's old lady running into a room and addressing the brothers as though she's one of them means there's not just trouble, but big fucking trouble. And this is what being voted in means—it means your problem is the club's problem, and they won't think twice about having your back. It's the closest any woman will ever get to wearing a Forsaken patch.

"What's up, Ma?" Dad says.

"Is the room secure?" Ruby asks.

Shit. The last thing I need is for them to come peeking around the corner to make sure. Dad may yell and scream, but Aunt Ruby is sure to tan my hide. The only times in my life I've ever been spanked have been by that woman.

"Yeah, it better be," Dad says. Maybe I'm just paranoid, but with that comment, it almost seems like he knows I'm listening.

"Gloria called, and she said Leo Scavo showed up at her house asking questions about me and Mike. He wanted to know what our history is, if there is even is one, and if she knows the real reason he was sent out to California."

I know enough about Alex's aunt Gloria to know that this Italian guy showing up at her house is bad news. Gloria is the one who orchestrated Alex's escape from New York and transport to California. She put her neck on the chopping block to keep Alex safe, and that's something that Forsaken won't forget.

"He hurt her?" Dad asks. His brows furrow together, and his expression is grim.

"No, she's fine. He just wanted a little bit of history. Which, by the way, she gave him. I'm fucking worried because I don't know how long she has until somebody else starts sniffing around and asking the kinds of questions that could get her killed."

"It's fucked up, I know. We're going to do everything we can to keep her safe," Wyatt says.

I hate to say it, but the way everything's going lately, that doesn't mean a hill of beans to me. Nobody is safe, especially not Gloria.

"How did Scavo react to the history lesson?" Dad asks.

"Like he believed it. Told her on the way out he had some shit to think about," Ruby says.

"Okay, enough of this shit," Dad says. His eyes cut a little too close to my direction as he focuses in on Duke. Quickly, I slide to my left to ensure I'm hidden behind the wall and hope Dad didn't see my movement. "You and Nic figure out what you're having? Holly keeps busting my nuts about buying baby shit. She needs to know—pink or blue.”

“A little asshole, judging from its parents,” Wyatt says. I peek back around in time to see him focus in on Dad as he smirks at Wyatt.

“Don't know yet. Nic wants to be surprised,” Duke says. “But it's fucking killing me. I just want to know already.”

“Sweets going on about baby shit is trouble for you, brother,” Wyatt says with his eyes on Dad.

Dad just shrugs like he doesn't care, but I want to think he's just putting on a front for the guys. “Best way to keep your woman happy is to give her what she wants. You might have one if you'd learned that lesson, Wy. Besides, she gets knocked up, I'll just be busy when the kid cries. Worked with Layla when we had Chey.”

“How is the ex?” Wyatt asks. Ruby scoffs.

“Fucked up but breathing, which is about all I can ask for these days,” Dad says.

A smile finds its way to my face for a brief moment before a sinking sadness overcomes me, and I decide that I've heard enough. It's not that I can't talk or hear about my mom. It's just that it reminds me that she's not here. And even worse, I don't even want her here. She doesn't ride my ass about homework, she doesn't watch movies with me that I know she hates, and she isn't here for me to talk to about Jeremy and every screwed up thing that's happening around town. She's not a mom, but she's all I had. Until Holly.

My head falls softly against the wall in front me as I close my eyes and take a deep breath. Tears sting my eyes, but I refuse to let them fall down my cheeks. I've cried enough over her and won't let myself go down this road again. She's ruined enough of my life. It takes a moment, but I pull myself out of that place I'd rather not be and stride down the hall and back into the garage.

My only exit routes are the garage or Dad and Holly's room on the bottom level. I can't really explain being in the parental unit's bedroom, nor can I reasonably explain hanging out in the garage, but there's an exterior door to the side of the house from the garage that can at least get me in the backyard where I can hang out for a while and make it seem like I was locked out of the house and had to go around front to get in via the security code. I don't know if it sounds as good as I think it does, but it's better than the alternative.

Darting across the garage and out the door to the side of the house takes but a moment. I'm heading for the backyard when the telltale sound of a branch cracking behind me alerts me that I'm not alone. I swing around quickly, a scream building in my throat as I prepare to swing at anything and everything within reach.

"Chill!" a masculine voice, not especially deep and not particularly confident, says. I calm my crazy eyes down long enough to see the Forsaken patch on the leather vest that rests on his shoulders. Beneath FORSAKEN is another patch that reads DETROIT. He's young, can't be more than twenty-five if I had to guess, and he isn't an officer judging from the lack of additional patches.

Uncle Rig—this guy must have come into town with Uncle Rig.

"Sorry," I say, now more than a little embarrassed. I smile apologetically as I appraise him. He's tall and lanky but carrying a fair amount of muscle. He has light blond hair and a pair of kind blue eyes peer at me inquisitively.

"Detroit, huh?" I nod my head to his patch. "Escaped winter?"

His smile widens and his eyes dance with mischief. "Heard a lot about the fine women in California. Glad to see the rumors are true."

His smooth talking causes a blush to rise to my cheeks. I'm so much more than the little girl Dad and my uncles want to think of me as. It's nice to have a member of Forsaken appreciate my more feminine qualities. I'm not counting Jeremy since we're the same age and all. This guy is definitely not a teenager.

"I got an idea who you are, but why don't you tell me your name, babe?"

I smirk at his forward attitude. This guy has a thing or two he can stand to learn about Forsaken women.

"You first, handsome." I purse my lips while I fold my arms across my chest.

"You see my patch?" His tone is bored, but his smile gives him away.

"I ain't blind," I say. "This is my house and my town, pal. Name please." We're flirting, so it makes all of this okay. If he were old or serious, I'd be heading for my dad to take care of this for me, but this guy seems safe to tease.

"Daniel," he says with a shake of his head. The smile on his face never fades.

Giving him a sexy smile—at least I hope it's coming across as sexy—I rake my eyes up and down his frame. He's surely attractive, and I've no doubt that if I weren't already crushing so bad on Jeremy I'd be hoping the end result of all this flirting would be heated kissing and some light petting. But I am crushing on Jeremy, and I doubt Daniel's idea of a happy ending is light petting. The thought of a man who I'd bet has more experience than I can fathom having his way with me scares me a little and calms the urge to flirt shamelessly as I've been doing.

"Cheyenne," I say and point to my chest. "I take it you're here for my dad."

He gives a low whistle. "Bloody Knuckles's kid. Should have known. A babe like you learned to bust balls early in life, didn't you?"

"You know it," I say and head for the front door. Being busted by this guy makes it impossible to go sneak into the backyard now. Crap. I don't know how I'm going to play this off. If it were six months ago, Dad wouldn't give a shit what I was doing. But now? Everything is too dangerous, and I really, absolutely can't handle another lecture from Aunt Ruby—because that's who Dad sends in when he gives up—telling me how I'm going to get myself or someone else killed by wandering off all the time. I don't care if this dude is charming and cute. I'm just no longer in the mood to be social now that I have to fabricate yet another freaking lie.

"This way." I say lead him around the front of the house and toward the front door. He follows closely, almost too close, and when we're less than twenty feet from the front porch, he wraps his hand around mine. I spin around in confusion and stare up at him.

Leaning in close, he says, "You got an old man?"

I suck in a deep breath, the motion causing his attention to redirect from my eyes to my mouth. Instinctively, my tongue darts out and wets my lips. The near-constant smile on his face darkens as he steps even closer. The cool leather of his cut grazes my thin cotton shirt. His warm, sour breath basks over my face, and despite how much I think I could like him in another time and another place, this doesn't feel right.

"I'll take that as a no," he says and slides his hand up around the back of my neck as he guides my face toward his.

I'm not scared to tell him no. I just don't know how. Grown men, especially Forsaken, don't hit on me. Like ever. Dad makes sure they all know who I am so they can stay away. Before Alex stormed into town, I even had Ryan tell me that, no matter how cute I've gotten, he'll never touch me because my dad is such a fucking asshole. We weren't even talking. I was just sitting at a picnic table at the clubhouse and eating some fried chicken Aunt Ruby cooked up. He came up, plopped down, started eating, and then proceeded to tell me that I shouldn't like Forsaken men because Dad's gotten me blackballed.

"Relax, sweetheart," he says, obviously noticing how tense I am. His lips barely touch mine, but he doesn't press. "I'm not an asshole." Then he pulls back and places his hand beneath my chin. "Don't ever be afraid to tell me no. I'm not that kind of man. You're safe with me."

I nod my head, still trying to catch my breath from what could have been something incredibly hot or super intimidating. His words slip over me, providing little comfort. Everything just happened so fast. One moment we were walking, and the next, he was practically dry humping me in the driveway.

"Miss Priss is off limits," Jeremy shouts as his footsteps rush toward us. I hadn't even heard the front door open much less hear the guys. I glance behind me to find that not only is Jeremy charging toward us, but so are Dad, Uncle Wyatt, and Duke.

"She yours?" Daniel asks with raised eyebrows. Jeremy's jaw locks in place as his nostrils flare. Daniel smirks. "You're a prospect, boy. What's yours is Forsaken's."

A wash of irritation wafts over me. What a freaking asshole.

"I'm mine," I gripe as I stare Dad down like he created

the Black Plague from scratch. My eyes widen, and I nod my chin to Daniel and Jeremy because things are about to get out of hand. Part of me wants Jeremy to tell Daniel I am his, but that would be a lie. Plus, I'm really not a fan of the whole idea of ownership.

Dad nods his head at me and then strides toward Daniel, blocking Jeremy's line of sight. I take a few steps back and find myself sandwiched between Duke and Uncle Wyatt. "Actually," Dad says with his attention on Daniel, "she's mine. Back off, boy."

Daniel raises his hands in the air as he takes a few steps backward. Jeremy's shoulders heave in agitation as he glares in Daniel's direction. Dad just shakes his head. His eyes are locked on mine. The closer he gets to me, the more irritated he seems.

"What the hell are you doing out here?" he asks.

"Um," I say, unable to finish.

"Explanation. Now."

"I was trying to sneak a beer in the garage when Holly stormed in all pissed off at you, so I came out here to sneak in the front door, when this guy found me," I say as quickly as I can and hike a finger in Daniel's direction.

Duke chuckles on one side of me while Wyatt shakes his head and mumbles, "Shit."

"The good shit or the cheap shit?" Dad asks, surprising me.

"You don't have good shit," I say, slightly perplexed.

Dad's eyes narrow. "Buy your own fuckin' beer, kid." A sick smile slides over his features. "Oh, that's right. You can't."

"I'm thinking really rude things about you right now," I say quietly without breaking eye contact.

"I want your ass at the kitchen table. Now," he barks loudly.

My lungs expand and collapse in quick succession. My face heats up, and my hands clench into fists at my side. I'm in fucking trouble for something I didn't even do. Then again, I'd be in way more trouble if I told him the truth. So I'll take my punishment, but I don't have to like it.

"Can you please send me to a surface you haven't had sex on?" I snap, careful to keep my voice low. Dad doesn't care if family hears me being sassy, but if an outsider overhears, it'll be my ass.

"Then you might want to wait in your car," he says slowly as he licks his lips and leans in so that his nasty-ass breath covers my face. I love my dad, I really do. Grandma says we're just too much alike to get along sometimes. "Shit, sorry, baby girl. Guess you can't sit there either."

My face pales as my stomach churns. I hope that, at the very least, it was Holly he's been with in my car.

"Kitchen table, right now, or I'm going to find a much less comfortable place for you to wait for me."

"Fine," I say in a huff and stomp off toward the front

door, already formulating a plan to move out and never come back.

CHAPTER 7

December

16 months to Mancuso's downfall

Cheyenne

I DRAG THE thin brush full of polish up my fingernail and consider whether I really want my nails to be Paris Pink or not. It's softer than the shades I usually go for, and in fact, it's not even mine. I swiped it from Holly's small collection in her and Dad's room. She always wears these really classy shades that are soft or muted in tone. In comparison, my colors are all loud and sometimes even neon. They seem childish next to Holly's more adult choices.

The interaction with Daniel last week made me think twice about the way I've been going about things. Daniel is a man. He doesn't have any trace of boy left in him like Jeremy still does, and that kind of scares me. My eyes survey the hot pink and black decor of my room. I loved the way it looked once, but now I feel stifled by it. It's so childish.

My cellphone chimes, alerting me to an incoming text message. When I carefully maneuver the phone into my hands with my still-drying nails, I find the message is from Jeremy.

U WITH ASSHOLE?

My brows pull together in confusion. What the hell does he mean by asking me that? I swear, he's so hot and cold I never know what to expect with him. This inconsistent behavior is one reason I've been inclined to keep texting Daniel despite my feelings for Jeremy. When he sent me a random text message after our first meeting, I was put off by it. He didn't do much to apologize but rather explained himself. For some reason, I'm still having doubts that the things he said are true.

I LIKE YOU, Daniel sent a few days ago.

Then yesterday, I WAS JUST MESSING W/THE PROSPECT.

WE GOT A CONNECTION, he followed it up with.

To be fair, I haven't exactly been radio silent on my end of things. I think I'm half in like with Daniel, but mostly just in like with the idea of him. He hasn't said much about Jeremy, but the few times he has, it hasn't been very kind. Jeremy on the other hand has been totally MIA. While Daniel isn't the perfect biker by any means, he's at least present.

DAD NOT HOME, I respond back to Jeremy and banish my thoughts of Daniel.

WRONG ASSHOLE, he says. I knew that, but I'm not about to get involved in this ridiculous pissing match they have going on. It's not about me—it can't be—because neither of them have actually asked me out.

U IGNORING ME?

Apparently I'm taking too long to respond. I huff before my cheeks turn a reddish pink. Even when he's being a jerk, I like him. I really need to talk to Holly about all this. The only problem with that is she's attached to Dad's hip, and he's the absolute last person I want advice from. His answer is pretty much always, "He touches you, you kill him," regardless of who the "him" is.

NO, I type back. I give it a few minutes to see if he's going to respond or try to continue the conversation. Once my nails are dry, I know I've waited long enough, and I decide to give up. He's so infuriating. My phone tells me his stupid ass read my text, but he chose not to respond to it.

Daniel responds to my texts.

HEY, I type out in a message and hit send. Daniel should respond any minute. He always does. The moment I set my phone down, it chimes.

HEY BEAUTIFUL, the text reads. A light blush covers my cheeks. For whatever reason, he's not just trying with me—he's trying hard. Holly's opinion matters to me, even if her judgment is questionable—she is dating my dad after all—and I can't wait to talk to her about Daniel and Jeremy and this whole being mixed-up thing.

WHAT R U DOING? I text and wait for him to respond. The little bubble pops up immediately, telling me that he's typing a response.

JERKING OFF TO YOUR TEXTS, Daniel says. I freeze with my phone in my hands and stop breathing. I stay like that for a while until my phone chimes again with a follow-up text. SORRY. TOO HONEST?

My eyes bug out. I toss my phone to the side and do an epic face palm into my pillow, all the while being wholly incapable of breathing. He did not. He so did not just text me that.

A few minutes pass before I work up the courage to look at my phone again. The messages he's sent still take my breath away. I just don't know what to do with this. High school boys don't send me texts like this. Jeremy certainly doesn't send me texts like this. Hell, I've never even been to third base, let alone being the recipient of dirty text messages!

This is too much, but I don't know how to say that without sounding like a baby.

SORRY. I'M A JERK, he says in another text.

CAN WE NOT USE THE WORD JERK, PLS? I ask.

DON'T WANT ME TO SAY I'M A JERK-OFF? he responds.

I peek at the message and decide I just can't take any more. This entire conversation is making me feel like a child, which I don't like. My heart is beating way fast, and even though my toes are curling, I'm not convinced that this is a good thing. With that, I shove my phone back under my pillow and head downstairs.

"WE COULD GO shopping or something?" I suggest. Holly's getting better. It's been a while since the attack happened. Still, she's not leaving the house for things when she doesn't have to if it's not with Dad. It took her a few weeks to leave the house right after it happened. I get it and all. I just worry that she's going to become a recluse if she keeps this up. Dad isn't much of a shopper, and I swear he's reaching his breaking point. Last time she dragged him into a clothing store, he was so bitchy that he scared the crap out of the poor sales clerk when she tried to upsell Holly on shoe inserts and Holly paused to think about it. Not only does Holly need to get better, but Dad needs his life back, and the entire town needs Sterling Grady to not go clothes shopping ever again.

"Where would we go shopping? There's nothing here," she says. We do have stores to shop in, but if I had to guess, I think she just doesn't want to leave without Dad.

"We have places to shop."

"I mean places that your dad hasn't almost gotten us banned from," she says with a bored expression on her face.

She has a point, but that doesn't mean I can't find an excuse to get out of the house. Besides, almost banned and banned aren't the same thing. She might think I'm nuts, but I'm considering this a stage-four crisis. I just want her to get better, and better means getting back to her sassy self when she starts reminding Dad who's boss again and doesn't put up with his shit. His stunt with the beer last week is proof that he's getting too big for his britches.

"I don't know. There's a bookstore downtown, and we can always go have lunch or something. There's no reason we just have to sit here and stare at the TV." Really, at this point I'm so desperate that I'm willing to hang out at a library.

"Your dad is going to be home soon. I don't want to get out and leave before he gets home and then have him worrying about where we're at."

"He's not going to worry! We'll have Diesel with us. Sheesh."

"Meh, I think I'll pass. But thanks for trying to get me out of the house, kid."

I sigh heavily and decide to let it drop. If Holly's really not ready for another outing, then maybe I shouldn't be pushing her. After all, I wasn't the one in that room seeing what happened to Mindy.

"Hey, Holly. I have a question." She looks at me curiously because she knows that anytime I start by telling her I have a question, it's probably not good. I may or may not have earned a reputation over the last few months as being a slight pain in the ass, but I'm Sterling Grady's daughter—what else can anyone expect from me?

"Hey, Cheyenne. What's up?"

"What do you think of Jeremy?"

"He's cute, he's earning his cut, but I think he's trouble," she says.

This is something I respect about Holly. She never

really bullshits me, and she's never really mean about it either. I'd say that, all in all, Dad found a good one. Not that I don't like Elle, because actually I had been hoping for a really long time that he and Elle would get together. It just didn't happen, and there was probably half a second where I was upset about it. Elle's been coming around here for years, and she's really awesome and all, but with her job, she's gone a lot. I used to think there was no way Dad would find anybody better suited for him than her. And then I met Holly. Holly is strong and tough and super sassy. She is basically everything my mother could've been if she weren't so fucking screwed up.

"Are you saying he's trouble because he's prospecting, or are you saying he's trouble because you think every boy I'm interested in is trouble?"

"Well, the day you're interested in a boy who isn't trouble, you'll have to let me know." Holly's smile nearly overtakes her face. Now I really don't want to tell her about Daniel. If she thinks Jeremy is trouble, then she'd definitely think the Jerk-Off King is major trouble. Holly's really funny when she wants to be, even these days, but I doubt her sense of humor will extend that far.

It usually just takes a little bit more time to pull Holly's funny side out now. Dad says we just have to be patient with her and hope her demons don't get the best of her. He doesn't mention Mom, but I know he must be thinking about her. Mom let her demons get the best of her and look where she is—somewhere up north whoring herself out for her drug of choice. Not that I think Holly would ever go down that path, and I know Dad doesn't. He would never have brought her home to me if he had even the smallest inkling. Still, in the back of my mind I worry this is something she's never going to be able to get over. She stronger than I am, though, so maybe I'm not giving her enough credit.

Just as I'm rolling my eyes at her, heavy boots sound against the hardwood floor in the entryway, and I know instinctively what that means. Dad's home. Everybody else announces themselves, but not Dad.

As he rounds the corner into the living room, he sees us sitting on the sofa. He gives me a smiling head nod, but soon enough his attention drifts toward Holly. I might've missed it if I didn't know him so well, but I've spent the last seventeen years looking into this man's face. And I know what it means when his eyebrows draw together, just slightly, before he carefully corrects them and resumes that mask of indifference. He's worried. He has every right to be, though I know he doesn't want to show it. Holly keeps saying she's fine and she's working through it. Even right after it happened, she told Dad she was okay because she did what she had to do. It had something to do with her protecting him, and I have to admit that my soon-to-be stepmom is badass enough to think she has to protect my dad, who is one of the scariest and most intimidating men anybody could ever hope to meet, makes my heart swoon. Her strength is exactly why I have to help Dad and the club figure out what happened with Holly and Mindy. I need Holly to be strong, not just for Dad but for me as well. I've never had a mom before, and I like it, so I need her to be okay. She has to be.

This is just who Holly is. She doesn't care how many muscles he has or how tough he acts in front of everybody else. She knows him in a different way than I do, but she knows that beneath all the angry rants and grumpy stares he's actually a lovable guy. But I won't let him catch me telling anybody that.

"What are you two up to?" he asks.

"Nothing, baby," Holly says. She smiles softly and reaches her arm out toward him. It's the only invitation he needs. His face covers hers, and he places a big sloppy kiss right on her lips. When Holly starts to giggle, Dad smiles wide. I'm smiling, too, before I decide I'm officially grossed out and turn away. I can still hear the swapping of spit, which is just plain disgusting but at the same time kind of not.

We had a way things worked around here for a long time. Dad went out and took care of club business whenever he needed to and partied with my uncles whenever he felt like it. He spent enough time at home, and he was always good about making sure that I knew I mattered. But he's never been much of a homebody, and as far back as I can remember, he's never been a one-woman man either.

Not that he couldn't be. It's just not who he has been. And Holly has obviously changed that. I love having him around more, and I love even more that he's happy. But even better than that, I actually like her, and that's saying a lot. Because as much as my dad thinks that nobody's good enough for his little girl, his little girl thinks that just about nobody is good enough for her dad.

"Well, you two kids have fun. I'm gonna go upstairs and do something that's not watching you guys make out like teenagers." I stand from the couch and cross the room. At the foot of the stairs, I turn back and realize they haven't even paid attention to the fact that I've gotten up. I'd like to think they heard me, but Dad is still bent over the couch trying to inhale Holly. And that's when I realize that, despite the thinking I'm mature for my age, I'm still not mature enough to have to watch my dad suck face with my school secretary. Even if I do adore her.

I trudge up the stairs to my room and close the door behind me, trying to forget that they've christened the entire house like a couple of teenagers.

I've been kind of bored lately because, unfortunately Holly has ratted me out to Dad about every time I've been absent from class this semester. I agreed to be on my best behavior, and part of that means actually getting my butt to class, but girl code takes precedence over relationship code. Whatever that is anyway. So now I'm grounded. That means staying in the house with the horny twosome, with little else to do. Thankfully my grounding is coming to an end in a few days, and it can't come soon enough. I'm just grateful there's an entire floor between my room and Dad's room. Tracie, the bestest best friend ever, says she can hear her mom and her new boyfriend going at it at least twice a week. And Tracie's really screwed in the head, so I'm thinking that having an entire floor between my room and my dad's room is going to save him on some serious therapy bills for me in the future.

I pull up the legs of my sweatpants, kick off my socks, and throw myself into bed. I grab my cell phone and wonder if anybody called while I was downstairs. As it turns out, my friends have been kind of silent ever since I got put on restriction. But that text—that one from

Daniel—is still there.

But an idea comes to me. I can call Jeremy. I think on it for just a minute before I decide not to call him. I'm at home and Dad's here, so I can't really use the whole "I'm in danger" excuse to get him here or talk to me. Plus, if Dad found out what I'd done, he would kick my ass. And not in the way where his eyebrows wrinkle and he gets all grouchy and tells me that I'm going to see the end of kingdom come if I ever do it again, because that's a total joke. No, Dad would get the kind of pissed at me where he calls Aunt Ruby and she kicks me in the ass. She's not the tallest woman I know, but her boot definitely reaches my behind.

So if I can't call Jeremy, I can probably send him a text. That's less intrusive, right? I don't know if I should. I mean, either he's going to respond back and talk to me for a little bit because he wants to, because maybe he likes me as much as I like him, or he will respond back because my dad is the club's sergeant at arms. That may not mean a whole hell of a lot to the other guys I'd be interested in, but it means the world to Jeremy. As a prospect for my dad's club, Jeremy's ass, testicles, and every other part of him belong to Forsaken. And Dad never lets him forget it.

HEY, I text. I shouldn't be texting him considering he ignored me earlier.

God, that was stupid. What a lame message. It's not like I've never talked to a boy before. I don't even know why I'm getting so flustered over trying to send him a text message. I've sent guys text messages before. I'm no chicken. I've even sent Jeremy text messages before. But this feels different. I'm texting with a purpose. Plus, I am a total feminist. I can take the lead. I can ask guys out. There is nothing wrong with being a strong, independent woman.

But what if he does think I'm stupid?

He thinks I'm stupid.

As time passes, I become convinced he's going to forever ignore me and think I'm a dumb little girl. Well, maybe I should give up on him and put on my big girl panties and redirect my attention to Daniel.

After five minutes, I decide he's out with another girl. Maybe she's giving him a hickey right now. Because unfortunately I've seen him sporting them before, so I know he's gotten further than I have. And even worse, maybe he's with a Lost Girl at the clubhouse getting his dick sucked. Because as much as Dad doesn't want me to know that that stuff happens there, people talk and I'm not a baby. Besides, what kind of stories did he think Ryan was going to share with me when he used to babysit?

My phone chimes, half frightening me. I grab it and check the screen.

WHATS UP? the text reads from Jeremy.

I let out a little squeal before I realize how stupid I sound. How can I ever convince anybody I'm not a baby if I'm squealing like a fourteen-year-old? Because really, that was so three years ago.

Pull it together, Cheyenne.

NOT MUCH, I text back.

This time, I don't have to wait long for response.

WHERE U BEEN?

What the hell does he mean where have I been? It's more like where has he been. For three weeks straight Dad has had him on what the guys call "bitch duty" here at the house. But ever since that one night where Dad came home to find us on the porch talking, Jeremy's been MIA. After a while I became convinced that he just had better things to do or the guys put them on another detail. I've only seen him a few times since his detail changed. He's been flirty, dismissive, and even downright territorial. But has he asked me out?

No, he hasn't.

Pussy.

Oh man, I've spent so much time in this house I'm starting to think like my dad. I need out. Now.

HERE, I text back in irritation. I'm not going to argue with him or call him on it. There's no way around not sounding like a pathetic, jealous girlfriend if I ask him where he's been. But how dare he ask me where I've been when I have been right here and he hasn't shown up. I got used to having him around, and his absence is pissing me off. It's pissing me off so bad that Daniel is looking better and better every day.

REASSIGNED.

Well, that explains it.

FIGURES, I say.

HOW SO?

DAD IS A HELICOPTER.

WHY? the text reads.

BOYS. HE'S NUTS.

U TRYING 2 TELL ME SOMETHING?

Okay, so maybe getting my flirt on in a text message isn't that hard after all, but still, my hands are practically shaking. What if he's just tolerating me because he's afraid to reject me? Maybe he thinks Dad's going to break his fingers or whatever the hell he does to scare and intimidate people he doesn't like. I don't know the specifics of Dad's "job" with the club—only that it's half-illegal and he's not afraid to get his hands dirty.

DON'T PLAY DUMB, I text back.

God, for some reason this is harder with him than it is with anybody else. Maybe it's because he's not playing the game like the other guys have. Daniel plays the game really well. Hell, he's so good at it he might have invented the damn game. Normally when I try to flirt with a guy, he flirts back by taking my innuendo and running with it. But not Jeremy. No, Jeremy Whelan is the kind of guy who makes you spell it out for him and then tells you exactly how it's going to be.

He's a total motorcycle brat through and through. Bossy, self-assured, and a wee bit narcissistic.

He's perfect.

NOT PLAYING, CHEY. TRYIN 2 FIGURE U OUT.

Oh. My. God.

He is insufferable. Still, the grin that spreads across my face is totally ridiculous. Because if there's anything that's hot about a guy like Jeremy Whelan, it's the fact he can basically do what he wants, how he wants, and when he wants. And he knows it.

ASK ME OUT. I am so nervous that my toes could literally fall off my feet, roll away, and end up in my cereal tomorrow morning, and I wouldn't even notice. And I know how gross that is, but that's how screwed up I am over this stupid boy. That's the big difference between Jeremy and Daniel. Daniel just exists and does as he pleases but invites me along for the ride. Meanwhile Jeremy is growing and learning. He's moldable, but not Daniel. I don't want to be with a man who has all his life figured out. I barely know how to wash my own clothes.

NO, his response reads.

My stomach drops, and I toss my phone beside me and then bury my face into my pillow. I can't believe I just got rejected. By a prospect. This is humiliating. My phone beeps, letting me know that I have a message. Very slowly I drag my face from the center of the pillow and try to breathe normally. It's hard, though, because my heart is beating a million miles a minute, and I think I'm about to die.

U ASK ME OUT, his text reads.

I shove my face back in my pillow and squeal maniacally. I'm done with being gentle with this boy.

WE R GOING OUT. FRIDAY, I text.

Holy crap.

PICK U UP AT 7. WEAR PINK. U LOOK HOT IN PINK. NO LIPSTICK.

Holy crap.

I'm going out with Jeremy Whelan.

Holy crap.

I stare my phone down, unable to figure out when I got the lady balls to do that. Only one thing perplexes me, though. Why the hell doesn't he want me to wear lipstick?

CHAPTER 8

December

16 months to Mancuso's downfall

Cheyenne

"ARE YOU EXCITED?" Holly asks. I'm looking in the mirror, and she's standing behind me. Her reflection is partially covered by mine, but I can see her well enough to tell she's smiling.

"Yeah, I am," I say. Because I am. I *so* am.

I would be more excited if I didn't know that Dad and Holly were going to be tailing me tonight. Because Dad always tails me.

And I mean always.

At first I think he really thought I needed him to follow me on my dates, but now I think he just enjoys it. Before Holly came along, he would come in my room as

I was getting ready for a date, and he would be smiling in this really unnatural way—it's really creepy—and he would just say, "Hey there, are we ready for our date?"

The first time it happened, I thought he was joking. The second time it happened, I thought he would calm down eventually. Now I know he's just a little bit demented. It's all those special brownies he likes to eat.

"Is there any way that maybe you could distract Dad? Enlist some of your super special awesome girlfriend powers?"

"Girl, I don't have enough special powers to convince your dad not to follow you tonight. Sorry. You're going out with *Jeremy Whelan*. Of course your dad's going to tail you."

Well shit. If Dad's being totally in love with Holly and Holly's living here now can't get him off my back even a little bit, then what good is this whole them falling in love thing anyway?

"Then at least keep him at a reasonable distance."

"I will see what I can do."

Sure enough, Dad walks into the room. His dark brown hair is greased back, and it looks almost black from where I stand. His dark eyes are gleaming, and he's smiling that same maniacal smile I know so well. He's wearing dark jeans, a long-sleeved flannel shirt, and his Forsaken cut. Because even when I go on dates with regular boys, Dad makes sure to follow us and let everyone know whose daughter I am.

"Are we ready for our date?" he asks. He actually is looking at me like he thinks I'm going to respond positively. I won't do it to his face, but the moment he turns his back I am flipping him off. Asshole. I swear he deserves something bad to happen to him, like maybe he'll walk into a wall. Nothing truly horrible because, despite how I feel in this moment, I still love my father. But, man, do I want him to suffer just a little bit.

"You're not funny. Nobody else is smiling. And there is a part of me that thinks you hate me," I say.

One would think that if your child tells you they're convinced, even a little bit, that you hate them that you would stop smiling. One would think it's the courteous thing to do. One would think they were talking to somebody other than my father. He stands there full of smiles and laughs.

I turn away from my reflection in the mirror and decide not to worry about the way I look anymore. I'm just wearing a plain pair of jeans, knee-high flat-footed boots, and a pink long-sleeved top. Jeremy asked for pink, so I'm giving him pink. And he's so right. I do look hot in pink. The long-sleeved top is courtesy of Dad's orders. I believe the exact words used were "if you're not actually charging for it, then don't act like you are." I came close to telling him that he should take his own advice. Because before Holly, he and I both know he was no saint. The chicks he used to "spend time with" at the clubhouse sure dress and act like they charge for it. Thank God they don't, or I wouldn't have a college fund with how much Dad used to like their company.

"You know," I say to Holly, "I wouldn't blame you for ditching this one and finding somebody less crazy." As the words leave my mouth, I realize that's the last thing I want. I couldn't handle it if she left. I'd track her down and refuse to leave her side. I can't go back to the way it was before. She's a part of us now, and I'll do anything to keep her.

Even if that means figuring out what happened to her and Mindy on my own.

A guilty smile spreads across her face as she tosses her head back in laughter. It's really awesome seeing her smile and laugh like this. But what's even better is that she's laughing at Dad's expense. He deserves it.

Dad rolls his eyes. He looks ridiculous and like a total drama queen. If we didn't look so much alike, I could totally ignore the fact that perhaps I probably look like a fool when I do it. But I'm a girl, and it doesn't look as stupid on me as it does a grouchy biker. At least I hope.

"Well, out with it. I know you want to say something. First up, it's always the speech. The speech about respecting myself and how I shouldn't let boys take advantage of me. But I know you're going to have an even better speech prepared because I'm going out with a prospect, so let's not pussyfoot around it. Just say what you got to say so I can go, and just follow me like you always do, you creeper."

Holly purses her lips, her face turns red, and she looks away. Her shoulders shake, giving away her silent laughter.

"I said you could go out with the kid. I'm not saying you can't, but I want you to understand that he's not just some mouthy eighteen-year-old. He's a prospect. You should know what that means."

"Dad, I do know what that means."

"I don't think you do."

Dad is obviously uncomfortable, and I can't really blame him. I'm not exactly comfortable either. But he's not going to let this rest until he's sure I know what I'm doing. Even though I might be eighty and he might be in a nursing home by the time that happens.

"Dating a prospect means I'm dating the club. I get that. I know he might have to leave at any time, and sometimes the stuff he has to do for the club is dangerous. Give me a little credit."

"You will never come first," he says. "I don't want that for you."

"But you want it for Holly?" I fold my arms over my chest.

"Don't want it for Holly either. But I'm a selfish prick," he says with sorrowful eyes.

That I can agree with.

"I'm going out with Jeremy," I say.

Dad stands in an awkward silence with an obviously uncomfortable stance. His shoulders are slightly hunched forward, with his hands on his hips and his head tilted down but his gaze to the side. I know that stance. He's recognized defeat. The thing is I know what he really wants to say. What he really wants to say is that dating a club member, even if he's still prospect, is a commitment to more than just a man. I've heard the speeches, and I know how this goes. The thing he needs to understand is that I'm ready for this.

I'm not sure exactly what happened, but I used to think there could be nothing more attractive than a man in uniform. You know, like the football uniform with the tight spandex pants. Or even the baseball uniform with the cup and the hat. Hockey uniforms aren't really all that hot, because you can't see anything. But I sure don't mind watching them body-check each other up against the Plexiglas in the rink.

But that was before. Because once things started getting dangerous for whatever reason with the club and the prospects started hanging out here, I started to wonder what it would be like to date a club member. If Dad knew the thoughts that have gone through my head, he would have a coronary and fall to pieces on the floor right now.

"You're starting to act like an adult, and I don't like it," he says.

I offer him a sad smile and shrug my shoulders. "And you're starting to sound like a sane person."

He lets out a brief chuckle before he shakes his head, points his finger at Holly, and directs her to the open door. He does a lot of pointing with her, and she does a lot of eye rolling with him.

As Holly walks past Dad, his hand comes down and smacks her on the butt, creating a loud slapping sound in the room. She gasps and turns around, giving him a dirty look. But I'm starting to figure out what Holly's dirty looks mean. She gives them constantly. To me, to Grandma, but to Dad most especially. Holly's look right now is one more of disapproval than of actual anger. When she's really angry, she doesn't even give him a dirty look. She just kind of looks past him blankly. It's a little intimidating, and I don't want to ever be on the receiving end of that look. So I shut my mouth, stay in the corner, and decide if she's happy getting spanked in front of her boyfriend's teenage daughter, then who am I to judge?

The doorbell rings loudly from downstairs as Holly is leaving my bedroom. But I can't let her get to it first, so I push past her, offering my apologies on the way down the stairs. By the time I get to the front door, I have to pause for a moment to stop myself from hyperventilating. Did I put on lipstick? Jeremy said no lipstick. I press two of my fingers to my lips just to make sure I didn't and thankfully find a pair of dry lips. I guess Jeremy just doesn't like the look of lipstick or something. I don't know, really.

Dad moves slowly but purposefully behind me, his heavy footsteps getting closer and louder with every moment.

I open the door and am met with a smiling Jeremy on the other side. My face flushes, and I lose my breath for just a moment. He's that good-looking.

With his strong jaw, straight nose, and dark navy-blue eyes, Jeremy Whelan is hot as hell. He's what Holly keeps calling a heartthrob. He's what grandma called a babe. But I'm not old and I'm not prehistoric, so I'm not using either of those terms. He's the kind of hot you can't manufacture with expensive clothes or arrogance. No, Jeremy is the kind of hot that radiates out of his skin and infects everyone around him.

"Looking good, babe," he says. A breathy sigh escapes me, and my face reddens. I might not survive the night if he keeps looking at me like this.

"I wore pink," I say.

He nods and grins. "Yeah, you did."

———◄✦►———

THE FIRST PLACE Jeremy took me on our date was the arcade. Dad didn't make an appearance inside, thankfully. I think Jeremy chose it because he knows that it's busy enough that we can get lost in the crowd but not so bad that we can't even talk while we're in there.

We are leaving the arcade when I spot Holly waving at me as she climbs out of Dad's truck. She's frantic, with wild eyes and her hands flinging around. My heart drops. It's not like I didn't know they followed me, but I don't know why she's out of the truck. Normally he stays put inside the truck and doesn't bother me too much when I'm on a date. I think his objective is just to let the guy I'm with know that my dad is always watching.

Jeremy spots them and grins down at me. "We could put a show on for him."

"You're not funny," I snap. "He's such an ass."

With an amused chuckle, he pulls me into his side and throws an arm around my neck. Our steps falter slightly as he bends down and places a kiss on top of my head. I give him a weak slap to his stomach but can't help the budding smile that threatens to overtake my face and the blush that shows my excitement.

"*What?*" I mouth to Holly while looking her way. She points at the other end of the bushes where Dad is standing, his back resting against a tree. His arms are crossed, and he's shaking his head. The fact that he's not happy doesn't tell me anything, because for the most part, he's always unhappy. I narrow my eyes at him and shake my head. He's been worse this time because it's Jeremy. No doubt.

What an asshole.

Jeremy places his hand on my lower back and leads me toward my father. My nerves shoot to the roof, and I start to panic. I knew he would see Dad by the bushes, but I didn't think he would approach him.

We're barely five or six feet away when Jeremy says, "Sir."

"Prospect," Dad says. Holly slides up beside him and jabs him in the ribs. He doesn't budge or even acknowledge her arrival. His eyes are hard as they fixate on Jeremy's arm around my neck. I'm mildly uncomfortable with the attention until Jeremy clears his throat.

Dad folds his arms across his chest. "You remember the rules?"

"Yes, sir," Jeremy says. "Gave you my word."

"Dad," I hiss. He doesn't even look my way. Holly gives me a sympathetic pout and shakes her head.

"Where we going next?" Dad asks, his eyes still on Jeremy's arm around my neck.

"Hell," I shout in annoyance. "We're all going to hell!"

"Chey, it's cool." Jeremy tightens his grip around my neck and places another soft kiss to my hairline. His voice is quiet and soft when he says, "Your dad just wants to make sure I'm doing right by you."

Dad straightens and nods his chin at Jeremy as if he's

pleased with him. But Holly and I both know what total bullshit this is. Jeremy's kissing Dad's ass, plain and simple. It just so happens Dad enjoys a good ass-kissing every now and then, so he's not calling him on it.

"Well, we better get going. Once traffic picks up, it gets harder to follow you two in the truck," Dad says, claps his hands together, and smiles deviously.

Holly's face turns beet red, and she looks away in obvious disbelief that Dad's actually acting like this. She never did believe me when I told her that he's batshit crazy. Well, she's stuck with him now.

"Yes, sir," Jeremy says. He's starting to sound like a fucking robot. It's making me want to give him a titty twister or something just to see some emotion from him. I duck out from beneath his arm, grab his hand, and give him a tug toward his bike. He follows silently. After he straps on his helmet and climbs on the bike, I get on behind him and try to ignore that Dad and Holly are behind us watching our every move.

WHEN MY AND Jeremy's date comes to an end, it's not nearly as romantic as I had been expecting it to be. I got a text from Daniel halfway through our date, which I ignored but Jeremy caught notice of. It took a good five minutes for the scowl to leave his face after that. I didn't even see what it said before I clicked the screen off. And despite Dad and Holly's following us, I didn't think he would be so cruel as to watch our every move while Jeremy tells me goodnight on the front porch. I don't even get a chance to ask him why he was adamant that I not wear lipstick.

I lean in for a quick kiss but find that Dad's already clearing his throat and telling Jeremy if he doesn't get going, then he won't have feet to move with. As Jeremy leaves and Dad starts commenting on how well the night went, I decide it's for the best to just head upstairs and plot my escape from this loony bin. If I stay down here with my father, he and I are going to have a huge fight, and nobody, especially Holly, is ready for that.

I'm up in my room less than a minute when my phone chimes from my back pocket. The overhead fixture above casts a warm glow of light around my room, illuminating the hot pink and black tones that have been used to decorate my personal space. Shutting the door behind me, I pull my phone out and smile at the message on the screen from Jeremy.

U SHOULD HAVE KISSED ME.

With a deep, happy sigh, I shuffle to my bed and plop down. My fingers work swiftly over the touch screen. IF U WERE HERE I WOULD.

I have barely sent the message by the time I hear the quiet *clink, clink, clink* of small rocks hitting my bedroom window. My phone chimes again.

OPEN WINDOW.

I can't stop the blush that comes to my skin from just the suggestion that Jeremy might be outside. I shuffle to the closed window and peek down at the grass below, surprised that Jeremy made it past the security alarm. Dad has the entire property pretty well alarmed, especially these days. But I suppose that's the benefit of dating a prospect—he knows where the alarms are and how to avoid them.

Anticipation builds in my gut as I drag up the aging wooden window casing, clearing a path for Jeremy's entrance. I look down alongside the house and realize one of Dad's ladders is already propped up.

I cast a look at Jeremy and shake my head ruefully. He planned this. And I couldn't be happier. I place my index finger to my lips and make a shushing sound, hoping he gets the gist of it. And he does, because when he climbs up the ladder, it's in near silence.

At the top of the ladder, he smiles widely, his blue eyes gleaming in the artificial light. I take a step back and gesture with my hand to welcome him in. Part of me can't believe I'm actually inviting a date into my room. This has never happened before. Not that I never wanted it to happen, but with how overbearing my dad is, no other boy has had the balls to do something like this.

"You planned this," I whisper accusingly.

He shrugs his shoulders, tilts his head downward, and crooks his index finger for me to come closer. His feet are placed shoulder width apart, and he stands with such confidence that I can barely believe he's only eighteen.

As if I have no choice, my feet carry me forward until I'm practically pressed up against his muscular frame. We're so close. We've never been this close before. My hands find their way to the still-fresh leather that hangs off his shoulders. When I look up and catch the devious smile on his lips, I instinctively press myself into him. His face moves closer to mine, slowly and purposefully. My chest constricts, and it's difficult to breathe. I reach up, even going so far as to stretch on my tiptoes, and lightly drag my desperate lips against his.

As if reading my mind, he whispers, "This is why I didn't want you to wear lipstick."

He takes over then, slamming his lips to mine. My hands reach out and wrap around the back of his neck, pulling him closer to me, so desperate for more. I peek my tongue out and drag it along his lip. Eagerly, he opens his mouth to me, and our kiss moves from sweet to sinful. Kissing Jeremy is everything I thought it would be and more. I've waited for this for so long that actually having it makes me feel as though I'm about to combust.

His hand reaches out and cups my ass. With a firm grip on my pliant flesh, he pulls me hard against him and bucks his hips. I'm not prepared for it, and I stumble backward. Jeremy stabilizes me, pulls in closer, and resumes his handsy and deliciously sexy ways. My body yearns for his touch and attention, but in the back of my head, something doesn't feel right. He's being too aggressive. Still, he walks me backward until my knees hit the edge of my bed, and I'm forced to bend at the knee and sit down. Bending down and parting my legs with his knee, he covers his body with mine, leaving me little choice but to lie back and allow his heavy frame to cover me. His leg further parts mine as he rocks himself into my core.

His lips command my heart, and his body commands my attention, but it's all too much too soon. We've only been on one date, and it wasn't like we got any time alone. This doesn't feel like the start of a relationship. It feels like a hookup, and I don't like that so much.

My hands press into his chest as I try to force him off of me. He's insistent in his attempts, but so am I. With every ounce of strength I can muster, I push him off me and take his surprise as an opportunity to slip away and scramble off my bed.

"What is your problem?" he asks quietly but with as much malice as if he had screamed it.

"No, what is *your* problem?"

I was the one being mauled, not him.

"You let me in your bedroom. What did you think was going to happen?"

I'm left speechless. I don't know the code for making out with guys in your bedroom, so I'm caught off guard by the suggestion that I've done something wrong. Jeremy's hard stare redirects to the window. His feet follow, and before I know it, he's out the window and staring at me in annoyance. He opens his mouth, but I have no desire to hear anything from him right now. I should have believed the rumors that float around school about how he's only ever interested in one thing.

"Don't open your mouth," I warn him, "or I will push this ladder to the ground and then scream for my dad."

CHAPTER 9

December

16 months to Mancuso's downfall

Cheyenne

"BEHAVE YOURSELF," HOLLY says as she stands in the middle of the open front door. Dad's on the other side slowly making his way to the edge of the porch and toward his awaiting bike. He smiles softly—as softly as Dad can, anyway—and gives her a wink. "I'm not kidding."

On my left, Tracie huffs quietly. Her arms are folded over her chest, and her brows are knit together. I let out a heavy sigh, and my body slinks into the wall beside me that separates the kitchen from the family room.

"Define that," Dad says and steps closer to Holly. He

places his hands on her hips and pulls her flush against him. They're so in their own world that neither of them sees Tracie and me watching their exchange.

"God, I hope he doesn't screw this up," I whisper-shout. Dad normally asks Holly to come with him to the clubhouse parties, but he didn't this time. It's put me on edge just waiting for him to ask her to go. She always says no, but that's not the point. If he's always asked before, he should ask now.

Tracie's brown hair is pulled up in a messy bun, just like mine, and her face is makeup free, also just like mine. Sometimes, when we do our hair similarly or wear our makeup a certain way, I swear we look so much alike we could be sisters. Hell, if Tracie had been born in town, with the way Dad used to get around, I wouldn't have put it out of the realm of possibility. But Tracie wasn't born here. Her fancy-pants douchebag father lives somewhere south of San Francisco with his new wife and new kids. Tracie's mom is kind of loose, so they had a paternity test done. Wishful thinking. I guess I'm just sick of being Sterling Grady's sole focus for torture.

Holly places her hands on Dad's chest and pushes him back just slightly. "I love you in ways I can't explain, but if you have to ask me to define cheating, then whatever you're thinking is okay for you to do isn't. Got it?"

"It was just a question, babe," Dad says. "Parties like this can get wild. Bitches walk around naked, they jump into laps. Tits gets shoved in faces. Shit happens. I'm not looking for an out. I'm just asking what's going to get me into trouble."

"That's it," Holly says in a loud voice. She throws her hands in the air, turns around, and heads for the staircase that leads to her and Dad's bedroom.

"What the hell?" Dad snaps as he follows her with one grouchy as hell look on his face. I'd never shoot my own father, but suddenly the handgun that's tucked into the back of my jeans feels heavier, like its presence is more obvious and uncomfortable all of a sudden.

"You want to know what's going to get you in trouble? Leaving this house without me is going to get you in trouble. Give me five minutes, baby. I'll be ready!" Holly's voice trails as she descends to the lower level.

Dad stops at the top of the staircase, peering down, and muttering to himself. "Fuck!" He kicks at the topmost spindle, which makes a cracking sound but remains intact. As his body pivots around, he finds us watching him. I can't help the smile that takes over my face. He's so damn pissy over Holly inviting herself to a club party—something I didn't think she was even allowed to do—that he can barely breathe. His face is beet red, and his hands are clenched at his sides. "You could have decided to come earlier, ya know!" he shouts down the stairs. His eyes slide over to me. "What are you two looking at?"

Tracie's eyes slide from side to side as she focuses elsewhere. I think I would, too, if I were her. But this is my dad, and if he thinks snapping at me can scare me, he's so freaking wrong. It'd be like he doesn't even know me.

"You're in love," I say. It doesn't come out as teasing as I intend for it to. Instead, I sound almost surprised and amazed.

"What tipped you off?" he says with more snark than Tracie and I combined. Yeah, I'd never shoot him, but it's a tempting thought.

"I'm perceptive," I say, "like my dad."

Slowly, his breathing regulates, and he grunts in irritation. Thank God. I hate to fight with him over such little shit. We get into it enough over everything else— attitudes, messy rooms, disrespect. Everything.

"You did good," I say with a nod. "Letting her go. The old Dad wouldn't have let her. You'd have just dealt with the breakup like you didn't care."

"Since when do you give me relationship advice?" Okay, so maybe he's not changed that much. He's still bitchy when he feels like he's being judged.

"Just because you never brought women home doesn't mean I didn't notice every time you had to change your phone number." My comment goes too far. The redness in his face comes back in a flash, and he's breathing heavy again. I decide to change tactics because this isn't working out the way I wanted it to. I was trying to be nice. Over the years, he's alternated between regular hookups like he had with Elle and random chicks at the clubhouse—and the Lost Girls, of course—and when one of his regulars would get too attached and wouldn't get the hint that he was done with her, he'd change his number. The only woman he never had to change his number with was Elle, which is why I thought something might become more permanent between the two of them.

"I love her, Dad," I say gently. I wouldn't dare warn him not to break her heart, because no matter how much shit he lets me get away with, that's one thing he doesn't take lightly. Not even *I* can threaten him and get away with it, which is why it's a damn good thing he can't read my mind. Like a bipolar grizzly bear, he calms down again. It's a solid minute before he nods his head once and then leaves the room for the garage.

"Is he really that mad?" Tracie asks when he's out of earshot.

"Nah," I say. "He's not used to having to check in with a woman. Grandma says he doesn't like the loss of independence even if he's happy with Holly. He's probably going to enjoy himself more with Holly there. He won't be wondering if he's going to get busted for looking at some naked woman if it gets back to her."

"Makes sense," Tracie says.

We head into the kitchen, where we heat up some hot cocoa, and then to the kitchen table. I place my gun on the table, and we sit down. It's early yet—we have another hour or so before the clock rings us into the new year. I try to block out what happens at club parties, not just because my dad will be in attendance, but also because someone new is going to be there this time—

Jeremy. Even worse, it's not just a New Year's party at the clubhouse—which always gets really crazy anyway—it's also for Jeremy's eighteenth birthday. They're bound to do something special for him.

Everybody's going to be there, even Nic. She and the old ladies with small kids will be in the chapel where they can hang out in safety and without being surrounded by smoke and drugs and the Lost Girls. It's too dangerous for the old ladies and the kids to stay home. Dad's only letting me and Tracie stay home because he doesn't trust me to behave at the clubhouse. The deal was that I keep my gun on me at all times and Holly and Grandma stay here with us. But I guess we're down to Grandma now that Holly's invited herself. Can't say Dad doesn't have reason not to want me there. No way in hell would I stay in the chapel. This house is like Fort Knox anyway. He's not only got alarms on all the ground-level doors and windows, but he has a tracking service that tells him every time a door is opened or closed as well. He never checks that, though, so I guess it's more of a deterrent to keep me where he wants me—not that it works so well. I live by Aunt Ruby's motto—it's better to ask for forgiveness than permission.

Just as we're finishing off our cocoa, Dad and Holly walk into the room hand in hand. Holly's wearing knee-high black boots with skinny jeans tucked into them and a sexy but modest flowing black blouse. She has large hoop earrings, and her hair is teased. She looks awesome for how quickly she got ready. Her makeup is mostly light, but her mascara is thick. She wears the look well.

"You look great," Tracie says with a smile on her face.

"Thanks." Holly flashes us each a big beautiful grin. "I don't know what happened, but these clothes were already laid out when I went downstairs."

"Right, then why did it take so damn long for you to get ready?" he asks. Dad *hates* to wait on anybody, especially women when they're getting ready. "Longest damn five minutes I've ever seen."

"Makeup, baby. I had to do my makeup."

I suck air up through my nose so quickly that I snort and have to cover my mouth with my hand so as not to spit cocoa everywhere. She so didn't happen to have her outfit lying around. Holly totally planned this, probably hoping Dad would ask her to go. Dad fell for it hook, line, and sinker. Either that, or he didn't ask her on purpose to force her to invite herself so that she'd have to go. I wouldn't put it past either of them to try to trick the other. While Tracie asks Holly about her boots, I get Dad's attention and slyly mouth, "*Sucker.*"

Dad gives me a resigned smile as he slaps the kitchen table and says, "Come on, baby, or I'm going to take you on the table again." Holly's gasp of surprise is drowned out by the sound of my and Tracie's chairs shoving back against the wooden floor as we scurry away from the defiled table.

Just when I had blocked that shit out, he has to bring it back up.

Asshole.

"Keep that gun on you, baby girl," he says and points at me.

I nod and say, "Shoot first, ask questions later."

"That's my girl." He gives me a proud grin and a wink that makes me feel like a little girl all over again.

They disappear out the front door, sneaking a chaste kiss on the way and laughing happily. When Dad thinks no one but Holly is looking, he smiles a lot. Even though it's not *at* me as much as I'd like, it's nice knowing he saves it for her. It makes it kind of special. Maybe he won't destroy this relationship.

"Dude." I elbow Tracie as I grab my gun and we walk up the stairs toward my room. "Dad left us alone. Totally unsupervised."

Just as the words leave my mouth, my phone chimes. I shove the gun back into the waistband of my jeans and pull the phone from my front pocket. A message from Holly mocks me. DON'T FORGET GMA IS IN HER ROOM. GROUCHY SAYS YOU SNEAK OUT, YOU GO TO CONVENT. CONVENT=LAME=STAY HOME. BE GOOD.

My entire body turns to gelatin as I laugh heartily at the message. I love it when Holly calls him Grouchy. I bet anything Dad made her send me that message—he does that a lot—but I doubt he knows what she actually says in the messages. I show Tracie the message, which has her in stitches in a matter of moments, too. We give up on walking and park our butts on the stairs. I wince as my tailbone hits the barrel of the gun.

"Shit," I shout and pull the gun out from underneath me and set it beside me. My tailbone throbs in pain, and I adjust my position on the stairs to lessen the discomfort. I could be missing my left ass cheek right about now if I weren't so paranoid that I'd already checked the safety about twenty times since Dad made me get the damn thing out.

Tracie shushes me. "You're going to wake up Lisa."

"Grandma won't wake up unless we throw a house party." My fingers work quickly over the digital keyboard on my phone's screen as I type out, DEFINE GOOD.

GROUCHY JR, she texts back with a sad looking emoticon at the end. I send back a heart emoticon and shove my phone in the pocket of my sweatpants.

"What are you thinking? All the good eighteen-and-up clubs are too far away, and you're not even eighteen yet," Tracie says. Ever since she turned eighteen, she's been reminding me of all the things I can't do. "Plus, you can't go into a club packing." She shifts her eyes to the gun between us. Tracie doesn't know anything about the inner workings of the club, but she knows enough about the occasional danger that creeps up due to club-related problems. That doesn't mean she's comfortable having guns out in the open around her. She knows the score, though. It's part of being connected, even loosely, to Forsaken.

Desperate to change the subject, I mentally inventory our options for the evening. "Well," I say slowly. The idea's forming in my head, but it's stupid. I shouldn't be thinking about this. Ever. The only thing that can come out of this is a majorly broken heart.

"Yeah?" Tracie says, eyes widening and waiting for me to finish.

"What if we... sneak into the party at the clubhouse..." I shove my face into my hands. I feel like an idiot. Jeremy and I had one date—one truly awful date—and we haven't had a kind word to say to each other since I threatened to push him out of my bedroom window after he tried to maul me. But the idea of him turning eighteen at the clubhouse with all the Lost Girls and the wannabe whores who haven't earned the title yet leaves an uncomfortable feeling in my gut. I just want to know, to see what's happening for myself. Daniel's going to be there, too. He's still texting me, and I'm texting back now, so I kind of also want to know what he's up to. If he's hooking up with someone during the party, then he doesn't like me enough for me to continue to let him pursue me.

"You don't actually have to *sneak* in. The doors will be open," Tracie says. "It's so loud and dark in there, I doubt anyone will notice us."

"No, they'll have security this time. Things are kind of tense with the club." I wave the gun in the air. It's a fine art, telling the truth without telling too much.

"They have prospects at the gate, and I *highly* doubt any of them would be stupid enough to turn you away."

I lift my head slowly as some things over the last few

months start to make sense. The times Tracie was MIA, and when she started to tell me that there's a major difference between sex and love. Then there's the looks she gives Dad and my uncles when they're around and how many times she's commented on how attractive they all are.

"You freaking slut," I say, still half in disbelief. She so hasn't partied with the club. She can't have. She's still in high school. That's so... wrong. She's *my* age. Ugh.

"Stop being such a prude. How is it possible that you're *Bloody Knuckles's* daughter and yet you're so sheltered? Your dad is a legend among the Lost Girls."

"That's gross." I slap at her knee. "And I'm not a fucking prude. But come on! That would be like *me* hooking up with one of them."

"Not really," Tracie says. "You're being a baby."

"Who have you hooked up with?" If she says she hooked up with my dad, I'm going to push her fucking ass down the stairs and call it an accident. I know my dad better than that, but until I have verbal confirmation, I'm keeping my options for retribution open. Like sisters or no, you don't hook up with your best friend's dad. Ever.

"Diesel," she says quietly. I cast a glance long enough to find that she's staring at me nervously. I've always liked Diesel. He's fun to be around, got some pretty awesome muscles, killer tatts, and his video game knowledge is out of this world. I squeal and grin, slapping at her legs like a crazy woman, demanding that she tell me everything. I can totally handle her sleeping with Diesel. As long as she keeps her hands off anyone I call "uncle," I think I can live with this.

"It was... hot," she says in a breathy tone. "I mean, I thought high school boys knew what they were doing— but I only hooked up with two guys at school before I started hanging with the club."

"Is he the only one you've hooked up with?" I ask.

"No," she says and lets out a breath. "I hooked up with Aaron before…" Her voice trails off, and we stay silent for a long moment. She can't bring herself to say it, but what she means is before Aaron died protecting Holly and Mindy. Before some sick bastard shot him in the back of the head. Before everything went to shit.

"Did you like him?" I ask, because if she did, I should probably offer some kind of condolences. I can't say I've made peace with what happened to him, because we were friends. He was funny and kind and was completely devoted to the club. But I cried my ass off at his funeral, and I promised Uncle Jim that I wouldn't waste any more tears on the dead. Aaron wouldn't want it, he said. So I try not to do something that Aaron wouldn't like. Instead, I'm dedicating myself to finding out what happened to him. It's too late to fix that crap for Aaron, but there's still time to fix it for Holly and Mindy.

And by fix it, I mean once I find out who did it, I'm turning the evidence over to the club so Dad can kill them. Because he would, and they'd deserve however he makes them suffer.

"Okay, and I'm afraid to ask, but how exactly did you

end up partying with Forsaken?"

"It was one of those days when Diesel was here. You were off somewhere with Holly when I caught him looking at me. We flirted. He invited me to a party. I went and we hooked up."

"You make having sex sound so simple and easy," I say in disbelief. "I never get a freaking moment alone with a guy because my dad is a helicopter, always hovering. Even the few times I have managed to get a base or two in, I barely know what I'm doing."

"That's because you're hung up on this idea of being in a relationship. That's the difference between us, Chey. You're Holly and I'm Elle," she says, referring to my dad's on-again-off-again hookups with Elle. While I don't care for her using my dad's relationships as an example, because that's just awkward, I know what she means.

"Why do you think Elle doesn't want a relationship?" I ask. Then I correct my question to what I actually mean. "Are you saying you *want* to be a club whore?"

"Some women are built for relationships, and some of us just want to have fun. If it's right, it'll happen, like with Duke and Nic."

My heart rate speeds up in fear that we're about to get into a fight. I hate fighting with Tracie, and it's been happening more and more lately.

"Do you know how many women show up at the clubhouse thinking they're going to whore their way to being some guy's old lady?" My voice is soft. My heart hurts for her if she thinks whore to housewife is an easy road.

"I didn't say I want to be someone's old lady." Her tone is defensive. "I just said if it's right, it'll happen."

"Okay. I just hope you know what you're doing," I say.

"I do, and speaking of knowing who I'm doing... we better get ready if we're going to crash this party. If we get there too late, all the hot guys will be taken for the night."

I don't say a word as we stand from the stairs and head for my room, which we ransack in search of the right outfits in order to blend in. I waffle on how sexy I should be. If I'm wearing too little, I might be more visible. But then if I'm dressed like a nun, I'll stand out. By the time we're ready, it's nearing in on midnight, and if we don't hurry, we're going to miss the countdown.

Do they even do a midnight countdown at these things?

CHAPTER 10

December

16 months to Mancuso's downfall

Cheyenne

WALKING INTO THE clubhouse in this outfit makes my palms sweat and my breath catch. I shouldn't be here and especially not dressed like this. If Dad catches sight of me, not only will I be embarrassed that I'm treated like a child, but I'll never get over Dad seeing me in these clothes. Even though it's almost officially January and cold and wet outside, Tracie convinced me to wear a pair of my cut-off jean shorts with one of Holly's numerous pairs of high-heeled leather boots. I have my black-and-hot-pink plaid shirt that I wore on my and Jeremy's one and only date rolled up and knotted atop a tight tank that shows a few inches of my midriff and is cut low at my breasts, showing off some cleavage. My thick brown hair is down and teased, held in place with half a pound of hairspray.

High heels suck. They are so uncomfortable, but at least I look taller and hopefully more mature, too. Between the heavy black eye makeup and the dark red lipstick, I'm hoping it's not as easy to recognize me. While Dad is Public Enemy Number One, I wouldn't put it past any of my uncles or the other club members to make this situation really suck for me. Thankfully this place is crowded, and just like Tracie said, it's too dark in here to really shine a spotlight on anyone. Rink gave me a little crap at the gate, but I promised I'd bake him some cookies the next time he was at the house, and he let us go with the warning that I'd pay for it if Dad finds out and reams him for not ratting on us. I don't know where the nickname came from, but Greg's nickname should be Oink or something rather than Rink. He's got a worse sweet tooth than anyone I've ever met.

I've never really seen the clubhouse like this. The lights are low, smoke fills the room, suffocating me the first few minutes until my lungs adjust, and the temperature is higher than I expected. Pulling at the knot of my button-up, I squirm under the heat of the other bodies in the room.

"Take it off if it's that uncomfortable," Tracie says, catching my movements. She threw on a pair of tight jeans and some hot pink pleather heels she had stored in her trunk—especially for this occasion apparently—with a low-cut pink tank. She's pushed her boobs up in her bra as far as she can without her nipples falling out.

"I can't," I say a little louder and with more fear in my voice than I should have. I know I'm being a baby, but my tank top is so small and the men around us are so... manly. They're adults, not stupid teenage boys that count their blessings if you let them get to second base. Well, most teenage boys do, just not the Forsaken ones.

A woman passes by fully naked with two beers in her hands. My eyes follow her naked body, half in disbelief and half in jealousy of her confidence, as she places the beers on a table in the corner of the room. She parts her legs and climbs up on the lap of a large man I don't recognize. I turn away when she lifts herself up and, through the gap between her body and his, a dark hand sneaks out and rubs the flesh tucked between her butt cheeks, then sinks in between them. Her head falls backward as her hips jerk from the motion.

"Oh my God," I say and elbow Tracie. I turn my attention back to the bar area across the main room and try to block that out.

It's not working.

"What?"

"Some dude just shoved his finger in that woman's butt." My face is beet red, and the stifling heat gets to be too much. I unbutton my top and slip it off and choose to deal with the tiny tank I'm sporting that provides very little coverage—even less than what Tracie's wearing.

"It happens," she says casually and tugs me toward the bar. I nearly trip over a couple making out and another doing lines of something off a naked woman's inner thighs. I can't believe my dad hangs out here. I can't believe *I'm* hanging out here. Knowing this shit goes down and seeing it firsthand are two totally different things.

"Since you're the expert, why don't you tell me where Jeremy is." I don't regret the words when they leave my mouth. No, I regret the curiosity and nervousness I feel in my heart. I shouldn't want to know.

"Ah," Tracie says with a smirk. "Birthday boy should be around here somewhere. Let's grab a few beers, and then we can track him down."

The bar is so crowded we can barely squeeze ourselves up to the counter. It's not a true bar, because the club doesn't take any money for the alcohol they dole out. Apparently it's served up for favors—sexual if you're a woman, and *otherwise* if you're not—no exceptions. Aunt Ruby says they don't keep tabs on who owes them what. They just kind of expect whoever shows up here to be available to them when they need or want it.

"Two beers," Tracie says with a smile at the chick behind the bar who looks around for the fridge. She must be new. My eyes slide down to the other end where I see Chel serving up a drink to Squat. He leans over the bar, and she grabs ahold of the back of his head before shoving her tongue down his throat. I back off from the bar and cover myself from her view by the dude from the Oakland charter who has his back to me. The woman behind the bar nods and sets two beers down in front of us.

We each grab one of the cold bottles and turn around. I take a single step and slam into a hard chest. My nose presses into the dirty black leather vest that I know means I'm in trouble. Out of the corner of my eye I can see the

Fort Bragg patch. Any other charter, any other club, and I'd be fine. But not *this* charter. Not one of my dad's brothers. Please, no. I thought maybe I could get a solid half hour before getting busted.

As my eyes travel up the leather cut and up the man's neck to his chin, I let out a heavy sigh. Ian.

"Unless I'm drunker than I think, you're not legal." His cool voice is soft as his brown eyes take in my attire.

"You gonna rat me out?" I ask, batting my eyes and flashing him my best sweet smile.

He just shakes his head and tosses an arm over my shoulder. He glances at Tracie and says, "Go party," before turning back to me and leading me away from the bar.

When he doesn't make a move to take away my beer, I take a small sip and try to convince myself that I like the taste of it. I've only ever really liked beer after I've had enough of it that I can't really taste it anymore. Still, it's my best friend right now since I know if I drink enough, it'll calm my nerves. I take a large gulp and fight off the bitter aftertaste.

Ian's always been good to me, but I know he has a dark side that puts people on edge. I try not to walk on eggshells around him, even knowing everything I know about him, but it's hard. Forcing myself to see past his damage, I smile at the man who once felt very much like an older brother.

"Checking up on Baby Boy?" he asks.

I shrug my shoulders and decide to just be honest. "Yeah, but I'd also like to know where Daniel is."

"Detroit is in the palace," Ian says. "Not sure about Baby Boy."

"You're not going to tell me I'm too young to be here or that I don't want to see this shit?" Honestly I'm a bit surprised he isn't pulling some big-brother routine. With his arm that's draped over my shoulders, I'm slightly turned to see Jeremy at the far wall where Ryan is standing with a brunette who can't be much older than me. She's wearing jeans and boots with a tight tank top.

I swear the chicks at this party created some kind of freaking dress code or something. The whores are either naked or almost there, and the old ladies look classy as ever next to their badass biker men. There's no mistaking Ryan's companion is Alex. Her dark brown hair is up in a casual bun with strands falling and swooping out in places. Her brown eyes that look so much like Ian's and Ruby's stay focused on Ryan. He isn't doing much talking, or if he is, he's talking slowly. He has all of her attention, and she has his. I almost didn't recognize her at first—it's been a few months—but I saw her at both Chief's and Aaron's funerals. Both of those days were hazy.

"Is it weird having your sister here?" I ask.

"No weirder than having *you* here," he says. His voice sounds tight and uncomfortable. We close in on Ryan and Alex, but when we're a few feet away, Alex makes eye contact with Ian and smiles. He gives her a casual head nod, but then we've suddenly taken a jerky turn toward the hallway. Maybe I shouldn't have asked him that. It's really none of my business, and it's not like we're close friends who share secrets or something.

"You want to know why I'm not trying to scare you out of here?"

In my experience, I've learned that if someone asks you a question that requires a simple yes or no, they are going to tell you the answer whether you want to hear it or not. So instead of fighting it, I just agree that I want to know why.

"You're going to do what you want anyway," he reasons. "And this way, at least you'll be fully informed of what you're getting yourself into."

"And what do you think I'm getting myself into?" It's been months since Ian and I have had really any conversation. It's not like we've ever been really chatty with one another, but I know what he did for Holly. He talked her through that awful night. He heard Mindy's screams. Even after, he's been gentle with Holly. He talks softly to her, and he was patient when she clung to him weeks after it all happened. I've always liked Ian, but now I have a newfound respect for him.

I know the clubhouse well enough to know what awaits us beyond the doors that line the hallway. Most of the rooms belong to the brothers. It gives them a place to crash or have sex with the Lost Girls—and for some, their old ladies. At the end of the hall is the chapel. I'd go say hi to Nic since I know she's holed up in there, but there's no telling who else might be in there who'd be more likely to tell on me. Still, I'm tempted to go say hi anyway since Duke quarantined her due to her super-pregnant state.

They hold Church meetings in the chapel, where they formally discuss club business. It's also the room where they'll decide whether or not to vote in Nic and Holly. I've only been in there a few times, and truthfully I have little desire to be in there normally. It's as sacred as any place can get to these men.

One door, though—one door isn't sacred, nor is it a personal space. The palace is where the nastiest of the nasty shit goes down. And we're headed right for the door.

"Trouble," he says and lifts his arm from my shoulders then takes a step away. My nerves get the best of me, oxygen catching in my throat, unable to make its way down to my lungs, and my palms sweat. I bring the beer bottle to my lips and take another large gulp.

"He's not good enough for you, Miss Priss," he says with a blank stare at the wall beside my head. "Your dad doesn't want this life for you. None of us do." He leaves me at the door to hell and disappears into his room at the end of the hall.

I wish Tracie were here with me. Instead, she's off somewhere, doing something—or apparently someone— and not by my side like I need her to be. Maybe this is what Ian is talking about. I don't do things on my own. I finish my beer quickly and wrap my hand around the doorknob. If I wait any longer I won't have the nerve to do it.

CHAPTER 11

December

16 months to Mancuso's downfall

Cheyenne

THE KNOB TWISTS easily under my direction. A heavy body bumps into me from behind and shoves me into the room before I'm ready. So much is happening around me and there's so many people in here—almost all of whom are naked—that I can't find a single familiar face.

I move deeper into the room, too curious for my own good. A Lost Girl whose name I don't know hangs from one of the stripper poles. She twirls around effortlessly in front of the mirrored wall with nothing on but a G-string and a pair of bright red heels. At first glance, her body looks to be totally free of ink, but then I see it—one of the Forsaken symbols tattooed on her hip. It's a smiling skull with the helmet of a Nordic warrior on top. I know some of the Lost Girls have them—these tattoos—but I don't know how the club goes about deciding who gets tattooed and who doesn't.

Across the room, also reflected in the mirrored wall, are two Forsaken—one I know and one I don't—having their way with a naked woman. Bear has his mouth wrapped around her left breast while the man I don't know has his fingers rhythmically moving between her parted legs. She jerks as her back bows up, and she reaches down to rub Bear through his jeans. I can't turn away. It's so intimate and yet out in the open. Nobody cares, though, and in a way, it sort of makes the act more beautiful. Nobody here is ashamed of seeking out and giving pleasure to another. It's only me.

A firm hand cups my hip, causing me to jump in place. Familiar blond hair tickles at the side of my face as Daniel's voice fills my ear. "Do you like what you see?"

I want to say no, that I'm horrified by what's going on here. But I'm not. I'm fascinated.

"Yes," I say breathily.

He presses against my backside in a move that both shocks and excites me. My hands shake at my sides, and the empty bottle in my hands falls to the floor. The clink catches Daniel's attention, but his only move is to kick the bottle under a nearby chair. As he lifts his leg, his hard body presses into the bottom of my butt. It's not his built thighs that catch my attention, nor is it his muscular lower legs. It's his dick that surprises me. I don't even like Daniel half as much as I like Jeremy—which is a lot—but he doesn't scare me the way Jeremy does. Maybe it's the beer or the casual nature of it. Maybe it's the place we're in or the fact that I'm not looking at him. I count my blessings that we're at the wrong angle to see anything in that stupid mirror. It just makes everything so visible in here. I can see people and things I wish I couldn't. So instead of focusing on all the bullshit around me, I let myself drift into this and enjoy what Daniel might have to offer.

Right now I'd be okay with seeing where this goes because I don't worry what he's going to think of me tomorrow or if my dad is going to approve of us. Not sex exactly, but a little fooling around and maybe third base. There won't be an us, and I'm not pairing my first name with his last in my head, getting attached to a future that is sure to fail because he's Forsaken and relationships don't start like this. Well, unless you're Nic and Duke, but those two are screwed up and do everything backward anyway.

"I'll go slow. I'm going to make you feel good, baby," Daniel says. His voice sounds slick, like he's selling me a car or forcing me to listen to his pyramid scheme. At some point, I thought he sounded charming. But not now. Now he's not the guy who flirts with me and pushes my buttons. No, he's the man who wants to take my virginity. It's not something I'm ready to give up, and that's frustrating the hell out of me because I feel like a damn child.

His hands slide up and down my sides, up to just beneath my breasts where he drags a finger along the lower line of my bra, then back down to the top of my jean shorts. His warm breath covers my neck as his lips softly trail from my collarbone up to my jaw. I let my eyes close and just enjoy the moment. They briefly flutter open long enough to see Tracie and Diesel pass by. Diesel's gaze catches mine just before my eyes close. His angry stare bounces off my dueling desires—to let loose and to be smart—and I find myself suddenly insecure. Diesel's basically been my babysitter the last few months. He's either taken me to school or has let me follow him in my Bug, but he screwed my best friend, so I'm not sure he can really serve as some kind of moral compass.

Soon the image of his disapproving glare fades from memory, and it's just me with Daniel's lips on my neck, his hands traveling the curves of my body. His hands slip under the legs of my shorts a few inches before circling most of my thigh and then dragging down a little lower on my leg. He's careful not to touch me any place too private, which helps keep this being okay in such a public place.

"Happy birthday, big boy!" Chel's voice rings loud in my ears. My eyes snap open and immediately search my surroundings before landing on her barely clothed frame. Her dyed red hair is down in waves, and her makeup is heavy, which I assume is typical on a night like tonight.

She's slowly swinging her body in sultry dance moves with her eyes focused on something in front of her.

The crowd slowly parts as Fish brings a folding chair through the throngs of people. He sets it down in the center of the room, and it's only then that I see Jeremy. The back of his cut stares me down, judging me for letting Daniel touch me in ways I wouldn't let him. I want Jeremy to turn around and see me, to stop Daniel, and to tell me how sorry he is for pushing me when I wasn't ready. I want his arms around me. I want his lips on mine, marking me, claiming me as his. I want him to turn to his right and to see me in the mirror. Just a few degrees and he'd know I was behind him.

But he doesn't turn around. His shoulders roll as he claps his hands together and shouts, "Hell yes, baby!"

Not even Jeremy's booming voice breaks Daniel's concentration. His mouth moves up to my ear, where he sucks gently on my pliant flesh. One of his hands gently rubs my right breast as he bucks his hips into my ass. I give him a small moan that I'm unable to contain. It only serves to encourage and hasten his movements. His hand roughly pinches and twists my breast as he moans into my neck. I wince, but not at the pain. It hurts, sure. But it's Jeremy being pushed into the folding chair and his pulling Chel into his lap that causes the flash of pain in my chest. He doesn't care about me.

I'm an idiot.

Chel strips her tank top off and then her bra. She presses her breasts together and shoves them in his face.

Greedily, he grabs hold of them and sucks them into his mouth.

"Enough of that," Duke says as he moves to Chel and taps her shoulder. She nods and taps Jeremy's nose so he lets go. "You can finish her off later if you want. Right now I got something to say."

Duke commands the attention of the room with ease. Even the man next to Bear removes his hand from between the naked woman's legs and looks to Duke. Only Daniel ignores him.

"Butch Whelan is a hell of a man and an even better brother," Duke says. Jeremy jumps up from his chair and gives Duke a hug, obviously knowing something I don't. From the angle he's standing, I can see the blinding grin on his face through the mirror. His eyes sparkle that beautiful dark blue with excitement.

"What the fuck, prospect?" Ryan shouts from someplace I can't see.

"Suck his dick, prospect!" my dad shouts. My dad. My freaking father is in here. I knew he was in the clubhouse, but I didn't expect for him to be in here. But he is. I don't know why I'm surprised. This is some kind of birthday deal for Jeremy.

My eyes travel around the room to see that they're all here. Every single member of my dad's club is here. Even Ian is by the door, watching from the back of the room. I guess because it's a club party, and not only a prospect's birthday but a member's son's birthday as well, that they kind of have to be here. If they're all here, that means all their girlfriends and wives are here, too. Either that or they're in the chapel. Party or no, Forsaken won't leave their women totally unprotected at a time like this.

My eyes nearly bug out of my head when I see Ruby and Holly sandwiched between Uncle Jim and Dad. The two women are chatting about something and barely paying attention to what's going on around them. I have no clue how they can just pretend all this isn't happening. I guess my theory about Aunt Ruby babysitting all the kids is bullshit.

"You got it?" Jeremy shouts excitedly. Duke confirms, and they do that manly hug thing where they practically chest bump and slap each other's backs. When they break apart, Jeremy turns to the room and throws his arms in the air in victory. I tilt my head so I'm better hidden behind a couple in front of me. There's a large enough crowd between us, but I don't need him seeing me right this second.

"Butch gave me his blessing," Duke shouts with a smile on his face. Oh, Butch's blessing. That makes sense now. It's a tradition the brothers take incredibly seriously. Nobody gives a shit if the chick is new, but if she's a member's kid, you ask for your brother's blessing. Period. Not asking is a big deal. Duke could marry Nic, and they already have a kid on the way, but wanting to officially make her his old lady without asking her father first is bad news. A smile takes over my face. I don't remember much about Butch, just that he always gave me gum even after Dad said I wasn't responsible enough for it anymore. I'd always get it in my hair, or his hair, or in the couch. But Butch would always say that nobody gets to decide what you're responsible enough to handle but you, and then he'd sneak me a piece. Despite how weird all of this is, I wish Butch could be here to see his son. He'd be proud of Jeremy. They all are.

I am.

Duke shoves Jeremy back in the chair and clears his throat. "Prospects don't normally get this kind of shit. Because you haven't earned it. But this fucking prick," he says and points to Jeremy, "is family. The only thing his dad asked in return for his daughter is that I make sure this asshole gets a pleasure Butch has been denied for too damn long."

I can't stop the smile that overtakes my face when Duke shoots Jeremy a huge smile and then winks at Chel. Forsaken really is a family. I crane my neck, ignoring Daniel's irritated grunt to get a better view of what's going on. Chel takes the attention away from Duke when she lifts one of her legs to expose the large slit in the crotch of her G-string and places her heel-clad foot on Jeremy's leg. She purses her lips, her attention wholly on him.

The smile slides off my face, and I'm back to feeling like total shit. It's not a punch to my gut this time. It's not a twisting of my heart. It's more like the breath has been sucked right out of me and has been replaced by acid. The only thing keeping me from running out in this moment is Daniel, who is still bucking at my ass and trailing soft kisses up and down my neck. He's moved to the other side now and has slipped my bra strap off my shoulder as he peppers every inch of my flesh he can find.

Chel drags her index finger along Jeremy's jaw and smirks. Then she drops down so quickly that I barely follow her movements. Her fingers work at his jeans, and before I can convince myself that she's not about to do what I think she is, her head disappears and then bobs right back up. Jeremy's neck looks like it turns to Jell-O as it flops backward. He moans loudly, his mouth trying to say something. It seems like he can't form a coherent thought much less vocalize it. Duke's laughter brings me back to the room. This is happening in front of so many people. Why? Why would anyone do this?

I focus in on Duke, whose laughter dwindles to nothing. Ruby's voice can't be heard across the room, but her face has morphed into a scowl. She points at Jeremy, shakes her head, and then points at Duke's chest. By the time she turns around, I notice that Holly and Alex are already near the door. Dad lumbers after Holly and does his best to ignore Ruby as she walks beside him, still obviously displeased with Duke's "gift" to Jeremy. Good. I'm glad somebody is as disgusted by this as I am. Uncle Jim is shaking his head and barking something at Duke. Then he leaves the room, hot on his wife's tail. Duke's just lucky Nic isn't in here, or they'd end up in an epic fight. She's going to find out eventually, and the best I can hope is that I'm far away when she does.

A couple moves away and crosses the room to grab a few beers. In their absence, I have a clear shot of Jeremy and Chel. Her hands link together around his shaft, effectively blocking the crowd's view of his dick.

I guess there are some things even Dad and Uncle Jim aren't cool with here. I'm not surprised that Holly and Aunt Ruby take issue with it, though. The problem certainly isn't nudity, nor is it sex that has set them off. But Jeremy is practically a baby to them. So even though he has his cut, seeing him get his dick sucked in the middle of a crowded room.

My fingers tingle, and soon enough, so do my arms and legs. A cramp starts in my stomach that travels up to my chest and forms a lump in my throat. It's not sorrow. It's not tears. I clamp my hand over my mouth and hunch forward. Daniel's hands are on me in an instant, helping me stand upright. Maybe I drank my beer too fast, or maybe the sight of the boy I've convinced myself could be mine getting his dick sucked in a room of strangers is just too much to take.

Daniel whispers, "Oh shit," into my ear. He disappears for just a moment before he's back with a plastic red cup. It's full of something, but he dumps it out on the floor and places it below my chin just in time for me to relieve my stomach. I gag over the cup for a moment, just frozen in place and terrified that Jeremy is going to turn around. He can't know I'm here, much less that I'm freaking yakking because he's such a stupid boy and Chel is a worthless whore.

I never knew why Elle had a problem with Chel.

Now I do.

Whore.

Idiot.

I hate them both.

CHAPTER 12

December

16 months to Mancuso's downfall

Cheyenne

DANIEL LEADS ME out of the room and into the hallway, where I finally stop gagging over the cup. Pushing the foul thing away, I turn toward the brick wall and press my face against it. Daniel awkwardly holds the cup before gently placing it on the floor beside me. Somebody is going to run into it, but I can't bring myself to pick it up and move it to save them the trouble. Maybe Chel can clean it up.

Whore.

My foot slides to the side and *accidentally* tips the cup

over.

Stupid cocksucking slut.

"You okay?" Daniel asks.

"Perfect," I mumble into the brick. Tears prick at my eyes, and frustration overtakes me. I pull my head back just a few inches and then let it fall forward against the brick. It takes Daniel one more head slam into the wall before he realizes what I'm doing, and he pulls me back, spins me around, and forces me to look at him.

"What the fuck is your problem?" he snaps. His attention is on my forehead as his fingers slide over the sensitive skin.

"No, what the fuck is *your* problem?" I snap back. "You guys think shit like that is funny? It's cool to watch a guy get his dick sucked? Really?"

"This is about that fucking prospect," he says and lets go of me so quickly that I stumble back to the brick wall. The back of my head throbs with the impact, but it's nothing compared to the intensity of my heart beating in my chest. I say nothing in response because there's nothing I can say. A tear falls down my cheek as I try to regroup.

"Your head hurt?" he says, the frustration obvious in his tone. His blue eyes fall to my brown ones as he cups my chin in his hands. I shrug my shoulders and refuse to verbalize my pain. "That guy is a fucking asshole whether he knew he was going to get blown in that room or not. He's a child. I don't give a shit that you're the same age. You're too good for him, too mature for him. Too beautiful and too everything for him."

He reaches out and takes my hand, leading me down the hallway to the bathroom. He yells at the people inside and gives them a minute before clearing them out. Once the bathroom is empty, he opens the door and I step inside. Maybe I misjudged him and he's not really as much of a perverted jerk as I assumed a few weeks ago. Maybe Daniel and I could be more than friends and I should put more effort into him.

Inside the bathroom, I clean up as best I can. I rinse my mouth out several times until I realize that my breath isn't going to get any better and, without an aid, I'm still going to be tasting my own vomit.

When I leave the bathroom, Daniel is nowhere to be found. My phone chimes in my pocket. I pull it out just enough to see he's sent me a text.

HAD TO GO. SORRY.

Being alone here—again—puts me on edge. I stare down the hallway to find it's completely empty save for me. With Dad and Uncle Jim already dealing with Aunt Ruby and Holly being on the warpath, it's probably a bad idea for me to be so out in the open. There's no telling what kind of hell I'll have to live through if Dad knows I saw what happened in there. *With that whore.*

I eye Ian's door at the end of the hall, bouncing from one foot to the other before I blow out a heady breath and decide that he's my best bet to get out of here. I haven't seen Tracie since she disappeared into the crowd with Diesel, and since we took her car, I'm kind of stuck. I would have opted to take my Bug except that if Grandma *did* happen to wake up, she would freak if she saw my car gone. So Ian it is.

My feet carry me to the doorway quickly. I curl my hand into a loose fist and knock on the heavy wooden door and wait. And wait. When the door swings open, a bleached blonde stands before me. She raises her eyebrows and looks me up and down in clear disdain.

"You're not his type," she says with narrowed eyes. Her eyes are rimmed with purple bags, and they're glassy and red. She looks drunk. Or high. Maybe both. I don't really know. Dad always kind of looks drunk and high, so there's no telling.

I have so freaking had it with whores in this place. I just want to go home. *Now.*

"Ian," I shout as loud as I can without screaming.

"Shit," he says in a ragged voice that's followed by a grunt.

My eyes fall shut as I bow my head. There's nothing but sex and drugs everywhere, and I want none of it anymore. I don't want to be someone's old lady. I don't want to help the Lost Girls during special occasions. None of it.

A minute later and Ian steps behind the chick in the doorway. His brows crinkle, and his lips form a flat line. He says, "We're done here," and reaches into the pocket of his jeans. His bare chest stares at me, full of scars that are laced with tattoos that depict bloody scenes of revenge and torture. He produces a few hundred-dollar bills and hands them to the skanky blonde in front of him.

"Don't fuck it up," he says. She pushes past me, shoving me into the doorframe, and then disappears from view. With his attention back on me, he says, "You're going home."

I nod, wanting to tell him what I saw and what happened with Daniel. For some reason I even want to tell him I knocked over that red cup in hopes that Chel would have to clean it up.

With her fucking tongue.

But I don't. Because Ian isn't the kind of guy who seems like he shares his feelings or bitches about petty stuff. His scars practically jump from his flesh and smack me across the face. Some of them are muted by the surrounding tattoos, while others seem to be accented by the ink surrounding them.

He slides back into the room for a moment and grabs a shirt and his cut. Another woman slinks out of the room. She doesn't meet my eyes, and she clings to a large piece of fabric that is larger than a robe but smaller than a sheet, I think. Ian disregards her as he pulls the shirt over his head and then slides the cut on. I back up and give him room to lead me out of this horrible, disgusting place.

"You look like you could use a pick-me-up," he says, leaning down so I can better hear him.

"Unless you can erase my memory of the last few months, I doubt anything will make me feel better."

"Trust me," he says, and I swear I can practically hear a smile in his voice. "And don't worry, I won't let you get busted."

"Thanks." Realizing how pathetic I sound, I try to force myself to lighten up a little. I got myself in this mess. I'm the one who decided it was a good idea to come here. I wanted to see what Jeremy's birthday party would be like. *Now I know.*

Ian leads me through the main room, careful to disguise me from his brothers as we pass, and into an offshoot that's only half-enclosed and holds a large, worn pool table. Ryan is standing against the far wall with his hands raised in the air. He's shaking his head at the woman in front of him—the same bleached blonde who just left Ian's room—as she drags her hands up and down his cut and then presses herself up against him.

"I will run your skanky ass over with my fucking bike if you get me in trouble with my woman," Ryan says with narrowed eyes. The blonde laughs and tosses her head back. "Seriously. Move, bitch," he orders loudly.

But she doesn't move. "Come on, baby. Let me suck your dick, and then I'll let you fuck my ass." Her voice is practically purring. She sounds pathetic, but this is kind of funny.

Ian elbows me, and when my attention briefly turns to his face, he's almost smiling. He nods his head to the back entrance of the room. Alex and Ruby are standing side by side, both wearing grim expressions.

"Oh crap," I say, my eyes darting between Ryan and the skank and Ruby and Alex. Aunt Ruby is a freaking bulldog when it comes to her boys. She takes a step forward, and Alex reaches out and places her hand on Ruby's arm.

"No," Alex says softly. "I got this, Mom."

Ruby nods her head and smiles at the sight of her daughter striding toward the blonde. She doesn't look angry, nor does she look like she can do much damage. Alex doesn't particularly carry herself with confidence, and she's definitely not assertive.

"Look what you've done," Ryan says with an irritable expression on his face. He shakes his head at the blonde, his hands still raised in the air.

"Excuse me," Alex says a little louder than I expect as she stands next to Bimbo Barbie. The blonde looks her over, purses her lips, and turns up her nose.

"Come on, Trigger," the blonde says. "Let's have some fun."

Alex looks back at Ruby, who gives her a nod. Alex smiles softly at her mother before turning back to the blonde and placing her hand on the bimbo's wrist. The blonde looks at her wrist blankly and smirks at Alex. I almost miss the movement, it's so sly, but Alex's fingers slide further around the blonde's wrist as her grip tightens and her knuckles turn white. Realizing the trouble she's in, the blonde turns to Ian with a fearful expression on her face. I sneak a peek at him to catch the subtle shake of his head.

An order of silence.

Holy crap.

"If you bust this up, I'm going to hand deliver you to Daddy," Ian whispers to me.

"I wouldn't—" I protest, but he cuts me off.

"She's my sister," he says. "He's my brother, but it's different. I just want to make sure he's going to be good to her."

"That's actually really sweet." My voice betrays my mood, sounding so light and soft. Happy almost.

The blonde regains her confidence and leans in toward Ryan, her lips pursing like she's going to try to kiss him. Alex's white-knuckled grip pulls the blonde away from Ryan in a scary-fast and effective move that I can't believe she's managed. Her face is calm, but her chest rises and falls rapidly as she uses the force of her grip to back the blonde up to the pool table. Alex continues to twist her wrist until the blonde's knees give out and she's fallen on the floor. Even then she doesn't lessen her grip.

"Please excuse my poor manners," Alex says a little louder now. She's inches from the blonde's face and practically spitting on her. "My name is Alexandra Mancuso, and this one belongs to me."

"Okay, I'm sorry," the blonde shrieks and pulls back. She jerks away, breaking free, and scrambles underneath the pool table. When she stands on the other side, she's holding her wrist, and tears fall down her cheeks.

Ian crooks his finger, summoning her, and pulls out three more hundred-dollar bills. His eyes are focused on Ryan as he hands her the money and tells her to go to urgent care to get her wrist checked. I eye Ruby to see that she looks not only happy but relaxed as well. I haven't seen that in a while. Ryan's gaze could cut glass he looks so pissed at the realization that this was a setup. Alex ignores his mood as she grabs ahold of his cut and drags him away.

"Damn, baby," Ryan says, his voice trailing off in the distance. "That was hot as shit. I so want to fuck you right now."

I smile at the lovebirds. This is what I like about this world—the love, the super intense, awesome, passionate love these people have for one another. Grandma says she thinks they fall in love so fast and so deeply because they're all suffering PTSD or something because it always seems to happen during the worst possible time. Like Ryan and Alex and their crazy love story that only makes sense if you bore witness to it yourself. Or Dad and Holly—two people who make no sense on paper but are like magnets when they're together, either pushing each other away or totally inseparable. Duke and Nic are so cute together that it sometimes makes me sick. There's this way he holds on to her baby bump whenever he can, like he's thanking her or something. And Nic? She's just perfect for him. Before tonight when I had delusions of becoming Jeremy's old lady, I wanted to be like Nic. Even Uncle Jim and Aunt Ruby who have been together forever find small ways to stay in physical contact. It's beautiful, and I want it.

More than anything.

"Cheyenne Grady," Ruby shouts. My back straightens, and I look up at Ian with wide eyes, intent on avoiding Ruby's gaze.

Ian mouths, "*Run*," and I take off without another thought. I can still hear Ruby shouting in the distance as I bob and weave around as many people as I can. My feet are killing me as I force them into action on these stupid heels, but I don't slip, and I suppose that's something. Dad and Holly nearly catch sight of me, but I duck behind a burly man before curving behind a table and out the front door. Once out of the clubhouse, I take a deep breath and thank God that I made it out of there alive.

With much slower steps, I walk to Ian's bike and plan to wait until he comes out. A second later, he bursts out of the front door. With a wicked smile on his face he says, "She's pissed," and climbs on his bike. I climb up after him, and he starts her up.

I catch sight of movement on the picnic table. A mess of shaggy blond hair hangs in his face as his hands grip the shoulders of a half-naked woman he has bent over. His jeans have been slid down just enough, and her skirt is tossed over her ass as he rocks himself into her. I already knows it's him—Daniel—so when he lifts his head and grunts, I'm not surprised. No, what surprises me is the look of pure satisfaction he has on his face as he grabs ahold of the woman's hair, and without breaking eye contact, he slams into her hard. His lips part, and his eyes roll back in his head just a moment before they're back on me. Just as we pull out of the parking lot and peel out, I let my face rest on Ian's back and close my eyes.

I am so done with bikers.

So done.

The ride home is short, and Ian helps me disengage the alarm. My Bug is still in the drive. Maybe Dad won't know I was there after all. Ian's taken notice of my sullen mood, and just before he closes the front door on me, he says, "You're better than that shit. Remember that. You deserve good, so don't settle for fucked up."

He leans in and places a kiss to my cheek and then strides away. I close my eyes and shut the door, not even worried that I'm going to wake Grandma up. It takes everything in me to climb the stairs to my room. I fall into my bed, shove my face in my pillow, and sob uncontrollably for the next hour. The only reason I think I'm able to stop myself from crying and have the good sense to clean myself up and wash away the evidence of sneaking out is because of the words that won't stop ringing in my head.

You deserve good, so don't settle for fucked up.

Just as I'm drifting off to sleep, I manage to send Ian a quick text. THANK YOU.

CHAPTER 13

January

15 months to Mancuso's downfall

Cheyenne

MY LEFT ARM curls around my notebook, and my right furiously scribbles a messy stick-figure drawing of Jeremy being beaten by a hammer. Drawing-Jeremy is tucked in the corner of the page, surrounded by a carefully constructed code I created in order to try to piece together the mystery of Mindy's rape without fear that someone will find it. Drawing-Jeremy is almost finished as I detail the blood oozing from his head. In the other corner of the page, Drawing-Daniel has been beheaded and is missing his right hand.

I may or may not be in a bad mood.

Everything is hectic and upside down right now. I barely know which direction I'm turning in anymore. Between avoiding Jeremy like the plague—because holy crap, I'm a chicken—to digging up every tiny piece of information on Mindy's attacker that I can, I'm worn out. If things had gone well on our date, I was going to try to pry a little into finding out what Jeremy knows about the whole thing. But things didn't go so well. On top of the ill-timed text from Daniel, that disaster after-date incident cemented our first date into the history books as our last. Not that the public blow job didn't make everything even worse.

Only, I hate the idea of that date being our last. Even despite the blow job. I'm so pathetic. I don't want to let him go. I really don't, and I can't figure out why. I don't want to like him, but there's just something there that has me in knots over what happened. Holly told me once to be careful because every girl marries a guy like her dad, and by her estimation, Jeremy shares more than just a cut with Grouchy. Maybe she's right, because I can see the protective side of Jeremy that I've come to expect with my dad. I see his playfulness, and even his bossiness isn't a turnoff. I'd never admit it, but I secretly love it when a guy goes alpha on me. Unfortunately, Jeremy's sidestepped alpha and rushed right into dirtbag.

I was hoping to be able to confide in Jeremy about my investigation. It's come to a standstill, and without a little more intel on the situation, I'm kind of stuck. I thought I'd hit the jackpot when I found Dad's manila folder full of hospital records in the garage, but that turned out to be my last solid lead. Even trying to look into this Scavo character has me banging my head against the wall.

Thanks to Google and the general public's fascination with the Italian Mafia, I was able to stumble upon a few things that might be of help. Maybe I'm not a detective down in my bones, because it took a few days of research to figure out that I was going about everything all wrong. I have been looking into Carlo Mancuso's thug roster to no avail. The only information I could find was on guys who had been pinched or who'd been "taken care of." No Scavo to find. Anywhere.

Eventually it occurred to me that I had no information on this guy—not even a first name—but I do have a lot of information on one person who is deeply connected to the Mancuso organization. Alex.

Now she has a pretty long internet trail. I was able to find bits and pieces on her life, including some rather disturbing candid photographs that were taken while she was out and about with various people. There's research and then there's stalking. I tried to avoid those sites as much as possible. Nothing good turned up at first. A few mafia fansites led me to newspaper reports from the day her cousin was shot. Dad would rather I not know, but I'm fully aware of why Alex is here and that the club has put their lives on the line to keep her safe. I even know why Dad doesn't want her here, but I keep that to myself to avoid a fight. The problem is that Dad hasn't let me go over to Aunt Ruby's house since Alex came to town. But that's just fine. I have a plan. Only, I have to wait until the bell rings to get the hell out of this classroom for good.

"Miss Grady," Mrs. Cowger says from the front of the room. Letting out a heavy sigh, I set down my pen and raise my head. Mrs. Cowger is an okay teacher. I mean, she tries. I just don't really care about Shakespeare. Romeo and Juliet were morons.

She raises an eyebrow and points at my notebook. "Miss Grady, I'd like your attention on me rather than your desk."

"No offense, Mrs. Cowger," I say. "I just don't have the energy for this crap."

The words leave my mouth, and I'm not entirely certain what I've just done. Half the room either gasps or snickers. My eyes shoot to Tracie, who sits across the room from me. She shakes her head and mouths with a grin, "*Bitch.*"

When we've managed to end up in the same class, our teachers have refused to seat us together. It's my last day here anyway, so it shouldn't matter. All my extracurricular investigations have taken away from the time I'm supposed to be in class. With over thirty unexcused absences—ten this semester alone—not even Holly can save my ass. Which is fine. We're only a month into the new semester, so I have no way of making that time up. Nor do I want to. The sooner I get out of this place, the sooner I can figure out where I'm going next. First my GED and then eventually culinary school in the city. Dad's pissed as hell that I'm basically being expelled less than a full semester before graduation, but I'm pissed as hell at life in general. We'll deal.

"I think you should visit Mr. Beck's office, Miss Grady," she says in response.

"Good idea." I smile and happily pack up my stuff. Fuck Mr. Beck. He and Holly already arranged for today to be my last day. What's he going to do? Expel me? Mr.

Beck and Dad already reached the agreement that in exchange for not expelling me that I would leave of my own accord.

Across the room, Tracie is just staring at me in astonishment. Drawing-Jeremy and Drawing-Daniel get shoved into my backpack, and I stride out of class without looking back. I wish I were badass enough to flip her the bird on the way out, but as it is, I'm already a train wreck of nerves. My hands begin to shake the moment the classroom door closes behind me. There's only ten or so minutes of class left, but it's enough to get to the office to tell Holly that I've been unceremoniously excused early. She is not going to like this.

But really, I was blowing this Popsicle stand anyway. Still, I'm going to be in for it when I get home. I don't know why they're going to care. I just know that they will. Parents are strange creatures who give a shit about the dumbest stuff. I can't even begin to think about Grandma. She is going to tan my hide—that is if she's even home. She's been curiously busy and absent from the house lately. I don't like it one bit.

The office door feels heavier when I open it, and the air feels stuffy when I walk up to Holly's desk. She is smiling down at her phone in her hands and so engrossed in whatever she's reading that she doesn't hear my approach. God, I hope she and Dad aren't sexting again. After the last time, I won't be peeking at either of their phones anytime soon.

"Please tell me you're in a good mood," I say with my best innocent smile plastered on my face.

Her head shoots up as her eyes land on me. She places

her phone upside down on her desk and clears her throat. Her cheeks are red, and her breathing is a little shaky. Yeah, sexting. Christ, that's freaking gross.

"Hey," she says with a smile. Her eyes slide over to the wall clock and then back to me. They're narrowed now, and she's looking back at me.

"You're supposed to be in class," she says in that "mom" voice she's been using a lot lately. I swear, she's picking up this "mom" shit so quick it's starting to freak me out. But I also kind of like it. A lot. For only a few months under her belt, she's picking it up pretty quick.

"Yeah," I say. "About that. Mrs. Cowger let me go early."

"Let you go or kicked you out?"

I shrug my shoulders and look over at Margot, who's pretending not to listen in. "It could have gone either way."

"Uh-huh," she says, pulling open her desk drawer. She takes out two pieces of individually wrapped chocolates and tosses one to me. I easily catch it in the air, unwrap it, and pop it in my mouth. She lets out a happy sigh and then looks at me again. "Fine. You were leaving today anyway."

"That was my point," I say. "She didn't get that. Why do I care what Romeo and Juliet did? They killed themselves? Okay, fine. Why is she even teaching us about a story that glorifies suicide? It's not romantic—it's stupid."

"Holy crap, what is your problem?" she asks with wide eyes.

"I'm just saying. We have classes on suicide prevention, and then we're reading this junk about these *children* who kill themselves when they only wanted each other because they couldn't be together anyway."

"Chey," Holly whispers. She pats her desk and leans in close to me. "Let's have a talk."

"I don't want to have a talk." I fold my arms over my chest.

She stands from her desk, circles round, and takes my elbow in her hand. I allow her to lead me away from the center of the room and into the nearby bathroom. She locks the door behind us.

"I'm not your mother," she says in a firm voice. My head snaps in her direction as her words cut at my heart. I know she's not my mother, but for some reason, her verbalizing it only makes everything that much worse. "But I love you."

"Yeah, love you, too, Holls," I say and tap my foot on the floor. My tone is biting, and I can't stop myself from huffing. If I do, I might cry.

"I wish I were your mother," she whispers.

Crap. She's doing that loving thing again, and it's going to make me cry. I don't want to cry, though. I want to kick something. I want to throw something. I want to hit Jeremy with a hammer. Repeatedly.

"Shut up," I mumble. My eyes are focused on the floor as they well with tears.

"No," she says sweetly and takes a step forward. "I do. You're awesome, and I hate seeing you so upset. I wish I knew you better so I could do more to help."

"You should be used to grouchy Gradys by now," I say with a pathetic laugh at the end.

It's been almost a month since Jeremy's birthday party. I might be able to get over everything that happened if he would just leave me alone. But he won't. He shows up at the house with bullshit excuses but then ignores me. He keeps taking over for Diesel, picking me up from school, and pretends like he hates it with all his being, but then Diesel tells me otherwise. I try to keep my interaction with Diesel limited as he keeps asking pesky questions about the party. I don't dare, but I really want to tell him it's none of his business. And really, I feel like such a stupid baby for thinking the stories I'd heard about the legendary Forsaken parties were exaggerated. Dad always kept me away from anything that wasn't PG-13, so how was I supposed to know?

"There's grouchy Gradys, and then there's depressed Gradys, and you, missy, are depressed." She takes another step forward. She's less than two feet away when she reaches out for me.

"I'm not depressed. I'm just... done," I say, barely able to find the right word for it.

"Ruby told me," she says even quieter. The mention of Aunt Ruby makes me feel about two inches tall. Everything in me feels hollow, like all my insides have been carved out. "You shouldn't have seen that. Any of it."

"I didn't see anything." I wince at the memory of Chel and her nasty ass and those panties with the slit up the center.

"You don't have to lie to me," she says softly.

"I don't want to talk about it."

She nods her head, then takes another step forward and sweeps me into her arms. She hugs me tight and doesn't let go. Eventually I sink into her and rest my head on her shoulder. I don't move to hug her back. I don't feel like I can give anything to anyone right now, but I need this hug. I need her kind words and her soothing voice. I just need Holly.

When she's content that I'm not going to talk any more about it, she lets me go and kisses my forehead. The words and the hug I can handle, but it's the motherly kiss to my forehead that sends a few sneaky tears down my cheeks. I stop myself quickly, though, and regain my composure. I'm not crying over Jeremy or even Daniel. I'm not even crying over my own mother who is gone. I'm crying because I'm terrified Dad is going to screw things up and I'm going to lose her. Because he's Forsaken, and they're all really good at screwing up relationships.

"Who's picking you up today?" she asks as we leave the bathroom.

I shift the weight of my backpack on my shoulder. "Diesel." At least it's supposed to be Diesel, so here's hoping Jeremy doesn't show instead.

"Good." At her desk, she retrieves another two pieces of chocolate and hands them both to me. "Nothing fixes a broken heart like chocolate and revenge, but you're in enough trouble, so let's stick with the chocolate, shall we?"

I smile at her and give her a wink. "Oh, don't worry. I've moved on from Jeremy."

Her eyes narrow as she surveys me. I'm lying, of course. I wish I were over Jeremy, but I can't help myself. I clear my throat and nod my head, tossing a piece of chocolate in my mouth. "I have my eye on a new man."

"Tell me or I'll read your diary," she says with a stupid giggle.

It's not that I don't love Holly. I do. It's just that nothing makes me feel better than to torture someone else. I guess I really am my father's daughter after all.

"Ian," I say with a musical laugh and practically skip out of the office. Her face falls as she grabs her phone and starts typing furiously. She's telling Dad, and he's going to crap himself. I know Ian has damage, and a small part of me feels kind of bad about using that to scare them. I scrub my face with my hands in frustration. Once the door closes behind me, I'm back to feeling like crap. But at least now I no longer want to stick my head in the oven.

The hallway is crowded now since classes have just ended. Students scatter from one end to the other, desperately trying to escape school property in favor of some place more appealing—so basically, anywhere. I almost want to tell them to just stop showing up and eventually you'll get out. One way or another, you'll get out.

I head toward the parking lot, my eyes scanning the crowd for Tracie. She should be around here somewhere. When I see her high ponytail bobbing through the crowd, I give her a wave and wiggle through the students to get to her.

"You are *such* a crazy bitch," she says with a huge smile on her face. "I so can't believe you did that."

"Neither can I." We start heading for the parking lot side by side.

"You've been off for a while now, babe," she says.

I don't respond. She's been hinting at this conversation for a while now, and I guess if both my best friend and Holly are bugging me about my attitude, I should probably do something to straighten myself out. The only thing worse than being crabby is everybody pointing out how crabby you are.

I've asked Dad why Jeremy keeps coming around but only get grunts and looks of disapproval. Dad doesn't know that Jeremy came by after he dropped me off after our date, and I *hope* Aunt Ruby and Holly have both kept their mouths shut and not told Dad I was at the party. If he knew about either of those things, he'd have a total conniption fit.

"When can we go back to everything being normal?" Tracie asks. She's started to get annoyed with the fact that I'm making a point to let everybody know how grouchy I am. Jeremy dropped out of school the day after he turned eighteen, saying, in his own words, "Nic can't twist my balls about it anymore."

"When everything *does* go back to normal," I say. The bitterness in my tone is unmistakable—and, unfortunately, becoming common.

"Okay," she says slowly. "And what exactly is normal?"

She has a point, even if I don't want to admit it.

"Six months ago—that was normal."

"Oh yeah, because your new mommy wouldn't be here," she says. "I know you don't want that. So I guess you're going to have to figure out how to deal with the new normal."

"You're supposed to be a stupid bimbo," I whine. Because she's right. And I hate that.

"Sorry, this bimbo has brains," she says and pushes my head away. "Is it possible you're being a little dramatic about the party?"

Is it possible? Sure, it is possible. But that doesn't mean it doesn't hurt. The fact that Tracie is asking me if I think I'm being dramatic tells me one thing—she likes Jeremy. She's been defending him and the cocksucking queen for weeks now. This is how it has always been with us. When we were kids, if Tracie had a toy, I wanted it. If I had a new bike, she wanted a new bike. It was all fun when there were enough Ken dolls to go around, but now it's becoming a problem. I admit to having developed a brief crush on the first baseman of the high school's baseball team back when Tracie liked him, but it was fleeting. He's a nice guy and all—he just doesn't do it for me.

No, I'm an idiot who falls for men in worn leather who have sex in public places.

CHAPTER 14

January

15 months to Mancuso's downfall

Cheyenne

JUST AS WE round the corner behind the library and are about to step into the school's back parking lot, I see *his* familiar Harley off to the side. It's old and a little beat up, but Jeremy loves that bike, and I don't blame him. I have a lot of good memories of that bike. But that's not what I should be focusing on right now.

Diesel is across the lot near the entrance, resting against the side of his bike waiting, telling me that there's been some kind of mix-up in the schedule today. I feel like a kid who has to choose between Mommy and Daddy in the divorce. I guess if that's the analogy I'm going with, then Jeremy is Mommy because he's a huge bitch.

There is an annoying, distracting giggle coming from behind us. Tracie's face hardens as she turns around. It's maybe half a second before I turn around, but by the time I'm barely catching the sight of the leather vest, Tracie's already trying to block my view and drag me in the opposite direction. I won't be moved, though.

I look back, wishing I hadn't. Jeremy has a girl whose name I don't know pushed up against the lockers, with one of his hands on her hip and the other pressing against a metal locker beside her head. His body is leaning into hers, keeping her in place. I can't see either of their faces, but their actions and intent are unmistakable. Flashbacks of that night in the clubhouse slam me from all sides. I'll bet he's going to get laid. She'll give it up easily for him because he's Jeremy and he's on his way to being Forsaken. And maybe it will break her heart, or maybe she won't give a damn. But it doesn't matter how she feels. I'm too consumed with my own humiliation at thinking he and I could have been something to care if she's going to be the next one he hurts.

From here, it looks like he's trying to inhale her. They're kissing pretty hot and heavy for being on school grounds—especially since he doesn't even go here anymore. And all I can think is that he is a serious fucking asshole, and if he likes inhaling things so much, maybe he should inhale his own dick. It's not like he has no idea that I could see him, but he doesn't care.

The girl runs her hands down his arms as she leans in and presses her body against his lower half. She lets out a breathy sigh and giggles again. And I want to smash her fucking skull into the metal locker behind her head. What a stupid bitch. It's not like he's saying anything charming or trying to woo her. All he's doing is shoving his tongue down her throat.

Not that he's so bad at it.

Still—asshole.

Tracie tries to gently guide me away from them, but I can't help myself. I can't help but hate her even though she's likely to fare no better than I have.

"Come on," Tracie whispers. "This is what I'm talking about. You're so upset, and it's not like you're together."

I don't move. I want him to know I've seen it. If there's one thing I've learned from Aunt Ruby over the years, it's this: Forsaken men are tough, but Forsaken women are tougher. Old ladies are expected to handle shit that nobody else can or would be expected to. They have to be both a raging bitch and know their place. I don't want to be someone's old lady, but I don't know what else I'd be, then. I grew up with the club and all it means. I know better than to talk about club business, and I know the score if any of the brothers gets busted. Having a little taste of what it's like to be with a Forsaken man, I don't think I'm cut out for life with a civilian. Honestly, I don't think they're going to be able to handle my temper tantrums. Grady tantrums are something special. Even if I don't want the heartache of being with a biker, I don't know anything else.

"Hey, asshole," I shout. If the wrong person were to hear that—Forsaken or school official—I could get myself into a good bit of trouble. But I don't care. I'm always in trouble these days for one thing or another anyway.

Jeremy pulls away, and his eyes shoot to me immediately. He zeroes in on my presence but doesn't even have the decency to look upset about my having caught him. Then again, this is the jerk who got a blow job in front of about thirty people. We're not dating, and we're certainly not a couple. I thought he gave a shit about me, but it's becoming painfully obvious I was wrong. It's only my heart that can't let go of us. Everybody else—especially he—has moved on.

"Excuse me?" Jeremy says. It's like he's taking tips on how to be a jerk with the way he's reacting. Then again, he does live with Duke. Or maybe he thinks that because he's got that cut on his shoulders he is somehow better than the rest of us for being in such an exclusive club. Well, newsflash, jerk. As long as my dad is Sterling Grady, that cut doesn't intimidate me. I doubt he's earned the right to prospect on a formal basis anyway. He wasn't hanging around the club the way prospects do before they're officially invited to start earning their top rocker.

"You heard me," I shout with my arms folded over my chest. Now that he and his cocky attitude have turned toward me, I can feel myself about to snap. Now I know why Ryan likes to start fights so much. My heart is racing and my blood is pumping in my veins. I feel like I could do anything right now, including ripping his arm off and beating him with it.

Seeing how angry I'm getting, he smirks and then licks his lips. This hallway isn't big enough for the four of us and Jeremy's ego as well. God, he looks so freaking cute like that. The realization that I can't stop looking at his lips as he stares at mine has my right hand twitching with the urge to slam it into his nose.

"Just so you know," I say and look at the girl, "he's going to use you, and then he's going to toss you out like you're garbage. He's done it to everybody. Don't be stupid enough to assume you're more than his newest slut."

Jeremy pushes off the lockers and strides toward me. His voice is quiet as he speaks. "Why are you acting like this?"

"Because I hate you," I grit out. Having him this close makes me feel insecure and like the immature brat I keep telling myself I'm not. "You acted like you like me, but you don't. You just wanted to have sex. If that's all you wanted, you could have said so and saved me the headache."

Heartache. I mean heartache, but I won't admit to that.

"I do like you," he whispers. "But you don't get to throw your daddy in my face every time I do something you dislike. Grady's not just my boss. He can do more than fire me if he thinks I've fucked up. He. Can. End. Me. I don't make the cut, what do you think is going to happen to me, huh? This is my life, my entire fucking future, and you run around acting like the most important thing is getting your feelings hurt."

"Don't put your crap on me. You chose to prospect."

The snake-like smile that slides over his features is almost disturbing. His gaze is calculating and vicious. He leans down and gets right in my face. His nose is a few inches from mine, and his breath warms my mouth and chin. My eyes fall on his lips for a brief moment before I redirect them. Looking at Jeremy's lips reminds me of how searing hot his kisses are. And that's not a good road to go down.

"We've grown up together. Seen you at the clubhouse, around town, at school. And you didn't look my way until I put this cut on," he hisses. The veins at his temples bulge, and his face reddens. "I chose to prospect, but if I hadn't, you'd never have been interested in me."

"That's not true," I insist, though he might be right. We have grown up in the same town and roughly the same circle, but it wasn't until he started on security detail around the house that we started talking. Now, thinking back on it, I'm not sure why we hadn't hung out before. "You haven't *earned* that cut, prospect. The only reason you want it is to get laid, which is just pathetic."

"Fuck you. Everything I have I've earned, and this cut means more to me than easy pussy. It's about family, and let me remind you that, prospect or not, I still rank above you—so watch what the fuck you say to me and how you say it."

"You may rank higher in the club, but you're nothing to me," I snap. I suck in a ragged breath and fight off the frustrated tears that want to escape. I was already a little raw from my conversation with Holly and now this, so the tears might come easier than I'd like, which could serve to be mighty embarrassing.

"You're full of shit," he says, noticing how wet my eyes have become. "If you're upset, why don't you text *Daniel* about it?"

"What the hell does that mean?" I lift my hands and push on his chest. He doesn't even budge. He reaches up and grabs ahold of my wrists. His breath washes over my face as he gets as close as he can.

"You texting him on our date? You want him, Cheyenne?"

"You really want to go down this road?" I eye his hands on my wrists and let my gaze travel to his strong arms and up to his thick neck. "Daniel sent *me* a text. I ignored it, which is the polite thing to do."

"That it?" he asks with narrowed eyes. It's the same look Dad gives me when we're wrapping up a fight. But Jeremy and I most certainly are not wrapping up anything. He's still an asshole, and this is so not settled.

"No," I say and pull my wrists down slowly. He doesn't let go. Instead, he just lets his arms drop. I bring my wrists back so he has no choice but to lean in close to my face. Now we're closer to being the same height. I press my nose to his. My chest heaves in fury. "You disgust me. You want to get your dick sucked by a whore, that's on you. Next time don't do it in a room full of people, asshole."

He flinches at my comment and lets go of my wrists. I shake my head, unable to take my eyes off him. His face pales as he sucks in a ragged breath. He practically whispers the words as he says, "You saw that?"

"Yeah, I did." His shock and embarrassment only makes me that much more angry. Why does he get to feel bad about it? I don't want him feeling bad. I want him to have never let it happen. "I didn't stay, though. Turns out Daniel is the better man after all. Hell of a kisser, too."

"Nothing I hate more than a bitch who doesn't know her fucking place," Jeremy says in a sneer and backs up. His eyes land on Tracie, and a wicked smile crosses his face. He licks his lips and nods his head at her. "You know your place, don't you, T? You like your place on my dick?"

Tracie shakes her head slowly. Her eyes dart from his to mine as her face scrunches and tears pool in her eyes.

"I don't understand," I say quietly. I can't really feel anything right now. It's all happening around me, and I know I should feel something, but I just don't. I know Jeremy's had plenty of casual sex. I know Tracie's hooked up with Diesel, but she never said if she's been with anyone else from the club.

Earlier I had assumed she liked Jeremy because she's been defending him for the last few weeks. But maybe it's not that she likes him...

Maybe it's because she's a slut and he's a whore.

And I'm an idiot.

I turn around and walk as quickly as I can, and once I hit the parking lot, I run straight to Diesel. He slides his phone into his pocket, abandoning the game I bet he was playing, and rushes toward me. I slam into his arms and cry into his chest.

Diesel's deep voice reverberates in his chest as he says, "Baby Boy did this?"

I nod my head and don't even care that Diesel could really hurt Jeremy. He deserves it.

But he's not the only one.

"He slept with Tracie," I say. Diesel stiffens and unhooks me from his cut and the shirt underneath.

"I'll take care of it," he says. "Follow me."

He's off and walking as quickly as he can in the direction I came from. I walk behind him at a slow pace, not giving a shit what he does to them. I'm barely absorbing all of it, but it's enough to make me bitter and vengeful and want to watch Jeremy get his nose broken.

In the distance, I see Diesel walk up to Jeremy, and without missing a beat, he closes his hand into a fist and swings at Jeremy's face. Jeremy ducks and weaves out of the way just in time, but Diesel's screaming at him, and Jeremy finally screams back. Then he stands still while Diesel delivers a blow to his gut. Tracie screams off to the side, which sends Diesel in her direction. He grabs ahold of her by the back of her neck and is saying something to her that has her crying her stupid, lying ass off.

As the school security guard rushes up through the thinning crowd of students, who all are trying to pretend they're not watching but don't seem to be moving away from the chaos, I realize there's too many witnesses. Everybody is watching, so many people are seeing this play out. I hope Diesel doesn't get in trouble for this. Then up walks Holly from the crowd with her eyes on me. I hope *I* don't get in trouble for this.

The security guard tries to get Diesel's attention, but he ignores him and makes his way back to me. When we're side by side and walking to his bike, Diesel says, "One of my bonus lives expired before I got to use it. I hate that shit."

A laugh escapes me as we climb onto his bike. I strap on my pink helmet and hold on tight as we leave Fort Bragg High School for the last time.

"So you had a bad day, too, then?" I scream over the roar of the Harley beneath us.

"Nah," he says with a smile in his voice. "Violence makes me feel better."

I'm getting off the bike at my house when I say, "I'll gift you my free life. I'm not going to use it. Best I can do to thank you for taking care of the trash."

He smiles and points his finger at me as he backs his Harley out of the driveway.

"You're a good woman, Cheyenne Grady."

And he's gone. The moment I'm inside the house, Grandma is on me and hugging me like her life depends on it. I hug her back knowing that she's talked to Holly, but I don't care. I just need a Grandma cuddle to make everything a little bit better.

CHAPTER 15

February

14 months to Mancuso's downfall

Cheyenne

I TENTATIVELY PEEK my head out around one of the wide columns that line the front porch of the Jennings residence and wait until I'm certain that I don't hear or see anybody coming. I'm not supposed to be here. Like *really* not supposed to be here. In the weeks following my departure from Fort Bragg High School, I have split my time between studying for the GED test and listening in on every conversation about club business that I possibly can. But that wasn't enough, and that's why I'm here.

The best thing about your best friend betraying you and your not-boyfriend being a dirt ball is that it frees up a lot of time I would have spent socializing. Tracie's sent me a bunch of text messages apologizing for the aforementioned betrayal, but I eventually got so tired of hearing about it that I blocked her number. That's when she resorted to coming to the house. Dad was about to jump down her throat, but he couldn't get there before Holly, who singlehandedly chased her to the curb. After the drama, I got some studying in for the GED, which I took yesterday. I'll know whether or not I passed in a few weeks. So here I am. Today's a new day, and I have nothing to do. My nails are painted, my hair is done, and I had nothing better to do after lunch than to put my detective skills to work.

Though Mr. and Mrs. Jennings' house is fairly close to the road, the wide columns should hide me well enough while I survey the scene before me. There's a neat pile of newspapers stacked near the front door and a few package delivery notices attached to the door. I swipe my cell phone from my pocket and snap a few pictures of the door before stepping closer to take photos of the individual items. The oldest package pickup notice is dated as far back as several weeks ago. A few other notices stick to the door, but only just barely, while several more have fallen off and are crumpled atop the welcome mat. Two pieces of paper with bright red bands at the top hang from the door knob. One is a notice from the water company that the water has been shut off in the house. It's from last week. The other notice dates back to the middle of December. The bill was overdue back then, and the company was threatening to cut the water. That was two months ago.

With the water shut off and all the stacked up newspapers and the notices hanging about, I can't imagine that the Jenningses have been here since then. Which is weird, because their son is still in the hospital and the news has reported he's awake. The local stations claim they don't know specifics about his condition and what he remembers, if anything.

Once I have enough pictures of everything, making sure they're all clear and show the dates, I stand awkwardly on the porch trying to figure out what to do next. The club needs to know about this. They probably already do, but what if, for some reason, they don't? It's awfully strange that Mr. and Mrs. Jennings haven't been home in probably months now, and yet the news left that off the report. If Dad thinks the Italian mafia hurt Darren like I think he thinks they hurt Mindy, then how could he not know that Darren's parents have left town?

Frustrated and unsure what to do next, I cautiously head down the walk to the driveway. There are more scattered newspapers on the lawn that have deteriorated into the grass with the winter rains, leaving behind soggy chunks that look like they're going to be a pain for someone to clean up. At the end of the drive is the mailbox. It's one of those custom-made ones that's shaped like the house—built in a colonial style with impressive columns that serve as handles to open it up and retrieve the mail. Pulling on the handle, I peek into the box. It's stuffed full of envelopes, stray package notices, and even a small box. I take a picture of the packed mailbox and close the door.

I take one last look at the Jennings' home. Across the street is a chunk of land dotted with redwoods and sharp rocks. Beyond that is the Pacific Ocean. The salty ocean air is strong here, much stronger than it is in town. In one of Dad's folders was some information on the Jennings family. I don't really know what my house is worth, but the Jennings' house seems awfully expensive on paper. Seeing it in person, I can understand why.

The white colonial doesn't really fit in the neighborhood but pays tribute to Mrs. Jennings's Southern roots. At least that's what the newspaper said when they did a feature on the family shortly after Darren's beating. Most of the homes in this neighborhood are set far apart—so far, in fact, that you'd have to squint to see much detail about a neighbor's house without a pair of binoculars. They're all set far back from the road, too, and none of them are really very large. Nice, but not large. Yet the Jennings' house sticks out like a sore thumb with its ridiculous columns and fancy-pants flowers everywhere. Not that the flowers are in great shape right now. Every inch of the property looks like it was well cared for and perfectly designed at one time. Now the grass is overgrown, and the weeds are out of control. The flower beds would be worse off had it not been raining a lot recently. But nothing appears to have been kept up in the last few months.

Without any major leads at the house, I'm kind of stuck. I don't know what I was hoping to find, but an abandoned house is definitely not it.

At the next house down, a woman is bent over what I think is her flower garden and working away. Her home is a one-story ranch with fresh paint and sturdy shutters. It looks a little bigger than Jeremy's house, though it can't be by much, but it's definitely better updated. As fast as I can, I make my way over to the woman. The closer I get, the more nervous I become. I have no idea what I'm going to say to her or how I'm going to convince her to talk to me.

"Excuse me," I say loudly but without being too rude or invasive. The woman stops her work and pushes herself up from the dirt. She reminds me of Grandma in a way. She's definitely Grandma's age, and judging by her khaki pants and brightly-colored floral top, it looks like they probably shop in the same store.

"Hello," she says politely with a smile on her face.

"Do you know where they went?" I ask, hitching my thumb toward the Jennings residence.

"Oh, them?" Taking a step forward, she removes her gardening gloves and holds them in her right hand while slapping them into her left repeatedly. "No, I don't."

"Okay." I blow out a frustrated breath. I need something here—anything would help. "Take a wild guess—what would you come up with?"

"I'd guess that man got himself into some trouble," she says. "There a reason Forsaken wants to know?"

I look down at my hoodie, realizing that she thinks I'm asking for the club. I guess I am, in a way. I just have to keep her talking as much as I can. I'm on eggshells over here. One crack and I might be done for. I can't tell her the club is asking, because they don't take kindly to people using them for their own gain, even if this is kind of for them, and I can't try to bully her. She doesn't look like she's one to be bullied.

"Forsaken is my family. The woman who was raped at Universal Grounds is my stepmom's cousin and best friend. Nobody tells me anything, and it's scary. I was just hoping that maybe Mr. and Mrs. Jennings knew something that might link what happened to their son to what happened to Mindy and Holly."

The woman's face falls, and she sighs. When she nods her head, I know honesty was the right way to go. The only fib there was that Holly isn't technically my stepmom. Yet.

"I've told the police, but they blew me off like I'm a nosy busybody. That man built that god-awful house, and then he bought himself a Porsche. Then he bought his wife a new car. They redid the whole front yard and then got approval for some kind of man-made safari thing in the backyard. And do you know what they used on the soil? Pesticides."

Okay, once she decides to talk, she really talks. I nod my head and scowl in what I hope are the appropriate places. She doesn't even seem to notice.

"The homeowners association banned the use of pesticides, but *that man* paid somebody off to get that stupid safari plan approved. He had to. Nobody's happy with them."

"So," I say slowly, "do you know where they went?"

"Oh, right." She taps the index finger of her free hand to her lips. "No, I don't know where they went, but I think he has a gambling problem. Don't tell anybody that came from me. Anyway, they left early one morning and only took a few bags with them when they went. Why would they leave their son in the hospital like that unless they had to?"

"That's what I'm trying to figure out," I say.

She nods her head and then squints at me. "What's your name?"

Come on, Cheyenne. You know how to lie and how to be evasive, so figure it out already.

"Um, maybe it's best we don't exchange names." I give her a smile while making a hasty retreat. "Thanks!"

Pulling my phone out of my pocket when it chimes, I read the message that awaits me. It's from Jeremy. WHERE R U?

Crap.

OUT, I text back.

I FUCKIN KNOW THAT. WHERE R U?

I so don't want to tell him where I'm at or what I'm doing, but he can be relentless. I think I need his help anyway, so I give him the address of the neighbor lady. I hope he doesn't recognize the street name as the Jennings' street, but knowing my luck, he will.

DON'T MOVE, he says.

ON WAY HOME. I hope this will calm him down.

It doesn't.

DON'T FUCKIN MOVE, he says and finishes it off with, I GOT 2 HUNT U DOWN, I WON'T BE HAPPY.

That makes two of us, dude. He shouldn't be looking for me. He's not on patrol at the house anymore since Dad caught wind of Jeremy's antics about switching out detail with Diesel anytime he was supposed to be keeping an eye on me. If Dad sent him to find me, then I'm in even more trouble than I think.

Oh well. All I know is that I'm fed up with running into one roadblock after another. I'm basically getting nowhere with everything I'm doing, and if Jeremy can shed some light on some of this, then maybe working with him won't be so terrible.

I shouldn't want to share this with him, but I kind of do. For some reason, I trust that he won't rat me out. I shouldn't want to share *anything* with him, especially considering I've already shared him with the former bestie. The pain from that betrayal is still too fresh to think about without getting upset. Still, this is information the club might need, so I'm going to try to set my feelings aside. I'm not getting very far on my own, and Holly is too important to me to not keep trying. For Holly, I can be mature enough to work with that stupid idiot. I just won't call him that to his face.

CHAPTER 16

February

14 months to Mancuso's downfall

Cheyenne

I'M WAITING ON the Jennings' front porch when I hear Jeremy's bike in the distance. I couldn't very well have hung out at the neighbor's house. That would have been awkward. His bike is loud, but not as loud as Dad's bike or even Duke's. I think Ryan's bike is the loudest, which doesn't surprise me in the least. Jeremy's bike sounds a little rougher than the other guy's bikes. It probably needs a tune-up and some work. I know Duke's been teaching him how to take care of her, but he's still a little green around the shop.

When he pulls up, his expression is unreadable. My heart beats faster and faster the closer I get to having to talk to him, to really seeing him. The last time I saw him, I was so angry and then so hurt. He cuts the bike off and dismounts, then takes off his helmet and sets it on the seat of the bike. He's wearing dark sunglasses even though it's cold and overcast. It's freaking February in Mendocino County for crying out loud. Why on earth is he wearing sunglasses?

He strides up quickly, his jaw firmly set and his cheeks pinched in a manner that leads me to believe he's tense. Underneath his cut is a black sweatshirt with the Forsaken symbol across the chest. I look down at my own black Forsaken hoodie and blush. Wearing the same thing is a little embarrassing for some reason. Maybe it's because it reminds me of our connection—to the club—and that we'll never really be able to go our separate ways and be out of each other's lives. Not that I really *want* to be out of his life.

"Hey," I say and clear my throat, trying to get rid of the hoarse nervousness I hear in my voice.

He doesn't say a word as he reaches the porch, steps up, and turns toward me. His stride doesn't falter the closer he gets. Wide footsteps close in on me, never slowing, and he is on me in a moment, his chest bumping into mine, pushing me backward. I stumble into the column behind me and am caught between the cool plaster and Jeremy's warm, hard body. His tangy breath washes over my face, engulfing me in the sweet smell of whiskey. He doesn't even look down at me—nothing. He just stands here like he's shielding me from the world.

Jeremy's arm lifts at his side, and a hard object brushes against my stomach. The quiet click of the safety releasing tells me he's pulled out his gun. His free hand lifts, barely tracing the curves of my body from my hip up to my ribs to the sides of my breasts and up above my head as he slaps it against the column and anchors himself to me. His tangy sweet breath comes harder and faster on my face now. His chest rises and falls quickly. His heartbeat is so fast that I worry for him. Our torsos push together, letting me share his adrenaline. He's been drinking and riding, and this isn't what I expected.

I don't know what I expected.

Reaching up, I place a hand over his heart. It's stupid, but I just want to feel his heartbeat. I want to know he's human and not entirely cruel. Still, he doesn't look at me. He leans in and turns his head to the left and then the right. His skin is so close I can almost feel him. I want to feel him, and I hate myself for it.

For every time Aunt Ruby showed me what it means to be a strong woman. For every intimate moment I've witnessed between Dad and Holly where I see who really wears the pants in that relationship. For how hard Nic made Duke work to earn her forgiveness, and for how strong Alex fought to have something with Ryan. They each took a chance on something they didn't know would work out, but they did it anyway. I don't have that kind of faith, so whatever I'm doing here is just torturing myself with what I want, but never will be.

And I'm here letting myself get sucked into the beat of Jeremy's heart and the way he smells, even now. I feel pathetic and weak. Dirty even. I should want nothing to do with him. But he's here, covering me with his body, and it doesn't feel scary or like he wants to hurt me. It feels like he's guarding me. Why is he so intense? Why won't he look at me?

Carefully, I reach up and grab ahold of his sunglasses and slide them off his face. With the loudest voice I can muster, I say, "Look at me."

He doesn't move, and for some reason, I feel even more determined at his refusal. I pass the glasses to my left hand and then place the thumb of my right hand on his chin and pull down until he's forced to face me. His red, swollen eyes stare down at me blankly. His eyes are misleading because his chest still expands and compresses quickly.

"You"—his deep voice comes out in a low growl, and he sucks in a breath—"fucked up."

The commanding way he looms over me, the way his eyes come alive as he speaks, and the way he presses himself into me makes it hard to breathe. He's so much man in this moment that it's both exciting and intimidating. He's still Jeremy, but he's a Jeremy I'm not sure I know. This is Jeremy, the guy who's prospecting for the club, not the cute teenage boy I usually see him as. And I fucking love it.

"I want to help," I whisper.

He leans in and lowers his face to my neck where he sucks in a deep breath. "You should not be here," his hisses into my ear.

"But I am," I say stupidly. It's the only thing I can think of with his face in my neck and his hot breath washing over my skin. I close my eyes, forcing myself to focus on why we're here and not what my body wants to do. "I need your help."

"You need me?" He holds his breath for a moment

while he waits for my response.

"I need your *help*," I correct. Quiet. We're so freaking quiet. It's making this moment private and weird all at the same time. "I have to find out who raped Mindy."

His body goes completely still as my words register, and then he tenses and sucks in a deep breath. He grits his teeth as if he's struggling to control himself. "Club business. We're taking care of it. It's fine."

"Liar," I say before I can stop myself. I hate that word, *fine*. "It's not fine. Dad said it was fine when Scavo showed up at school, and he said it was fine when Holly moved in. He promised me we were safe, and then Mindy was raped." Now my chest is rising and falling quickly, my heart rate is picking up, and I'm on the verge of tears. I hate how that word—*fine*—makes me react. Everything is so not fine.

"You're safe," he says, his voice softening just slightly.

"No, I'm not. None of us are." My voice shakes.

He pulls his head back and looks me in the eye. "I *will* keep you safe."

His words feel like a vow, like he really believes them. I'll bet he does, but that's the problem. They all think they can make that promise and keep it. I'll bet Ryan made that promise to Alex, but then she was taken by her brother and beaten. I'll bet Dad made that promise to Holly, but then she had to watch Mindy be violently raped. We're all just sitting ducks.

"Whatever you're doing here, you need to stop it," he says. I give him a noncommittal sigh and continue looking in his eyes. I'm not going to stop what I'm doing, I can't. He must sense this, because the fire in his eyes comes back and he's back to looking at me blankly. I'm learning that this means he's angry and maybe even a little scared. "I mean it, Cheyenne."

"No," I say loudly.

He removes his hand from the column and replaces the safety on his gun. He slides the gun into the back of his jeans and reaches around, grabbing me by my upper arms.

"You need to understand," he barks loudly in my face. "You could get yourself killed."

"I could get killed anyway!" I shout back. My arms ache as the adrenaline pumps through them, and my legs tingle with the desire to run. He's not intimidating or scary now, just so freaking intense that it makes it hard to breathe.

"Either I'm going to have to show you how very bad of an idea it is for you to be poking into club business, or I'm going to let your father make you understand," he screams. Veins pop out of the sides of his neck, and a blue line appears on his forehead. He's snapping. I can see it.

"Do what you have to do, and I'll do what I have to do," I scream back.

The anger fuels me, pushing me to lose my temper. Still with his sunglasses in my hands, I shove against his chest to give myself some space. He steps back just one solitary step before reaching out and pulling on my arm. He spins me around with my arm behind my back and pushes me into the plaster behind me. His glasses, still in my hand, crack from the impact. The sky breaks with the crashing sound of thunder. Droplets of rain thump against the top of the covered porch. The welcome chaotic, rhythmic drumming provides a blanket of privacy over us, making me feel less exposed to the nosy neighbor next door.

"Are you going to listen to me now?" he says roughly in my ear.

"Are you?" I shoot back. "You don't even know what information I have. I could help the club."

"Last warning, Cheyenne." His voice drops as his mouth falls to my ear, lips ghosting the shell.

I turn into his face, letting our cheeks touch as I whisper, "You need help. Admit it."

He pulls back, but his grip on my arm is as strong as ever as he spins me around, pushing my face into the column. The warmth of his body disappears, and a cool wind picks up, chilling me. His hand slams down on my ass, pushing me forward.

I gasp, shocked and unsure how to respond. It's just a moment before I struggle against him, but that only encourages him to bring his hand down to spank me again. I throw a leg back and kick him in the shins. Jeremy loses his grip on my arm, and I pull away, spin around, and lunge for him, swinging with an open hand. I make contact with his cheek. The force of my slap surprises me, and my flesh stings in response. He grabs me by my wrists. I pull away but lose my footing and pull us both to the brick pavers below. He lands on his butt. I'm falling backward when his strong arms yank me forward, bringing me down on top of him. He groans beneath me.

"You spanked me," I say breathily, wholly incapable of focusing on anything else at the moment.

"You slapped me," he responds on a ragged breath.

"But you actually spanked me," I repeat, this time a little more forceful.

"I like your ass." He sucks in a struggling breath.

I cast him a dirty look to find that my elbow is jabbing into his gut as I lie across him with my hip on top of his. It's only my side that's touching his front, but this feels more tender than when he was up in my room mauling me. Testing the waters, I shove my elbow deeper into his abdomen. He responds by scrunching his navy eyes shut and wincing, but he doesn't move to stop me.

"This is for being a jerk," I say and dig in as hard as I can. He kicks at the brick beneath him but still doesn't stop me. "And for sleeping with my best friend when you know I like you. And for coming up here and fucking spanking me."

"I deserve that," he manages to say on a gasp. "You still like me?"

Forgetting all about the pressure I'm supposed to be applying to his stomach, I retract and demand, "Say it. Say you're sorry and mean it, or I'll figure out a way to crush your windpipe."

He opens his eyes, and while they're still red and swollen, like he's been drinking and not sleeping very well, they're still so very blue and so very deep. They're one of the reasons I fell for him so hard and so fast. His eyes are absolutely gorgeous. I place my arm along his ribs and redistribute my weight so he can adequately breathe, but I don't move off of him just in case he decides to be a dick again.

"I'm an asshole, okay?" he says. "I liked you, and I fucked it up. You made me mad, so I did what I always do. I shouldn't have said shit about what happened at my party."

It's not an apology. Or maybe it is in a fucked up way, but it's not enough. I don't have the energy or time for halfhearted bullshit. He's not sorry for what he did. He's only sorry he threw it in my face.

"She was my best friend, and you could have been my boyfriend," I say and shove my elbow into his gut again. His legs kick up as he hunches in and whines in pain. I stand and watch him recover from his fetal position to straighten out, suck in a large breath, and stand beside me.

"I was wrong," he says. His face has fallen, and he looks sorrowful all right. It's just not enough. Ian's words ring in the back of my head, and I find the strength to not let him suck me into his web again.

You deserve good, so don't settle for fucked up.

"I deserve better than that," I say.

"I know." He stands and reaches to cup my jaw. "So I'm going to take you home because I promised you that I'm gonna make sure you'll be safe."

I could argue and tell him I'm taking my car home, but I don't want to. I want him to try to show me that he can protect me, even if I know he can't.

His phone beeps from his pocket, signaling that he's got a text. It's a little sad that I still remember the tones he has set for different notifications. He withdraws his hand from my cheek and pulls his phone out, reads the screen, curses, and sends a text back at a furious pace. I watch quietly as he curses again and makes a frustrated grunting sound.

"Let's go," he says as he takes my hand and drags me off the porch.

My hair and sweatshirt absorb the rain quickly, soaking me to the bone. I have to work to keep up as he pulls me toward his bike at a rapid speed. She's drenched from the downpour, but she's a trooper and will work just fine. He hands me his helmet, so I place it on my head and wait for him to climb onto the bike. He swings a leg over and starts her up quickly. Revving the engine, he pops up the kickstand, and I climb on, wrapping my arms tight around his waist. He's without a helmet, which is hugely illegal in California, but nobody says shit to anybody in a cut around here. All it would do is earn them a headache to mess with the club. Still, I worry about him. Being on this bike with him feels like I'm home. I refuse to accept that has anything to do with Jeremy, but more to do with the bike itself. We speed away, passing my Bug on our way out. I don't doubt that she will be returned to me soon.

Soon, we pull up the house, and the rain has stopped. Jeremy doesn't even get the bike cut off before Dad's outside and screaming at us. His deep, hysterical voice demands to know where we've been.

Jeremy coolly cuts off the bike. "Miss Priss's car broke down. Had to pick her up."

"You got shit to do, prospect," Dad says.

Jeremy's relaxed face hardens as does his entire body. I extract myself from him and his bike and take off his helmet. He puts the kickstand down and nods at Dad. "Yes, sir."

"You tell me if my kid's car breaks down. You wait for orders. You don't go fucking missing on a job," Dad screams a little too loudly. Our neighbors are cool as hell, but still. They know the club does some shit they probably wouldn't approve of. At least, I can't imagine they don't, but that doesn't mean we need to take out an ad on the highway to advertise it to everybody. "Get out of my fucking sight."

I hand him the helmet and watch as he straps it on his head, gives the kickstand a shove, and then starts up the bike again and takes off all in a matter of moments. Jeremy's gone, and I'm left with Dad, who's pissed as fuck and wanting to know where I was that my car broke down. I could lie, but if he sends someone to get my car and it's not where I said it was, I'll be in even more trouble. So instead, I lie and say I have a friend who lives two doors down from the Jennings family. I don't tell him that exactly, but I give him the address of my supposed friend's house. His face pales and his breathing catches when I say the street name,

With a hard glare he points at me and says, "You're not going over there again. I don't give a fuck how good of friends you are with this bitch. No more. And especially not fucking again without a man on you."

"Yes," I say quickly. "I'm sorry, Dad."

"Do you understand me, Cheyenne? It's not safe. It's

really not safe. I'm not fucking playing with you."

"Yes," I snap and throw my hands up in the air. "I get it. I'm sorry!" I stomp off in the house and up to my room. Something about Dad's reaction makes me feel weird about having been over there, like there's something more that I'm missing. I just wish I weren't so dense and I could actually put my finger on the missing piece of the puzzle already.

CHAPTER 17

February

14 months to Mancuso's downfall

Cheyenne

IT'S BEEN A few weeks since I last saw Jeremy. And it's killing me. He sent me one text message on Valentine's Day. I've probably brought that text up and stared at it a hundred times since. It still gives me butterflies every time I read it.

STILL THNKNG BOUT UR ASS.

It's not mushy or romantic or anything, but it's perfectly Jeremy. I'm the biggest freaking idiot on the planet because I've convinced myself that was his way of telling me to have a good Valentine's Day. I never responded because by the time I could breathe again, it had been so long since he'd sent it. I didn't know if it was too awkward to respond that late or if I should just not respond at all. I still don't know if responding would have been better. He didn't try to text me again, so now I bet he thinks I'm ignoring him.

I *should* be ignoring him like I'm ignoring Daniel, who for some reason is still trying to talk to me. Despite the fact that I've made it super clear that seeing him screw someone on a picnic table was enough for me, he won't let it go. He just pretends that we're fine. He says we have plans to go out next week, but that's so not going to happen.

I got ahold of Alex's cell number from Ryan's phone the last time he was at the house. I thought I'd been really sly until he tracked me down and yelled at me. Apparently Alex freaked a little when she got crazy excited text messages from me and didn't really trust that it was legit. He said something about not getting laid that night because, once she knew it was me and not some crazed killer, she and I spent the entire night texting back and forth. I'm working up to asking Dad to let me hang out with her, but he's been on edge about something lately, and I know better than to ask for shit when he's in a pissy mood. It doesn't matter, because we're on our way to being besties—once I can knock Nic out of the top spot—and after I decide whether or not to give Jeremy another chance, we might be able to double date.

The loneliness from losing Tracie is clearly getting to my brain. If I don't find someone else to hang out with soon, I might start accompanying Grandma to her flower-lady meetings where they sit around and talk dirt and plants all day.

I have tried to keep myself busy with helping the club put away all the Christmas decorations Aunt Ruby put up. For the most part, the clubhouse isn't a place I spend a lot of time at, but during the holiday season, Ruby makes sure the guys keep it mostly family friendly. With one charity run after another and all the visiting family members that seem to make it into town, the clubhouse becomes a hub of activity for all ages. Aunt Ruby is typically one hard-ass lady, but during holidays, she turns into a leather-clad biker version of Martha Stewart, just with a foul mouth and a mean right hook. But once New Year's Eve comes around, apparently all the family joy fizzles from the place, and it turns into a whorehouse for dick-sucking sluts.

Shoving a broken Santa ornament into the plastic trash bag I'm holding, I force myself to take a deep breath. Being reminded of Chel and her oral skills is not helping me get over all the bad shit that went down with Jeremy. It's just that the day Jeremy picked me up at the Jennings' house, he seemed so angry and worried. And he let me elbow him and snap at him. I know enough that Forsaken—prospect or not—don't let a chick do that unless they care about them. So he cares about me, but the question is by how much.

I've stowed myself away in the game room, which is set behind the main gathering room at the front of the clubhouse. I chose this room because of the large, worn pool table that serves as an expansive table top for organizing all this junk the guys call memorabilia. There is everything here from old beer cans to women's lingerie to Santa hats. I think I even saw a used condom earlier, but I threw that entire box in the dumpster out back. I don't even care what was in there.

I'm a good two hours into the project when I decide to give up. I didn't *technically* volunteer to help clean up, it's more like Dad grounded me for distracting Jeremy and this is my punishment. But I didn't argue, and that should count for something, so it's kind of like I volunteered.

The clubhouse is quiet right now, with the guys all out doing God only knows what. Peeking around the corner, I double-check that I'm alone. When I'm confident I won't get busted, I go for my best casual walk across the main room to the bar area and grab a cold beer from the fridge. I'm already grounded and expelled from school, so what can Dad really do to me at this point? Tell me I can't see my friends? I mean, they're all in school still, so it's not like I get to see them much anyway. Still, I run back into the game room with the beer and use the bottle opener on my key ring to pop it open. I doubt Dad would let me keep it if he knew I had a bottle opener, but oh well. It's not like he sets the best example. I take a sip of the beer and grimace. It tastes like total shit, but the guys drink it all the time, so maybe it'll grow on me.

Hardened rubber claps against the concrete, growing louder with every step, in an unmistakable rhythm of a walk so distinctive that I already know it's Jeremy. I shove the beer behind the box I was sorting pre-beer break. He rounds the corner at his usual gait, then slows, does a double take, and gives me the signature Forsaken chin nod. I sense his mood before I really see the expression on his face. I force my hands to start moving, organizing this crap so that I'm not as distracted with knowing that he's here. Which is a feat in and of itself because he's incredibly distracting, especially because he's giving off these sullen vibes, like something's wrong. He just keeps staring at me, and I'm doing everything I possibly can to ignore him.

It's not working.

"Are you lost?" I ask.

He raises an eyebrow as he retorts, "I work here."

"Right." I haven't forgotten that he has as much right to be here as I do, but I'm more than conflicted about being in the same room with him. I don't want to like him, but I do. Enough to argue with him over just about anything. He likes to argue. He talks when he's mad.

"So—what do you want?" I ask.

He shoves his hands in his pockets and blows out a breath. He stares off into nothingness for a solid minute before he finally turns back to me and raises both eyebrows.

"You," he says.

Now I'm the one raising an eyebrow and working hard to keep my composure. The butterflies are flipping the fuck out in my stomach, and I'm turning bright red. I can't freaking breathe, and my hands are shaking. Dad always says to listen to the words that people speak, but take their actions to heart. Because people are full of shit, and they'll tell you whatever they think you want to hear, but it's the way they behave that will show you who they are. Jeremy acts like a dick, but he's here. For me. And I want him. I want there to be an us. But I also don't want to be a stupid girl who falls for a jerk's lies.

"You could have had me," I say. "Before you fucked my best friend. Before you let Chel suck your dick. Before you were a total asshole."

I want him, but apparently I still have some anger issues to work out.

"We weren't together," he says and pulls his hands out of his pockets. He walks forward, casting a shadow over me. I prepare myself for him to bump into me like he did the last time I saw him. When he stops just before touching me, I fight back the disappointment. I was a little excited over the idea of him walking me back to the brick wall and mauling me. I'm ready for it this time.

"I still want to shoot you for it." Because I do, but only just a little.

"Let's get this straight," he says. "When you're my girl, you're *my* girl. Stop texting that fucktard. You tell him who you belong to. When you belong to me, I'll keep my dick wherever you want it—preferably in you— but I guess that can wait for a little bit. Point is once we're together, we're fucking together. Until then, you got no reason to be pissed at me, and if I fuck up when we're together, then you can go ahead and fucking shoot me."

Now gasping for breath, I look down at his boots to try to hide how his words affect me. He's freaking insane. So bossy and assertive. He came in here looking like he was going to apologize and ask for forgiveness. This total alpha-male mood swing catches me off guard.

It's hot.

Really fucking hot.

"Tracie was my best friend," I say and look up to meet his eyes. He had me the second he started barking orders, but I'll die before telling him that.

"Your friend is a whore," he says. "She fucked Diesel right before fucking me."

"Yeah, her place is on your dick, right?" My voice is so small. The words he said to me don't make me angry. They just make me feel sad. Like there's no way I'm ever going to get over that.

"That was fucked up." He takes another step forward. He cups my face in his hands and forces me to look up at him. "I didn't know Duke had set that blow job up for me. What the fuck was I supposed to do? Bitch out in front of the club? I look like a pussy in front of those guys and I risk my patch. They don't tolerate weakness. You know that."

"Not the point," I say. Though I am losing track of what my point is. He's a smooth talker, that's for sure. He knows just how to redirect the conversation the way he wants.

"You're done throwing shit in my face." His voice is taking on that hard edge again. "And I'm done fucking pretending that I don't miss you."

"You have a funny way of showing it." I sound like a broken record, but I want him to admit that he's fucked up. I mean, he kind of has, but it's just not enough.

"Look, the chicks I normally go for are some dirty bitches. They're down for whatever. I'm not used to feeling shit for someone, and I got a little... excited. I forgot how inexperienced you are."

"You're making this entire conversation worse," I gripe. My cheeks heat as embarrassment floods my face. Intellectually, I know I shouldn't be embarrassed for not being as experienced as him, but I can't help it. I just wish we were on a level playing field, and his being a jerk and pointing it out doesn't help one bit.

"Here's what's going to happen—I'm going to kiss you, and this time I'll respect your boundaries. You say no, I'll stop. You won't throw your dad in my face, and I'll try not to be an asshole most of the time."

"But we're fighting," I say in confusion. When Dad and Holly fight, they can go on and on for hours. Dad and Mom don't really fight because she's never around, so I don't really know how they fight, or how they used to. Aunt Ruby and Uncle Jim fight like cats and dogs, and Forsaken members fight one another all the time. But it's just not the same as what's happening here. Usually there's a lot of screaming before they start making up. We're not even screaming right now. I don't know what to do with this.

"Not anymore," he says.

Waiting for him to kiss me is beyond frustrating, so I take matters into my own hands and stand on my toes and press my lips against his. I don't know that his explanation is any kind of apology, or even if it's one that I should be forgiving, but I decide to let my heart lead. My head leads me to being alone, but my heart gets me to second base, God willing.

His arm circles my waist, and he draws me nearer. My arms wrap around his neck, keeping a firm hold on him. The kiss is mostly chaste, with a few peeks of our tongues here and there. His hand travels down to my ass, and even though my nerves are on edge with the idea of going *there* with him, I can't bring myself to tell him to stop. My hormones are getting the best of me, but I don't care. He grips my ass firmly and pulls me up against him. A tingly feeling starts in my belly and shoots down my legs, urging me to pull myself up his body. He bends slightly, not breaking the kiss, and grips me more firmly. He lifts me up easily as I wrap my legs around his waist. He turns us to the side and sets me on the pool table.

He pulls away and pecks at my lips as he whispers, "You have beer."

"Not important," I whisper back and peck at his lips.

He kisses me again and nibbles at my bottom lip with teeth. With ragged breath, he pulls back and says, "Shut it."

"Excuse me?" I ask him between pecks.

"You're ruining"—peck—"this for me."

"What?" I nip at his lower lip.

"Talking," he says and kisses me in a much less chaste manner. His tongue slides between my lips. My thighs clench around his legs, and it's getting harder to breathe. I just want to kiss him until I'm numb everywhere. I choose to ignore his comment even though he was the one who started talking first. He can win that battle because I'm about to win the war.

"Who do I belong to?" I whisper as I pull back from his lips. He sucks in a ragged breath, and his cheeks are flushed.

"Me," he says and leans in to kiss me again. I lean backward and shake my head.

"And who do you belong to?"

He smiles wide. "I belong to you."

"Don't forget that," I say and smash my lips against his.

I'm finally letting myself believe that this might work out between us when I realize that we have company, and I pull away. Ryan is like a spider, the way he sneaks up on people. It's like, you may not have proof that he's in the room, but you just know he's there. Watching and judging and plotting. And then you see him, and all your suspicions are confirmed.

He stands in the corner of the room near the entrance from the main room. A satisfied smirks plays at his lips, and his gray eyes are clearly amused. He's an odd one, and he's only getting worse as he ages. Back when Dad and Uncle Jim would ditch me in his and Ian's care, he wasn't so bad. Well, maybe he was, but Ian kept him in line. Ryan has always kind of been like the aloof big brother that I never asked for, never wanted, and tried to get rid of. But I wouldn't want to get rid of him now. He's grown on me.

"Shouldn't be doing that. Miss Priss is just a baby," Ryan says.

Asshole.

"At least he's my age. Your girlfriend is practically still in high school."

"Wishin' we hooked up?" he asks while pointing at himself.

I roll my eyes and wave him away. "Hell no. Don't you have someone else to irritate?"

A smirk covers Ryan's face. As far back as I can

remember he's had a ridiculously huge ego. On his way out, he says in a mocking voice, " 'Who do you belong to?' 'Oh, you Cheyenne Grady, I belong to you. I got no fucking balls, and I'm a total pussy. My name is Jeremy Whelan, and my favorite thing to do is to suck Ryan's dick.' " His laughter trails behind him as he leaves.

"He really lets you talk to him like that?" Jeremy asks in surprise while trying his best to ignore the goading.

"What is he going to do about it?" I'm careful never to embarrass or disrespect Ryan in front of his peers, so I don't see why he would get pissy about the stuff I say privately. Besides, it's not like he doesn't deserve it. "Plus, he's obsessed with himself and probably doesn't hear a word I say anyway."

"I heard *that*." He gives Jeremy that head nod and says, "We got Church, and you got clean-up duty in the shop."

"I'm going," Jeremy says and takes a step back. He mouths, *"I'm sorry,"* and walks away without another word.

Ryan stands with his arms folded and looking at me with the most serious expression I've seen on his face in a while. "He good to you?"

I shrug my shoulders and give him a smile. "I don't know yet."

"He's not, you tell me."

"Thanks," I say softly, touched by his kind gesture.

"His sister sucks dick like her life depends on it. Always wanted to see if Baby Boy can do the same."

"Oh my God, what the fuck," I say in shock.

Ryan gives me a wink and walks off. I sit there for a few moments before pulling out my cell and texting Alex.

UR BF WANTS JER 2 SUCK HIS DICK.

She responds immediately. HE'S A CHILD. IGNORE HIM.

NOT THAT EASY, I text back.

I'LL GIVE U TIPS. I can't help but chuckle at her response.

Everything is working out really well now. I mean, I know I'm letting myself get caught up in the excitement of a new relationship, but it's ridiculous how much things can change in just a few minutes. I've barely had him, but already I know that it would break my heart to lose him. Everything is working out except for my investigation. That's still at a standstill. I grab my beer and take another drink. It's not as cold now and tastes even worse, but I power through it.

I wish I had access to more club business than I do. It's just hard because Dad doesn't like paper trails, so he only has what he absolutely needs to have. The clubhouse gets loud as the men all trail in for Church. One deep voice barking orders after another fills the space, making it feel much smaller. When their voices fade, I can only assume they're in the chapel now. If only I could be in there with them.

I hop off the pool table, and I grab my phone out of my pocket again and send Alex another text. NOBODY TELLS ME NETHNG.

THEY NEVER WILL, she says back. I'm trying to

fish for information on how to get further in my investigation, but she didn't really bite. Maybe I just need to be more upfront.

I NEED INFO, I say and pray she doesn't tell her sadistic guard dog.

DANGEROUS, she says back.

I KNOW. MY CHOICE. NEED TO KNOW.

PAY BETTER ATTN, she says. NO MORE TIPS. TROUBLE.

Gah, she isn't freaking helping me at all. I read her last few texts again and blow out a frustrated breath. The guys are all sitting around the chapel and talking about stuff I could really use to help Holly and Mindy. It's not fair. I just want to help, and nobody is making that feat any easier on me.

Pay better attention, she said. I think on that for a minute. Maybe that's her way of helping? I think back on what she told me about getting in trouble for listening to her father's business. Scrolling up, I find the text and eye it until the idea comes to me.

They're in Church, down the hallway, discussing club business.

Club business I could use.

If they catch me, I'm in some serious trouble. I take a sip of my beer and set it down. Freaking gross. I don't think I'm ever going to like that crap. I nervously tap my foot and think it over.

I'm still thinking it over as I walk into the main room. I'm certain this is a horrible idea as I make sure no one's around and turn the corner down the hallway. My hands shake. I shouldn't be doing this, but I crouch as silently as possible in front of the double doors to the chapel anyway. I press my ear to the left door and close my eyes, doing my best not to bump into the wood.

"Jennings is awake and recovering," Dad says. His voice barely makes it through the thick wooden doors. There's a few displeased rumbles from around the room and some cursing. "Apparently, since FBPD doesn't have any solid enough leads to arrest anyone, they kept the asswipe's progress quiet to keep him safe."

"Why the fuck didn't we know about this sooner?" Wyatt snaps.

"Gonzales was taken off the case," Dad says.

"That asshole Mercer?" Wyatt asks, referring to Lieutenant Harry Mercer, who is Holly's uncle and Mindy's dad. "I'm fucking sick of that prick."

The room is quiet for half a minute before Jim pipes in. "Mercer complicates shit, but he's a friend to the club."

Damn straight he is, Uncle Jim! I can't say I have any personal positive stories about Harry Mercer, but Holly loves him, and he's been fiercely protective of Mindy since her attack. Dad says he can respect a man who guards his kid like Harry's been doing. The club barely got to see Mindy after she was released from the hospital, and even then, it was a short visit. I managed to get it out of Holly that she was allowed more time with Mindy but that Harry thought it was enough for the day when he and Ian had some words. But that was a while ago. Nobody's said a word about Mindy in weeks, and it's starting to worry me. Out of nowhere, a hand wraps around my face and seizes my mouth, clamping down and suppressing my scream. My stomach lurches, my heart beats frantically, and I desperately try to breathe, but the hand not only covers my mouth but my nostrils as well. Before I can kick at the door to signal someone that I'm in trouble, I'm dragged backward down the hall as my lungs fight for air.

CHAPTER 18

February

14 months to Mancuso's downfall

Cheyenne

I KICK MY feet in the air in a pathetic attempt to free myself but can't make contact with anything. The hand at my mouth moves slightly, allowing me to suck in a ragged breath through my nostrils. I'm assaulted by a familiar masculine musk that I know all too well. My body relaxes instantly as it recognizes his scent. It takes my mind an extra moment to realize who it is.

Jeremy.

Shit. This is so not good, but I guess being busted by the brand-new boyfriend is better than being busted by anyone else. Snooping on Church won't just get me grounded. It'll get me in hot water at a club level. I knew I was asking for trouble when I walked down that hallway. I knew the risk and decided it was worth it. But now, after having gotten very little information, I regret my choice. Knowing that Darren is awake and recovering doesn't do much to help me. I mean, I guess I *could* go talk to him. But then I risk exposing myself if he's not cooperative. Either way, I fucking blew it. I can't take another chance to listen in on Church.

"Keep your fucking mouth shut," he whispers in my ear. His hand slides away from my mouth. I take a deep breath and let myself feel the stress of the situation. I'm still hauled up in his arms. There's a creak as he walks us through the now open door. *The palace.* I hate this room.

Once inside, he sets me on my feet and reaches past me to close the door. I don't dare turn around for fear of seeing the angry look on his face. I'm trying really hard, as I take one deep breath after another, to not act like the baby that everybody still thinks I am. I'm an adult, and I can accept responsibility for the things I've done—but that doesn't mean it won't suck to be yelled at.

"What the fuck were you thinking?" he hisses in my ear. The pure disgust in his voice makes my stomach churn.

The tension in the room is so thick it's uncomfortable. Too thick. I fold my arms over my chest and focus on the doorknob in front of me. If I thought he was mad the last time he caught me somewhere I shouldn't have been, then I was dead wrong.

The clanking of metal objects sounds behind me, and a child's voice whispers something inaudible. I spin around to find Chel and her son, Xavier, on one of the long couches. Xavier has a pair of toy metal motorcycles in his hands that he's clanking together in his lap. He's still little, just barely three. He's got naturally tanned skin and jet-black hair. His brown eyes shine as they land on me. He smiles wide and waves a motorcycle at me. I like the kid well enough. He's always been easy when I've babysat him, and until last month, his mom was always good to me. Not that she knows she did it, but girl did me wrong.

My attention redirects to Chel, who has a textbook in her lap. She's nervously tapping a pencil on a notebook that hangs off the side of her textbook. She's studying to be a nurse, and I'll give her credit for that, but for the time being, she's just a whore. I let my inner bitch rage and think over the fact that I've never heard her give mention of Xavier's father—that is assuming she knows who that even is.

Chel gives me a tentative smile that falls the longer I look at her. I turn my attention to the wall of mirrors to my side. The expression on my face is clear as day. I'm not happy. My mouth is turned down in the corners, and my eyes are narrowed. My jaw is set in a hard line, and my nostrils are flaring just like my dad's do when he's mad. Seeing a miniature female Sterling in the mirror is almost enough for me to force a fake smile to my face. *Almost*.

"Everything okay, Jer?" Chel asks. Her eyes shift to Jeremy, which just raises my hackles even more.

"Why are you asking him and not me?" I snap. She shrinks back, clearly taken aback by my response. She and I have never had a problem before now.

Jeremy wraps a hand around my upper arm and softly tugs me backward as he whispers, "We can talk elsewhere." Though his voice is soft and he's speaking quietly, I can feel the tension in his hand as he guides me out of the palace and down the hallway. He grabs my pink helmet from the table near the front door where I left it after Dad escorted me here. He doesn't trust my car to get me anywhere safely now thanks to Jeremy's lie.

Even out of the clubhouse, Jeremy's still frustrated as all get out. He leads me to his bike, throws a leg over, and crooks his index finger at me. I affix my helmet to my head just as he does his own. We're staring each other down like our lives depend on this eye contact.

As rebellious as I'm prone to be, even I know not to argue in this moment. Without a single word, I climb onto the rumbling bike, place my feet on the foot rests and wrap my arms around his midsection. He signals to Dunce, a prospect who's been absent as of late, as he opens the gate for us, and we take off through the Forsaken Custom Cycle lot and down Main Street. The wet ground is slick beneath the tires of the bike. It's been raining here fairly regularly the last few weeks—and thank goodness, too—but it seems like folks forget how to function in the first rain of the season. It could be three weeks without any rain, and the first rain is always the most dangerous. I never understood why until this moment.

Time has a way of making us forget the danger and the pain. I was so angry with Jeremy right after our date and then just disappointed when he never made the attempt to apologize. Then at the school, and with Tracie, and at the Jennings' house a few weeks ago... after everything, I still like the feel of wrapping my arms around him. I like having my face pressed into his cut. I like his smell and his smile. I love his eyes, and I'm becoming quickly addicted to his bossy nature. But it's a slippery slope, because the wounds are still so fresh and I'm not the best at letting things go. Chel didn't technically do anything to hurt me, even if her actions did end up causing me pain. And I know how it is with the Lost Girls, so I really shouldn't be surprised. Still, it's going to take a while for me to be mature enough to not hate her.

But I've seen her fucking vagina, and if I could see it clear enough from where I stood, then Jeremy definitely got a good peep show. And that just pisses me off to no end.

"Stop it," Jeremy shouts from in front of me. One of his hands leave the handlebars as he swats at my hands on his abdomen. We swerve slightly before he corrects us, now with both hands on the handlebars. I should be frightened since he's only been riding since summer, but for some reason I trust him. Maybe not totally with my heart, but definitely with my life.

It's only now that I realize that the more I think about Chel, the harder I dig my nails into his flesh. I retract my claws and close my eyes and enjoy the ride. As an apology, I trace small circles over the place I was scratching him. We slow down as the road gets bumpy, and the salty tang of the air grows stronger. Opening my eyes, I see we're at the beach.

Jeremy cuts the bike off and pushes down her kickstand. I reluctantly let him go and push myself off the bike and onto the sandy concrete. He climbs down, and we remove our helmets and rest them on the seat side by side. There's barely enough room for both of them, but he makes them fit. When he turns toward me, he looks down at my thin cotton long-sleeve and shakes his head. I didn't think to grab a jacket before he dragged me out of the clubhouse, not that he gave me the opportunity to think about how cold I'd be. I didn't even know where we were headed. He shrugs off his cut and hands it to me. I take the leather in my hands and marvel at the weight of it. I always forget how heavy they are until I'm holding one. It's substantial, that's for sure. It doesn't weigh quite as much as my dad's, but I'm guessing that's partially because it's maybe a size smaller and doesn't have as many patches on it as Dad's does. It will, though. One day Jeremy will have his top rocker and maybe even a few more patches. The only patch I don't want him to collect is a memory patch, because that means he's lost a brother.

"You'll be cold," I say as I realize he's unzipping his Forsaken hoodie and handing it to me. He shakes his head and reaches out with both hands. Grabbing his cut, he shoves the hoodie in my face again, so I take it. Slipping the hoodie on, I bask in his scent and the size of the item. I curl the ends of the sleeves around my closed fists and huddle in when the winter wind picks up.

"I like seeing you in that," he says with a nod.

"I like wearing it." As awkward as I am, I'm not totally understanding exactly what he's saying. Does he like seeing me in Forsaken stuff or *his* stuff?

It doesn't matter, I realize. Because we're here together, and he's being sweet. He takes my hand and leads me off the concrete lot and down the jagged shoreline to Glass Beach. It's a gorgeous spot, really. Millions of little shards of glass have shored up here, morphing and chiseling themselves into beautiful rocks that look like priceless stones. Individually, they're pretty enough, but all together as they blanket the shoreline, they're incredible.

He walks us to a spot that's fairly dry and sits down. He leans up against a flat rock and motions for me to come to him. I lean down and go to sit beside him, but he reaches out and pulls me into his lap. I screech and laugh at the sudden change in direction, then settle in. Even though I know his good mood won't last, I want to enjoy this calm before the storm.

"Warmer?" he asks. I nod my head, not wanting to speak. Anything I say is going to ruin the moment, I just know it. "Good, so now maybe you can fucking explain what you were doing listening in at the chapel while Church is in session."

"Are you going to yell?" I ask quietly. He wraps his arms around my waist and pulls me close to him. "Because quite frankly I'd rather just sit here and cuddle if talking leads to yelling."

"I got reason to yell," he says.

I squirm in his lap and get comfortable, then place my head on his shoulder. "I still have to find out why Mindy and Holly were attacked."

"Club business, babe. How many times do I got to explain that shit?"

"Don't give me that crap." I sound like a petulant child, but I can't help it. "I'm doing what I have to do."

"I told you that I'd keep you safe," he says in a rather unkind and sterile voice. I don't want to lose soft Jeremy, but at least this is a Jeremy I can fight with.

"Dad said the same thing about Holly," I say. "He swore she was safe and nothing bad would happen to her, but something bad *did* happen. Leo Scavo raped Mindy and forced Holly to watch. He probably hurt Darren Jennings, too. At least he's getting better and can maybe tell someone what happened."

"Wait," he says in a firm voice that silences my whining. "I don't even want to know how you know that name, but before you keep running your mouth, let me school you on something. I'm sure Scavo's done a lot of fucked up shit in his life, but one thing he did not do is rape Mindy."

"But you guys talk about finding him and how he's so awful. He showed up at the—"

He tightens his grip around me and shushes me into silence. "Jennings," he says. "That asshole is no fucking good. He's not a goddamn victim."

Nothing makes sense, and suddenly the last several weeks of my life feel like a total waste. How in the hell is Darren *not* a victim? He's been in the hospital since the end of summer.

"Nic dated him back in high school. I didn't fucking realize what was going on. Right under my fucking nose. That asshole made her feel like shit. I think I knew something wasn't right, but I never really paid any attention. Nic's a tough bitch. She doesn't need no sympathy or help or nothing. She's always able to take care of herself."

"Who put him in the hospital?" I ask, afraid of the answer. Jeremy ignores my question. His refusal to answer is as much of an admission as if he'd actually said it. Forsaken did it.

He takes a deep breath before he continues. "Few months back, Jennings came by the house to clear something up with Nic. I was watching TV and kept turning the volume up because they started yelling at each other. I didn't want to be bothered by it. Her drama was an inconvenience. I didn't even like what I was watching, but she was a fucking inconvenience." His words don't come out spiteful but rather remorseful. The shame that radiates through his voice is something I've never heard before. Forsaken don't express shame or regret much, because it would mean they did something wrong, and that's not something any of them are comfortable expressing. Even Aunt Ruby has a hard time saying she's sorry. I guess in a way I'm as much Forsaken as the rest of them, because I don't do great with *I'm sorry* either.

"I hear this crash and get up to tell the assholes to keep it down because he's fucking up my night. As it was, I was already having a bad fucking night. It was the day I found out Nic was knocked up and accidentally spilled that shit to Duke before she had a chance to tell him. That did not go over well." He takes a break from talking and places a kiss to the side of my head before continuing. A shiver runs up my spine, likely from the cold but possibly from the conversation. "I get in the hallway and all I can see is this preppy bastard standing with his back to me. He's got my goddamn sister—my sister who doesn't let *anybody* fuck with her—on the fucking floor. She's on her knees, holding her stomach and sobbing. He has a hand in her hair and the other holding his dick. By the time I get ahold of him, he's got his fucking dick shoved against her lips. She's fucking sobbing and refusing to open her mouth, and he's just fucking forcing himself on her."

My heart breaks for Nic as tears slip down my cheeks. Every word Jeremy speaks is annunciated and sounds more painful than the last. He leans over, eyeing my face. Turning my head to him, I stare into his eyes and let the tears fall freely. I'd rather he not know I'm crying, but I think he wants to see it so he knows I'm listening and absorbing what he's telling me.

"I wanted to kill him," he says.

"Forsaken did it." I'd already figured it out, but feel the need to verbalize my findings. Everything becomes so much clearer. Every time Jeremy would get annoyed at the news reports and how Dad would just turn off the TV and tell me to ignore it make so much sense. Jeremy just nods.

"I beat the guy down and got Nic's keys from her. Shoved him in the trunk and took him to the clubhouse. I wanted him dead, but he hurt Duke's woman, so it wasn't my call."

"That's why they let you prospect early, isn't it?" I ask. He nods again. I knew he had to have done something impressive for the club to give him a cut before he was legal. That's always been the rules— nobody underage prospects. But then... Jeremy. And knowing he's the youngest to ever prospect for the MC— in its entire history—made him desirable instantly. Getting to know this side of him is big trouble for me, because I'm getting sucked into him quickly.

"We're at the clubhouse, and Wyatt—the fucking VP—looks at me and says, 'Show me you got enough heart for this club,' and has me hold Jennings's head up while Knuck and Diesel held the fucker in place. Nobody wanted Nic to see the shit that was about to go down, but Duke fucking brought her in anyway and let her have first crack. She fucked him up good, and it looked painful, too. But the shit she was saying, like she was repeating Jennings's words back to him? I won't forget that shit. Not ever."

We're silent a long moment before Jeremy gives me a squeeze and whispers, "So after Nic's done fucking him up, Duke takes his turn. Gotta tell ya, I've never respected the dude more than in that moment. He fixed my sister's shit when I didn't."

"I'm sorry," I whisper because I don't know what else to say.

"No, I'm sorry. I'm going to do right by you. I won't let that shit happen to you."

"What exactly did he do?" My voice falls so quiet I'm not sure he hears me over the ocean.

He clears his throat and buries his face in my neck as he whispers, "He raped her. More than once. He beat her, too. I used to see the bruises when I was younger, but she'd say she got into another fight with some random chick when I asked. He never gave me reason to really think he was hurting her."

"It's hard to picture your sister like that." Because I don't know Nic any other way.

"Right?" he says, his mood lifting slightly. "Pissed her off once, and she shoved me in the fucking closet and locked it until I cooled down."

"What?" I ask, letting out a small laugh. I just want to forget everything he's said before that. I've always known a large part of my dad's job involves violence and intimidation, but hearing the details of it is startling. Yeah, he's got a loud bark and he can be a serious asshole, but he's still just my dad. He's the man who taught me to dance and played tea party with me. I'm not allowed to talk about it, but he did it. He's the guy who holds Holly while she cries herself to sleep some nights, and he's the man who never lets me forget how loved I am. The man who watches a person—even a disgusting parasite like Darren Jennings—be beaten within an inch of his life isn't the man I know. But I guess that's how they all are. There's always two sides to Forsaken men.

"I want to say it was a while ago, but it was last year," Jeremy says with a snicker.

I let out a short giggle at the mental image. Nic's a foot shorter than Jeremy, so there's no telling what tactics she employed to actually force him into a closet and lock him in. I might need to call her for tips.

"I won't let anything hurt you, not even me," he says. His mood darkens again, and he's back to speaking in that sullen way where his words drag out painfully slow and so weighted with meaning and promises that I'm drowning in my own insecurity and desperation to have him love me the way I think I've fallen for him—fast, deep, hard, and without a safety net to limit the destruction when this all goes to shit. Because we just got together. Like… *just*.

"Not hurting me means not shutting me out," I say.

"You're scaring the crap out of me, Chey."

"Then *help me*," I plead. "Holly's getting better, but she's still struggling, and God only knows what's going on with Mindy. Nobody can seem to get ahold of her."

"Club's handling it," he says firmly. Like that's supposed to stop me.

"You're not saying anything new. Quit shutting me out."

"Meth heads who raped Mindy kept calling her Nic while they did it, so the club thinks it's revenge for his prick kid."

I let my eyes fall closed so I can block the world out for a moment. I'm under no delusions that Forsaken is a club full of angels. They may be assholes, and they use women and lose them before the condom comes off. They may even sell pot by the fucking ton, but so what? It's weed, not heroin. Even if it were, they don't have women raped or send their men out to kill their own children. They don't do those things, so why is all this awful shit happening to us?

"Tell me what you're thinking," he says.

"I'm just trying to figure out why so much crap is happening to the club is all."

Neither of us say a word for a long while. The sun starts to set as the temperature drops. Jeremy must be freezing, but he doesn't move to leave.

"I got a job to do," he says. "And for me to do that job, I got to know you're not poking into shit you shouldn't be. Got it?"

"One night, less than a week after the... attack." My voice drops lower with every word as I figure out how to word what I'm trying to say. "Holly woke up screaming. Dad was outside with Ian. Whatever they were talking about had them both really upset. I didn't want to bug them, so I went downstairs to see if I could calm her down. She let me crawl into their bed with her, and as we were lying there, side by side, she was crying. Not like screaming anymore, but her face was covered in tears. She looked so out of it, like she didn't really know what was going on around her. Then something clicked, and she looked at me and just said, 'I'd do it again,' and then she mumbled the numbers seven and one. It was totally creepy and really weird, but she did something for my dad, which means she did something for me. And I love her, and I can't lose her."

I let that settle with him for a long moment before saying, "Holly did what she had to do for us. Now I'm doing what I have to for her."

"Christ," he mutters. "If I promise to keep you up-to-date on shit I find out, will you promise to fucking leave it alone?"

I think that over for a moment before nodding in agreement. I feel lighter now, less frustrated and more hopeful. Being able to share my fears with him and to have him promise to keep me up-to-date makes me feel better than I have in weeks. He twists me in his lap so I can face him better, and very slowly, he leans in and presses his lips to mine. Letting out a happy sigh, I press back, and we begin to move in a practiced rhythm. It's a few minutes of wandering hands and heaving breathing and a kiss that quickly moves from chaste to something that should most definitely be private. Just as my hands trail down his arms, rubbing his practically frozen flesh to warm him up, his phone buzzes from beneath me.

We pause, and I wiggle off his lap and onto the cold-as-hell sand and curl up to his side. He pulls the phone out, stares at the screen, and says, "Fuck." He pushes a few buttons and then brings the phone to his ear. He closes his eyes and places his head in his hand. All is quiet for a moment before Duke's voice shouts through the line in an angry string of curses.

"Yes, sir," Jeremy says, sounding so freaking upset.

"You fucked up, boy," Duke barks so loudly that I can hear him without even straining to listen in.

"Yes, sir," Jeremy repeats.

"Where the fuck did you go?" Duke demands.

Jeremy kicks at the sand in front of him and mouths, "*Fuck.*" He hasn't met my eyes, which may not be so bad after all. At least if he's not looking at me I don't have to see his eyes. He's in trouble and, from the sound of it, *lots of it*—and it's my fault.

Shame assaults me for not even thinking about the fact that Jeremy was supposed to be working this afternoon. I know he got in trouble when he picked me up from the Jennings' house. He was supposed to be on security detail that afternoon, but instead he was picking me up. Dad was so pissed he even grounded *me* over that because I lied to Dad and told him I begged Jeremy not to tell anyone I'd left the house without a detail on me. Knowing how pissed Dad was that day, I should have stopped Jeremy earlier when we left the clubhouse. If he's not going to think of the consequences of going rogue, then I'll have to do it for him.

"Miss Priss was in trouble," he says.

It's weak, and Duke knows it. He gives Jeremy the riot act about responsibility and makes a snide remark indicating that maybe Jeremy isn't mature enough for his cut yet.

"It was a fucking emergency."

But Duke doesn't care. He's fired up, and it sounds like there's no stopping him as he says, "Not my fuckin' problem. Good luck explaining this shit to the Pres."

The call ends, and Jeremy just sits there, staring at his phone. I don't push him to move or speak. I just watch as he mentally chides himself for fucking up with the club. Regret and sorrow fill me up until I'm choking on my own self-deprecation. Maybe I should stop poking into things if having to save my ass every time I find myself in hot water is going to get Jeremy into trouble. If there's one thing he wants more than anything else, it's his top rocker. I don't want to be the reason it doesn't happen for him.

CHAPTER 19

March

13 months to Mancuso's downfall

Cheyenne

IT'S BEEN BLISS, just being with Jeremy these past several weeks. I wasn't sure about his commitment to us at first. Everything had begun so rocky that I almost couldn't believe he was for real. Above anything else, I wanted to believe him. He'd confided in me, saved me—more than once—and he'd protected me from my dad and the club finding out what I've been doing. But he's still Jeremy, and his reputation leaves something to be desired. After a few weeks, Holly sat me down and asked me what was going on. Every time he'd leave for work or for home, my mood would make a drastic turn and I'd sulk for the next day or two.

As a prospect, he's busy. I get it. Nic just had her and Duke's baby—a little girl they named Robin. She was born just two days after my eighteenth birthday, and holy crap, is she freaking cute. I've only seen her twice in the week since she's been born, but I love her already. Holly and I went shopping for baby gifts, and I already know Dad's in major trouble because Holly totally has baby fever. I'd kill for a sibling so that somebody else on this planet can understand the pain of having Sterling Grady for a father.

When Jeremy isn't pulling sixty-plus-hour weeks at the shop and doing God knows what else for the club, he's on baby duty. I just want… time with my boyfriend. And now that I've gotten my GED test results back and I've passed, I have more time to spend with him—not that I actually spend more time with him since Duke's passing off baby chores on him. Apparently baby crap smells worse than big people crap, which is nasty. I don't even know how it's possible considering the clubhouse bathrooms are always questionably unclean.

It's not really club business—making Jer babysit—so technically not a part of his duties with the club, but I'm not about to tell Duke that. I believe the phrase Duke used was "own your balls and asshole." So instead I whined to Holly about it. I told her all about how I worry what he's doing when I'm not around, and who he's doing it with. I told her I want more time with him— more alone time—and that no matter how he swears he's been faithful, I'm terrified to find out he's not been. He's so freaking hot and such a great kisser, and even though I haven't gotten all that far with his lower half, I've seen it up close, and it's mighty impressive. Then again, what do I know? But telling him it's big and thick seems to make him happy, so I don't question my judgment.

Holly was gentle but firm in her assessment. Part of me wished Grandma had been available to talk to, but when I tried, she didn't even know Jeremy and I were a thing. She said last she checked, I still hated him after he was an epic douche canoe. She's been so absent lately that I'm starting to think she's seeing someone.

Apparently I was suffering from a bad case of self-doubt, which she drilled into me was only going to serve to hurt my relationship. While Dad never opted to say it to me himself, I've overheard him telling Holly that he agrees with her. That was kind of big, because until I had heard Dad admitting he was worried I was going to sabotage my relationship, I was convinced he would've been excited if Jeremy and I would break up.

But that was a few weeks ago, and ever since then, our relationship has been nothing but perfect. I know perfect won't last, because everybody keeps reminding me the first love is fleeting. Eventually our relationship will have to evolve, or it will end.

Their words, not mine.

A firm thud sounds against my bedroom door followed by Grandma's soft voice. "Knock, knock." As always, she doesn't wait for permission to enter. She just does. And she has the nerve to talk about Dad's manners. But I keep that to myself because she's been MIA lately, and any time I can score with her—and maybe some of her bomb-ass snickerdoodle cookies—the better.

Shifting on my bed, I turn to the door and raise an eyebrow in question. She stands with her hand on the doorknob and mimics my look with her own raised brow. "Well, well, well," I say. "Funny seeing you here. At home. Where you left me. With Dad. And Holly."

"Is this your mature way of saying you've missed me?" she asks. I check out her outfit and roll my eyes. She has some kind of glitter-glue thing going on that matches on both her jeans and her button-up. It's all silver and hot pink swirls and flowers and crap that I wouldn't be caught dead in. I fucking hate puff paint with a passion—and I hate it even more that Holly got her a new set of paints for Christmas. It's like they're trying to kill me.

"Well, like I said, you left me here with Dad. I mean, what did I do to deserve that?"

She crosses the room and takes a seat at the foot of my bed and smirks. "From what I hear? You've done plenty to earn a little time under house arrest. Sneaking beer, cutting class, and being a brat to everybody you come into contact with?" She whistles and then grins. "Your father did the same crap. Good job throwing that back at him. It's about time he got as good as he gave."

"Thanks. I've been working on giving him an ulcer," I say. "But really, where have you been? You keep disappearing. It's kind of pissing me off."

"That's what I came to talk to you about," she says. "I love you, baby girl. I do. But I put my life on hold to help your dad raise you. I wouldn't trade that for anything in the world, but Grandma is done checking homework and grounding your stubborn ass. You're an adult now, and you have Holly. Lord knows Sterling won't be letting her go."

"So you're ditching me?"

"You're ditching me, sweetheart. Pretty soon you'll be off to school in the city." The mention of culinary school is both exciting and scary. San Francisco is a huge city, and life would just be super different there. I wanted to go when Holly and I first talked about her time living in the city, but now I don't know.

"It's not the same," I whine.

"Okay, real talk?" she asks. I nod my head. "I'm tired of hearing my son talking about having sex on every surface in this house. I don't care how old he is—it's not something a mother wants to hear."

"How do you think I feel? It's awful! I have to wipe down every surface before I touch it," I gripe.

"You mean to tell me that you've learned how to clean? Well hell, guess it's not such a tragedy after all. Besides, you're escaping soon enough," she says without any sympathy. "Plus, you don't need me hovering over you all the time. You're grown."

"Congratulations, you're the only person who doesn't think I need supervision anymore." My attitude sucks, I know. But I don't really care. She basically abandoned me with my father. Who does that?

"You are just like your dad. If you two weren't such a pain in my ass, I'd think it was funny. I love you, and I'm not exactly moving out just yet. But this is your dad and Holly's house. They need time and space to be a couple, and I just don't think Holly is ever going to think of it as hers as long as her boyfriend lives with his mom."

I snort because Grandma has a great way of making Dad sound like a loser. I know I'm hard on him, but I can't help myself.

"Can you tell Dad that I'm an adult, please?" I ask.

"Baby girl, I'd need to be twenty years younger to have enough time on this earth to convince him that you're not still five years old. Doesn't matter how beautiful you are or how mature you get. Your dad is always going to see his little pig-tailed, button-nose brat on her first day of kindergarten."

"Well, that sucks," I say. She's trying to be nice, but I want some alone time with Jeremy, damn it, and she's not freaking helping.

"No, baby. It's one of the best things you could ever wish for in life. He's nearing forty, but Sterling is and always will be my baby. I don't care what anybody says. I'll always remember the day he was born, his first day of school, and every other important milestone he's had, and I'll hold those close to my heart."

"Lucky Dad," I say with a biting tone. It's great that she remembers all this shit about my dad, but I'm betting my mom doesn't remember a damn thing about me. Not that she was there for any of my milestones, except my birth. I'm pretty sure she didn't have the option to ditch out of that. Grandma wraps her arms around me and pulls me in. I let myself sink into her and take a deep breath so I don't tear up.

"Missing your mom?" she asks. I shrug my shoulders, not wanting to answer that question. I have nothing to miss, but the idea of Grandma being less available is fucked up. It's making me feel bad, which is why I don't like talking about Layla. "You got screwed out of a mom, but my son got screwed out of a dad. We do the best we can with what we have, and maybe you don't have Layla, but you do have someone damn special."

"My grandma," I say. I press my eyes into her button-up to dry the tears that are forming in my eyes.

"Nah, someone whose clothes you actually want to steal. You have Holly."

"Yeah, I guess I do," I say quietly.

"You might not understand this just yet, but a mother isn't always the one who gives birth to you. She's the one who fights for you even when you don't want her to, and that woman has been fighting for you since before she even met your dad, and when he got in her way, she ran right over him."

She's right. I do have Holly. And Holly does fight for me. In everything. Truth be told, it wasn't until recently that I realized how much Grandma's been gone. She spends a few more minutes telling me how much she loves Holly, not just for Dad, but for me as well. I want to ask her if she's seeing someone, but I figure I can always get it out of Holly later. She's likely to be more truthful anyway.

When she's gone, I slip back into my thoughts. If Grandma's dating, that means everybody around here is getting some except for me. Even my freaking grandmother. People with gray hair and wrinkles should not have a better love life than I do. They really shouldn't.

The last time Jeremy and I snuck away for a little while, we spent a few hours on Glass Beach just watching the water and talking about everything from his favorite superhero as a little boy to my favorite pastry. It's sort of become our spot. Somewhere in there we started talking about the future, but that went to a place I don't really want to go, so I changed the subject, and now I know more about Ryan's relationship drama than I ever wanted to know—not that I wasn't already aware of most of it. The future is a scary subject because there's so much that I want in life, but the only thing I need is Jeremy. And I don't know how to say that without everybody thinking I'm a foolish child who's going to regret her choices. I'd much rather stick my head in the sand and let those pesky school deadlines pass so I can pretend I just missed the admissions cut-off as opposed to the truth—that I can't imagine going to school so far away. Despite how attractive San Francisco once sounded, now it's just too far away.

My fingers move swiftly over the touch screen of my phone as I try to conquer the second castle in Level-V of Candy Castle. I now regret gifting Diesel my extra two lives the game had given me when I hadn't played in a while. I'm low on energy level, and I've made a series of ill-timed moves that have my character's health in the red. My character in the game jumps too soon—due to no fault of my own—and misses the bridge I'm aiming for. A message comes on the screen telling me that I'm out of lives unless I want to buy more credits, so I decide to give up on the game for now. Damn it. I only gave Diesel those lives because he bitched that chicks think he's a good listener and he can't properly concentrate on the game when we're all blabbing in his ears. I had a momentary feeling of guilt that ended with my being more generous than I actually am.

Now that I'm without the distraction of Candy Castle,

I find myself immediately suffering from a bad case of boredom. My fingers twitch and my toes dance in search of purpose. There is nothing to do around this house, except for watching TV or sitting around and talking with the parental units. Neither of which is really all that appealing right now. If I had my way, I'd be lying next to Jeremy, wrapped his arms. Dad gets to live with his girlfriend, so it's pretty fucked up that I can't even have some alone time with my boyfriend. We're both adults for crying out loud. Jeremy isn't allowed in my room, and I'm certainly not allowed in his. Dad's taken the "my house, my rules" thing and extended it beyond the laws of reason. It doesn't matter to him one bit that Jeremy's room is in Duke and Nic's house. We've been pretty lucky so far with Nic. She may not actively lie to Duke about anything, but she certainly isn't rushing to tell him the truth about all of our activities either. And even though Nic's cool about our sneaking off into Jeremy's room for a few minutes, it's never enough. I just want some more alone time with him, and I don't think that's too much to ask.

I check the clock to find that it's after eleven, which means that Dad and Holly are likely in their room. Having sex and the freedom to do whatever they want. Who knows if Grandma is even still in the house.

I pick my phone back up, open the messaging app, and start to type out a text to Jeremy. But then I stop.

I'm a legal fucking adult, and this level of strict supervision isn't necessary. Dad certainly didn't get this kind of supervision from Grandma, and even though I know very little about my mom's family, I know she ran wild. There's no reason I can't clock a few more hours a week with my freaking boyfriend.

Frustration builds, and I find myself lying on my bed and staring at the ceiling while resenting every adult around me. It's not fair. They all get to go out and do whatever they want, whenever they want, and in most cases whoever they want, but God forbid they extend the same courtesies to me.

So screw this crap.

I'm done being the perfect little girl who does most of what she's told. Even though Jeremy has been really understanding with the boundaries so far, I'm getting sick of them. I just want to be able to make my own choices and be treated like the adult everybody tells me I am.

I want to have sex.

Jeremy has had sex, which he doesn't really like to talk about. I'm not really up for hearing about it either, but the irritation of being unable to share that with him is driving me mad. I mean, I guess I know he enjoys it. Otherwise, why would he want to do it all the time? I just want to have that with him. We are so good together in every other way that I want this experience, too.

I've tried to figure things out on my own, for myself, but it's hit or miss. Tracie told me that I could watch YouTube videos about it and that the internet has a wealth of information, but that just seems a little bit too pathetic. It's bad enough to be terrified that I'm not going to be very good for anybody else, but knowing that I can't even be good for myself makes me want to give up entirely. If I can't manage to have sex with Jeremy soon, I'm going to just become asexual, if that's even possible.

Grandma always says practice makes perfect, so I figure it only stands to reason that I should practice before Jeremy and I get so frustrated that we end up giving up on our relationship altogether. Not that I want to think he will dump me if we don't have sex, but I'm not an idiot. He's hot, and he could get it from just about anywhere, especially with that cut on his back. Unfortunately, I know that all too well.

Without thinking, I hop out of bed, shove my phone in my pocket, and grab my sweatshirt from the back of my door. A pair of flip flops rest a few feet over in front of my dresser. I shove them on my feet without even checking to see if I match and slowly open my bedroom door. I'm practiced enough that I make it down the stairs and through the living room and out the front door without triggering the alarm or making much noise. I've timed myself, and I'm now able to get from my bedroom to the front porch and reset the alarm in under forty-five seconds.

Shrill guitar riffs and a heavy drumbeat sound from the basement level where Dad's room is, and I say a little thank-you to whoever is listening, because I know from experience that he can't hear my Bug starting up when his music is that loud. My keys and my license are already in the pocket of my sweatshirt, thankfully. I didn't even think about grabbing them on my way out, which could've turned out really bad. With a practiced ear, I listen to the sound coming from the basement level and wait until the chorus, which seems to be louder than the rest the song. Right when the chorus starts up, I slide into my unlocked Bug, fire the engine, and back down the driveway as quickly as I can without hitting anything. The first few times I tried to sneak out, it was not without disastrous results. I did everything slowly, with fear that I would get caught. But then I finally learned that faster is better, because at least if I get caught, I can get away first and have a chance at freedom. I've since had a much higher success rate.

Jeremy's house is less than a five-minute drive, and there's no traffic in a small, boring town like Fort Bragg. Soon enough, I'm pulling up to the yellow ranch house whose driveway plays host to two Harleys and a Toyota Corolla. The living room light is on, and through the front window, I can see the TV is on as well. I'm hoping Jeremy's not in there, because there's no way I'm going to the front door if Nic and Duke are awake. Nic would keep her mouth shut, but Duke would personally escort me back home. I used to like him, but he's kind of a wet blanket these days.

I opt for parking in front of their neighbor's house in order to avoid getting busted. My stomach flips uneasily with the worry that I might get caught, so I'm particularly quiet as I cross the front lawn and press my nose up to Jeremy's bedroom window.

Somewhere in the back of my mind I wonder if ambushing him like this is a good idea. He could be with another girl. That would break my heart, and as much as I don't want to believe it, I think a part of me is waiting for it to happen. Even Jim screws around on Aunt Ruby at times. I know Uncle Chief was hooking up with Chel on the regular before he died. Aunt Barbara knew about it, and she disliked it, but it was something she accepted. Until I met Holly, I'd never known a woman who had demanded exclusivity. Most just demand silence.

I can't see much of anything through the shrouded

window. There seems to be little movement in the room, if any. Holding in a deep breath, I check my nerves and tap the window just hard enough to make a distinct clicking sound against the glass. Anticipation builds in my gut, and my hands practically shake. I'm working myself up into a frenzy over a fear I don't know I'll ever be able to shake.

CHAPTER 20

March

13 months to Mancuso's downfall

Cheyenne

THE AGED FOREST-GREEN curtains rustle from behind the glass and swoop to the side, revealing Jeremy's tired face. He looks like he's been put through the ringer, which motivates me to get through this glass barrier and wrap my arms around him that much faster. He blinks twice before smiling wide and working the window open with fast, knowledgeable movements.

"Hey," he says as he slides the glass to the side and reaches an arm out. His fingers curl around the back of my head as he pulls me in for a kiss. I slide my lips over his and savor the calm that overtakes my entire body. This is right. This is us.

I want him more than I've ever wanted anything before. I lift my arms up and pull him in closer, needing more. My tongue traces the inside curves of his bottom lip. He opens to me immediately and gives a low growling noise. It's the same noise he makes when I know he wants to go further but restrains himself for my benefit. Pulling away slowly, I lick my lips and look into his hazy eyes. My heart practically thumps out of my chest, and my palms are sweaty when I place them on the window sill.

"Help me in," I say. My foot finds purchase on the brick retaining wall that holds the budding yellow daisies that Duke had a few prospects plant for Nic. I'm careful not to disturb the flowers as Jeremy reaches out and helps guide me in the window and around the crap he has piling up on his bedroom floor. Once I'm inside with my feet firmly on the carpet, I snake my arms around his neck and grin up at him.

Jeremy's wearing sweat pants and an aging Forsaken Custom Cycle T-Shirt. His hair is damp and slicked back from his face. He always looks good in my eyes, but right now he's especially attractive. Maybe it's because I've had a sort of epiphany since the last time I saw him.

"What's wrong?" he asks. His brows draw together, and a scowl forms on his face. I notice the beginnings of a nasty bruise on his temple that extends down to his cheekbone. With a light touch, I trace the slight discoloration of the bruise. I hate seeing him hurt, especially not knowing how it happened. I don't ask because it's club business, and I'd rather not be told that. He knows I only want to know if it has to do with Mindy's rape. The rest is up to him whether or not he feels he needs to share.

"Nothing. I just wanted to be with you," I say and let my fingers slide from the bruise on his face down the line of his jaw to his chin and then down his throat to the center of his chest. He's silent and fully aware of my touch, but he doesn't move. For weeks now, we've been dancing around the physical aspects of our relationship, sometimes careful, sometimes cautious of the limitations of privacy. Now that I've staged my breakout and I'm here, I just want him. No explanations, no talking—nothing. Just him and me, together in a way I don't want to be with anyone else.

I step out of my sandals and then slowly unzip my hoodie. Jeremy watches me cautiously, like he's not sure I'm really here in the room with him. The hoodie falls to the floor. My hands shake as I lift my shirt over my head to reveal my old and faded sports bra. It's not what I expected I'd be wearing the first time I had sex, but that's okay. It feels right with him. In fact, I can't imagine it being right or better with anyone else.

Jeremy's eyes widen just slightly before he regains his composure and purses his lips in appreciation. I give him a soft smile and slowly unbutton my jeans. They slide down my legs and collect at my feet. My thighs feel like Jell-O as I step out of them. My panties aren't the newest in my collection either. So that kind of sucks, but he doesn't seem to mind.

Following my lead, Jeremy reaches up over the back of his head and pulls his shirt off and lets it fall beside him. His sweats are next, leaving him in a pair of light gray boxers. Despite his experience, he seems as nervous as I am, which actually soothes my nerves some.

"Are you sure?" His voice is full of hope and restraint. I've barely nodded my head before he's on me with one hand on my ass and the other tilting my head up to kiss him. Rubbing my thighs together and pressing myself even further into him, I relish in the feeling of his hard dick. Jeremy gets hard about as often as I assume any teenage boy does, but it's something altogether different when I'm enticing him on purpose.

I reach up and press my lips against his. Our kiss soon evolves from something chaste that we manage to sneak in when Dad's not looking to a wild frenzy of tongues and lips and even a clank of our teeth. We smile together through the kiss and slow our movements. Jeremy's hands move up and down my nearly naked body, caressing my pliant flesh. I press into his warm skin and bask in his muscled frame. He's always been well built, but the last several months of maintaining a rigorous weight-lifting routine is paying off big time. He reaches around and unhooks the wide clasp of my bra. Any other sports bra and I'd be awkwardly trying to shimmy out of it and likely elbowing him in the eye. A bundle of nervous anticipation, I hold my breath until my lungs strain for air, trying to be grateful for at least having chosen accessible, if not pretty, undergarments.

"It's okay, baby," he whispers, putting me at ease.

"I've just been thinking about this for so long." I drop my shoulders and peel my bra away. It falls to the floor without a sound.

"You think about this?" he asks with a husky voice. He keeps his attention on my face, surprisingly, and doesn't let it veer toward my chest. Somewhere in the back of my mind, I expected him to practically maul me. But he isn't, and the fact that he's being so slow and gentle makes me more confident in what I'm doing. I just have to get past the wobbly feeling in my knees, and then maybe I'll be able to fully enjoy it.

We slowly and awkwardly peel away the remainder of one another's clothing. My panties and then his boxers join the rest of our clothes on the floor. I've fantasized about having this with him. I've even tried to plan it. None of those fantasies or plans worked out so well. We kept getting busted and thwarted at every turn.

Feeling brave, I reach down between us to feel him, but he guides my hand back up at the elbow.

"I love you," he blurts out. His navy-blue eyes slide over mine, his brows draw together, and his expression darkens. His arms lock in place, and it's like he's turned to stone.

Then I realize that he's told me he loves me. And I'm standing here like an idiot. I breathe in deeply, smile widely, and laugh happily like a moron.

"I'm naked," I whisper with wet eyes.

"I mean it," he says. "I love you."

I nod my head before realizing that I should probably say something back. I barely get the words out as I say, "I'm so totally in love with you."

He smiles in a way I've never seen. The corners of his eyes crinkle slightly, and his cheeks are so high up on his face it almost looks painful. The nervous energy fades into the background as we move toward the bed, still holding one another, and still smiling. Kissing is great, but this is better. As he lays me on his bed, I try not to think about how he learned his moves. The way he runs his hands up and down my thighs to the light touch over my dark brown curls sends blissful waves through my entire body. His lips press light, purposeful kisses to every peak and valley of my pale flesh, and when he finally crawls up my naked frame, I wrap my hand around his silk-soft member as he shows me how to roll on a condom. Everything about this is as perfect as perfect can be. Bringing him inside of me stings for a moment before it dulls to a raw ache. Still, I won't let him stop. No pain could make this so uncomfortable that I wouldn't want this with him.

Through all the new sensations and the buzz of my building orgasm, I make myself a promise that I won't ever leave him and I won't ever hurt him.

IT'S NEARLY THREE in the morning when I realize that I really need to get home. Dad won't stand for my being out all night, especially if he finds where I've gone. Not that he would have any doubts. Duke and Nic—but more importantly, Robin—are all asleep, so once we're dressed, Jeremy leads me out the front door. It feels slightly more respectable than sneaking in his bedroom window.

When I pull up to the house, I breathe a sigh of relief that all the lights are off. Thankfully it seems like Dad and Holly are tucked safely in their bed. I cut the engine and slowly climb out of the car. My thighs are sore and I feel little bit grimy, but I wouldn't change it for the world. Being with Jeremy like that was better than I even could have imagined.

I want to do it again. Only, I hope it doesn't hurt so much next time. And maybe next time I'll actually orgasm and it won't fade away at the last moment.

The front door unlocks with ease, and I cancel the alarm before it makes a sound. If Dad really wants to keep me in the house all night, he should probably change the code. I'm way too good at this for his own good.

I make it past the kitchen and into the living room, at the foot of the stairs, before it happens. The light switch clicks, and the room is suddenly basked in artificial light from one of the end-table lamps. I've been caught sneaking out and sneaking back in before, so that's not such a big deal. It's the fact that my hair is a complete disaster, I'm pretty sure I have a few hickeys on my neck, and I smell like Jeremy that worries me.

"You better have a good fucking explanation for this," Dad says.

I still haven't turned around to meet his eyes, both out of fear and embarrassment. My heart beats loudly in my chest, and my hands shake at my sides. This is going to be bad.

With a stiff upper lip, I turn around and face my fears. Dad is wearing a pair of his old black sweatpants that Grandma's asked him to throw away more times than I can count. As always, he hasn't worn a shirt to bed, and his wavy hair is pointing in a hundred different directions.

"I'm an adult," I say. Something moves in the corner of the room, and it's only then that I notice Holly in the chair by the fireplace. She's wearing one of Dad's big T-shirts and, from the looks of it, nothing else. Of course it's okay for him to have sex with his girlfriend, but it's not okay for me to have sex with my boyfriend. At least we've had enough respect for household furnishings not to do it on the fucking kitchen table. He is such a hypocrite.

"You are way too wrapped up in that boy," he says. He folds his arms over his chest and shakes his head. I can tell that he's trying his best to hold back his temper, but it looks like it's barely working. That's okay because my temper is shot, so this is about to get real good.

"What's your problem with me and Jeremy? Is it because I want to spend every minute with him? Is it because I don't want to be away from him? What is it, Dad?"

"Yeah," he says. His tone is more biting than it was a moment ago, but that's probably in reaction to mine.

"Then what the hell are you doing with Holly? You're always together, you hate to be away from her. You live together. If I need to take a step back, so do you."

I think I'm going to throw up. My stomach is uneasy, and my back is stiff. I don't talk to Dad like this very often, and when I do, we always end up in an enormous fight that leaves us not speaking for weeks at a time.

"What did you just say to me?" he barks and strides across the room so fast that I almost don't expect it when he's in my face and breathing rank breath down on my cheeks. My stomach flips, and my body feels like it's weighted down with hundreds of pounds of concrete. I just want to sink to the floor and play dead.

"I love him," I whisper. Because I do, and Dad needs to know it.

"What about school?" he asks.

"I got my GED. I can work in town." I know how it sounds to his ears, even if I don't want to admit it. It sounds like I'm giving up my dream of culinary school to stay in town with a boy. But it's more than that. So much more.

"Fuck that," he says. His eyes travel down to my neck where, sure enough, he spots the bruises that are forming. "He use anything tonight besides you?"

"We were careful, and he didn't use me," I yell, leaning in to him. I know men Dad's size and bigger who won't say a cross word to him. I wouldn't piss him off if I wore a patch either. But I don't, and I'm not afraid of him. "He loves me."

"The hell he does," Dad seethes. "You gonna feel real grown up when your dad shows up and rips his dick off? You gonna feel like an adult then, huh, Chey?

"Is this the first time?" he asks. I'm tempted not to tell him. It's none of his business, but this is bad enough. Refusing to answer is only going to earn us a longer fight and a trip to Nic and Duke's, which will wake up the baby. And that, I've learned, is worse than scratching Duke's bike. Sleep is precious these days in that house.

"Yes," I say. Tears well in my eyes. This isn't how the night of my first time was supposed to go. I was supposed to crawl into bed and reminisce about it, not stand here and fight with my dad over something this private.

Asshole. He is such an asshole.

"Is this shit the reason you haven't applied to that school you been talking about?"

"I changed my mind. I just don't want to go anymore."

I can't tell him that I've not gotten far enough on Mindy's case to leave. I can't tell him that I want to be here when he and Holly have a baby—because she's so going to snow him into that one. I can't tell him any of this, so we go back and forth and back again. He asks a question, and I respond with increasingly unkind words. I don't want to talk about this with him, but even if I run upstairs, he'll just follow me. Because he won't listen, and I can't find the words he needs to understand.

"You're throwing your future away for a boy who isn't going to give a shit in six months. You want me to stop getting in your business, then you need to start making better choices."

"You're wrong," I say through falling tears. "He loves me."

"I'll bet he thinks he does," he says. "But you're going to school. Holly has worked too hard to keep you on track with your education for you to throw it away because you want some asshole's attention. As it is, you had to get your GED because you couldn't get your ass to class."

"It's not like that," I wail. I don't even bother to wipe the tears away. Every word he says is meaner than the last. They slam into my gut and practically pierce my heart one after the other. He needs to stop before his words split me in two. Maybe if he knew the reason I missed so many classes he would understand. Maybe then he wouldn't look so disgusted with me. No, then I'd have to deal with the entire club's disapproval.

"I was eighteen once," he says. "It's always like that. He wanted your pussy, and now that he's got it, he's going to leave you behind. He's Forsaken now, Chey. He won't be faithful." Dad's words have fallen to a whisper. His shoulders have dropped, and the intensity of the moment has passed. He just looks pained.

Good. Misery loves company.

"I'm not going to leave him no matter what you say," I mutter through a series of hiccups. "You don't get it. It's painful thinking about going away, and I won't do it to him or to me. I love him, sometimes so much it hurts. It feels like it's crushing me from the inside out."

"You are going to regret this," Dad says. "I don't want you to make the same mistakes I did."

I sniffle and wipe my nose. Dad reaches out to hug me, but the last thing I want is his comfort. I just want Jeremy.

Dad backs up and blows out a heavy breath. I shake my head at him as I pass and head for the front door. On my way out, I hear him calling for Holly, who screams something at him before her voice trails off, probably downstairs to their bedroom. I hope she's angry at him for how shitty he just was to me. But even if she is, I'm not all that happy with her for sitting in the corner and not saying or doing a fucking thing. So much for having my back.

I'm back in my car and speeding to Jeremy once again. This time when I pull up, I park in the driveway and don't bother cutting the lights until I turn the car off. The porch light flicks on, so somebody is obviously still awake. As if he sensed me coming, Jeremy opens the front door wearing only his boxers. I run out of the car and let the tears fall openly as I crash into him. He wraps his strong arms around me, holding me to his chest.

"What's wrong?" he asks. Concern fills his voice.

"My dad, he... he wants me to go to culinary school. I don't want to leave you. Not ever." I sound like a whiny baby who isn't getting her way, but I don't care. This is Jeremy. He isn't going to think I'm stupid.

"Don't go," he says lowly. It sounds so easy. To just not go and defy my dad. But then what happens to me? Where do I live? What if Dad actually makes me go? What if Jeremy gets in trouble for all of this—because of me? What if he realizes he's not the only reason I want to stay? That aside from Mindy, my jerky father and Holly, and Grandma, I'm terrified to be so far away from the club. Up until recently, I'd always felt safe here. But regardless of what's going on, I have to be safer here than anywhere else. San Francisco is huge, and nobody will know they're not to mess with me. Nobody will know me, and nobody will care when they hear my last name.

"Stop worrying, baby." He kisses my forehead and then my eyebrow and my cheek. He tilts my head back and places a final kiss on my lips.

"But what if he tries to make me go?" I need some reassurance and maybe even some muscle here. I can fight Dad to the end of the earth, but at the end of the day, he has the cash to keep me in the finer things in life—like food and electricity.

Jeremy becomes still, and his grip on my chin tightens. I'm about to say something to him, but then he opens his mouth. He's working through something in his head, but then he speaks. And he blows me away.

"We'll get married. Tonight. Just run away with me and fucking marry me."

"You mean it?" I ask. "You want to marry me?"

"More than anything," he whispers and rubs his nose against mine.

Voices sound from the other side of the open front door—one masculine and one feminine. We've woken up Duke and Nic, but I don't give a damn. As long as we don't wake up Robin, I don't think they can be too mad. Still, the look on Nic's face is murderous. The extra baby weight she hasn't lost yet shows through her nightgown, emphasized by the way she folds her arms over her chest and purses her lips. Duke looks too exhausted to even swat at a fly, and I say a silent prayer for that. I've heard him yelling at Jeremy before, and there's no doubt that Robin gets her set of lungs from her dad, even if Duke begs to differ.

"Knuck know you're here?" Duke asks through a yawn.

"Yeah," I say because he'd be stupid to think I'd go anywhere else. Duke will check with Dad, I know he will, so at least the cranky asshole won't think I'm dead in a ditch somewhere.

"Then come in, shut the fuck up, and don't wake up my kid," he says slowly, losing his train of thought halfway through only to recapture it a moment later.

"I have ways to make you both wish you were fucking dead if my baby wakes up before she's supposed to," Nic says and drags Duke down the hallway to their bedroom.

Gulping, I look at Jeremy nervously and whisper, "How does she know when Robin is supposed to wake up?" As far as I know, babies are unpredictable little creatures.

"She doesn't," he whispers and takes my hand as he leads me toward his bedroom. "So I hope you like baby duty, because they're going to find a way to get out of changing the next dirty diaper."

"I gave you my virginity, Jeremy Whelan. The least you can do is spare me a poopy diaper," I whisper-shout as I carefully close his bedroom door behind me.

I want Jeremy as my old man, and I want to be his old lady. I want what Duke and Nic have and what Ryan has with Alex—that deep kind of love you fight and sacrifice for. I want what Dad and Holly have and what Uncle Jim and Aunt Ruby have—the kind of love that doesn't have to make sense and can last forever—and I'll crawl over their destroyed Harleys to do it.

CHAPTER 21

April

12 months to Mancuso's downfall

Jeremy

I FLASH MY girl a million-dollar grin and wiggle my brows, saying, "Mrs. Whelan."

Her smile is blinding, so fucking wide it's practically ear to ear, and she giggles a high-pitched giggle that morphs into a squeal. It's not quite four in the morning, and if she's up for it, I could totally go a round before we crash. She recognizes the change in my demeanor—from playful to pervy—and her expression darkens.

"We should probably, you know, practice for our wedding night," she says through a quiet laugh that tapers off.

I lunge for her, causing another round of squeals. I'm careful with my landing so I don't crush her with my weight. She wiggles to the center of the bed as I swiftly brace my landing with my elbows on either side of her head and my knees propping up my lower half. She parts her legs for me, letting me slide between them. She's completely dressed, and that just won't do.

Just as I'm unbuttoning the top of her jeans, Robin starts wailing from Nic and Duke's room. Her cry is so damn loud you'd think somebody was stabbing her or something. I actually used to worry that she was hurt when I'd hear her cry, because fuck if I knew what a baby's cries are supposed to sound like. But now, after even a week, I can figure most of her noises out. She's just hungry, or maybe she wants to be held right now. I don't really know, but it's getting easier to figure out that she's not sick or something—she just makes it sound like she is.

"Crap," Chey whispers. "We should probably just try to get some sleep. If Robin's awake, so are Nic and Duke."

"They're not going—"

My bedroom door swings open. My heart spasms in surprise. In the open doorway is Duke, who is wearing only a pair of worn flannel boxers and holding a whimpering infant in his arms. His eyes are narrowed and rimmed by purple bags that appeared right around the time the little ball of chub did and haven't gone away since. Dude looks like shit, and Nic doesn't look much better these days.

"Woke up the baby," he says. His expression is anything but pleased, and his voice is flat. "I should shoot you both."

"I, uh, I'm sorry," Cheyenne says quietly. Her eyes travel from his tired face to Robin's small body.

Duke catches the change of focus and turns his attention back to me. A small smile forms on his lips before it's gone and he looks at Cheyenne. His feet carry him toward us. Every foot he gets closer, I move farther away from Chey, until I'm sitting up at the other end of the bed. She scurries to sit up and pull her shirt down to cover the open top button of her jeans.

When he's close enough, he leans forward and extends Robin out to Chey. It takes her a moment to catch on, but once she does, she carefully scoops Robin into her arms and holds her safely tucked to her chest. Duke mumbles, "You wake her, you hold her," as he turns and leaves the room.

Cheyenne's face is turned down toward my infant niece. She's a cute baby as far as babies go. I mean, she doesn't really look like a conehead anymore, and when I talk to her, she listens. Not sure her mom and dad would like the words I'm teaching her, but that's part of what being an uncle is about—teaching the kid shit her parents won't. Chey shushes and coos at Robin until her discontented cries become restless squawks. She turns into Chey's chest, opening and closing her mouth in frustration.

"What is she doing?" Chey says with wide downcast eyes. Her arms are stiff, like she has no clue how to hold a baby. I'd actually be surprised if she did. As far as I know she has less experience with babies than I do. The kid's on like day eight of life and has produced an obscene number of dirty diapers, at least half of which I've had the pleasure of fucking dealing with.

"She's just hungry," I say and glance at Robin for just a moment. "Every time she gets around tits, she tries to eat."

"Is she bigger than the last time I saw her?" she asks. Her voice is soft, so soft in fact that I can barely hear her words over Robin's crying. She tilts her head to the side and gives Robin a soft smile. "Sorry, kiddo, I can't really help you out."

"She can tell you don't know what the fuck you're doing," I say and gesture for her to hand the kid over. She's going to be pissed until she gets fed, but at least she has baby ADHD or something and can be distracted by other shit, which shuts her up for at least one single fucking minute. Chey turns toward me but doesn't move to hand her over. She was just as fucking awkward when she held her at the hospital. When Chey's eyes meet mine, I instantly feel like an asshole. She looks hurt, and I'm not so stupid to think it's not because I'm an insensitive prick.

Reaching out and taking Robin into my arms, I say, "You just need more practice. Watch me." I cradle Robin to my chest with one arm and wrap the other around her side so she doesn't wiggle away from me. She's not wiggling yet, but Nic's read that she will at some point, and fuck if I'm going to drop Duke's kid. I'm still paying for that scratch on his bike. Keeping my arms relaxed, I put a hand under her butt to do this pat-bounce thing that gets her moving a little and calms her down. She whimpers between cries, and she even cuts out the short screams.

"Babe, you're nervous, and she can tell," I say and try to give her a small smile. The sad look on her face changes into something different, something hopeful.

"You're good with her," she says, reaching out and running the back of her pointer finger over Robin's cheek.

"Shit," I say and make a funny face at the baby. "You listen to those screams every few hours, and you'll be trying anything to shut her up." I give Robin a glare, and even though I've been told at least twenty times that she's too young, I swear she's fucking smiling through her tears. Chey won't know she's too young to smile, so I tip her toward Chey and say, "She's smiling because she knows she's a shithead."

My girl blushes before stumbling over her words. "Do you want kids?"

I stop breathing, stop moving—even doing the pat-bounce. I don't know what to say to that. Heard it from a couple of the brothers before. Don't ever mention marriage to a chick unless you're ready to have kids, because that's all she can see in her future. Probably should have listened to that shit before opening my mouth.

"I want to be a mom," she says.

Fuck. I still can't move, and Robin's starting to scream again. She's greedy with the pat-bounce, so I force myself to make my hand move. It barely calms her.

"Not now, but someday," she clarifies.

"Eh, why not," I say like it's no big deal. "I'll be a fucking pro at this shit by the time I'm thirty."

"Thirty is probably young enough to have kids," she says through a yawn. And I swear, my fucking heart starts beating again, and I relax my arms around Robin. "Let me try again," she says and reaches for her. I hand her over, hoping Chey's better with her this time, because that crying has got to fucking go. When she cradles Robin against her chest, she moves her around a bit before settling in and doing the pat-bounce. Robin is still crying, but it's nothing like before.

"There you go," I say and smile at her.

"I can't believe my mom didn't stick around for this," she mumbles. She doesn't talk about her mom, but for some reason she is right now. I don't got shit to say because my mom didn't stick around either. It's not like I have anything encouraging to say. "Nic's probably going to remember every single thing about her daughter, from her favorite color to her worst nightmare."

"Yeah, I give her shit, but Nic's like a fucking grizzly about the kid. She's a good mom."

"I'm glad Robin has that," she says.

"Me, too."

Duke strides back into the room with a baby bottle full of pumped breast milk in one hand and the last bite of a sandwich in the other. He shoves the final bite in his mouth and chews like his life depends on it. Fucking asshole made himself a sandwich while his kid is in here having a fucking fit. He places his pointer finger over the nipple of the bottle and shakes it up a little. I always try to avoid Nic when she's pumping. It's just awkward. It's not like I like to look at my sister's tits. They're just there, and it's just... uncomfortable.

Duke bends in front of Chey and takes Robin in his

arms and then swiftly shoves the nipple of the bottle into her eager mouth. She sucks at it vigorously, and her red face calms to her normal pink. She's pretty for a baby.

"You made a fucking sandwich?" I can't keep the irritation from my voice.

"Fuck you," he says. "We're on the same feeding schedule, and if I had to depend on your sister to feed me, I'd starve. Besides, she was in good hands."

I go to open my mouth and argue, but I can't. Not only is he not making excuses with the club, but he's putting his time in at the shop, and he gets up at least once every night to feed the baby. Dad would have mad respect for him if he were here, and knowing that Duke trusts me with his most prized possession means something to me. He knows she annoys me, but I won't let a goddamn thing hurt her.

I also don't tell him that Nic knows how to cook but just chooses not to. He'd have a huge-ass fit, and it's not worth how funny it would be.

"Can you tell Uncle Jeremy to wrap his shit so he doesn't give you any cousins?" Duke says as he snuggles her in his arms. He doesn't do that baby voice shit or anything. He just talks to her like she's an adult, and he doesn't even bother to censor his language.

I think I vaguely remember my mom chastising my dad for cursing in front of us when I was little, but I have so many memories I'm not certain actually happened. For years I could have sworn Mom came back to visit us one Christmas. Nic and Dad are adamant it didn't happen, but in my heart it's as real as anything else. The fact that I can't distinguish fiction from reality fucks me up just enough so that I try to numb out all of my memories from when I was a kid. Something about being around someone and their mom is a big fucking reminder of all the shit I never got. I just hope Chey doesn't feel half of what I do right now, because between Nic and Robin and Ruby and Alex, I'm all kinds of fucked up and moody.

"We, um." Chey's cheeks are bright red, and she's trying to babble, but she's so embarrassed by Duke's comment—which I've heard before, mind you—that she can't even make her tongue work well enough to babble.

"Right, of course you can't talk," he says flatly, his eyes completely focused on her. "You're eating." Like if her mouth wasn't preoccupied she could actually talk. I don't say shit about the fact that he has full conversations with her. It's goofy as fuck, but it makes my sister smile, and the more she smiles, the less she bitches.

"You heard me?" he says as he lifts his head. "I'm not fucking kidding. Club's got enough fucking drama. We don't need you knocking up Knuck's daughter on top of it. I change enough goddamn diapers around this house."

Liar. Every chance he gets, he passes the dirty diapers off on me. If a crying baby isn't a suitable reminder to wrap my dick, the nasty mudslides she creates are plenty sufficient.

"I know how to wrap my shit," I say and nod to the baby in his arms. "Seems I should be giving you the talk about safe sex."

Chey squirms uncomfortably beside me, but she remains silent. I wish Duke hadn't jumped to the conclusion that we've had sex, but it's not like there's anything I can say to stop him from making this awkward, so it wouldn't matter anyway.

"Riding your sister bare is one of life's greatest joys."

"Dude. Shut the fuck up. That's nasty," I gripe and scrub my face with my hands, ignoring the pain from the bruise that's forming. I'm fucking tired, and the sun is going to be up soon.

"Seriously, though. No fucking when I'm awake. Makes me feel all parental and shit, like I should be stopping it or giving pointers or something."

Because when Duke isn't yelling, he's finding ways to make me consider hanging myself. Fucking prick.

"Really? Even if I had the energy to pound one out, your kid killed the mood," I say.

He grins. He fucking grins.

"Oh my God, shut up!" Chey snaps. Her face is still beet red, but she's giving me a look that even I know to interpret as I'm definitely not getting laid again anytime soon. Maybe not even on our wedding night—whenever that might be. I know I said tonight, but I need sleep, and maybe we can wait until tomorrow or the next day to do it. I have to figure out how to even go about doing it.

Wedding night. Shit, that makes it real.

Duke walks Robin out of the room and tells her through muffled yawns that she has to be quiet because if Nic wakes up, then nobody is going to get any peace. Word, brother. Motherfucking word. Before he makes it into the hallway, he turns back and says, "Got that job later today."

"I remember." Of course I fucking remember. Today's

the day I help the club right a very big fucking wrong. Thankfully Chey's yawning, and her eyelids are dropping. She's not paying the least bit of attention to us anymore.

Slowly, I climb off my bed, cross the room, and shut my bedroom door that Duke so rudely left open. My body drags, and my thoughts are scattered and barely make any sense.

When I turn back to Chey, she shakes her head slowly in obvious judgment and says, "I'm going to sleep." She hogs more than her share of my twin bed and hogs my pillow.

I mutter to myself about being too tired for anything anyway. It's only half a lie, and I feel like crashing the minute I crawl in bed beside her. My mind is racing with everything coming up tomorrow, from the job with Duke to the whole getting married thing. It takes way too long to fall asleep, and when I do, it's not a deep sleep by any means.

When I wake, all I can think about is being married and what that means. I'm getting married, and I don't even know how it works or what to do. The sudden panic that overtakes me is almost painful, but I try to smile through it and grit my teeth as Chey slowly comes to life. I want to do this—for her, for me—but for some reason I feel like I'm about to shit my pants. Thank fucking God Duke and I got shit to do today.

CHAPTER 22

April

12 months to Mancuso's downfall

Jeremy

CHEYENNE HOLDS MY cut in her hands, clutching it furiously against her chest as she glares at me. Her eyes scan my appearance, appraising the plain black hoodie I'm wearing and the dirty, gray ball cap that rests on my head, covering my dark brown hair. In all this black and plain shit, the only thing that really looks like me are my eyes. They're still that same dark blue that gets chicks wet even from a distance. But the thing that defines me most is in my girl's hands.

I can't wear my cut into that hospital, and it pisses me off.

"But you wear it everywhere," Chey says with a ruffled brow. I can't tell her why—it's an order—but she's not making it very fucking easy to keep my mouth shut. I just want to get in, get out, and get back here for a fucking nap.

"I just can't, okay?" I snap. Because, shit, I already want to wear my cut and can't, and now she's giving me the riot act over it. Cheyenne's green eyes bore into mine, making me feel like shit. I don't like not telling her shit, but Duke said not to. Nic knows what we're doing, but not because he wanted to tell her. She has a pushy fucking temperament and outright asked him when Forsaken was going to finish the job on Darren one too many times, and the dude cracked. With any other chick, I'd say he was pussy whipped, but I know my sister, and it's a fucking miracle he held out as long as he did.

"I want to tell you things, okay, baby? I want you to know what's going on and the shit we get into, but I can't. I have orders." I let the words fall between us and allow the tension in the room to rise. Something about this is upsetting to Chey in a way I didn't expect. She's always been Forsaken, and that means she knows when to go along with the program, but she's not doing it right now. "Why are you this upset over my cut?"

"Last time Dad left the house on a job and he didn't wear his cut, he got locked up for thirteen months and seventeen days," she says firmly.

My shoulders fall, and I cross the room, immediately wrapping her in my arms. She's still clutching my cut to her chest, both limbs and leather squished between us as I hold on to her like my life depends on it.

"I sound crazy," she admits. And yeah, she does, but fuck if I don't like it. She's worried about me, and she doesn't want me to get hurt or to get locked up. For that, I'll take crazy.

"I'm coming back to you tonight," I say and place a kiss to her forehead. Reluctantly, I release her and take a step back. She gives me a nod and a fake smile. It's not confident enough for me to believe it, but it's going to have to be enough for now.

When I turn to leave, Nic is waiting in the doorway with Robin in her carrier. She and I have never been especially affectionate, but something's changed since she gave birth. Before, she was always so tough and mean and bitchy. But now she's someone's mother. She fusses over my niece the way I hope our mother cared for us when we were infants. I can't imagine Nic leaving her kid, though. Not with the way she watches her sleep and checks on her breathing. Seeing this side of my sister makes me want to be better to her and for her. I didn't expect to feel any different about the whole baby thing after she was born, but I do. Robin is this tiny little human, and she can't do a damn thing for herself. It's up to us—all of us—to be good to her. I want to be good for her, just not with any more fucking diapers.

As I pass, Nic reaches out and places her hand on my covered bicep and says, "Let's go." The ferocity in her eyes is surprising, and I choose not to argue.

Robin and her carrier are kind of heavy, so I don't know how she balances it without any issue, but she does. My sister has taken every bit of her anger and protective nature and channeled it into being the mother I wish I had. Her conviction takes hold of me in a vice grip of emotion, but all I can do is nod. Everything that led up to Darren's hospital stay floods my mind. He threatened to beat the baby out of Nic that night. So cold and calculating in his abuse, Darren had wanted to make not just Nic suffer, but her baby as well. And because of him, Mindy and Holly suffered, too.

I zoom down the hall and through the living room to the front door where Duke is standing with the front door wide open. He's leaning against the doorframe, his expression flat, and he's fiddling with his phone. Without looking up, he says, "When I say to be ready at noon, I fucking mean twelve o'clock, not ten after."

"Sorry," I mumble and slip past him out the door, trying to get away from the blowup Nic's about to cause by tagging along. Meeting up with me, Duke shoves his elbow into my side. He looks up from his phone for a moment, digs into his jean pocket, and tosses the keys to the black van at me. I catch them easily and walk to the street where the club's van is parked. The same van he and I used to dump Darren in his daddy dearest's driveway.

"Quit apologizing. You sound like a fucking pussy," he says. I climb into the driver's seat of the van and start her up just as Duke climbs into the passenger side.

"Okay." If Duke wants me to stop apologizing, then I will stop fucking apologizing. I wish I could stop screwing up, but that's unlikely.

Nic approaches the van and gives Duke a huge grin as she catches his eye. Just when I think Duke's going to fucking lose it because she's taking their newborn on a job, he smiles at her and reaches back to open the door for her.

"Least you could do, asshole," Nic says, and she

climbs in and settles Robin's carrier into its base in the seat directly behind mine. If I had noticed the base of the car seat was already in here, maybe I wouldn't have been about to piss myself at the fight I was sure would ensue.

"You're cool with this shit?" I ask Duke.

He shrugs his shoulders. "Let's just call it 'Take Your Daughter to Work Day.' "

"Chill, Jer," Nic says, buckling up and shutting the door. "You two need a reason to be at the hospital."

The drive to the hospital is quiet, so quiet in fact that it starts to get tense inside the van. I hate when any of the brothers are this silent, because it means they're thinking about shit—likely shit I've done wrong—and that usually leads to bitch duty. I fucking hate bitch duty, mostly because I usually end up on bitch duty with my sister. And if there is one woman on this planet who doesn't like to be watched over, it's her.

Upon our arrival, I swing around to the maternity ward and park in the underground garage. Last week when Nic delivered Robin, we scoped out the best point of entry and found the fewest number of cameras between here and Darren's room. Nic dislodges Robin's carrier from the base and climbs out of the van with her in tow. Duke and I hop out and meet her on the passenger side.

Duke eyes me and says, "Nic's going to cause a distraction while you and I pop into Jennings's room and take care of business."

"Mercer's got a uniform on Jennings's room." I've gone over this again and again in my head and don't know how the fuck we're going to work this out. "Not to mention hospital security."

"You're so fucking new," Nic says with a snicker.

Duke smirks at his girl and takes the carrier from her hands. He peers down at Robin and makes a funny face for her. "Your butt buddy is taking care of security. Gonzales is on Jennings, and she'll leave to take care of Nic."

"Would you fucking quit with that shit? Trigger's got a hard-on for my ass, and the last fucking thing I need is you reminding me of that shit."

"Relax, Jer. I don't think he really wants to fuck your ass," Nic says.

Duke purses his lips and looks down at Nic. "Do not get yourself arrested."

She smiles.

"I mean it, babe. That's a fucking order. Distract them—that's all."

Nic takes Robin back and heads for the hospital while mumbling something about ignoring Duke when he gets bossy. The sappy fuck just smiles at her as she walks away bitching. Fuck, I hope I don't look like that.

Nic beelines for the nurse's station in the maternity ward, raising her voice as she gets closer to the large wraparound desk. She's screeching about fevers and poisonous diapers and something about toxic formula. She even sounds like she's crying. Christ, she's a fucking psychopath if she can turn that shit on that quick.

Duke and I dart down a hallway in the opposite direction and through two sets of heavy double doors that signal our exit and entrance into different departments. The hall is lined with Critical Care patient rooms. Right next to a life support station that houses a defibrillation machine and a few locked boxes of shit I'd love to get my hands on is a closed and unmarked door. I stride up to it and push it open, revealing a set of narrow stairs that Duke and I dart up as quickly as we can. By the time we reach the third floor where Darren's room is, I'm huffing and puffing and ready to pass the hell out. But Duke? No, that motherfucker takes a deep breath and smiles at me.

"Your sister gives me a fucking workout every goddamn night," he says.

As gross as it is, I know that's not true right now. "Liar. I read that book. You got another five weeks before you can bust a nut." I shove my way out into the hallway, desperate to get away from this conversation. I didn't want to read that book—swear to Christ I didn't—but Nic made me. And fuck babies. Fuck riding a chick bare. Fuck it all. A bitch's asshole should only get torn because she's getting pounded too hard, not because a leechy human is escaping her vagina.

Fuck.

No.

At the end of the hall is Detective Angel Gonzales. When she spots us, she nods her head and leaves her post for the small desk that passes for a nurse's station in this two-bit hospital. Informing the nurse of an issue downstairs, Gonzales asks for backup in figuring out what's going on. The nurse is angled away from us, facing a filing cabinet behind the desk. She huffs and explains that she's not to leave her post. I slip behind a thick square pillar near Jennings's room and make room for Duke. He and I each pull out a pair of black gloves and slip them on.

No fingerprints.

The doors to the rooms beep, so we have to wait it out until Gonzales gets rid of the nurse. It takes longer than it should before Gonzales gets her out of here and they disappear into the elevator.

Duke shoots out from behind the pillar and into Jennings's room. The door beeps on entrance, and I grab ahold of the handle to slip in behind him. Jennings is lying in the bed in the center of the private room. He's looking pretty good for a guy who got fucked by a flathead less than a year ago. I expected a breathing tube and maybe a million wires and machines surrounding him. But that's not the case. He's not hooked up to an IV, and he doesn't even have a heart monitor attached to him. The most I can see is a small red button attached to a cord sitting on the side of the mattress.

His brown hair is slicked back and wet, his skin is paler than I remember, and his brown eyes appear lethargic despite how wide they've become. Slowly, he blinks. His finger moves toward the red button, but he's not quick enough. He must be medicated. I dart toward the bed and grab his icy hand. He trembles under my touch, egging me on to grip him tighter.

"Remember me?" I ask with more cheer in my voice than I feel. Being around him makes me tense as fuck and ready to end him. In theory at least. I've never hurt anyone outside of the heat of the moment before. And I've definitely never taken another person's life. Grady tried to tell me once that taking a life will fuck you up, but I didn't believe him until I was witness to one of Holly's panic attacks. Crazy chick beat a dude's face in with a brick, and it took her weeks to come to terms with that. If she's that fucked up over the one, I don't know how the brothers deal with the shit they do.

What we do is important. We protect our town. We protect our own. We keep order when the cops can't or won't. But that doesn't mean that what I'm about to do isn't fucking me up.

I move the red button to the table beside his bed and let go of his hand. As predicted, he reaches for the button again, fast at least this time, but doesn't make it. Instead of moving the button out of his reach, I wrap my fingers around his throat and squeeze as hard as I can.

"Release him," Duke says firmly, still standing near the door. He hasn't done shit since we got in here. Reluctantly, I let go and watch as Darren struggles to suck in pathetic breath after pathetic breath. His eyes are bugged out as he strains to move up the bed. Cringing, he claws his way into a sitting position.

"You've been awake for a while now, and there's no telling the shit you've been telling people," Duke says.

Darren gasps and says, "No, no. I haven't said anything to anybody."

"You believe him?" I ask.

Duke grins and pulls a flathead screwdriver out of his pocket. "Not a word. Good thing I'm not here to talk."

"Please," Darren begs. Tears stream down his face as Duke pops the flathead into the air and catches it. Unable to help myself, I reach down and slap him across the face.

"Act like a bitch and I'll treat you like one," I hiss.

Duke whistles, catching my attention, and tosses the flathead to me. I catch it easily and hold it by the handle, pointing the tip at Darren's mouth. His breathing comes more ragged and strained now. He's not saying a word, but his eyes beg for relief.

"Lick it," I bite out. Panic seizes him, forcing strangled cries from his lungs. Fucking asshole can't ever do what he's told. Wrapping my fingers around his neck again, I squeeze and lean in, smiling wide. "Lick it and act like it's my dick, asshole."

I pull back and watch as his tongue slowly peeks out and touches the metal of the tip of the screwdriver. Lightening up on my grip around his throat, I watch the depravity I'm forcing on him. My stomach rolls as the sight, and for half a second I have to close my eyes. Killing him might be easier than torturing him like this. It's not that I don't think he deserves whatever comes to him. It's just that the idea of hurting someone is different than actually hurting them. The club has a debt to settle with Larry Jennings, and in typical Forsaken fashion, we're going through the person who matters to him most to do it.

"Got a problem, Baby Boy?" Duke asks from the foot of the bed. He's got Darren's hospital chart in his hands and is studying it.

"Just hit me, ya know? Darren hurts Nic, we hurt Darren. Larry hurts Mindy, we hurt Larry."

Duke nods and sets the chart back in its slot. He walks

up the other side of the bed and places a hand on Darren's chest. Darren's eyes bug out as he stares nervously at Duke's hand, his mouth still working the flathead like a pro.

"Nic won't tell me much about what happened, and you were too young to see it all very clearly, but this guy? I'm sure he remembers it all. I'll bet he remembers waiting until Butch got busted to take Nic's virginity. I'll bet he remembers telling her the only man who will ever love her now is him."

Every ounce of guilt and fear that I'm feeling slowly disappears, and in its place is a numbness. It makes me want to barf, but I feel my conscience dying every second that Duke speaks. It's like my body's gone on autopilot as I slowly slide the flathead farther into Darren's mouth.

"Did she ever tell you that this prick told her he was going to kill my baby? She ever tell you that my baby being inside her made him sick, sick enough to brutalize her until my fucking kid was dead?"

My muscles tense as the flathead darts into his mouth quickly, hitting what I think is his tongue. Duke's iron fist reaches out and pulls me back. Darren coughs and lunges forward as the flathead leaves his mouth. The blade and shank are covered in blood. Unlike before, the reality of what I've done doesn't seem to creep up on me as I watch him choke on his own blood. He leans to Duke's side, spitting it out all over his bed. Duke lifts the bed sheet to cover himself from the blood splatter and says, "We're not ready to kill him yet."

"Right." I tuck the screwdriver into my pocket.

"It's in your best interest to get your bitch daddy and

cunt mommy back in town. Either they come home for your release from the hospital or for your funeral. It's your choice. You have two weeks," Duke says and swiftly throws his clenched fist into Darren's face before he walks away. Darren folds in on himself, blood streams now from his nose as well as he cries into his hands.

Grabbing ahold of his hair, I hiss into his ear, "I don't have to tell you that telling anyone about this visit is a bad idea, do I?"

Darren shakes and sobs simultaneously as I pull the syringe from the pocket of my hoodie and pop off the cap. Ryan suggested a sweet coke/meth powder combo, but that just seemed like too much work. Taking a deep breath, I grab his arm and position him as best I can to make it look like he's injected himself in his stomach. I don't give a fuck if the stomach is a place people shoot up—I wouldn't fucking know—but his arm is stiff and uncooperative.

"Save a place for me in Hell," I murmur as I plunge the concoction into his body. He shakes mercilessly, cries booming from his throat, and stares down at the needle in his stomach with wide, fearful eyes.

I take a step back and reach over, handing him the red button to make sure he doesn't end up dying just yet. His fingers struggle to push the plastic piece down, but he finally makes it, and I bolt out of there before I have to stare at what I've done any longer.

Duke's just outside the door, and together we race to the same stairwell we just came from and down to the second floor where the cafeteria is. A few minutes after sitting down with a pair of nasty hospital burgers, Nic comes in, escorted by a frazzled nurse. My sister has the good sense to look sheepish as she sets Robin in a chair between her and Duke.

"She has gas," Nic says quietly.

The nurse clears her throat. "Ms. Whelan, please call the nurse helpline next time you're worried. We're here to help."

I raise an eyebrow at the nurse, who tucks a stray hair behind her ear and feels around ensuring the rest of her hair is still up in a messy bun. The woman diverts my gaze and turns away. When she does, I realize where I know her from. She's got an angel tattoo on the back of her neck. The last time I saw that, she was naked and swinging around a pole at the clubhouse.

"What did you do?" I ask, curiously.

Nic smiles down at Robin and says, "It wasn't me. She really did have gas. Wouldn't stop screaming. I just acted like I didn't know how to deal with it."

Duke and I smile at my sister, who can't take her eyes off her baby. My eyes drift to his, and when he turns toward me, I say, "It's worth it."

He returns my words with a nod before digging into his nasty burger. We fall into conversation about the upcoming party at Pres's place and whether or not we should bring food or beer.

"I can't drink, so food," Nic says.

"But I can, so beer," Duke retorts.

"This party is half in honor of the human I birthed, and she can't do either, so I get her vote. Chey isn't legal to drink, so she automatically votes food. That means we win. Food."

Duke and I throw our hands up at her reasoning and laugh easily. Not that Chey won't drink just because she's not legal, but Nic's crafty and I'm in too good of a mood to argue. It should always be like this. There's just one person missing—my girl.

CHAPTER 23

April

12 months to Mancuso's downfall

Cheyenne

THE AGING CAR radio crackles under the strain of the weakened signal the farther we get from town. Fort Bragg doesn't have any good radio stations, but that doesn't stop us from turning on the radio and trying anyway. It's sad really. You would think we would have learned by now.

The news personality, whose name I don't even know, blabs on and on about the fucking weather like it's some big surprise that it's raining in Mendocino County in winter. Frustrated, I reach over and change the station, hoping for something more entertaining. There are few choices, and even fewer that sound appealing, but one word catches my attention, and I dial back to hear the story.

Sure enough, the station is delivering a news report, too, but this one is far more interesting than the last one about the rain. The whiny newscaster voice chirps through my Bug's speakers, but I push through the annoyance because just a moment ago he said the name Darren Jennings.

"Quoting an unnamed source who reached out to us earlier today, 'the attack on Darren Jennings appeared to have come out of nowhere, but without a statement from the police department, our community is forced to assume it was a gang-related attack, possibly in retaliation for Jennings's father's supposed gambling debt.' Again, this statement is coming from an unnamed source in the community. Rumors have circled our small town since Darren Jennings was admitted to Coast Hospital last summer. While the police appeared to have a few leads initially, they have since reported no further progress in determining who is behind the former football star's attack. St. Mary's Catholic Church has asked on behalf of Jennings's absent family that the people Fort Bragg continue to keep an eye out for suspicious activity and an open heart for the grief the Jennings family is suffering."

They're not reporting anything I haven't heard already. Two days ago, I was left alone at Duke and Nic's house while the three of them took Robin to the hospital for a supposed fever. But when they got back, Nick said it was just gas. I don't know anything about babies, but even I know you can't possibly confuse a fever with gas. Later that night, when the news reported that Darren Jennings had been found in his hospital room with a needle of methamphetamine pumped into his stomach, I knew it was the club. And I didn't give a shit. That bastard hurt Nic, and he tried to hurt Robin. I may not be a brother, but I am Forsaken. That means he hurt my family, and fuck him if he expects any sympathy.

I want to ask Jeremy about Darren, but I don't dare. He seems freaked. He did well to shower right after he came back from the hospital, and then he basically forbid me to even ask what happened. I wanted to press the issue, but he just crawled into bed with me and held me as if his life depended on it. Later that night, when he had fallen asleep, I lay awake, restless and fearful. That's the worst part of being a woman in this world. We can ask questions and even beg for answers, but if the club doesn't want to give them, they won't. And there's nothing we can do about that. Sometimes, it feels like I'm being punished by straddling the edge of the world but never been fully welcomed into it.

I choose this, I tell myself. Because I do. I choose Jeremy. I don't regret it, even when he flops around for hours, struggling to find peace and refusing to tell me why he is so troubled. I suppose if it is this difficult for him to deal with, then I should respect his wishes and let him have his privacy.

So when we pull up to Ruby and Jim's house and Jeremy cuts the car, I lean over and place a kiss on his cheek. I don't really have to say anything to let them know that I'm here.

I climb out of the car and head directly for the house, but Jeremy doesn't follow. He wanders off toward Ryan and Squat for some kind of crazy intense conversation that I want no part of. So instead, I sneak into the house through the sliding glass door that opens into the hallway near Alex's room. I don't think I'm supposed to know that, but the brothers are a bunch of chatty bitches. I figure if Jeremy is busy, then maybe I can actually hang out with Alex for a few minutes. We have been friends long enough but have never actually hung out. It's kind of sad, really.

I close the door behind me and tiptoe down the hall but pause at the sound of a familiar gruff voice. Dad.

I peer around the corner to the game room and find that Dad and Holly are tucked into the corner. Neither look terribly pleased, but I can't help watching anyway. It's been three days since I've seen him, and as much as I want to say that I'm an adult and it doesn't hurt, I would be lying. He's my dad, and even when I don't want to admit it, his opinion matters to me. He made me feel like a cheap whore and acted like Jeremy only wants me for my body. But I know that's not true. Still, it was terribly hurtful and mean for him to say it. What's worse is that Holly saw it all and didn't say anything. She's supposed to be on my side.

"You have to talk to her," Holly says. Dad huffs and rolls his shoulders like he's going to put up a fight, but Holly doesn't give him any time. "One of the reasons I fell in love with you was because I got to see the kind of father you are. I know how much you love your little girl, and I know it kills you to see her grow up, but making her feel like crap is only going to push her away."

"We still on this?" he asks.

"I can't live with you being this grouchy. You need to talk to Cheyenne. You're upset, but she's upset, too.

She's not one of your brothers, so handle her with a little more care, will ya?"

"You telling me how to care for my own kid?" Questioning his decisions is one of the things he hates most. It doesn't even matter that it's Holly. I can tell it's pissing him off, but I give him credit where credit is due, because he keeps his mouth shut when I know he wants to tell her off.

"Yeah, I am," she says.

"You gonna make a habit out of it?"

"When I need to."

Dad nods his head and rubs the back of his neck. As much as I wish she had stuck up for me during our fight the other night, I'm grateful she's doing it now. I'm lucky to have her. In fact, Dad's lucky to have her, too.

After an appropriate amount of time of listening in, I decide to make my presence known. Walking into the room, I clear my throat and avert my eyes. Showing up here doesn't mean I'm caving. I meant what I said the other night, but unfortunately, I think Dad did, too.

From the other end of the hall, Jeremy strides toward me but stalls when he turns to see who's in the game room. He wasn't there to hear what Dad said, but I certainly wasn't shy in relaying my frustration.

"Talk," Holly says quietly as she elbows Dad in the side.

He turns to her and narrows his eyes before focusing his gaze back on me. He takes note of Jeremy in the room and crosses his arms over his chest. Without thinking about it, I mirror his stance. I want to move my arms and do anything aside from looking like the spitting image of Sterling Grady, but I don't want him to think I'm backing down. Because I am so not.

"Haven't seen you in a few days," Dad says with a nod in my direction.

"Yeah, I figured we needed a few days of space." Truth be told, I wish he had shown up at Duke and Nic's house right after our fight and apologized. But that's not my dad, and I know better than to hope for an apology like that.

"I was hard on you," he says. "Went too far, didn't say what I wanted to."

I swear the man is capable of forming complete sentences but definitely not when he struggling with his emotions. "Well, I'm listening now."

"You two are so young. There's no reason you got to rush into being adults. Trust me, it ain't all it's cracked up to be. I just want you both to slow things down and focus on the shit you need to instead of each other all the time."

"I love him," I say in absence of the more eloquent response. It's simple and it's the truth, so really it's all that I have. Dad's eyes shift to Jeremy, totally ignoring my declaration.

"Jeremy, you've been fucking up the last few months. You're not where you're supposed to be, and when you are, you're on your fucking phone. Spent a good year fucking begging for a cut. Did good with it until you got distracted. But the way you're going, the brothers are never going to vote you in."

I suck in a sharp breath and try to keep my composure. I don't want him to know how much what he's just said hurts. Jeremy's gotten in trouble because of *me*, not because he's lazy or disrespectful. He hasn't forgotten where he is supposed to be and when. It's only been to protect me.

"You get that?" Dad asks, his eyes now having traveled to Jeremy's.

"Yes, sir," Jeremy says like a goddamn parrot.

"Prospecting isn't a time for hooking up. Your only priority should be the club, and if you can't tell me without a doubt that you choose the cut over your girlfriend, then you might as well hand it over now."

"Fiancée," I snap. I shouldn't let them get to me like this, but I can't take it back. The word I so callously and carelessly threw out is probably the worst thing I could've said right now. Well, not technically the worst. I bet telling him I was pregnant would be worse, but only slightly.

"Fiancée?" Dad bellows. First, his face turns red, then his neck, and pretty soon his hands that are clenched at his sides have turned an unnatural combination of red and white.

"You heard a single word I said?" he screams. Holly jumps back half a foot, her eyes flutter closed and her entire frame goes rigid. While I don't suffer such a violent physical reaction, I certainly feel his disapproval deep in my heart. "You are throwing your entire fucking future away for a little bit of a dick. I raised you better than that, Cheyenne. I don't fucking understand where I went so wrong that you are this intent on destroying not just your future but his as well."

Staring at him numbly, I try to figure out exactly what he's telling me. It feels like he's not so subtly dancing around what he really wants to say, which is surprising. He's never been a man known for self-control.

"I'm going to marry him because I love him. Because the future you want for me isn't the future I want for myself," I say. The words fly from my mouth in a pathetic whine I can't really control.

"Not without my vote, he won't," Dad says.

Very slowly, Jeremy turns his attention toward me. He shakes his head slowly and mouths, "*Just stop.*"

"It doesn't take a club vote to get married," I say. It's his club—he should know the rules little bit better than that.

"No, but it does take the club to vote in an old lady. And as long as you keep acting like a spoiled fucking brat, I won't ever allow you to be voted in."

"Grady, man," Jeremy says. His voice wavers, careful not to insult my dad, but fearful and pleading.

"No. I'm fucking done with this shit. I am the only one who's noticed you can't keep your dick on straight. You want to be Forsaken? You want to marry my girl? Only fucking way either of those is ever going to happen is if you can get your shit together long enough to not fuck up your entire future."

"Wow, you can't even be a little bit happy for me, can you?" I say. I fight back the tears that threaten to slip down my cheeks. I'm an adult, and I'm strong. I refuse to let any of them see how weak I really feel inside.

"It's not about being happy for you, baby girl. It's about doing right by you, and right now that means giving you some hard truths. You need to know that if you keep going like this, you're going to cost that boy his patch. Best thing you can do for him is to just go to that goddamn school I told you I'd fucking pay for and let the kid earned his top rocker in peace."

Dad raises an eyebrow, daring me to keep arguing. Honestly, I could argue with him for days. We've done it before, and I'm not afraid to do it again. Unfortunately, there doesn't seem to be any point in it. He's got himself convinced that our relationship is going to destroy both our lives, and I don't think there's anything I can do to change that. So instead, I let my frustration get the better of me—I throw my hands in the air and stomp away.

Jeremy follows after me and pulls me aside into Alex's room. I only know it's her room because while there are posters of naked women on the walls, there are also competing department store photographs of flowers, the beach, and even one 5x7 of Ryan and Alex together. I never wondered what Ryan's decorating style was, but now that I know, I'm really grateful that tiny little crush I had on him years ago has since faded and that nothing ever came of it. I totally couldn't live with waking up every day to a woman's fake rack.

"This is so fucked up," Jeremy says. He's scrubs his face with his hands and groans. "Maybe he's right. I've been spending so much time trying to keep your ass out of trouble that I haven't even been worried about mine."

I have to turn away from him to stop myself from totally breaking down. We've been engaged for, what, three days? And he's already got cold feet and changed his mind. I was afraid of this, even if I never wanted to admit it. Something in the back of my mind told me that this is what boys do. They make commitments they can't keep. They tell you they'll be with you forever, when what they really mean is that they'll be with you until it's no longer convenient. Because that's all this is with my dad—inconvenient.

"Are you serious? Are you really going to let one argument stop us from being together the way we want to be?" I think I already have my answer, but I'm not willing to accept it.

"You heard him," he says. "When have you ever known Grady to threaten shit he doesn't mean?"

"So this is it? Our relationship means so little to you that you can just throw us away at the first sign of trouble? Well, I guess it's better to find this out now."

"No, I'm not throwing us away. I'm fucking telling you that we're rushing into shit."

"So, what—you asked me to marry you and you didn't mean it?"

"No, that's not what I mean. I fucking love you, but I don't know how to do this and not fuck everything up at the club."

And here it is, in terms so black-and-white that even I can't pretend I don't see it. He's choosing the club over what we have. The pain from his rejection cuts me like a knife, slicing through my flesh as smooth as it would butter. I refuse to cry in front of him, but that doesn't mean it's easy. I just want him to know that I believe in us, and I'll fight tooth and nail for there to be an us—

always.

"I'm sorry," he says as he closes in and reaches out for me.

I swat him away and beg for him to leave. Because if he stays, I'm going to cry. And today isn't supposed to be a day of sorrow but a day of celebration.

Jeremy leaves. His absence practically suffocates me.

It doesn't matter anymore. Because my father thinks I'm an idiot, my boyfriend doesn't want to marry me, and every hope I had for my life has just shattered in a million little pieces. I would've thought something that hurts this bad would've come with a bigger hammer. But I guess not.

Minutes pass with me alone in Alex's room, careful not to touch anything, just standing around and sniffling. I wish I had asked Jeremy for my car keys so I could go home, even if I know I'd get in trouble for being at the house by myself. I don't really give a shit right now. All the men in my life are so keen on telling me what they think is best, but none of them are willing to listen to what I think is best for myself. So they can all go to hell.

"Cheyenne?" Alex says in a soft voice.

I spin around and stare at her sheepishly, then refocus my attention on her walls.

"I see you hired a professional decorator," I say. I don't know how to act with her, especially not right now. I formally met her once, but she's my texting buddy, and I feel closer to her than I ever did to Tracie. And that's saying something. She understands shit about my life that Tracie never could.

"Yeah, it's a good thing I refused to pay him, right?" she says with a kind smile on her face. "Hey, are you okay?"

"I'll be fine," I say sarcastically. "Jeremy just asked me to marry him a few days ago, and now, faced with Dad's disapproval, he's changed his mind. But I'm totally fine. Don't worry about me," I mutter, folding in on myself.

"Ouch," she says, "but can I give you a piece of advice?"

No. I don't want her advice. Alex has always encouraged me to go to school since I have the opportunity. She thinks I will regret not going, but she can't possibly know that.

"Yeah," I say. I want to refuse, but even I can't figure out how to be that impolite.

"If Jeremy is willing to give up what you have so easily, then maybe that means he's not ready for that kind of commitment just yet."

"But I was ready," I say. "Now I'm just pissed."

"It's just something to think about."

It's weird how we completely skipped the pleasantries and moved right into the deep stuff, but what's even stranger is that it doesn't feel weird at all.

"Well, I'll be back in just a minute, okay?" Alex says hopefully. "I really want to hang out, but my mom needs one of my nonna's recipes."

"Oh, a recipe for what?" I ask. I'm being nosy, but I don't know Aunt Ruby to have a mother in her life, so I can only assume this is her Italian grandmother we're talking about. Alex has sent over enough yummy Italian dishes that I know damn well the girl can cook, so if Ruby is making Italiano, I want a piece of that.

She walks over to her dresser and reaches into the top drawer where she pulls out a small leather notebook. It has a multitude of old, yellowed papers stuffed inside. She flips through for a few pages before pulling a slip out and smiling at me. Her long brown hair cascades down her back, and her heart-shaped face almost glows. She seems truly happy, not just surface happy. I'm glad she has that, even if I kind of want to slap it off her right now.

"It's the frosting recipe for Italian cream cake," she says.

I've never eaten Italian cream cake, but it sounds delicious, so I nod my head enthusiastically and tell her to make sure I get a slice. She agrees and rushes off, yelling in the distance about finding the recipe and asking Ruby if they have all the ingredients.

Being in Alex's room alone makes me feel awkward, but she said she would be back in a moment, so I don't want to run out and miss the chance to hang out. In her absence, I pace awkwardly, unable to stay still. That fight with Jeremy is making me stupid needy, but I can't seem to help myself. I crave having a friendship with someone who doesn't have to "follow orders" all the damn time. Then again, I don't really know anybody very well who isn't under control of the club.

Muted voices bring my attention to the hallway. I try not to be nosy, but the masculine conversation draws me in. The men speak in hushed tones as if trying to hide, but they're not doing a very good job at it. I can hear them really well the more I listen in and the closer I get to the open doorway.

"Got everybody up here," the deeper voice says. "Fucking idiots don't know it's coming." I hold my breath and give it a moment, trying to place the voice. When it comes to me, it's like a freightliner crashing into my chest—Uncle Rig. I don't know who he's talking about, but something doesn't sit right with me.

"Good. He know I'm coming?" the other voice asks. The slight Midwestern inflection of his voice tells me it's Daniel. I close my eyes and pray that listening in on this conversation isn't as bad as it feels.

"No, couldn't get to him. Should only have one guard on Michael right now. Get in and get him out as quickly as you can."

"Where am I taking him?" Daniel asks.

"Get him to the Italian. He should be nearby if not already there. Keep your cover as long as you can," Rig says.

Get Michael? What the hell? Their heavy steps creep away from Alex's room and toward the sliding glass door at the other end of the hall. I suck in a breath and place my forehead on the wall before me. It sounds like Uncle Rig and Daniel are thinking about busting Michael out of the Ian's house. And even though I know that's what I heard, I'm having a hard time wrapping my head around it. That doesn't make any sense at all. They're Forsaken.

Still, I have to talk to somebody about it. Somebody I can trust.

I have to find Dad or Jeremy.

CHAPTER 24

April

12 months to Mancuso's downfall

Cheyenne

IN THE MOMENTS that pass after hearing of Uncle Rig and Daniel's betrayal, I find myself unable to breath. My lungs drained with the need for oxygen, but my body refuses to comply. My muscles grow tense, and it's difficult to move the longer that my body fights its natural need to care for itself.

Once I'm sure they are long gone, I dart out of Alex's room intent on finding anybody I think I can trust. That's not a whole hell of a lot of people, to be honest, but if I can find Dad or Jeremy or maybe even Aunt Ruby, I might be able to stop the entire world from imploding.

Rushing out into the hallway, I practically slam right into Alex. She laughs with the surprise shriek and asks if

I'm okay.

"Where's your mom?" I ask, not taking a moment to be polite about it.

"Outside, I think," she says.

I don't bother to thank her. I just push past her and rush out the front door.

Just off the deck, surrounded by a couple of old ladies and Chel, Aunt Ruby stands with a beer in her hand and a casual smile on her face. I push off the side of the house and run to her, tugging on her arm the moment I reach her. She jerks back violently with wide eyes and an explosive fear plastered on her face.

"What the hell?"

"Need your help," I say and tug her away from her conversation. With jerky movements, I survey my surroundings and make sure we're alone once we reach the garage. The door's open and nobody is in sight, so we should be safe. I hope.

"Problem," I say. "I have to tell you something, and you're probably going to think I'm crazy, but it's super important that you know I'm telling you the truth." It's not just kind of a big deal to tell somebody that somebody is betraying the patch—it's the kind of deal that wars start over and entire villages get slaughtered because of. Trusting Aunt Ruby with this should be considered a compliment, but I have a feeling she's not going to consider it as such.

"If it's important, just tell me," she says softly. Aunt Ruby doesn't do soft very often, but when she does, you know she means business.

"I overheard Uncle Rig and Daniel talking about getting Michael out of Ian's house. They called the club a bunch of idiots, and they said something about working with 'the Italian,' " I tell her in a rush.

Ruby appraises me. Everybody who knows me is well aware that I'm comfortable telling a little white lie, but I hope they all know I wouldn't lie about something this serious.

"Baby, I'm sure you heard them wrong. I know that sounds scary, but the club probably has a reason for what they're doing."

"No," I say, "I heard Uncle Rig call everybody a bunch of idiots. He's betraying the club, like right the hell now, and I need you to help me get Dad down there to stop him."

"Cheyenne, have you been drinking?"

"No! What the hell?"

She lets out of heavy sigh and nods her head. "Let me go find your uncle Jim, and you can tell him what you heard. That way we're not interfering with club business. I just have to find them first."

Every minute that passes is one minute closer to catastrophe where Rig and Daniel are betraying my family. I know Ruby wants to believe the best of Rig, but I'm not nuts and I'm not a liar.

"Never mind!" I shout. I don't know what I expected from her, but it wasn't that.

Now more desperate than anything, I scope out the backyard looking for somebody, anybody that I think will listen to me. Off by the red barn, Jeremy stands beside

Rink and Dunce, who have a couple of joints they're passing around a much larger crowd.

When I approach, Jeremy's attention is completely on me. I take immediate advantage of that and say loudly, "I need your help. It's important."

"With what?" Jeremy snaps. His attitude fucking sucks, and if I didn't need him so badly right now, I wouldn't even deal with his shit. But I do. I have no idea where my dad is, and Aunt Ruby was really no help at all.

Walking up to him, I place my hand on his lower back, close to the handgun he keeps tucked there. "It's important, and it's private. Please stop being such a dick," I say quietly. Okay, so that didn't come out exactly as I had planned.

"Giving the boy his balls back?" Dunce says with a smirk.

I narrow my eyes at him and flip him the bird. He's a fucking prospect, not a patched brother, and doesn't have shit over me. Unfortunately, he keeps forgetting his rank.

"Check your attitude, Cheyenne," he says in a dismissive tone. His eyes cut to the men around him like he's looking for approval or something. "Need to learn your place, babe."

Frustration builds, my hands shake at my sides, and I suck in an unsteady breath. Everybody's being so freaking difficult about helping me, and it's not something that I can shout out to the masses. Discretion, even with rowdy bikers, is important. I force my hands to steady and take a deep breath, telling myself all the while that I need to play nice.

"It's about Michael," I whisper-shout in Jeremy's ear.

His eyes grow wide and he nods, immediately turning and pulling me aside, out of earshot of everybody else.

"What's going on?"

"Rig and Daniel are about to take Michael from Ian's and give him to Scavo," I say in a frantic rush as low as I can.

"Rig?" Jeremy questions in disbelief. "He's Detroit's president."

"I didn't want to believe it either, but I know what I heard."

"Fuck. There's no way you could be wrong?" He kicks into the dirt below his feet.

"No," I say firmly. I wouldn't be here right now if there was a chance I was wrong.

Jeremy nods and pulls out his cell, dials my dad's number, and brings it up to his ear, waiting for him to answer. He groans, his eyes darting from Ruby and Jim's house to the tree line that hides Ian's cabin. His eyes travel across the property, eventually landing on Rig, who stands with a beer to his lips, talking to Uncle Jim near the tiny pond adjacent to the barn.

By the third ring, Jeremy's clearly lost his patience. With his eyes constantly darting to Rig and Jim, he takes off toward the trees, mindful of his speed. So far it seems as though Rig hasn't seen us. His attention is elsewhere for the moment, and I can only hope it stays that way.

When Dad answers the phone, Jeremy says quickly, "They're about to jailbreak Junior." Pause. "Right now."

Another pause. "Chey overheard Rig and Daniel." Then he's off the phone and moving faster to the tree line.

I follow Jeremy, picking up my pace to catch up with him, but my movements are too slow—they catch Rig's attention. He lowers the beer, gives Jim a nod, and turns his entire body toward me, walking away from their conversation. Rig pulls his phone from his pocket, types a short message, and then shoves it back in his pocket. He takes another drink from the bottle in his hand and then slowly walks back toward the house. Jim eyes him carefully before answering his phone. I can't tell if he says anything or just listens for the few seconds he's on the call. Then he hangs up and observes me and Jeremy as we nervously head for the trees.

Jeremy stops, but we're moving so fast that I don't notice until it's too late and I've slammed into his back. His eyes are affixed in the direction of the house. He sucks in a breath and mutters, "Shit."

I track his gaze to the line of men stalking toward us— all heaving muscles, grim expressions, and major firepower. Ryan, Ian, Diesel, Bear, Rink, Dad, Wyatt, Duke, and a few men I don't know charge forward on Wyatt's hand signal in the air. It almost looks like something out of a movie, all these dangerous men in full-on warrior mode. Jim stands in his same place he's been in, his attention focused on Rig. He raises his arm in the air, two fingers above the rest, and he points to Rig, who is now almost past the house and heading for his bike. Duke and Ryan fall back and pause a moment before taking off after him, both have their guns raised and ready to shoot if necessary.

I know what I heard, and I know there's no mistaking

the betrayal. Rig—who I've called uncle my entire life—had the nerve to refer to my family as idiots. Anger wells in my heart, spreads through my veins, and ignites a fire in me that I doubt I can control.

"We got this. Stay here, babe," Jeremy says, and he takes off at full speed, still several hundred yards in front of the angry line of men. I don't even have my gun on me. It would be suicide to go after him and willingly throw myself into the mix with these men.

Idiots.

The mere reminder of the insult Rig so easily delivered about my family heats my body, propelling me forward. I take off running after Jeremy, through the yard toward the back of the property where Ian lives. Jim and Ruby's property butts up to two separate roads, but it's not easy to get to the back road from their house unless your vehicle has four-wheel drive. Ian's house is more like a cabin, small in nature and made of a fine wood. It sits far enough back from the road and is shrouded in enough redwood trees that it would be hard for a stranger to even know it's there. It makes an excellent safe house.

So I run, my legs straining and my lungs on fire. Jeremy stumbles up ahead and loses some of his lead. The ground here gets hilly and dips in places you can't really see. There's a way to run over it without losing any steam—a lesson I learned from my days under Ryan and Ian's care—but without knowing to pick your feet up higher and jump from one hill to the next, you'll risk twisting your ankle thanks to the unpredictable terrain.

I clear the hills in record time, leaving Jeremy in the distance, and dash into the trees without thinking to pause. The thick redwoods make seeing anything or anybody out here difficult at any distance. If I were trying to sneak up on someone, I would hide in the shadows and trunks of the trees, but I'm not.

I'm the distraction.

I just hope the distraction doesn't get shot at in the process.

The cabin comes into view in the distance. A small lot has been cleared, giving the house maybe a twenty-foot clearance on all sides from the towering redwoods. The cabin sits up about five feet from the dampened earth with a large and inviting front porch and wide steps leading up to the mosaic-glass front door. The roots of the redwoods curve and snake through the dirt under the cabin, which is why it's raised. These trees are epic in size and have been known to destroy strip malls with their roots sneaking up through the earth, showing us mere humans who's the more powerful of the two.

I'm so focused on the roots under the cabin and checking their shadows for men who might be hiding that I don't even see the fallen log before me until my shin's gotten intimately acquainted with the damn thing. I fall forward into the mix of dirt and moss, the skin of my leg tearing as it drags against the dead tree bark. Instinctively, I cry out but don't move. If I crawl forward, I'll lose even more flesh. If I lift it, I'll spare myself more pain, but it'll be awkward at best, and I'm not certain I'll be successful. Giving the lifting method my best shot, I bite down on my bottom lip and fight the pained cries that build in my chest. Pushing up from the earth, I've managed to get my good leg bent and prop up my knee in the damp soil when a large, flat, and hard object shoves me back down.

I twist my head just enough to see a man with olive skin, brown hair, and a black suit towering over me with a gold gun pointed at my head. With a sneer, he says, "Don't fucking move."

Leaves crunch, branches snap, and heavy breaths sound behind me. A gun cocks from somewhere at a close distance, the noise of the metal sliding somehow sounding so foreign out here surrounded by all this nature. This should be a peaceful place, not a place for war. Jeremy was right behind me. It has to be him. Sure enough, his voice warms my cooling body despite the anger laced within.

"Let her go!"

"You could kill me, boy," the man with the gold gun says, "but then your bitch dies, too."

I focus on Jeremy's voice and his labored breathing, letting his presence bring me comfort. Anything else and I'll either cry or start cursing. I never wanted to be one of those girls who gets herself in trouble and has to be saved. I wanted to do the saving. It's why I got myself expelled from school in my last semester. It's why I put my freedom on the line with Dad by disappearing and lying about it all the time. It's what I've dedicated the last several months of my life to—helping the club—not being some damsel in distress.

"Tell your men to stand down at the trees. Once we have what we came for, I'll release her," the man above me says. In a fantasy world, Jeremy would be such a quick shot that this guy wouldn't stand a chance. He could shoot him in the head, and I could crawl away from his falling corpse. But realistically, I know if Jeremy takes a shot, I'm dead.

Turning my head to the side, I see Jeremy click the safety on his gun and toss it onto the ground near the man's feet. His eyes catch mine for half a second, and he gives me the most subtle nod known to man. Or maybe I'm imagining it, because that nod is telling me to grab for the gun. As Jeremy retreats into the woods, walking backward with his arms in the air, he shouts, "Stand down! They got Miss Priss!"

The man presses his foot even harder into my back, his attention focuses in on the gun just on the other side of his feet, and a sinister grin takes over his face. His eyes seem to dance with some kind of sick pleasure that I wish I didn't see. *Bang!* A loud and terrifying noise rings out above me. The pressure from the man's foot disappears as a shadow is cast over me, and a moment later, his inanimate body falls to the forest floor beside me. He lands with his face turned my direction and his torso twisted in an unnatural manner. The gaping bullet wound at his temple serves as a fountain for his blood that soon coats his lifeless features, turning this once cruel man into nothing more than food for the crows when they descend.

"Stand up," a thick New York accent orders from behind me. I jump in place, so wholly mesmerized and disgusted by the dead man who lies beside me. I scramble to my feet, terrified of delaying, and try to mentally brush off the ache from my battered shin. When I pivot to turn toward the voice, an arm shoots out and pushes me forward and demands that I not turn around. "You will live through this should you choose to heed my advice. I came for only one thing and do not wish war with

Forsaken."

"Could've fooled me," I say. Every word is laced with venom, fully intent on pissing him off. There's a reason this man killed the other guy, though neither are on my side, and that worries me. I barely understand why everything's gone to hell around here let alone entertaining the idea of more than one organization trying to get their hands on mafia royalty. This shit is probably why Dad and his brothers drinks so much and smoke so much of their own product. Otherwise, I don't know how they get through any given day.

"Chey!" Dad screams from beyond the trees. Rustling sounds explode, along with the sound of a herd of men trampling the untouched earth.

"Stand down, or she's dead!" the man screams as loud as I'm thinking he's capable of.

"It wasn't me!" I shout. "I'm fine!" Lies. I'm so not fucking fine, but what the hell am I supposed to say? No, please come and kill this psychopath who's going to kill me before you get here? I'll pass, thanks.

The sounds stop, and everything is quiet in the forest once more. Dad barks so loud that his voice echoes around me, saying, "We're gonna get you out safely, baby girl!"

The man pushes me forward with his hand once more. "Take me to the front door."

I comply, walking slowly and avoiding any more stray pieces of wood I could fall on. As it is, my shin makes walking uncomfortable with the way my jeans have torn and rub against the wound. But I don't focus on that, or else I might cave and lose my mind right here and now. No, one foot in front of the other and eyes on the ground. Jeremy's gun is less than five feet away, and I have to get back to it. He wouldn't have dropped it without being forced to if he didn't intend for me to grab it.

"Good girl," the man says in praise of, I suppose, my not fighting him. "That man would have killed you for sport. I'm not that cruel, but I will sacrifice you for the *principe* if I must." We come to a block of redwoods that forces us to deviate from our straight path to the house. I choose to go to the right, bringing me closer to Jeremy's gun, now only about three feet away.

"I wouldn't try it if I were you," he says, catching where my attention has drifted. He barely has the words out when another man approaches, disturbing the quiet forest with his heavy footfalls, from someplace behind me. The man behind me spins around at the noise and lets out a relieved sigh.

"What's with the gunfire?" the newcomer asks with a similar East Coast flair to his speech. I duck down quietly and cringe at the pain that radiates from my shin but am careful to stay as silent as possible. The newcomer's eyes fall to the dead man only feet away, and he lifts his gun toward the man who killed him. "Tony was right," he says to the killer. "You've turned on your family—and for what? A fucking rat and a prince who doesn't deserve the legacy he's been gifted."

My mind races to process this new information while I slowly lean toward the gun. It's barely out of reach, and I don't know if I can get to it without making more noise. I'm a pretty good shot—Dad's seen to that—but I'm no expert. I'm not Ian, who can accurately hit his target even in motion and without much visibility.

"You forget that Tony doesn't have the rank to give anybody orders. He's a fucking soldier running around like a capo or underboss, making decisions he has no goddamn right to make," the killer says. His voice is calm and smooth, triggering a memory from recent months. The same voice came from the man who stood against my Bug in the school parking lot telling me he needed to speak with my dad. Leo Scavo.

"Tony represents our future."

"If Tony is our future, then I want none of it."

"I'll make sure your mother remembers you as a man of honor," the man tells Leo as he cocks his gun. Even standing behind Leo, I can see how angry he is. His neck turns red, and his shoulders straighten like he's preparing for a fight.

If I don't do something to distract the unnamed man, he's going to kill Leo, and I'll be in a worse situation than I already am. Thinking quickly on how to handle the situation, I stretch my arm out for the gun but come up short by no more than three inches. I'm leaning too far to the side and lose my balance, falling on my hip. The rustling of the fallen leaves and twigs beneath me redirects the attention of both men.

The man I don't know narrows his dark eyes and lowers his gun until I'm staring down the barrel. Leo steps off to the side and moves to cock his gun as discreetly as possible. From his new angle, he's better equipped to take the other man out. The stranger keeps his gun pointed at my head but turns his body and face toward Leo.

"Prove to me that you're still a standup guy," he says to Leo.

I may have grown up with a rowdy motorcycle club and not a mafia family, but a lot of the language is interchangeable. This guy has already called Leo's loyalty into question once and got away with it, but doing it twice is no doubt dangerous. With any luck, Leo will take this guy out like he should. If it were my dad, he wouldn't stand for such an insult.

Sure enough, Leo raises his gun and points it at the guy's head. "I owe you nothing. Do not forget that."

The man steps forward, creeping closer to me, and with his attention still on Leo, he smiles. It's a sick combination of amusement and arrogance that I can't stomach. He seems to think Leo is the betraying the family because he's not on board with Tony's agenda. I may not be privy to even half of what's going on between the club and the Mancuso crime family, but I know the basics. Tony is the reason Alex had to leave New York. Without his bullshit temper tantrum, nobody ever would have had to know that Alex made the mistake of trusting the wrong person. As far as I can see it, if Leo isn't onboard with Tony, then he's not really that much of a threat to us. He told me the man he shot would have taken pleasure in hurting me. Other than keeping the peace—and right now that means keeping me alive—Leo had no reason to kill that man. He could have let him hurt me and then used him to help get to Michael, but he didn't. He didn't have to kill him right then—he chose to. Maybe, just maybe, Leo isn't really the enemy after all.

"Then you've made your choice." The man moves to redirect his gun toward Leo.

I have to act now, or I'll lose my chance. Reaching for Jeremy's gun, I lift it quickly, unlock the safety, cock the barrel back, and train it on the man who is set on killing the only person who might be able to stop the bloodshed.

The man's eyes slide over to me and widen in surprise. Shock registers on his face for just a moment before he masks it with a cool indifference and corrects his aim to Leo's chest. Leo has been still all this time, seemingly waiting to react to whatever may happen around him. There are three people, and all three of us have a weapon and know how to use it. Unless two of us can manage to form an alliance, these woods are going to get very bloody very fast.

"Put down the gun," I say to the man across from me.

He ignores me and snarls at Leo. "You would prefer the company of trash over your oath."

I really do hate to be called trash. People in fancy cars and pricey suits always want to judge us because we would rather live it up in comfort without pretense than to force ourselves to pretend as though were something we're not. And I'm fucking sick of it.

I squeeze the trigger with my pointer finger, aiming the gun at the guy's chest. I know better than to shoot for any reason but to kill. That's one of the first lessons dad taught me when he first introduced me to the guns back when I was in kindergarten. Before that, we had always had guns around the house, but I knew better than to ask to touch one. It's not a toy. It's a weapon designed for destruction.

My bullet lands in the guy's shoulder, more than six inches left of my intended target. Leo raises his gun, and without a moment's notice, he's fired and landed two more bullets into the guy's chest. His body falls backward, and his gun spills from his hand.

CHAPTER 25

April

12 months to Mancuso's downfall

Cheyenne

LEO EYES ME, his gun still raised, and starts to turn toward me. I reposition and stand quickly, pointing my gun at him. We're at a stalemate.

"If you shoot me, you won't walk away from it," he says.

"You're outnumbered. You may kill me, but I'll scream before I die. You have a gun trained on the sergeant at arms's daughter. Do you really think you'll walk away from that?"

"It seems we have a situation, then."

"No, I don't think you want to cause any damage. If you wanted to, you could've hurt Mindy and Holly when you kidnapped them. But you didn't. You could've hurt

Gloria when you went back to New York asking questions. But you didn't. And you could have hurt me, but I'm still standing."

"I didn't realize how much of their business Forsaken shared with their women."

I smile, knowing full well this guy's history with Alex. He's young and attractive and obviously well built, but he's got some kind of major damage about women to think it acceptable to barter for one. Mancuso and his men would never willingly share details of their business with the women in their lives. They are to be pretty and seen, but most definitely never heard.

"They don't." Feeling brave, I smirk. "A good friend of mine once told me that men will never willingly share their secrets. So I took matters into my own hands." It's not like after this the club won't know anyway.

"Ah, I see you've made friends with my princess," he says.

I shake my head. "She's not your princess. She's our Alex."

"What do you hope to accomplish by pointing the gun at me?"

I'm so tense and terrified in this moment that I'm scarcely able to keep my target in sight. "The same thing you're hoping for—a means to an end. Now, what do you want with Michael?"

He's silent, holding out for several long, suffocating moments. His brow line is smooth, his jaw is relaxed, and his eyes seem decided. There is no confusion in this man.

"I belong to an organization that has failed to provide

a leader. An ignorant, self-absorbed, bloodthirsty twit has attempted to take over. Michael was sent here by that twit, and as it stands, he is the only person who remains in my family that I can trust."

"The way I see it is that you could be of use to my family. I'm tired of losing them to this war. If we don't figure out a way to put an end to it soon, there won't be any of us left—in my family or yours."

"You're not patched, and you never will be. You don't have the authority to create an alliance with me."

"No, but I am the only chance you have of getting out of here alive. The only way my father, my boyfriend, and my uncles will leave your heart beating is if I demand it. The way I see it, you don't have a choice."

"I need to speak with Michael. Gloria claims your club is treating him well, but I need to see him alive before I make any deal with you."

Think, Cheyenne. Think. I need something more for Leo to trust me. Crap.

I tilt my head slightly to the right and look to the house. From this angle, I can see the shadow of a man standing watch at the front door. He adjusts his position just slightly and moves into the light enough for me to see his face. It's Daniel.

"The man at the front door has betrayed my family. His president ditched his ass. Once Rig realized we figured out what they were doing, he ran. He's either dead or gone by now. Either way, you don't have them either. Daniel doesn't have the balls to face what he's done, so it's going to be your ass hung out to dry."

"Yes, I'm aware of Tony's involvement in forcing your Detroit president's hand," Leo says.

"I want your word that if I get you to Michael and promise that I'll keep you alive at least long enough to have a sit down with the club, you won't be a threat to us anymore."

"I can't promise an alliance, though I can promise an honest attempt at compromise," he says and lowers his gun slowly. I nod my head and do the same.

"Okay, don't judge me, but I don't know what the hell to do now," I say with a nervous laugh. We're facing the cabin, and I can't stop staring at Daniel. I'm not even remotely confident that he'll have my back, but I'm out of resources. "I'm toast."

"And you were doing so well," Leo says with a chuckle. He walks toward the house and signals for me to follow. I want to ask him if that chuckle means he's not planning on killing me or if he's figured out how to do it, but I think I've already used up all my courage because I'm fresh out of snarky comments and energy.

We step out from the trees and into the clearing surrounding the cabin. I move to stand beside Leo when suddenly he grabs me around my neck and pulls me up against his torso. Shocked by the sudden jostling, I forget the gun in my hand and close my eyes, fearful that this is the end. By the time I remember I have a weapon, it's too late.

"Hide the gun and just go with it," he says quietly.

I open my eyes and take a deep breath, clicking the safety on and shoving the gun into the back of my jeans. I squirm from the discomfort of the hard metal against my spine. I don't know how the guys walk around like this all the time. I'm going to have to get a holster if this kind of shit is going to keep happening.

He walks me to the front door with his gun to my head. Daniel catches sight of us as we round the side of the porch. He doesn't move to lift his gun or bother with taking cover. Like the traitorous asshole he is, he smiles.

A loopy sickness overtakes me, reminding me of the situation I'm in. The guys can't still be on the other side of the trees. I assured them I wasn't hurt the first time but didn't the second or the third time a gun was fired. I don't doubt that they are slowly making their way through the woods to me. I just have to ensure that Leo and I get to Michael before the club gets to us. I might be able to convince the club not to shoot him on sight, but if I have to convince them to allow him to see Michael and agree to a sit down, then I'm going to end up breaking my word. Leo's right, I don't have the authority to be making alliances on behalf of Forsaken. Thankfully, I'm all he has, and he knows it.

"Finally. Guards are dead inside, and the kid is detained. Put up a fight and had to knock him around a bit, but he's breathing. Fucker was walking around like he owns the goddamn place," Daniel says. The very sight of him makes me angry, but the sound of his voice forces a violent shudder over my entire body. I don't just hate him—I actually loathe his very existence. "Looks like you brought me a present." Daniel licks his lips and gives me a wink.

"How do I know I can trust you?" Leo asks. He forces us up the steps within feet of Daniel.

"Let me show you," Daniel says. He lifts his gun and points it at my head.

People say their life flashes before their eyes, but that doesn't happen to me. I experience a deep sense of regret and sorrow for the things I've never gotten to do. I don't know why, after so many men have died this afternoon, but it's only now it truly sinks in that I might not live to see nineteen. The realization eats away at me, taking small little chunks of my protective shield with it and leaving me desperate for an end.

I don't know what I was thinking, bargaining with a Made man. I don't know what I was thinking of running into the woods, into danger, without a weapon. I don't even know what I was thinking when I started investigating Mindy's rape. Every decision I've made weighs on me. I was a senior in high school and looking forward to graduation. I ditched class, spent too much time with my friends, and flirted with football players. Aside from the club, everything in my life was typical. I wasn't more beautiful than any other girl in school, I wasn't smarter than anybody else either, and I didn't stand out in any way I can fathom.

Not until I put my mind to righting a very big wrong. My friends' problems, like being so far from the mall, became trivial, and I started to find it difficult to listen to their childish whining. The football players were suddenly all talk with very little to back it up. And somehow the most important thing in my life became the thing I just spent a lifetime without—a mother.

I just wanted to show Holly that she could be safe here, with us, and that she could be happy. I never wanted her to be so damaged and so afraid of life. I thought if I could solve the mystery of who hurt her best friend, it would make everything better for her. But I didn't solve it, because the club already knew, and they were already taking steps to rectify the situation. I should have known better.

"Why?" I ask.

Daniel's smile turns predatory, and he rubs his thumb across his bottom lip. "Because Fort Bragg has fucked up peace treaties across the country with their unprovoked strike against the Italians in Brooklyn." He obviously knows nothing if he thinks that's what this war is about, which only confirms my suspicion that Rig didn't just lie to us—he lied to Daniel, too.

"Is that what your president told you?" Leo asks. All trace of humor is now gone, and in its place is a solemnness that I don't expect. "I suppose he left out the part about his kidnapped wife and children who are to be sold overseas should he fail?"

If ever there were a reason to betray the brotherhood, I suppose that would be it. Not that I agree with Rig's actions, but I don't envy the choice he had to make. I knew that if Rig was working with Mancuso, there had to be a reason for it. Brothers don't turn on the patch just because they get tired of the old regime.

"It's unfortunate that you committed yourself to a cause that doesn't exist and that you'll lose your life for a crime you no doubt had little choice but to commit," Leo says. Daniel's eyes flutter for a moment before it registers what Leo's words mean.

He's a dead man.

Daniel redirects his gun to Leo, who takes a step back from me and moves to point his own at Daniel. It worked last time, so I try again. Pulling the gun from the back of my jeans and clicking the safety off, I direct it at Daniel. I distract him just enough for his eyes to slide to mine, ignoring Leo's movements.

Just moments ago I wanted this man dead, but now that I know Leo's going to do it for me, I feel a small amount of pity for him. Daniel closes his eyes and drops the gun on the porch. I force the words from my mouth, though they come quietly.

"I'm sorry."

Leo's bullet shoots from the gun and wedges itself in Daniels chest. He tumbles backward, nearly falling over a metal folding chair in his path. Once he's down, he doesn't move. Leo steps in front of me, turns the knob on the front door, and swings it open before redirecting his gun to clear the room. He tugs me inside after him and continues to lead us farther into the house.

"Don't pity him."

"I don't," I say, "I haven't forgotten his betrayal. It just sucks knowing another person has died because they were lied to."

The fear that crept up on me as Daniel had his gun directed at my brain doesn't dissipate. I'm eighteen. I'm not trained for this, nor do I want to be. For the first time since Jeremy back down from my father, I consider that maybe it was a good thing. Because now, having nearly died a few times at the hands of different men, I want nothing more than to get the hell away from this life. I want to go to school, and I want to see the world—or at least other parts of California. I want to be a teenager, not a murderer. I guess I'm not cut out to be an old lady after all.

"Where is he?" Leo asks.

"I don't know. There's no basement, no attic, and no torture chamber."

"Okay then, I guess we're going to wing it."

Leo leads us out of the living area—it's smaller than I remember—to the kitchen and then around to Ian's bedroom. I try to recall the layout of the house and think where they would stash somebody they wanted to keep control of. Every room has a window, including the bathroom. The cabin has only one bedroom and no extra spaces like an office or anything. Decades before I was born, Jim's dad, Rage, built this place as a getaway for him and his wife, Sylvia. I force myself to remember the story Ruby told me about the cabin, thinking it might be somehow significant.

Rage and Sylvia had a place in town where they raised Jim until the day a social worker showed up at the house with a three-month-old baby claiming Jim was the father. According to Ruby, Jim was barely nineteen and hadn't yet started prospecting for the club. He was more interested in racing his bike in the undeveloped dirt track behind the high school and drinking himself stupid than he was in doing something to better himself. Ruby said Sylvia had told her once that Jim didn't want under his father's thumb any more than he already was. So Rage had this house built small enough to avoid people making themselves at home. The only indulgence Sylvia had asked for was her closet—she wanted a closet the size of a small bedroom.

"The closet!" I say loudly, and without thinking, I reach up to smack Leo's arm. He ignores my enthusiasm and strides across Ian's bedroom to the closed door.

"Michael?" Leo says with a shout.

From the other side of the door, muffled curse words sound. Leo moves to stand in front of me and swings the door open, keeping his gun drawn and ready just in case. When Leo's stance relaxes, he steps into the closet and allows me to see what he's dealing with. Michael is gagged and bound to a metal folding chair. His face has been pounded, and he's struggling against his restraints. "Hold still."

Leo pulls out a knife from his pants pocket and cuts away Michael's binds. When he's freed, he stands awkwardly, favoring his left foot over his right. I suppose it's not his face that got the brunt of it. Michael pulls the gag from his mouth and sucks in a desperate breath before saying, "About fucking time."

Feet fall against the hardwood floors, sounding like a herd of charging buffalo. Leo reaches his arm out and shoves me behind him, drawing his gun at the open door. The first person through the door is Dad and then Uncle Jim, followed by Jeremy. Jeremy has another handgun, but the others all have what I think are AR-15s. They're large and require two hands, too big to operate on a daily basis. Heavy firepower, that's for sure.

"Let her go, or you get a bullet in your fucking skull, Scavo!" Dad shouts. His face is a dark red, and I can see veins popping out from over here. Michael stands on the other side of Leo and raises his arms in the air.

"She's not a prisoner," Leo says. "It seems you raised a woman skilled in hostile negotiations."

"What the fuck did he just say?" Jeremy shouts.

Christ, this isn't good, and it's only going to get worse. *Deep breath, Cheyenne. You can do this.* I've made my proverbial bed, and now I can lie in it. Grounded. For the rest of my life. I really have to start thinking things through before acting. Dad doesn't even like me to sneak his beer let alone make deals on behalf of his club. Shit, even he's not allowed to do that.

I sidestep Leo, gun in hand, and turn my back to the club. I couldn't see everybody who's crowded in and behind the doorway, but I know it's a mass. More than there were earlier, I'm sure.

"Give me the gun," I say to Leo. "I gave you my word that I wouldn't let them kill you." To show him that I'm serious, I empty Jeremy's gun of its bullets and toss them one direction and the gun the other, onto Ian's bed.

"I give you my gun, I'm a dead man," Leo says.

"You can't show them you're not a threat if you have the ability to hurt me," I reply. "I'm going to need your knife, too."

Michael finally speaks up and says, "She came willingly," to the club and then to Leo, "Trust her." When he finally hands over his piece and knife, I toss the knife on the floor, keeping the gun in my hand, and then turn to my dad.

"Leo could have killed me, but he didn't. He just wants answers like we all do. I promised him you'd hear him out and we could see about a cease fire."

"Are you fucking kidding me?" Uncle Jim says. Anger floods his expression, and he stomps forward, repositioning himself with his gun still on Leo. Dad moves to the side, allowing more men into the room. Behind Dad, Jeremy flanks Uncle Jim, followed by Wyatt and Bear, all inside the cramped space with their AR15s in hand.

"He saved my life," I say again and move to stand in front of him.

"You can trust him," Michael says with a nod to Uncle Jim. Something flashes in Jim's eyes, and he lowers his weapon.

"I came here for answers, not a war," Leo says. "All I ask is that you hear me out. I have some intel you're going to need if you plan on making it out of this thing whole."

But we're not whole. We keep losing men, and women keep getting hurt, and everybody is afraid to go on living their lives. The rest of them can't really leave because they are the club and have nothing outside of it. Some were born to it and some purposefully tied themselves to it. Maybe they can't go, but I can. I can go to school and live my life. I can experience independence and see what life is like outside of this small town. Because I want experiences that don't include guns, and death, and so much fear.

"Stand down," Uncle Jim says. "Find a place to put the new guy."

"Playing hostage wasn't part of the deal," Leo says.

I shrug my shoulders and sigh. "You didn't barter for

your choice in accommodations."

It takes several minutes for all the men to lower their weapons.

Dad charges forward and knocks Michael out of the way, then shoves Leo into the open closet we just got Michael out of. Slamming the door shut, he says, "Fuck. Jim, I'm running out of places to put all the WOPs you keep adopting."

"Blame your negotiations team for that," Jim says and approaches Michael. His eyes slide to mine, and he smirks. I can't tell if it's a "Ruby is going to beat you" smirk or a "well done" smirk. He directs Michael into the living room with his pointer finger.

When I have Dad's word that Leo won't be harmed, I cross the room and rush into Jeremy's arms. He sighs deeply and crushes me against his body. To my surprise, all the tears I thought I would cry dry up, and the urge to freak out disappears.

"I can't stand to ever see you in danger again," Jeremy says.

"I know." He didn't say it, but I know he's thinking it. "I can't stay."

"No, you can't. Not until this is over," he whispers against my forehead.

"Don't tell me this is goodbye." I can't bear it if he breaks up with me. I know I have to go to school, because not getting to is all I could think about when I was certain I was a dead girl. "I don't want to lose you."

"You're not losing me, but I need to focus on my job here. The best way I can do that is if I know you're safe."

"Yeah," I say, my voice breaking. I shudder and take a deep, controlled breath, refusing to cry.

CHAPTER 26

January

3 months to Mancuso's downfall

Cheyenne

THE BLUE-GRAY SKY fogs over as the afternoon clouds roll in. Damn it. Dad always accuses the city of being foggy and hard to drive in. Honestly, I think he just hates every place that's not home. It's not like Fort Bragg is all that sunny and hot either. Oh well, he's just gonna have to deal, and hopefully he doesn't bitch too much.

Sometimes I miss him a lot. If I'm being honest with myself, I miss him all the time, though when he's more annoying, it's not so bad being three hours away. Still, it's been almost a year since I started school here, and while I love the program and the city, it's not home. I guess you never know what you have until it's gone.

I stretch my legs out and eye the worn wooden slats beneath my feet. Even after a year, this place still doesn't feel like home. I like the room Dad got set up for me in a rental house that Forsaken's San Francisco charter owns. I am lucky to room with only two other people—an impressive feat in the city this clogged and expensive. Unfortunately, one of those people is a bear of a man who stands over six foot five and weighs, I'm guessing, at least three hundred pounds. He goes by the name Ratchet, and he loves to talk about all the San Francisco charter's history. Ratchet is the sergeant at arms for the SF charter, and he does his job well. Of course, Ratchet doesn't babysit me for free. No, every time Dad comes down, he has a new bag for my burly buddy that's filled with some of the club's finest weed. All in all, it's a system that seems to work for both men. And Ratchet isn't so bad. We're definitely not hanging out and painting each other's toenails, but this was the deal. I wanted to go to school, and with all the danger surrounding the club, the only way I could go was if I was under club protection. And there's no place safer than in a house they own.

My other housemate isn't really a Lost Girl, but she is certainly on her way to being one. She helps out around the club and does a lot of favors for the guys. She's pretty nice and never brings anybody home, which I appreciate. At the end of the day, though, it doesn't matter how nice any of these people are. They're not my family, and it gets a little lonely here, especially because *he* isn't with me.

I wish things were different and I could live with my classmates near campus rather than in this rental across the city in the Sunset District. But I don't dare say that to Dad. As it is, he already likes to remind me how lucky I am to be able to go to school in the city on his dime, and the apartments near school are well above reasonable in his opinion. Plus, the whole warring-outlaw-empires thing kind of kills that fantasy.

Though Forsaken has made progress in recent months—creating an alliance with Leo Scavo and letting him and Michael work with the club to take down Tony and the rest of the Armani-wearing baddies—nothing is really settled yet. Dad says Carlo and Emilio have been quiet, which is never a good thing, so he's extra paranoid these days, being calmed little by the inside information Michael and Leo have provided.

After everything that happened at Ian's house with Rig and Daniel, Jeremy and I haven't talk too much. It breaks my heart because I think I love him more with every passing day, despite our distance, than I did the night I agreed to marry him. When he and I do talk, the conversations are short and we stick to pleasantries. At the end he always says, "You're still my girl, right?" Just before I hang up, I say, "Always." And every single time I end up in tears because even though he says the words faithfully, they sound hollow and do little to mend my broken heart. He says I haven't lost him, but it certainly feels like I have. With that void in my life, I need Dad and Holly now more than ever.

Even Grandma has stepped up her game and brought her new boyfriend down to meet me. Only I already knew the guy. I try really hard to block out images of Grandma and Old Man Hill making out like teenagers. Unfortunately, that which has been seen cannot be unseen. And I appreciate my vision too much to splash bleach in my eyeballs.

It's just a few more minutes of sitting and waiting. I'm bundled up in my Forsaken hoodie, enjoying the sounds of the city, sleepy as it may be around here. The familiar growl of Dad's bike sounds down the road, and I jump up from my seat and rush down the flight of stairs that brings me to the sidewalk. Excitement overtakes me—I might get a shopping trip out of this. Dad makes the trip down twice a month, and at least one of those is with Holly. His last trip down, he didn't bring her, so this time she will be coming with him.

My heart falls when he comes into view, rolling down the street alone on his bike. Holly's not with him, and that worries me. It's not like I keep track of which time she comes and which time she doesn't come, but she has consistently visited at least once a month. The times she doesn't come with Dad are normally because he's doing something for the club they don't want her to have to see. But her not being here right now makes me nervous, freaking me out that maybe he finally screwed up their relationship. And just when I was convinced she was so stupid in love that there was nothing he could do to mess it up.

When he pulls into the short driveway that ends at the single-car garage that's barely bigger than a queen-size bed, he cuts the bike off quickly, removes his helmet, and strides to me with a big grin on his face. I'm starting to think maybe he smoked a little too much before he left Fort Bragg, because there are very few things in this earth that can make Sterling Grady smile that wide when he sober. He envelops me in a tight hug, even lifting me off the ground like he used to when I was little. Yep, definitely high.

"How stoned are you, old man?" I love that he's happy to see me, but I can't help but question his strangely upbeat mood.

"Not very," he says. "I'm just happy to see you."

"I'm happy to see you, too, so don't take this the wrong way—where the hell is my Holly?" I pull back and give him a disappointed pout.

"Decided it was best she stay behind this time," Dad says. Asshole.

"Why would you go and do something stupid like that?"

"I needed to talk to you alone," he says. With everything ugly that's happened with the club lately and all the turmoil and grief, I can't imagine he has good news to share. He seems to be pretty upbeat, but his wanting to talk to me alone is troublesome. The whole situation is making me paranoid. If he tells me Jeremy is hurt or isn't being patched in, I'm going to lose my shit. I'll be back home faster than he will, he can bet on that.

"Because..." he says. Draping an arm over my shoulder, he leads me up the stairs and sits in one of the two wooden chairs on the front porch. I take the other, trying to give him the opportunity to explain himself before I get upset. It takes longer than I think it should for him to give me a reasonable explanation for his poor behavior, but when he does, I instantly regret being a jerk. "I could never ask a woman to marry me without first asking for your blessing."

I sit in silence, staring at him in confusion. He wants to marry Holly? That's why he didn't want her to come? My brain is slow to process it, but really, if there were ever an excuse for denying me my Holly time, this would be it.

"You say no, I won't do it, kid. I gotta know you're good with this."

"It's always been me, you, and Grandma," I say thoughtfully. Even before Holly, something felt like it was missing in our family. Now that we have her, I know she's the piece that was missing.

"Yeah, a lot of shit is changing. Club's lost people— *we've* lost people." His voice is so low it's barely audible. "She's pregnant. Due in June."

My breath hitches, trying to make sense of each bomb he's dropping. I search my heart for a clear thought but can't find one. I love Holly, I love Dad, and I'm sure I'll love the baby, too. But a very large, selfish part of me is suddenly terrified that a biological child she gets to raise is going to matter more to her than I do. And I'm so far away…

"That's awesome," I say, forcing myself to push through my own petty concerns. Dad notices the slight unease in my voice and raises his eyebrows.

"June? How long have you known?" I ask. The idea of being left out of this monumental event upsets me. I was just home for Christmas a few weeks ago. If she's due in June, Holly has to be like four months along now. She would have known over Christmas. She would have known at Nic's voting-in party, which I fucking attended back in December. She might have even fucking known at Thanksgiving. What the fuck?

"A while now, but there was some spotting and a chance she wouldn't make it. Holly didn't want to tell you about her until we knew she was going to be okay," he says. A soft smile takes over his entire face.

"I'm going to have a sister," I say in astonishment. The idea of having a mini Holly and not a mini Dad pacifies me some.

"Hey, you're still my baby girl, okay? I don't give a shit how old you get or whose old lady you become, got that?"

I nod my head and take the opportunity to change the subject. I want to feel undiluted happiness for Dad and Holly, but I just can't shake the fear that I'm going to rate second from now on.

"You been taking care of Jeremy for me?" I ask.

Dad gives me a flat look and shakes his head. "Fuck that kid."

"Come on, Dad. I love that asshole." I know he's only joking—I think—but I want to know. I *have* to know he's looking out for him.

"He the only asshole you love?" He smiles wide.

I choose not to squander his good mood. "Nah, you'll always be the first asshole I ever loved."

"About Holly?" he says.

"What about her?" I ask playfully.

"Yes or no, kid. Quit busting my balls."

"If you don't marry her, I'll disown you," I say and give him a soft smile. "Finally picked a winner." Because he has. Holly is nothing like my mother, and thank God for that. She's strong and loyal and already a great mom.

Once I get over the nagging jealousy of having to share, I know I'm going to be way excited to finally have a sibling. I've always wanted someone else to know that the struggle of being Sterling Grady's child is real.

"Layla's fucked up and missing out on the best thing she could ever have," Dad says. He raises his chin in the air and avoids eye contact, probably because I've started crying. The subject of my mom always does that to me. It doesn't matter how long she's been absent for or how old I get—she's still my mom, and I think I'm always going to have an empty spot in my life where she should be. "She's sick, baby girl. Only reason that keeps her away is her sickness. You gotta know if she could be here and be good to you, she would be."

"But she's not," I say in a messy, rushed mix of words and tears.

"No, she's not, but that's not on you. That's on her. Don't got to like the shit she does to love her."

"Fuck." I wipe my tears, and Dad chuckles lightly and leans over, patting my knee. Subject change. I need another fucking subject change. "Now about Jer..."

"The best I can promise is that I won't kill him and I'll try to keep him from getting killed," he says reluctantly.

"Fair enough."

We're quiet for a long while as we watch the sky darken. I can't really say the sun's setting since the Sunset District is under a perpetual fog due to its close proximity to the Pacific Ocean. It being late January doesn't help either.

Eventually, Dad stands and stretches out. I follow his

movements as he cross the porch and opens the front door, saying, "Now, I heard you're learning about frostings in your new class. Show me my money isn't being wasted."

My mouth parts and then spreads wide in excitement. Dad has taken special interest in my courses because they involve food. He says he likes to test how my skills are coming along, but I know it's really because he likes to be fed. Just as I close the front door behind me, he says, "By the way—before you get going in the kitchen, you should call your boy. He won't say it, but he misses you."

"He doesn't sound like he misses me when we talk on the phone." I'd love to call Jer. I just don't want to call and get the same bullshit I've been getting since I left Fort Bragg for culinary school almost a year ago. It's just not the same. *He's* not the same.

"Club's on its way to a good place—a safe place—but the shit that boy is going through to help get us there? Fuck, Chey. Call him and say whatever the fuck it is you two say to each other. Just *talk* to him. Let the little asshole know you want to know how he's doing."

"Since when do you give me relationship advice?" I ask, taken aback by his attempt at helping my failing relationship. This conversation takes me back to another conversation we had about this same thing—only Dad and I were on opposing ends then.

"Since he did the right thing and let you go so you could be safe," he says and disappears down the long hall toward Ratchet's room in the back of the house.

"Yeah," I whisper. "He did."

With Dad out of sight, I head for my room where I can have a little privacy. He isn't one of those people who gives advice freely. I doubt he wanted to say anything about it since he's not an authority on healthy relationships—he basically lucked out with Holly and her Stockholm Syndrome because, honestly, nothing else could explain it—so he must find this awfully important to bring it up. My cheeks heat at the idea that I matter so much to Jeremy that a few encouraging words from me could turn his mood around. I see it happen with Dad and Holly, but they're in a very different place than Jeremy and I are.

It was nearly a year ago now that I thought he and I were going to run away together and get married, but that didn't happen. Part of me wishes it had turned out differently and that, instead of being in the small room with unfamiliar walls and a rather impersonal décor, I were in another small room tucked into his side as we learn how to live together. But in my fantasy, I'm back home in Fort Bragg with a gold band on the fourth finger of my left hand and with the last name Whelan and maybe, just maybe, one day a baby of our own on the way. But that's not how life has turned out, and I'm slowly coming to terms with that. Like an idiot, the thought finally occurs to me that if I'm struggling with my new reality, maybe Jeremy is struggling with his new reality as well.

I grab my phone from the cheap, plastic bedside table where it's been charging, disconnect the cord, and sit at the foot of my bed. After bringing up my contacts and pressing the touch screen where Jeremy's face appears, I wait in hopeful anticipation as the phone rings. I shouldn't be nervous about calling him. I love him, and he says he loves me still, even despite the distance. Even despite how short-lived our quasi-engagement actually was.

I take a deep breath and force myself to shove off the impending disappointment when his voicemail picks up. When it's time to leave a message, I open my mouth to speak, but nothing comes out. Better not, I guess. I don't even know what I was going to say to him, much less how to convey exactly how I feel. Because I guess that's the point of Dad telling me to call him, so that I can tell Jeremy what it means to me.

The moment my phone starts ringing I swipe my finger across the answer button and I bring it to my ear. I didn't even check the caller ID before saying, "Hey." My voice is soft and encouraging. In an attempt to get him to talk to me—really talk to me. Not that bullshit crap he tries to pull where he always says he's fine and everything is good and that the club is settling. I know all that already. Just because I'm a few hours away doesn't mean I've been exiled from the club. I keep in touch with Alex and occasionally Aunt Ruby—though not as much lately. She's just not in a place where she's up for talking, and I don't really know what else I can say to her. Nothing seems to make anything any better.

"Hey, babe," Jeremy's deep voice says from the other end. "What's up?"

Relief washes over me, showing me how disappointed I was at not getting to talk to him. Sometimes I don't even realize how sad our distance makes me until he's on the other end of the line telling me bullshit stories about work that mean nothing, matter little, and don't do shit to make me feel any better.

"I miss you. I miss you a lot." So much for easing him into this conversation. But that's kind of the Forsaken way—bulls in a china shop.

"Fuck, I miss you, too," he says. We just saw each other a few weeks ago, but it's not enough. It's never enough. And just like that, the imaginary dam we built to keep ourselves safe and the scary emotions at bay during this time apart freaking bursts, and everything comes flowing out. "I was starting to think you were moving on."

"Never. I'm just scared," I admit. He sucks in a deep breath but doesn't say anything. "I'm scared we're going to drift apart, and every time I start thinking about what you're doing while I'm down here, I have the urge to flambé somebody's face."

"What the fuck is a flambé?" he asks, a light laugh echoing on the other end of the line, followed by static and what I think might be the whistling of the wind.

I settle in on my bed, not even trying to ignore the fluttery feeling in my stomach. "You know those kitchen blowtorches? The ones that make crème brûlée?" I ask. I almost tell him it's the thing that Dad forces me to carry with me in my purse. He says it makes an excellent weapon, and I have an excuse for having it. Got a problem? Light 'em on fire. That's his motto. Since my school doesn't allow firearms on campus, I can't bring my handgun with me. We don't have metal detectors or anything that could bust me for bringing it, but I'd feel like a prisoner if I had to carry it with me everywhere.

"Is that some kind of cake?" He has to repeat himself because I didn't hear him the first time. "Sorry the connection sucks. I'm outside waiting on someone."

"Someone special?" I ask, almost teasing but not really. I would hate to have to cut a bitch.

"Just my favorite girl is all," he says, and I swear I can hear the smile in his voice.

"Give Robin a hug from her auntie for me, will ya?" He must be on babysitting duty for my little buddy.

"Yeah, yeah," he says, brushing off my comment. "So anyway, the cake?"

"No." I try to think of how to describe flambé to him. When nothing comes to me, I say, "Alcohol makes fire in a hot pan. It's lighting food on fire."

"Babe, you get my dick hard when you talk about fire and food in the same sentence." He clears his throat and blows out a shuddered breath. I eye my closed bedroom door and scrunch my face up at what I'm about to do.

"Is your dick hard now?" I ask, stuttering through the entire sentence. God, I sound like a freaking moron.

I'm not the only one who wasn't expecting me to be this forward. "It is now," he says. "Good thing I got a few minutes."

"Aren't you outside?" I ask. He can't possibly be... considering... that... outdoors.

There's rustling on the other end, and a doorbell chimes in the background. His stomping echoes in the phone, and then a door creaks open and shuts closed. When I hear the lock slide into place, I almost giggle.

"Can you touch yourself for me?" I ask. Yeah, it's official. I have no fucking clue what I'm doing, but I'm not hearing any complaints so I go with it. I think he might be at the new coffee shop in town... in the bathroom... about to touch himself. I shouldn't encourage this kind of behavior, but he's going to do it anyway. Dad did say to make my boy happy.

His breathing escalates as he slides his zipper down and frees himself. At least, that's what he tells me he's doing. He tells me he's stroking himself,

"I don't know what you want me to say," I confess.

"Just talk," he says. "I want to hear your voice. Tell me how you make a flambé or whatever it is." I giggle happily at his difficulty at understanding the meaning of flambé. "I fucking love that sound. Do it again."

So I tell him, through giggles, how to flambé a dish. Trying to sound sexy, I note the heat of the fire and the wetness of the alcohol before it burns. I search for any aspect of the process that could help him along, but I'm pretty miserable at it, to be honest.

Finally, I give up trying to be sexy when I'm not. "I love you, baby, and I wish I were there with you right now."

He grunts on the other end of the phone, then gasps and sucks in a frantic breath. I wait until he's back with me, sounding breathless and pleased and obviously worn out judging from the series of yawns that escape him. Being able to give him this and to hear him pleasure himself is enticing. But I can't do anything with my dad in this house—it's bad enough what we just did—so I try to block out the telltale throbbing at the apex of my thighs and my heated skin. Jeremy and I have only been together a few times, and in a lot of ways, it feels like our relationship can't stay on course like normal adult relationships do.

"I love you," he says. He yawns again despite the early hour. "Sorry."

"Long day?"

"Long year," he says, I think referencing my absence in combination with all the club's shit.

And here it is, the topic he never wants to talk about. The toll the club takes on him with the Mancuso situation, and the devastation that's followed is painful. It hurts me to even think about what we've lost, but Jeremy actually lives through it every day. He's been there through almost all of it, and I know it must weigh on his heart that things are going this direction. It's just getting more violent and scarier every time he gives me an update. I worry for him so much sometimes that I curl into a ball on the floor and sob for fear that the next call I'll get will be my dad telling me he's gone.

"I'm sorry, baby. I wish I could make it all less painful," I say in absence of anything more helpful. "I know you don't want me to have to deal with all that shit, but I want you to talk to me about it. You *need* to talk about it so you can move forward and get the shit done you need to so we can have our always."

And he does.

I listen while he talks and tells me things I didn't know, and this time when he asks if I'm still his girl, I say, "Always," and I know it's the truth.

Just as I hang up the phone, Dad knocks and, as always, walks in without notice. He notices my fallen shoulders and sorrowful eyes. He blows out a breath and says, "You talk to him?"

"Yeah." I give him a small smile. "I just miss him. I still feel that crushing thing when I think about how long it's going to be until I'm going to see him again."

"Christ, you're fucking dramatic." With a huff, I eye the black throw pillow beside me and chuck it at his head. He doesn't bother with batting it away and lets it bounce off his head. With a raised eyebrow, he says, "If you're done throwing shit, I want to show you something I brought for you."

"If you're done being insensitive, I'd like to see it," I say and stand from my bed.

"Left it outside." He hitches his thumb in the direction of the front door. I nod my head and follow behind. "Just hope it hasn't gotten itself lost or run over by now, because I ain't finding you another one."

"Did you get me a puppy?" I ask, way too hopeful. I've been asking for a puppy for years, and he has always said no. The day I can afford a puppy on my own, I can have one. But with the dangers the club is facing, maybe he's changed his mind and gone to that breeder where they got PJ. I could totally dig having my very own PJ.

"I should have gotten you a dog years ago to avoid this, but no." He opens the front door halfway, blocking my view outside. I bounce on the balls of my feet and try to peek, but he flicks me in the forehead and shakes his head. "Don't think I'm happy about this or anything, but here's your early birthday present."

I shove past him, careful to jab my elbow into his side

extra hard, and stumble onto the front porch. Looking around, I can't find anything that might belong to me. Movement down below on the street catches my attention. Sitting on top of my dad's old bike—the very first bike I ever sat on—is Jeremy. Dad walks out of the house after me and closes the door. I make a move to head down the stairs when Dad places his gorilla-like hand on my shoulder and says, "Wait for it."

Jeremy stands from the bike and step away from it. He gives Dad a lift of his chin, which I catch Dad returning. The more time they spend together, the more similar their mannerisms become, which, frankly, freaks me the ever-loving fuck out. Jeremy lifts his arms perpendicular to his body and slowly turns around. His back comes into view, and the weight of this moment hits me like a sledgehammer to my gut. Dad removes his hand from my shoulder and lets out a small chuckle.

I place my hand over my mouth to cover the gasp as tears explode in my eyes. A wretched sob overtakes me as I find myself taking a single step forward. He's fully turned around now and a brand new FORSAKEN patch shines from the top of his vest. I got used to seeing his prospect cut with so few patches on it, that this new addition is startling. He finishes his circle and is facing me once again. He drops his arms at his sides and then crooks a finger, calling me over.

My feet have taken off, and I'm halfway down the stairs when I realize I'm in motion. Once I hit the concrete, I'm grateful that even on autopilot I can at least navigate a flat surface. I don't slow down when I reach him. Instead, I fling myself into his arms. He hauls me up and swings me around in a circle before placing me on the pavement again.

"Holy fucking shit," I say. I'm almost speechless but not quite. I gape at him for a moment before he places one hand behind my head and pulls me to him, crashing his lips against mine. I'm wrapped up in him, sucked into all that he is and what he's accomplished. I fell in love with a smart-mouthed boy in a prospect cut, and I continue to sink even deeper in love with this man. There's so little of the boy left in him now, but what's replaced the immature antics is a man whose word is his law, and his heart is as beautiful as anything I've ever known. But I won't tell him that. He doesn't like it when I get sappy and shit.

"When did this happen?"

"Few days after you left town." The grin on his face is almost unbelievable. I'm not sure I've ever seen him look so happy before.

"That was almost a month ago!" I scream, a rabid, angry-woman scream that I didn't know I was capable of until we got together.

"Had to take care of some shit first," he says with an attitude that makes me want to beat him with his cut. I was home for almost a month over Christmas break and that asshole didn't call me, come see me, or nothing. Fucking dick.

"That's your response? That's all you got to fucking say for yourself? Really, Jeremy Whelan? Really?"

"Would you shut the fuck up?" he shouts in my face so loudly that I'm startled into silence. Has he forgotten my dad is on the porch and can rip his goddamn head off for that shit? I slide my eyes to Dad, whose arms are folded over his chest that's heaving in laughter. No, really? The asshole gets a new patch on his back and suddenly I'm fucking chopped liver?

"You did *not* just scream in my face," I say quietly, readying myself for battle. Where's that damn blowtorch when I need it?

"Are you going to shut your trap so I can talk to you, or are you going to keep bitching at me?"

"Which do you suggest?" I say with more sarcasm than should be legal.

"Shutting your fucking mouth. Wanted to get the club's opinion on something before coming down here," he says. That cocky grin is back now. "And you're going to feel like a Grade-A bitch when I tell you why."

"Well, you picked me," I mutter and pout like an insolent child. Calming myself down, I place my hand over the new patches on the front of his cut that have replaced the PROSPECT patch. He's a full member of the club now and is entitled to everything that comes with that. I wanted this for him, even tried to pray for it once, and now that it's happened, I barely know what to do with myself.

"You deserve this," I say with a definitive nod.

"So do you," he says quietly. "That's why the night I was patched in, I asked your dad for permission to make you my old lady. So don't you dare fuck this up for us, because you've been on the clock since yesterday."

"You—" I stop. Now I really am speechless. I can't be angry with him for that. My head spins around to my dad, who smiles down at me. "You did that? They voted on me?"

"Please," he says with an air of confidence that's almost suffocating. "Leo told us how you handled him in the woods. You think any of my *brothers* were going to say no to you?"

"But Dad?" I say in a half question, half statement. But *my dad* voted yes?

"Well, yeah. You're a handful, and he's got another one on the way. Had to unload you somewhere."

"Fucking asshole," I say and grab the sides of his neck and bring his lips to mine.

He's a fucking asshole, all right. But he's *my Forsaken* asshole.

EPILOGUE

June

2 months after Mancuso's downfall

Jeremy

THE FARTHER WE get from the city, the hotter the sun beats on my skin. I suck in a deep, greedy breath and revel in the feel of my girl's arms wrapped tight around my waist. Chey's been riding her whole life, even in Layla's stomach before she was born, but her grip is murderous right now. Her tits are pushed into my cut, and her face rests between my shoulder blades. Her body is so relaxed, but she's squeezing the fucking life out of me. Still, I can't bring myself to tell her to lighten up. If she needs to hang on to me like this to know I'm here and I'm real, then she can break a fucking rib for all I care.

Because as much as she needs to know I'm real, I need to know she's real possibly even more.

The last two years have been rough. It seemed like

we'd made the decision that she would go to school on the spur of the moment, in the shadows of chaos and trauma, and that after the dust settled, one of us would tell the other it was a mistake. That she shouldn't go.

"My little girl ran into a war zone today," Grady said once we'd gotten back to his house that night. "Do the right thing and let her go."

I looked him in the eye and tried to be as strong as he was when I said, "I can't let her get hurt because of me. She has to go."

We're nearing town, having just left Willits, and the road is winding down through Jackson State Forest. The sun is blocked by the hills and trees above us. The memories of how we got here flood my mind. Grady's given me a wider berth since that day, treating me more like an equal than some punk kid he's forced to tolerate.

The day the club patched me in, over a year ago now, he said, "Don't undervalue the gift I'm giving you, son. It's the greatest thing you'll ever get." I remember shaking my head and asking to speak with him privately. When we were alone, I went right for it.

"Proud to have my patch, but I can think of a gift more valuable than your brotherhood."

He looked away and was silent for at least a solid minute. "You're doing this now?"

I nodded my head. "I'm not whole without her," I said. It was the truth then as much as it is the truth now. "I'd like your permission to ask the club to consider voting her in."

"I fucking hate you," he said. He didn't mean it,

because he gave me his permission and then called the guys back into the chapel for the vote. It'll be another year yet before she can be voted in, but she's earning her place at my side. Hopefully soon she'll share my name.

"One day, Grady, I'm going to ask her to marry me again," I told him to prepare him for it. I've found that the more prepared he is for something, the less angry he gets when it happens, even if he disapproves. That was about three months ago. He shrugged it off but pulled out his gun and took off the safety.

"One day, Jeremy, you're going to say the wrong fucking thing and I'm going to lose it," he had said. But that was it. We didn't talk about it again until I pulled him aside at the graduation ceremony two days ago.

Preparing Grady for Chey's return to Fort Bragg hasn't been easy. First I had to get the whole proposal thing out there for him. Then I mentioned bringing her stuff to my place. That one almost got me decapitated, but eventually he mumbled something about a pool table and moving the kids' rooms around. I didn't really follow it, but the following week, her bedroom was cleared out of anything Holly and Elle thought she might want to have around her new home. I drew the line at the shitty girly posters of half-naked actors she professes to like "because of their talent and not their appearance." Either way, those fucking assholes don't get to come to the house with us.

As we descend upon Fort Bragg, her grip relaxes some. My stomach muscles have gotten a serious workout this ride—and it was a long fucking ride—but the strain feels good. I haven't worked out the way Duke and I used to lately. Been too busy getting shit fixed up for my girl to come home. Haven't shaved properly in a while, but she's expressed interest in my budding goatee.

I veer off Main Street and head down Sherwood Road in the wrong direction of her dad's house. She notices immediately and pipes up, but I ignore her. Before we get to Ruby's long-ass driveway, I slow the bike and cut down a small service road that separates her from her neighbors and turn toward the family cabin. Ian lived here for several years before moving out for a bigger place and offering it up to me and Chey. He'd reasoned that we'd be better company for his mother than he ever was. The only other people to live in the cabin besides Ian and Mindy were Rage and Sylvia before she passed and he retired to Nevada.

"What are we doing out here?" she asks as I bring the bike to a stop in front of the small cabin. This place hasn't always held happy memories for her, but I'm determined to turn that around. Cutting off the bike and pushing down her kickstand, I pat her thigh for her to get up. She responds and climbs off, then steps back to give me room to swing my leg over. Once I'm on the dirt, I take her hand and lead her to the front steps. She's acting funny, just like she's been for months now. It's my own fault, really. But I want her to have this, so I'll deal with it for now.

"That's not what you want to say, and we both know it," I say. "Go on."

"Well, you're an asshole. You barely answer my calls anymore, you go MIA for hours on end, and nobody can tell me where you've been. You want me to pick up where we left off like nothing's fucking wrong, but guess what, buddy? Something is wrong. I feel like you're hiding something from me, and I'll overturn every rock in this damn county to find it."

"That's because I am hiding something from you," I admit, feeling rather proud of myself. She does this, sticking her foot so far down her throat she ends up offering to suck my dick on the regular after she realizes she's been an asshole. My girl's a little bitchy and a lot paranoid, but she's mine, and if she didn't prove that she's Forsaken-level difficult once in a while, I'd worry I picked the wrong chick.

I pause, waiting for her to start bitching, but she doesn't. She does narrow her eyes, though, and shake her head. "I'm not going to lay into you like I want to, because I have a feeling you're setting me up to make me into an asshole."

"And why would I do that?"

"You like getting your dick sucked," she says. I try to tell her that she enjoys it as much as I do, but she shoots that idea down pretty quick. "No woman likes sucking dick as much as a man enjoys it, and if they say they are, they're goddamn liars."

"Speaking of sucking dick," I say, trailing off and placing a kiss to the shell of her ear.

She shakes her head and pushes on my chest. "Nuh-uh."

"Fine, I'll just have to give you your real gift." I lead her up the steps to the front door. Pulling out a set of keys, I hand them to her and step back. A sheepish grin appears on her face as she draws her bottom lip into her mouth. Swiftly, she gets the door open and steps inside with a gasp.

I'm no expert with making shit look good, but I know several women who think they are, and they did a damn good job helping me out. The cabin had never been updated from when Rage built it, and while it was functional in a utilitarian kind of way, it wasn't what I wanted to bring Chey home to. Now, after months of work, the wood floors shine with fresh sanding and a slick polish. The walls have been patched where needed, and each room is painted a different color that Chey loves. I managed to veto hot pink from the design team, who almost went rogue and did it behind my back anyway, but almost everything else was a go. I don't give a shit that the walls are violet or that the sofa's gray fabric has a tiny bit of sparkle to it. Not that it's going to matter in a few months anyway. That shit is going to get so worn out the sparkle will be forgotten.

"Is that the rug Holly and I spotted in the city?" Chey asks, pointing at the black and white rug that sits in the center of the living room. Holly called it a chevron rug, but I think she's lost her mind. That rug doesn't look like it belongs in a gas station. Again, another piece that looks good now, but who knows how it's going to wear. More hard-earned money spent on shit I don't care about. It's my fault really—I told them to do something that would make Chey happy. And judging by the happy tears, it worked.

She walks around the corner to the kitchen and reaches for my hand. She gives it a squeeze and thanks me about a hundred times. I'm glad she likes the updated and extended countertop and the new appliances. It's just stuff, but it makes her happy, so it's worth every dime.

She leads me by our joined hands into the bathroom where she giggles over the rainfall showerhead and the makeup station.

"But all of this looks like this place is for me," she says. "What about you?"

"Baby, as long as I get to fuck you on that pretty couch and under that fucking shower head, I don't give a fuck what any of this shit looks like." Because I don't.

We walk into the bedroom, and she eyes the king-size bed. With a happy sigh she says, "There's your influence," in response to the framed mirrored headboard I had made in exchange for a new strain of bud we just started growing.

She turns around and places a soft kiss to my lips. Unable to control myself, I grab her by the hips and buck into her. A breathy groan escapes her, urging me on. I do it again, which earns me a desperate plea. "Make love to me in our bed," she says. Like she even has to ask.

We undress one another with frantic movements, pulling and shoving nearly to the point of ripping everything in the process. Soon I'm without my shoes, pants, and boxers and am left with my top half fully clothed. Her chest rises and falls in desperation as she gently removes my cut and tosses it at the foot of the bed, but once that's out of the way, she nearly chokes me trying to get my red shirt off. Her hands trace the outline of the tattoo I'm having done. Just three more sessions and all the tiny details will be complete. It's the scene from that fucking van, in that fucking moment when everything changed. But I didn't want faces because those distort bad as you age, so instead the van is empty.

There are no people crying, and no blood—just lines made up of names and dates that I can't ever forget, no matter how hard I try.

"It's almost done," she whispers as she slows down her movements.

"Yeah."

Chey leans in and places a kiss over the lines of the names of each of the men we've lost. She doesn't cry about it anymore because my girl knows it doesn't do us any fucking good to think about that shit. Instead, she does the best fucking thing she can—she honors our losses by making sure we all fucking live for the ones who didn't make it.

I'm slightly less rough with her as I free her of every one of her articles of clothing. When we're both naked and my dick is throbbing so hard it's almost painful, I lay her down on the bed so that I can see us in the mirror.

Yeah, this view is totally fucking worth the bud I had to give up for this.

She parts her legs, welcoming me in. I could slam into her right now, especially with how much I need this. But I'd rather not hurt her. She needs to enjoy this as much as I do, and with finals and all the bullshit with graduation and finishing the house, it's been almost a month since I got into her pussy. Almost a month would have been a godsend back when she first left for school. We were lucky if we got together every other month. But after her being gone so long and once I'd earned my top rocker, we made it a point to see each other more often. Come hell or high water I'd see her every other weekend at the very least. Sometimes on a transport down south, I'd sneak away and we'd have a quick fuck at her place. It was always too short and made me feel like shit for running in, busting a nut, and running out. When it upset her, she'd say it—loudly and until her throat went hoarse—but that was rare. Now, though, I'm not letting her get so far away.

I slide down her beautiful, naked body and kiss her hip before making my way to her slick center. No longer nervous about her body or afraid to ask for what she wants, she parts her legs even more and moans when I finally give in and tease her tiny bud. Soon enough, she's unable to stay still, close to coming and a panting mess. When I crawl back up her body and slide into her, my eyes roll back in my head. The best part of our lives is beginning now, in this bed, with just the two of us making this place our home.

"What's that noise?" she asks suddenly, barely able to suck in enough breath to form the question.

"What noise?" I try not to get distracted and to keep my rhythm going. If she's hearing other shit besides me, then I'm not doing my job, so I reach down and massage her clit in slow circles.

"It sounds like panting," she says with a scrunched face and through broken speech.

"That's you, baby," I say. She shakes her head, opens her eyes, and looks around the room as best she can. I'm sliding into her, going as deep as I can, when she lets out a terrified scream and uses her nails to claw at my exposed flesh. I look around and find the reason for her fear.

"Shit," I mutter without stopping my ministrations.

The little brown eight-pound ball of fat and fur stares at her from under his splayed, floppy ears. He growls, raises his butt in the air, barks, and brings his head down to the comforter. At this age, he's cute when he's being territorial, but it won't be so cute when he's a full-grown pit who thinks he runs this shit.

"Gentle," I command, still refusing to stop what I'm doing. The dog takes a moment to think about the command before he quiets down. When I order that he sit, he decides instead to walk around the bed to get a better look at Cheyenne. He's never seen her before, so this is new for him. He's barely three months old, so he's still learning his commands. He's smart, though, so I have no doubt that in time he's going to be an excellent guard dog for my girl.

"I'm guessing he's ours," she whispers, looking slightly less afraid now. Her back arches when I hit a particularly sensitive spot, and her eyes flutter. "Not in front of the dog."

"Fuck that," I say. "This is our bed, and I'm not going to stop fucking you every time nosy ass over here decides to enter a room." Really, he and I are pretty good friends at this point. I'm hoping Chey doesn't mind him sleeping in the bed with us, because since I got him last week, he's slept by my feet above the covers.

As creepy as it is, the damn dog watches us the entire time. In a few minutes' time, she seems to forget about his presence, until my dumb ass has to comment with, "Watch Daddy. I'll show you how to handle bitches."

"Asshole," Chey whispers, almost like it's a compliment, and reaches down to stroke the sensitive flesh behind my ballsack. A hot jolt rushes up my spine as she clenches down on me, and we come together in near silence with our eyes open and watching each other shudder and shake with the ripples of pleasure that pass over us.

"Thought the place was too big for just us," I say and nod to the dog when I'm able to speak again. "He doesn't have a name yet, so that's been kind of confusing for training purposes."

"Can I name him Leo?" she asks.

I pull out of her and shake my head in disagreement. If she wants to name the fucking thing Leo, she can, but I don't have to be happy about it. Somehow, she and Scavo developed a friendship while he was here. She says he makes her feel brave. I want to support her friendships, but I won't lie—that kind of pisses me off. I want to be her everything, and the idea that she bonded with somebody else doesn't sit right.

"Don't be like that," she says and crawls to the top of the bed where she buries herself under the covers. "You know it's not romantic or sexual. He's like a brother to me, and I'm sorry that he's gone. That's all."

"Yeah, I get it. Doesn't mean I want to name my dog after the guy," I gripe and crawl up the bed to join her beneath the covers. I stare into her green eyes, taking a moment to really see her and just be fucking grateful that she's here and with me willingly. Because I would have totally kidnapped her if she had objected to coming home with me. I told her once that she was my always, and I fucking meant it.

She smiles softly, leans in, and grabs ahold of the

goatee I've been working on, and tugs. She smirks as she says, "We could name him Ryan."

Back when I was a prospect, the idea of naming a dog after Ryan would have scared me. But now? Fuck it. I'm sure it'll be funny when he finds out. Plus, it wasn't my idea anyway.

"Ryan, come see Daddy," I say. Yeah, I'm one of those fucking people who treats their dog like their kid. Grady thought it was funny until he realized who little Ryan's mama is if I'm his daddy. The dog stares at me and then Cheyenne and then back to me before prancing up the bed to my lap. I give him a quick rub under his chin and then behind his ears before dropping my hand and letting Chey bond with him.

"Go to Mama," I tell him. Ian's dog training guy told me to familiarize him with her scent early on, so I did. We've spent the past week learning how to find Mama by her scent. Just yesterday he managed to complete the entire session without any issues. Next week we'll have to up the ante.

"Go to Mama," I repeat. This time he seems to understand, and he takes the few steps to sit at her side, tail wagging against the comforter, and waits for praise. I watch as she tentatively shows him her hand and goes about waiting for his acceptance. Once granted, she rubs him behind his ears, under his chin, and along his spine.

"I can't believe you did all of this for me." Her green eyes shine in the fading daylight, illuminating her pale skin and dark brown hair. She's gorgeous, even more so than when I first fell in love with her.

"Believe it, babe. I told you we would have our

always, and this is it," I whisper and lean over to kiss her.

"I'm never leaving this bed," she whispers back and presses her lips to mine. We're lost in slow, sated kisses for so long I almost forget what we're doing until she says, "Hey, don't you owe me a ring?"

Yeah, I do.

I really fucking do.

THE END

ACKNOWLEDGEMENTS

I tend to be chatty in these things, but this one is going to be short because it's nearly six a.m. and I haven't the energy to properly gush.

Thank you first and foremost to my readers who have taken a chance on me and my little stories. Thank you for allowing me to live my dream. To each and every one of you who held in there while dates kept changing and no answers were being provided—thank you. It's been a rough year, but I know I'm at the tail end of it. Your determination to drag this book out of me pushed me to give you absolutely the best book possible. I hope it's lived up to expectations. And yes, Ian is coming. Chill. #hiding

Thank you to my family who provide me never-ending support and encouragement: Mom, Britt, Mandie, Amy, Grandma (even though you purposely read the dirty parts out loud and then have the nerve to look embarrassed), Debbie, and Candace. And the rest of my extended family who have gone out of their way to show their excitement and support over me getting to live my dream.

Thank you to my author friends who commiserate with me over this beautifully chaotic career we've chosen. I'm a better businesswoman and writer because of you all. Thank you to the girls who read this story first and encouraged me to keep going even when I was certain that Jeremy was going to die in a car explosion in chapter seven because he wouldn't cooperate: Chelsea Camaron, Tracie Redmond, Lisa R., Judy Ruiz, Amber Vaughn, Michelle Chu, Danielle Plane, Julie Deaton, and Nicki DeStasi.

To my awesome team of ladies who stick by me no matter what I throw at them through this publishing journey: Dawn Johnson, A.M. Jones, Danielle Sanchez, and Cindy Emery. I'm turning into a pathetic little codependent baby because you four have shown me such great support and love that I don't ever want to stand alone in this again. If you run, I'll find you. Thank you to Brenda Gonet for these gorgeous covers. I love the way the entire series turned out and am on pins and needles wanting to show them off *right now*. Thank you to Michele Milburn for going over every word more times than you should have. I appreciate your dedication and thoughtfulness in every step of the journey. You're a keeper!

To anyone I may have missed—I'm terribly sorry. Please know that I'm an idiot.

About the Author

As a child, JC was fascinated by things that went

bump in the night. As they say, some things never change. Now, as an adult, she divides her time between the bad-ass bikers, sexy law men, mythical creatures, and kick-ass heroines that live inside her head. A San Francisco Bay Area native, JC has also called both Texas and Louisiana home.

These days she rocks her flip flops year-round in Northern California and can't imagine a climate more beautiful. Her dream is to own her own Harley and she feels compelled to tell you that she is Team Peeta all the way. JC is the author of the Bayonet Scars series and the Men with Badges line.